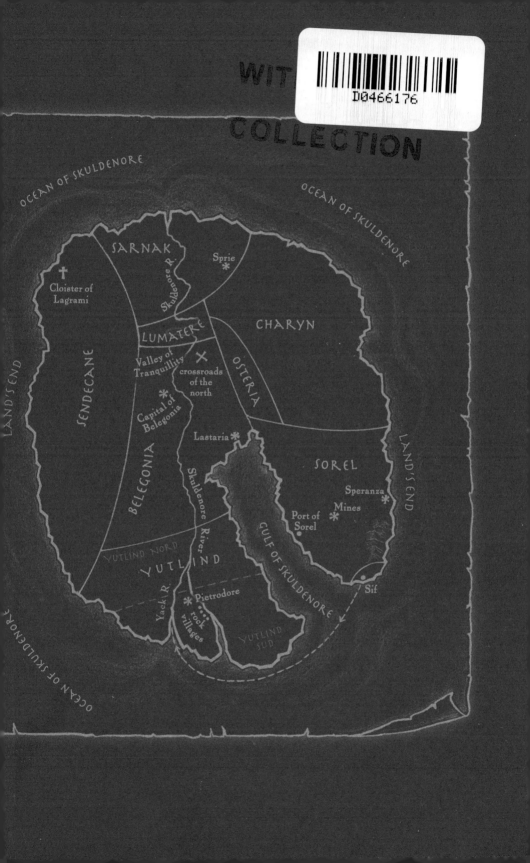

OCEAN OF SKULDENORE

OCEAN OF SKULDENORE

LAND'S END

LAND'S END

OCEAN OF SKULDENORE

SARNAK

Sprie *

Skuldenore R.

† Cloister of Lagrami

LUMATERE

CHARYN

Valley of Tranquillity

✕ crossroads of the north

OSTERIA

SENDECANE

* Capital of Belegonia

Lastaria *

SOREL

Speranza *

BELEGONIA

Skuldenore River

Mines *

Port of Sorel •

GULF OF SKULDENORE

VUTLIND NORD

VUTLIND

Yack R.

* Pietrodore

• • • • rock villages

Sif •

VUTLIND SUD

QUINTANA of CHARYN

BOOK THREE
of the Lumatere Chronicles

Quintana
of
Charyn

MELINA MARCHETTA

CANDLEWICK PRESS

First U.S. edition 2013

Library of Congress Catalog Card Number 2012955120
ISBN 978-0-7636-5835-9

13 14 15 16 17 18 SHD 10 9 8 7 6 5 4 3 2 1

Printed in Ann Arbor, MI, U.S.A.

This book was typeset in Palatino.

Candlewick Press
99 Dover Street
Somerville, Massachusetts 02144

visit us at www.candlewick.com

For Mum, Dad, Marisa, Daniela, Luca, Daniel, Brendan, and Andy,
who make it so easy to write about strong, passionate,
high-maintenance families with big hearts

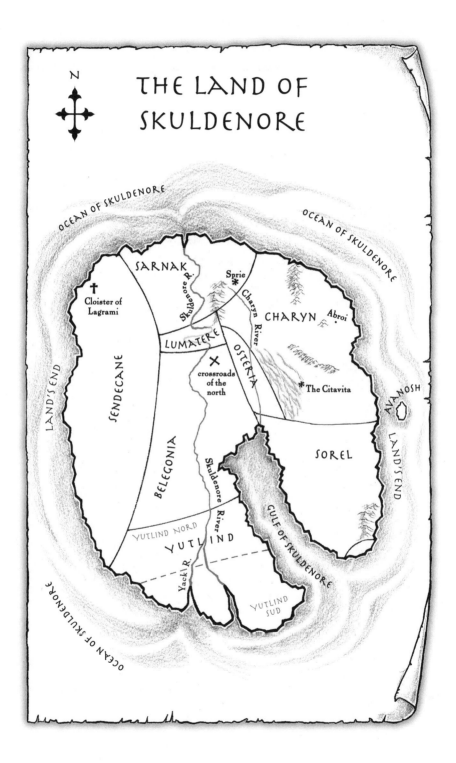

THE LAND OF SKULDENORE

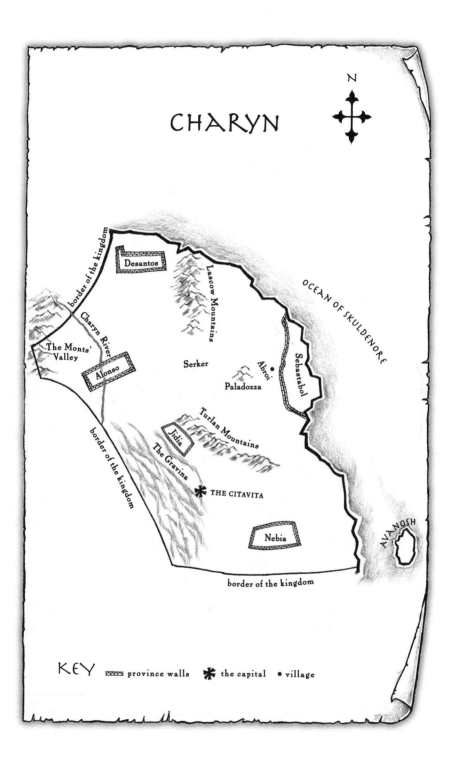

CHARYN

N

Desantos

Lascow Mountains

OCEAN OF SKULDENORE

border of the kingdom

Charyn River

The Monts' Valley

Alonso

Serker

Abroi

Paladozza

Sebastabol

Turlan Mountains

border of the kingdom

Jidia

The Gravina

✳ THE CITAVITA

Nebia

AVANOSH

border of the kingdom

KEY ▦ province walls ✳ the capital • village

prologue

There's a babe in my belly that whispers the valley, Froi. I follow the whispers and come to the road. And I travel for days on the back of a cart with the lice and the filth, and the swill of the swine.

But once in the valley, those pigs of the city sit high on their horses, not with a noose, but with swords at their sides. And still so forsaken, I rage at the gods, and I turn from the faces of those who take charge.

I keep to myself, but I find they are watching. I clench both my fists; I'll kill in a beat. Your words pound my brain, Froi; if they dare try to touch me, a knife to the side and a slit ear to ear.

Those in my cave, they grab and they drag me. They want me to bathe, but they'll soon know the truth. And the fear on their faces speaks loud of their awe, and I capture the crying and tell them what's true — that the men with the swords, who once held the noose, will cut out my king and leave me to die.

The girl with the smile, the one you once spoke of, she enters the cave and can see what is true. And she thinks with her heart and shouts out, "It's plague!" and calls for a man who has seen plague before. I beg her, I beg her, but the man named Matteo is the lad with the cats from when I was a child. "Your Highness," he whispers, his eyes full of wonder. "Did you mate with the last born I sent to save Charyn?"

And the women, they stare with fear in their hope, but it's hope drenched with tears, and it smothers me whole. And the Mont's wife, she covers my belly and speaks. "We'll be dead to all Charyn, from plague in the north." There's keening and wailing from those left behind: the men of the valley who lose all they have.

And here where we're hidden, I sleep in a corner. My dreams are consumed by She who has stealth. I feel her, I fight her, I grit through my teeth, "Keep far from my king or I'll tear you to pieces."

I call out your name to help fight this demon. I call out your name. "Froi! Save Charyn's son."

And day after day it is dull in my heart, for there's nothing to say when you're dead to the world. And the Mont's wife, she looks to the valley and mountains with pain and regret, but such hope and fierce love.

"Is it rain?" someone asks, and I wait for the answer. Though winter still shrouds this land, I've prayed for the sun.

part one

Dafar

CHAPTER 1

"Froi!"

In the dark of their chamber, Isaboe awoke. She heard Finnikin stir beside her and climbed out of their bed, pulling back the curtain that partitioned their sleeping quarters from the rest of their private residence. Despite the thickness of the rug, her feet felt icy as she tiptoed to the hearth. Her hands shook as she lit a taper with the embers of last night's fire, trying to understand the savage strangeness of her dream. But when she returned to their bed, she saw, through the flicker of the flame, what the darkness had hidden. Finnikin lay awake, staring at her with fury. And it made her shiver even more.

"What is it?" she asked, as if facing a stranger, not her king. And because she feared the malevolence of Finnikin's gaze, she gathered Jasmina into her arms and carried their daughter away, settling her to sleep in a moonlit corner of the room. There was a sound behind her, and Finnikin's shadow was on the wall. Isaboe despaired at the wickedness that had crawled into their lives this night.

"What?" she demanded to know, her mood eased only by the smile of sleepy satisfaction on Jasmina's face.

Finnikin didn't respond, and this time she turned to face him, the light of a cruel moon mocking her belief that she had nothing to fear from her king.

"You wake with another man's name on your lips and you ask me what the matter is?" he said.

Froi?

She could hardly remember it now, but she had certainly dreamed that she had heard his name.

"It's the walk," she said, pressing a kiss against the soft skin of her daughter's cheek. "Every night now it seems as if I'm in another's sleep, but they reveal nothing."

Unable to stand his accusing stare, she brushed past him and returned to their bed. "It's a mind full of strangeness," she mused. "There's cunning beyond reckoning there. Snarls. Whispers. And something else. I can't explain it."

"You've not bled for months, Isaboe," Finnikin said, his voice blunt. "Since you began carrying the child. How can you walk the sleep if you don't bleed?"

And then fear left her and anger set in and she matched the gray stoniness in Finnikin's eyes with dark rage.

"Are you calling me a liar?" she asked softly. "Because I'd be careful of that, my love."

They heard the sound of horses in the courtyard outside and she suspected it was Trevanion and Perri returning from the mountains where she had sent them to question Rafuel of Sebastabol. Finnikin walked away, without so much as a word. They had all been tense these past weeks after the return of Froi's ring by a Charynite brigand. They had also received news from inside the kingdom of Belegonia about the man who may have

4

planned the slaughter of Isaboe's family, thirteen years past: Gargarin of Abroi. Isaboe had insisted that they were to collect information about the suspect. She knew what her next order would be. Slowly, every man responsible for Lumatere's pain would be gone, and she prayed to the goddess that it would bring her peace.

When she heard the voices from the entrance of the chamber, Isaboe wrapped her fleece around her body and pulled across the curtain that separated their bed from the rest of the room. Informal meetings with Sir Topher and Trevanion always took place here in their private residence. It was Isaboe's favorite place in the castle, and when she had first seen the vastness of the room, she had insisted that they include a dining bench and settees to accommodate the closest of their friends when they came to visit. It was beautifully decorated with rich tapestries and ceiling frescoes, and Isaboe was proud of how at ease those nearest to her heart felt in her home. But there was little of that today.

She watched her lady's maid serve hot brew to Trevanion and Perri, who were hovering near the doorway.

"Your shoes, my queen!" Rhiannon reprimanded, turning her attention to Isaboe and staring down at Isaboe's bare feet.

She hadn't noticed. She had only noticed Finnikin brooding by the window. Isaboe greeted Trevanion, who embraced her, and she felt the icy wetness of his coat. Taking his hand, she led him closer to the fire, where Finnikin's hound pressed himself against Trevanion's leg in recognition.

"Where are your shoes, Isaboe?" he asked with disapproval.

Finnikin's father had one gruff tone for everything, and she was finally becoming used to it after all these years.

A bleary-eyed Sir Topher entered with a knock, and then they were all huddled before the warmth.

"Sit," Isaboe ordered everyone, and they made themselves comfortable before the fire.

"Rafuel of Sebastabol has become somewhat difficult to get alone these past weeks," Trevanion said. "Impossible, actually."

"Since Phaedra of Alonso . . ." Isaboe said.

Trevanion nodded.

"How are they all?" she asked quietly. It had been three weeks since the death of Lucian's wife.

"Grieving. I left Beatriss and Vestie with them."

"Yata sent a letter," Isaboe said. "Tesadora is taking it hard, I hear," she added, looking at Perri. He nodded but said nothing more. Isaboe had never known him to speak of Tesadora. Whatever it was that they shared was a private matter.

"Tesadora and her girls insist on going down to the valley again," Trevanion said.

Isaboe shook her head. "I want Tesadora here keeping me company until I deem it safe for her to return to her work with those Charynite valley dwellers."

She noticed the flicker of annoyance on Perri's face and stared at him questioningly.

"Tesadora claims they are suffering greatly," Trevanion said.

"The Monts?" Isaboe asked.

"The valley dwellers."

"Why so much concern for the valley dwellers?" she asked, exasperated. "They're not our problem."

"Well, they may just be," Trevanion continued. "The province of Alonso has stopped sending grain carts. The valley dwellers are sharing meager rations, and it's beginning to show. Tesadora says that in their weakened state and in this cold, they're more at risk of illness. The older ones are beginning to die far too quickly."

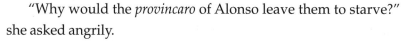

"Why would the *provincaro* of Alonso leave them to starve?" she asked angrily.

"Grief," Sir Topher said. "He believes his daughter's death would have been avoided if she wasn't in the valley. He blames the valley, and he blames us. Perhaps if we write to offer our —"

"I don't grieve for Charynites," Isaboe said, her voice cold. "I don't recall receiving a letter from the *provincaro* of Alonso when my family was slaughtered, nor was there a note of sympathy when my uncle Saro of the Monts was killed. I owe the *provincaro* nothing. He, on the other hand, owes Lumatere for relieving him of the problem of a crowded province. Write to him, Sir Topher, and demand that he feed his people. I will not have them dropping like flies on my land!"

Rhiannon returned with Isaboe's slippers and another shawl, and they all waited until she stopped her fussing.

"You're quiet, Finnikin," Sir Topher said after Rhiannon had left the room.

"I agree with Isaboe," he said, his voice flat. "Regardless of whose problem they are, the valley dwellers are Charynites, and Alonso has no right to stop the grain carts. Explain to the *provincaro* that every death in the valley will be recorded, and one day when a benevolent king sits on the Charynite throne, Alonso will be held accountable."

It was the wavering in Finnikin's voice that marked the difference between them both. Isaboe knew that. He was the better person. He wrote the letters of outrage to the king of Yutlind Nord about the injustices in Yutlind Sud. He wrote the letters to every leader of the land challenging the Sorellian laws of slavery. He was the only person she had ever known to use the word *Skuldenorian*. As if those in the land of Skuldenore were one people. But Isaboe could not think of being one with their enemies. Not with the memory of what had been done to her family. Finnikin's father was close at hand. Hers was dead and she had prayed these past years for the grace of forgiveness, but the goddess refused to send it.

"We're not here to speak of the valley dwellers," Isaboe said. "What else have we discovered about Gargarin of Abroi?"

Trevanion gestured for Perri to speak first.

"I've interrogated every Charynite prisoner we have," Perri said, leaning forward in his seat. The blaze of the hearth illuminated the scar that ran across his brow. "Those who have heard of Gargarin of Abroi all speak the same thoughts. He was the king's favorite adviser in the palace eighteen years ago. The Charynites in our prison say that the king favored Gargarin of Abroi's opinion over all others. It was well known in the capital that if young Gargarin of Abroi had a plan, the king would follow it."

"And what does the Charynite in possession of Froi's ring have to say?" Finnikin asked.

"Every word that comes out of his mouth seems a lie, so he's not the most reliable of sources, but he certainly knows who Gargarin of Abroi is."

Trevanion and Perri exchanged looks. "According to the Charynite, the ring was given to him by a lad to bargain for Gargarin of Abroi's life. And the province leaders paid three hundred pieces of gold as ransom to have Gargarin of Abroi returned to them when he was held hostage by these men called the street lords."

There was an uneasy silence in the room.

"Are we suspecting that Froi has joined the enemy?" Isaboe asked, trying to keep her voice even.

"We're suspecting that anyone can be an enemy to Lumatere," Trevanion said. "If it was Froi who bargained with the ring, then he was begging for the life of a man who could easily have been the mastermind behind events in this palace thirteen years ago."

"Easily have been?" Isaboe asked. "If we're going to hunt a man down, we need to be more certain than that."

"Gargarin of Abroi dazzled the king with his ideas," Sir Topher said. "Perhaps he has a way about him."

"Froi is the least likely to be dazzled by another," she said. "Even when he had a choice between life and death, he refused to be influenced by powerful men. His choices are about survival."

She heard a sound come from Finnikin and dared to glance at him.

"How is it that you came to speak about such things with him?" her husband asked.

She shrugged. "We were exchanging stories of horror from our childhood. I told him about my time as a slave in Sorel, and he shared with me some of his more . . . sordid moments on the streets of the Sarnak capital."

Again she felt Finnikin's cold stare. How could a man who stared so coldly possess a smile that made her mood change in an instant? But that smile was far away now.

"I'll say this again because it's the life of a man we are playing with," Isaboe said. "Gargarin of Abroi worked for the king of Charyn eighteen years ago and then disappeared. But he did not work for the king thirteen years ago, when Lumatere was attacked. How can we be sure he was involved?"

"We intercepted a letter he sent to the Belegonians, Your Majesty," Sir Topher said. "Gargarin of Abroi wants to talk to them about Charyn's unborn king. He has ambition."

"Is that a crime? Most people in this court have ambition," she said.

"He mentioned Lumatere." Sir Topher removed the letter

from his pocket and began to read. *"The Lumaterans need not know of our alliance. We'll talk later about what to do with them. Leave it to me, for I have a plan for Lumatere that will eliminate them as a threat."*

Eliminate Lumatere? Isaboe shuddered. "Then we must set a trap," she said.

Trevanion nodded. "Already done, my queen. We sent a letter in response to his, asking him to meet with us on the Charyn-Osteria border."

"And you don't think Gargarin of Abroi knows the look of an authentic Belegonian seal on a letter?" she asked.

Trevanion and Sir Topher exchanged a look.

"Our spy in the Belegonian palace managed to stamp the letter with a Belegonian seal," Sir Topher said, and she knew him well enough to understand that he was hiding something. She looked from her First Man to Trevanion.

"Who's your spy?" she demanded. "Lord August? On his last visit? Does Abian know?"

There was silence and she almost choked at the realization.

"Celie?" She stared at them in horror. "August will kill you."

Sir Topher sighed. "Celie came to us. She's bored. She says she's too plain to dazzle the Belegonian court but that they all confide in her. She says her insipid looks are the perfect weapon. Her words, not ours."

Isaboe rubbed her face, knowing that soon she would be dealing with Celie's parents, Lady Abian and Lord August.

"What about Rafuel of Sebastabol?"

"According to Lucian, the Charynite has made contact between us impossible," Perri said.

"I don't like the fact that he's out of our sight," Finnikin said. "He's still a prisoner, and the agreement was that he would be spying in the valley for us."

Isaboe agreed. "I want Lucian to send down the lads again. I want Rafuel's every movement noted."

"If you send down the Mont lads, Tesadora will insist on returning to the valley for good," Perri said.

"Last I knew, Tesadora was not in charge of this kingdom," she said coolly. "I'll say it again. I want her to pay me a visit. Can you ensure that she receives that request, Perri?"

He nodded. "I'll send Moss."

"Hunt Gargarin of Abroi down," she said to Trevanion. "I don't want him alive. And I don't want him in Lumatere. What needs to be done."

She spoke a few moments more with Sir Topher about their upcoming market day and then turned to find Finnikin packing.

"What are you doing?" she asked. "Where are you going?"

He refused to speak and continued to place items in his pack.

"What is wrong with you?" she cried.

She grabbed the cloak from his belongings and threw it back into the chest.

He stood her aside and retrieved the cloak and placed it back in his pack before pulling on calfskin trousers, which she knew he used only for travel.

"I'm going with my father and Perri."

"No!"

He laced up his boots, continuing to dress as if she hadn't spoken.

"You're not going to Charyn, Finnikin."

"I don't follow a wife's orders," he said.

"I'm not speaking to you as your wife," she shouted. "I'm speaking to you as your queen, and my order is that you are not going to Charyn."

In her corner, Jasmina awoke and began to cry.

"Ah, so that's what is meant by *the queen's consort*," Finnikin said with bitterness. "A page who answers to her demands."

She grabbed his arm, but he shook it free.

"Is that what this is about?" she asked. "Being my consort?"

He ignored her.

"Answer me!"

"You spoke another man's name in my bed!"

She stared at him, stunned. He had shouted at her this way once before when she had been disguised as the novice Evanjalin. It was almost four years past when he discovered the truth about Balthazar and had accused her of sedition.

"I go to Charyn with my father and Perri," he said, his voice hard. "Because I speak the language in a way they don't, and if we are fortunate enough to cross the path of our wayward lad, I'll bring him home to you safe and sound. Perhaps you can murmur his name to him while he shares your bed."

She slapped his face with a cry of outrage, and he pulled her close to him, his arms shaking.

"You've never spoken to me of your time in Sorel as a child," he said, and she saw tears in his eyes. "You've always said it was too painful. That apart from Balthazar's death and what you witnessed in Sarnak, it was your worst memory. Yet you told him. You trusted another man with your pain."

He shook his head, anguished and full of fury. "I've told you everything. Every fear I have. How can we be equals in this union if you can't trust me?"

"Not telling you about Sorel has nothing to do with trust, Finnikin!" she said.

He walked out the door before she could speak another word.

Soon after, she saw his fleece on their bed and knew he would freeze without it. *Let him,* she thought. *Let him.* But she grabbed the fleece and walked outside, flinging it over the balcony down to where Finnikin was already mounting his horse in the court-yard alongside his father and Perri. It caught him in the face, and her only satisfaction was that the weight of it almost toppled him from his horse.

"And don't expect any sympathy if you catch your death out there," she shouted. "You didn't even pack an undershirt."

"I expect nothing from you," he shouted back.

She was determined he would not get the last word and shouted a whole lot more until she had no idea what she was saying.

Inside, she walked to Jasmina's bed, thinking of her dream again. Not of the savageness and not of the confusion, but of the part that she remembered most of all. That it wasn't Tesadora and Vestie who had walked the sleep with her, as they had each month before her pregnancy when it was Isaboe's time to bleed. It was a different spirit now, one that almost shared her heartbeat. She stared down at her daughter but knew it hadn't been Jasmina. She felt a kick in her belly and almost buckled, imagining the truth.

Had she walked the sleep of some savage beast with her unborn child?

CHAPTER 2

F roi?"

"Yes?"

"Are you awake?"

"I am now."

"I can't sleep."

"What are you thinking?"

"About sad things, really. What if I never get to meet our little king, Froi?"

"Don't say that. Don't think it!"

"He'll never know that the time I felt most brave was when I knew he was in my belly."

"You were brave long before that, Quintana. Sleep."

"Quintana?"

"Yes."

"Are you awake?"

"I am now."

"I can't sleep," he said.

"What are you thinking?"

"That time . . . that time you let go of my hand in the Citavita," he said, "when you thought I would hurt you and the babe, where would you have gone?"

"Wherever our little king guided me."

"He speaks to you?"

"No. But he used to speak to my sister, the reginita. He liked the sound of her voice. He's very clever in that way. I think he's gods' blessed, like Arjuro."

"And where did our little king suggest you all journey without me?"

"You'll not believe it."

"But I will."

"Promise you won't think me a fool."

"With all my heart."

"Then you'll have to come closer, Froi. We can't have the Avanosh lot hearing."

"Quintana? I can't hear you. Speak louder. You've got to speak louder. I can't hear you. Quintana!"

"Froi!"

Don't wake up.

"Froi!"

Fight it. Don't let her go again.

"Froi, wake up!"

The times he loved most were when his eyes were closed. So he could imagine he was still in his quarters in Paladozza on that long night when they talked and talked and lay naked against each other. They were like a cocoon, she said. She had seen one in the gardens of their compound and had sat and watched it for hours. So there they lay with her rounded belly between them, protecting their little king, studying each other's face as if trying to work out which part of them would belong to the babe.

With eyes closed shut, Froi could also imagine Gargarin and Lirah down the hall in De Lancey's home and he could go back to that room time and time again and change everything that happened. Take back every word he spoke.

But sleep was already gone and with its loss came truth and a flatness to his spirit that rendered him motionless. Barely opening his eyes, he could see Arjuro crouched beside him, a cup of brew in the priestling's hands that was sure to turn Froi's stomach.

"She whispered it to me, Arjuro," he said, his voice hoarse, and Arjuro lifted the cup to Froi's lips. "I could almost hear her. I could almost hear the words telling me where she'd hide."

"Drink," Arjuro ordered gently. "She's just about told you every night, Froi. For weeks now. You beg her in your sleep over and over again. Let it rest or you'll drive us both mad."

Arjuro lit another of the oil lamps, and then two more, and placed them in the crooks of the wall. It was the only light Froi had seen these past weeks, and he wondered what it did to a spirit to not feel sun on the skin or the wind on one's face.

Although he shared the cavern with Arjuro, passages linked it to every other cavern in the underground godshouse of Trist. The rest of Charyn had been led to believe that the priests were hiding somewhere in the caves outside Sebastabol, but instead they lived beneath the city itself. It was a labyrinth so extensive that it had three main entrances: one through a grate in the ceiling that led to a hospital for travelers, and two through cellars of Sebastabolians who had an allegiance to the priests. It was outside one of those homes where Froi's bloody body was left.

"You have a habit of turning up on our doorstep, Dafar of Abroi," Simeon, the head priest, had told him the first time Froi woke. "Creating havoc in the kingdom beyond understanding."

They were unable to tell him who his savior was. "You were left and he was gone without a word," they said.

Froi dragged himself out of his bedroll and walked to the basin, where he dampened a cloth and wiped it over his face. Each morning had been a measure of how quickly he was healing, and his only relief today was that there was less pain than the day before.

"I'm ready," he said to Arjuro.

"You said you were ready the day you woke up with eight barbs wedged in your body," Arjuro muttered, mixing a paste that he coated on Froi's wounds each morning. It produced a stench that made them both want to retch, but Arjuro insisted that the scars would fade and Froi would heal quicker. The faster Froi healed, the closer he came to finding her.

"Arm up," Arjuro ordered.

Froi held up his arm as Arjuro smeared the paste onto the deepest of the wounds on Froi's side. "It's the one that brought you closest to death," Arjuro said most days, and Froi would hear the break in the priestling's voice each time.

The paste and Arjuro's fingers were cold on his skin, and Froi flinched more than once, although he tried hard not to. It was Arjuro who had to be convinced of his strength. Arjuro, Froi had come to understand, was respected by the compound of Trist, and Froi could see that the priests and their families were desperate to keep him. He was the last of the oracle's priestlings, and he still held a fascination for them all.

"Are you ready for the *collegiati*?" Arjuro asked. "You're the most exciting thing that's happened to them for quite some time."

"You mean my injuries are," Froi said.

"Yes, I suppose they will miss your wounds when you leave." Arjuro chuckled.

Each morning, a group of young men and women, a little

17

older than Froi, came to visit their quarters. Although not last borns, some were in hiding because they were believed to be gods' blessed. Others were the children of the priests and priestesses who had hidden their families all those years ago when the oracle's godshouse was attacked. That a school for the brightest minds in Charyn existed in the bowels of a province didn't surprise Froi. In the nook of any given cave in this kingdom were a people refusing to give up.

"The way they grovel to you makes me sick to my stomach," Froi said as he watched Arjuro arrange his tools of healing. Froi thought of them more as tools of torture. When he had first awoken from his injuries, one of the *collegiati* had told Froi how excited all in the compound had been when Arjuro returned to them.

"He was considered the greatest young surgeon in Charyn before the attack on the Oracle's godshouse," the girl Marte had explained to Froi. "My mother was one of his teachers in Paladozza and said that even as a boy he showed brilliance."

Marte and her fellow *collegiati* were hungry for any type of learning, and they hovered around the entrance of Arjuro's chamber all day long, just for a chance to spend more time with the priestling.

Arjuro found them as annoying as he found most people and would tell them exactly where he would prefer they go. But they returned each day while he treated Froi's wounds, which they analyzed and discussed, poking at Froi as if he were nothing but a slab of mutton. Froi would see their eyes blaze with excitement each time they saw his scars.

Whoever had taken him to these caves had tried to yank out the arrows, but once the shafts were pulled, they had come unstuck from their stems and Froi was left with eight arrowheads lodged inside his body.

"Catgut goes a long way, blessed Arjuro," Marte said that morning when they all shuffled in. "The stitching is perfect."

"But how did you remove the barbs, Brother Arjuro?" a *collegiato* asked in awe.

"With an arrow spoon," Arjuro said, showing them the instrument.

There was much oohing and aahing.

"The spoon is inserted into the wound and latches on to the arrowhead," Arjuro said, looking at Froi. "You might want to close your ears for this next bit, Froi." Arjuro turned back to the others. "Next moment, the barb is ripped out and look what we have?" Arjuro said. "Beautiful."

This was what produced joy for Arjuro. Inflicting pain.

"It's a work of art, Brother Arjuro," an annoyingly fawning *collegiata* said. "You're a genius."

"Yes, I'm going to have to agree," Arjuro said, pleased with himself. "See how clean this one is," he said, pointing to Froi's shoulder blade. "But I think it could have been a tighter stitch. I only wish I had a chance to do it again. If I could get myself some bronzed wire, rather than using sheep bone, I think I could have done a neater job of this sewing."

He caught Froi's eye, a smile crossing his lips. Froi knew he was enjoying himself.

Someone ran a finger alongside the dent at the back of Froi's head and Arjuro slapped the hand away. Froi had received an arrow to the head and they had been forced to crop his hair. Although not completely bare, it felt strange under his fingers. But what was even stranger was the *collegiati*'s reaction to it. Not a day went by without a hand attempting to feel its way across the cleft at the back of Froi's skull.

"Are you going to tell me what's there?" he demanded of Arjuro.

"A hard head," Arjuro responded, and Froi saw the warning look he sent to the others. "It's a good thing you have no brains and the arrowhead pierced nothing but empty space."

It was the same joke each time, and Froi rolled his eyes when the others laughed at it again. "Can I put on my trousers now?" he asked. Never one to be bashful about his naked self, it felt different when the *collegiati* scrutinized every part of his body. The topic of foreskin was the most difficult to endure.

"He grew up in Sarnak. It's what they do to their male young. A snip and then it's gone," Arjuro explained.

The men had flinched. The women were intrigued.

Arjuro ushered them all out.

"Brother Arjuro, what of warts?" one of the lads asked at the entrance of the cave. Nothing gods' blessed about that one. Some were quite delusional when it came to the degree of their talents.

Arjuro stared at the young man.

"I don't heal warts. If you want to learn how to heal warts, go to the soothsayer and she'll feed you with an old wives' tale or two."

When they were all gone, Froi pulled on his trousers.

"They're all half in love with you," he said. "Men and women."

"Yes, it's a pity you didn't inherit our looks," Arjuro said. "You, too, could be as popular."

Froi hid a smile.

"Gargarin was even more sought after," Arjuro explained, sketching today's image of Froi's gut wound into his journal. "It's because he ignored the world and, in turn, the world believed he was playing games."

"Were you jealous of him?"

"Gargarin?" Arjuro looked up, surprised by the question. "Never. I told you. I was jealous of anyone who took him from me."

20

"He could be happy with Lirah in Paladozza," Froi said softly.

Arjuro sighed. "I can't see my brother staying put while all this is happening."

Froi imagined that "all this" was the question of Quintana's whereabouts. He watched Arjuro carefully. "You know I'm ready."

"I'll tell you when you're ready. Sit." Arjuro pressed hard on the puckered skin across Froi's gut.

"Does that hurt?"

Froi pressed two fingers against Arjuro's shoulder with the same force.

"Does that?" he snapped in return.

"Oh, so we're bad-tempered this morning, as well. Always good to see the Abroi spirit living on in our sprog."

This time Froi couldn't resist a smile, but then he grabbed Arjuro's hand and pressed it against the back of his skull.

"What's there, Arjuro? What are you hiding from me?"

Arjuro pulled his hand away with a grimace.

"Nothing we don't already know, Froi. It was just hidden for so long. You were born with a mop of hair. Did you know that? It's probably been there your whole life and no one ever saw it."

"But what is it?"

"It's the same style of lettering as Quintana's," Arjuro said finally. "We didn't realize all this time that both of you were scorched by the gods or whoever it was."

"If not the gods, who else?" Froi asked.

Arjuro shook his head. "I don't know. I wish I did. I wish I knew what it meant."

He placed a blue woolen cap over Froi's head, almost covering his eyes and ears.

"Make sure no one outside these caves see it. Charynites are used to the sign belonging to last-born women," Arjuro said.

"I don't know what would happen if they knew the very last male born was walking among us."

Arjuro put his journal away under his cot. Froi saw a note poking out from one of the pages. He watched for signs of news all the time, and during the past day, Arjuro had received new correspondence.

"What's in the letter?" he asked.

Arjuro didn't respond.

"Tell me," Froi begged.

Arjuro sat on the cot and thought for a minute. "We've received word back from the Turlans. Quintana never reached them, Froi. She's not in the Lascow Mountains, either. We've sent out word to the *provincari*. She may have gone back to Jidia."

"Orlanda made it clear that she would not protect her," Froi said, referring to the *provincara* of Jidia.

"Regardless, if Orlanda's hand is forced, she will protect the future king."

"What of De Lancey? Quintana went searching for Lirah that time in the Citavita. Maybe she returned to Paladozza."

"I've written to De Lancey. Let's hope he responds with the news we want to hear."

"Arjuro—"

"It's all I know. Don't ask me again!"

CHAPTER 3

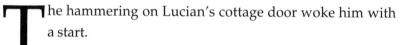

The hammering on Lucian's cottage door woke him with a start.

"Lucian! Lucian!"

The voices belonged to Lady Beatriss and Tesadora, he thought, stumbling from his bed. Something had happened to Yata. He felt the all-too-familiar taste of bile fill his mouth as his mind raced with images of the worst.

But Yata was there the moment Lucian opened the door, his relief cut short when he saw the looks on all three faces.

"Vestie's gone!"

"Taken from her bed, Lucian!"

He grabbed his coat and felt the sharp slap of wind against his cheeks as he joined them outside. Winter was outstaying its welcome for yet another day. He had never known it to drag on so long.

"One at a time," he ordered as they traveled the path down to Yata's home. "And everyone calm down! No one on this mountain would hurt Vestie, so there has to be an explanation."

Lady Beatriss nodded and tried to do as she was told, taking a deep breath that sounded more like a ragged sob.

"I woke up and her bed was empty, and then I woke Tesadora and we searched Yata's house. Nothing."

"The door was unlatched," Tesadora continued. "From the inside."

They reached Yata's compound, which sat at the center of the mountain, and Lucian hurried to the bell in the courtyard. It had only been rung once since their return, after the younger lads broke into the cellars and got drunk. It was unlike the bell that Isaboe had insisted be placed on the mountain halfway to Lumatere. That one was a means of alerting the guards stationed there that something was wrong on the Charyn border; Yata's bell could be heard only throughout the mountain village. Lucian rang it long and loud until the Monts emerged from their cottages, even from as far up as the slopes to the east.

Lucian's eyes met Tesadora's. She wasn't one for dramatics, but she looked pale and he knew that Vestie of the Flatlands was precious to her. Very few people found a place in Tesadora's heart. Finnikin spoke often about the love between Tesadora and Isaboe. Letters were exchanged between the two each week and it wasn't rare to see Tesadora laughing as she read her correspondence. Both Isaboe's and Tesadora's bonds with Vestie were strong because they had walked the sleep together during the curse. Lucian could not fathom the thought of what would happen if Vestie was hurt.

"She could have responded to a knock," Lucian said.

Tesadora, then Beatriss, shook her head.

"We would have heard it," Yata said. "There was no knock."

By now a crowd had gathered around them, calling out questions, realizing that this was no drunken foolery by the younger lads.

Lucian settled them down, knowing that their silence would be short-lived the moment he spoke the words "Vestie is gone."

24

And short-lived it was. Questions were shouted at him from all directions, the women crying out their fear as they surrounded Beatriss, alarming her even more. Worst were Jory and the lads, whipped into a frenzy of fury. Jory's response to Phaedra's death had been anger. The lad wasn't aware that it was grief he was feeling, and perhaps Lucian and the Monts had not realized until these past weeks that Jory was no longer a boy.

"Stop!" Lucian ordered above the noise. He pointed a finger at the lads, who were the last to obey. He waited for silence again. "Everyone search around your homes. Jory, ride down toward the valley and ask the cottagers to start searching the middle mountain. You lot," he said, pointing to his younger cousins, "check the woods. Knock on every door. Juno, take your lads and head toward Balconio."

Lucian turned to Lady Beatriss. "Maybe she woke up feeling lost and is trying to make her way home?"

Lady Beatriss shook her head, and he could see she was holding back tears.

"There is an explanation, Lady Beatriss. You know that. It's what Trevanion would tell you if he were here."

All morning, Vestie's name rang throughout the mountain. Every cottage was searched, every footstep traced, every shrine to the goddess filled with garlands. Lucian knew of Vestie's gift for walking the sleep, but he had never known anyone to become so lost in the dream that it took them from their bed.

And then, midmorning, Jory returned, his face pale, clutching a mitten in his hand. Lady Beatriss took it and held it to her face, weeping.

"She has to be in the valley, Lucian," Jory said. "It's the only explanation."

Lucian caught his breath. It had been weeks since Phaedra's

death, and he had only made the journey to the valley twice. At night, in a panic, he would wake up afraid that he had abandoned Phaedra's companions to the mercy of the cutthroat camp leader, Donashe, and his men. No matter how many times he reminded himself that the valley dwellers were not his people, Lucian felt a fierce sense of guilt.

"We should have had our sentinels down in the valley," Tesadora said, her voice blunt and accusing.

"But we don't," Lucian argued. He had used the threat of the plague as a reason to stop sending down the lads, but he knew there was no such danger anymore. He looked around at those waiting for the next order. "Lady Beatriss, you wait —"

"Don't ask me to do that, Lucian. I'm coming with you."

He didn't even attempt to instruct Tesadora. She was coming down to the valley whether Lucian liked it or not.

"Yata." He sighed. "Go back to the house, in case Vestie returns. Jory and Yael, come with me. Everyone else, stay."

When they reached the bottom of the mountain, Lucian did what he always did: asked his father for guidance. What would Saro do? Cross the stream and accuse the Charynites of taking a Lumateran child, after all the valley dwellers had endured with the death of five of their women and the slaughter of Rafuel's men? Would Lucian ask for help from the murderous camp leaders, or would he accuse them of taking Vestie? Could he trust Rafuel, who now seemed a stranger to them? At the campsite on the Lumateran side of the valley where Tesadora had once camped with her girls, he dared to look through the trees in the hope of catching a glimpse of his wife crossing the stream.

That's why you haven't returned here, Lucian. Because you see her everywhere.

"Jory, you cross the stream and see what you can find out.

They'll trust you. Remember, no accusations. I don't care what the camp leaders say — we cannot have Kasabian and the others thinking we believe that they hurt one of our own.

"Yael, you watch Jory from one of the trees and holler for me the moment there's trouble. Lady Beatriss, Tesadora and I will continue down this side of the stream and see what we can find. We'll meet you back here."

As they traveled farther downstream, he could see Phaedra's people in their caves through the copse of trees.

"She would never have come this far," Beatriss said when they were deep within the woods. "Perhaps . . . perhaps she tried to cross the stream. The ice is beginning to melt on the mountain, and the force of it could have carried her away."

"Beatriss," Tesadora said firmly, "she swims better than any child we know."

Lucian doubted greatly that Vestie had been swept away by the stream. Lucian knew that teaching Vestie to swim was the first thing Trevanion had done for Lady Beatriss and the child she bore during the curse, when they were reunited three years past. It had created a bond between the captain and his former lover's child. Today, they were a family, and the union had been one of the most joyous occasions for Lumaterans.

Suddenly he saw a movement, heard the snap of a twig and the rustle of leaves and the strangest of giggles.

"Vestie!" he called out, racing toward the sound. Beatriss and Tesadora were with him, calling out her name. "Vestie!"

But there was nothing. They stood a moment to listen, hearing only the sound of a bird mocking. Then he saw the movement again and Lucian was running, leaping over half-fallen limbs, avoiding the tree shoots that caught at his ankle.

"Vestie!"

"Vestie!"

"Vestie, my love!"

Lucian continued his pursuit until he heard the sound of heavy breath, rasping for air. But it was not the breathing of a child. He stopped and held up a hand to Tesadora, who appeared close behind.

"Vestie, it's Lucian! Are you hiding?"

Beatriss entered the clearing, and Tesadora placed a finger to her lips.

"I'll not be angry," Lucian said. "I promise, Vestie darlin'."

He knew she was close, but not alone, and that alarmed Lucian more than he cared to admit. He took a step closer, and there he saw them. Huddled in the hollow of a tree trunk. A girl with crazed eyes held a hand over Vestie's mouth. A bloody dagger was clasped in her other hand.

He heard Beatriss's cry behind him, and he saw Vestie look up, startled to see them all. Startled, but not frightened. Beatriss rushed forward, but the strange girl snarled, and Lucian gripped Beatriss's hand and dragged her gently behind him.

"Please don't hurt her," Beatriss begged the girl. "Please."

Lucian moved toward the girl, a hand at the scabbard of his sword. He knew with certainty that he would slice this wretch's hand clear off her body if she didn't let go of Vestie at his command.

"Vestie, step away from her," he ordered gently. Vestie stared at the sword and suddenly began to weep, confused. Was she waking from walking in her sleep? He moved closer and the most savage of sounds came from the girl, and she held the dagger out before her, waving it in Lucian's face. He retrieved his sword from its scabbard slowly, not once losing eye contact with her.

"Lucian, come back," Tesadora ordered. "You're scaring them."

But Lucian refused, and when he almost reached them, the savage girl clenched her teeth, dragging Vestie deeper into the hollow of the tree.

"Lucian, please stop," Beatriss cried. "She'll hurt her."

Lucian shook his head, refusing to move away.

"Do not let me have to explain to Trevanion why I put my sword down while someone held a dagger to his daughter."

Tesadora walked before him. His hand caught her arm to pull her backward, but she shrugged free.

"I know what I'm doing," she said, her eyes fastened on the girl, who stared, almost transfixed. When Tesadora was only a step away from Vestie and the girl, Lucian heard a bloodcurdling snarl, but suddenly Tesadora's hand snaked out and gripped the girl's face.

"Oh, you savage beauty," Tesadora said. "Where did you come from?"

Lucian wondered if Tesadora was bewitched. The girl stared, confused. Tesadora repeated the words in Charyn.

"We won't hurt her," Tesadora said, reaching out for Vestie.

Vestie gripped the girl's hand that was pressed over her mouth and removed it. Lucian expected a scream, but instead Vestie leaned forward and whispered into the stranger's ear.

The mad girl peered over Tesadora's shoulder to where Beatriss stood with Lucian.

"I just want to hear the little person speak again," the savage girl said coldly in Charyn. "I want to hear her voice."

"We need to take her home," Tesadora explained gently. "She'll be safe. You must get back to your people in the valley."

The girl shook her head emphatically.

"Tell no one, Serker Eyes," she whispered. "Or else they'll kill us all."

Small crooked teeth showed through a snarl. Before anyone

could speak another word, the girl scrambled to her feet and tore off. Lucian quickly gathered Vestie in his arms, his eyes meeting Tesadora's.

"What," he asked, "was that?"

Later, when Vestie was being bathed by Beatriss and the women, they found not a single mark on her body. She had recovered quickly from her ordeal.

"Who was she, Vestie?" Lady Beatriss asked as Yata wrapped the little girl up in a blanket while Lucian's aunts fussed.

"I don't know. I think I walked and slept, Mama, and then I was in the woods crying and I saw her. It was as though I knew she'd be there. And I said, 'Hello there. Hello there, I say.' And she looked so frightened. It was just like that time we first met the valley dwellers and they stared at us in such a fashion."

"They're not used to seeing little girls," Yata said.

"I spoke again and said, 'My name is Vestie,' and she wept and wept and she spoke in that funny way the camp dwellers speak."

Vestie turned to Tesadora. "I want to learn, Tesadora. I want to speak just like them. I only know one word. It means friend. I said it in her ear. '*Sora. Sora. Sora.*'"

Tesadora chuckled and gathered Vestie to her.

"And who taught you this Charynite word for friend?"

"Phaedra of Alonso did. She said it was the prettiest word in Charyn."

And Lucian ached to hear those words.

Vestie looked up at Lady Beatriss. "That time we crossed the stream together with you, Mama. Remember? Phaedra said not to be afraid because the camp dwellers only wanted to be my friend. My *sora*. I want to learn more."

"I'll teach you, Vestie," Jory said from the entrance of the room, anger lacing his voice. "So that when you see her again you can tell the witch we'll tear her limb—"

"Jory!" Lucian warned, while Beatriss covered Vestie's ears. Jory looked away, shamefaced.

"Go out to the lads," Lucian ordered, shoving his young cousin forward. "And calm them down. There will be no repeat of raids into the valley."

"Not their side of the valley, Lucian," Jory said. "Ours. She wasn't a valley dweller. You said so yourself."

"Go."

Jory left, a stubborn set to his jaw.

"We'll get supper started," Yata said, following the aunts out of the room. Lucian bobbed down to Vestie's height.

"Can you remember anything else, Vestie?" Lucian asked.

"Every time I spoke, she'd weep and weep with joy."

"She liked your voice," Beatriss said quietly.

"But whose blood was it?" Lucian asked. "It was the first thing we saw, and it frightened us all."

Vestie laughed with glee. "She taught me to slaughter a hare."

Vestie twisted her hands together as if breaking the neck of an animal and made the most gods-awful sound. "I'm going to show Father."

"Yes, Father will be overjoyed to hear all about this when he returns," Beatriss murmured, catching Lucian's eye.

"We caught three," Vestie exclaimed. "We caught them together."

"You did not," Lucian mocked, desperate to know more about their savage neighbor.

"I did, too," she said indignantly. "Can I play with her again?"

"No, my love," Beatriss said. "We're going home to Fenton in a few days. You've given us quite a scare."

"I told her about Millie and how I left her behind in my bed."

Lucian was confused. "Millie?"

"Her doll," Beatriss said. "I'll go get her." She pressed a kiss to her daughter's brow. "Don't do this to Mama again, Vestie. You scared me today."

When Beatriss left the room, Vestie turned to Tesadora.

"Why can't I take her home with us, Tesadora?"

"We know nothing about her, minx," Tesadora said, picking her up and swinging her around. "We don't even know her name."

"I think I do," Vestie said, indignant. "She's just like Isaboe, you know. Just like her."

"She's nothing like Isaboe," Lucian said.

Tesadora looked up at him. "How about you calm down the lads . . . and Vestie can tell me everything she knows about her new friend in the valley?"

CHAPTER 4

I come close to our cave with hands drenched in hare's blood. If they feast on fresh game for the first time in weeks, perhaps things may change and their hearts will be open. But the women are speaking, they're fighting, they're weeping, Froi. Their stone-hearted claws scratch at me whole. Though their voices are hushed, they scream with such hate. I hear them speak words, "We'll kill in her sleep." The little king kicks, a beat of great fear, and he begs me to run from these wretches of malice. The Mont's wife, she sees me, her face speaks of shame, and the hares in my hand are hurled in my fury.

And I run and I run, and I think of the girl child, the one they call Visti, and the trust in her eyes. I think of her voice, so much like Regina, my sister beloved who's left me behind. But Froi, have you joined her at the lake of the half dead? I fear that you have and she's not sent you back. The last time I saw you, eight arrows were piercing. You couldn't have lived; the gods aren't that kind.

And I hide in the thistles that tear at my skin, but finally I see her, the white-headed Serker. She knows I am out here but pretends she's not looking. I know she is looking and pretend it's a game. And finally I'm closer and I grip at her strange hair, the white of its strands a shroud around my fist. And my blood beats a dance because I've found it a kindred. So I vow to return and my smile aches my face. I know her: Tesadora. Will she love me regardless?

She knows me, she knows me, but does not turn away.

Phaedra of Alonso was running. Stumbling over an upturned stone once, twice. Praying with all her being for a glimpse of their strange princess. Up in the distance the whistle of the wind sang to her from the mountain. From Lucian's mountain. It beckoned and taunted, and she wanted to run toward it. To be enveloped in its coat of fleece and to hear its safe sounds.

And then she saw Quintana of Charyn and she stopped, almost crumbling from relief and fatigue and fear. It left room for anger, and Phaedra didn't realize until that moment how much she disliked Princess Abomination for what she had brought into their lives.

"Your Highness," she said quietly, fearful that Donashe and his men would travel downstream and cross their path. Despite the distance from both the camp and the road to her father's province, there was always a chance that someone would stray and discover their secret. From what Rafuel had told them, the one time he had managed to slip away since their "deaths," the Monts were no longer acting as sentinels on the Lumateran side of the stream. So there was nothing to stop Donashe and his murderers from hunting in the woodlands and crossing the stream to where Phaedra and the women hid. Worse still, Rafuel had advised that one of Donashe's men was feeling threatened by Rafuel's presence around his leader. The man followed Rafuel's and Donashe's every move, which had made it difficult for Rafuel to slip away. So here Phaedra and the women were, a mile downstream from the Charynite valley dwellers, not knowing what was happening to their people upstream except that Phaedra's father had stopped sending grain from Alonso.

Despite Phaedra's warnings to stay put, the Princess crossed the stream most days. It was as if she was drawn to the Lumateran side with its gullies and tall tree canopies. The girl had a tendency to disappear for hours upon end, which unnerved them all. And then they'd be unnerved again by her return.

Phaedra didn't know what was worse. Quintana of Charyn's absence or presence. This afternoon's behavior was quite dramatic: she had tossed one of the hares at Florenza and run off like a wild savage.

"Her father's daughter," Jorja had muttered. Jorja and her husband, Harker, despised the dead king more than anyone Phaedra had ever met, except for the Lumaterans.

Phaedra caught up with the princess near a moss-covered stone.

"You can't wander away, Your Highness." Phaedra used a brisk tone, despite the fact that she was speaking to the daughter of a king. "We must keep to the cave. We've been beside ourselves with worry."

The stare that met hers was hard and cold. Cora and the other women believed an entity inhabited Quintana of Charyn, and that deep inside, she was not quite human. It made Phaedra despair even more. What hope did Charyn have if this creature carried the first?

"I'm the queen, Phaedra of Alonso. Did I not mention that?"

Oh, you've mentioned it many, many times, Phaedra wanted to say. Once with a hand around Jorja's neck, squeezing tight because Jorja had dared to question what type of authority the princess had now that the king was dead.

"And I'm not going back," announced the princess or queen or whoever she wanted to be. "They'll kill me in my sleep. I heard them say."

Phaedra sighed. "They said no such thing, Your Majesty."

And there was the ice-cold stare again.

"I heard the words," Quintana said with a curl to her lip that spoke of a threat. "Are you calling me a liar, Phaedra of Alonso?"

Phaedra hesitated, choosing her next words wisely. "You frighten them," she finally said. "You snarl and rage and sometimes we believe that our sacrifice was for nothing. 'She'll kill us in our sleep.' That's what you heard. Their fear is that you will kill us all."

With as much courage as she could muster, Phaedra walked to the princess, pulled her to her feet, and dragged her along in much the same way she had seen a Mont mother drag her protesting boy toward the bathhouse. She was sick and tired of being the one to keep the peace among the women. It was about time everyone else did their duty. When they reached the stream, Phaedra tore a strip from Quintana's dress and soaked it in the water, then cleaned the girl's bloodied hands and face with it. If Quintana of Charyn knew anything, it was how to hunt. A frightening thought in itself, but Phaedra had to admit that the hares had filled their empty stomachs for the first time in days. And there was the satisfaction of seeing one of the hares lobbed at Florenza's nose. Jorja believed that she and her precious daughter were above everyone else, despite their journey through the sewers. "She was the most sought-after girl in our province," Jorja had boasted just the night before.

"Yes, but where are these suitors now that Florenza has crawled through shit?" Cora asked.

Each time Jorja and Florenza's escape was mentioned, Florenza whimpered and made gagging sounds, and Ginny would laugh. Ginny laughed at anything that was mean. Phaedra had learned to dislike them all since their so-called deaths. If she had to hear Jorja boast, or Florenza whimper, or Cora mock, or Ginny being snide one more time, she'd find a hare or two to throw at them all herself.

"What are you smiling about?" the princess asked, breaking Phaedra's thoughts. Quintana sat on one of the stepping stones in the stream, and Phaedra had no choice but to squat beside her. She felt the skirt of her dress soak but refused to allow her discomfort to show.

"It's a grimace, not a smile," Phaedra said.

"It was a smile."

She felt Quintana's strange gaze and met it. Months on the mountain had made Phaedra less afraid of bullies, and no people knew how to intimidate her more than the Monts. But as she returned Quintana's stare, all Phaedra saw was that the mother of their future king was nothing but a broken, bloodied girl.

"I think he's dead," the princess said quietly.

Phaedra froze. "The babe?"

The princess shook her head.

Phaedra waited, gently scrubbing Quintana's face clean.

"I looked back once," the princess continued, "and counted eight arrows, and I heard his cries and saw his spirit fight to leave his body."

Phaedra was confused. She had heard the princess tell Rafuel that the father of her child, the heir Tariq of Lascow, had been slaughtered in the underground caves of the Citavita. Who was this "he" she was speaking of?

"Is there a chance that Tariq of Lascow is alive?" Phaedra asked, hope in her voice.

"Tariq's dead," Quintana said. "I saw his corpse. I saw them all. They died protecting me . . . protecting this," she said, pointing to her belly. "Maybe I'll see your corpse, Phaedra of Alonso. Everywhere I go, I leave behind corpses." There were tears of fury in the girl's eyes. "I left him behind, dying."

Phaedra failed to hide a shudder. "Whom are you speaking of?" she dared to ask. She thought of Rafuel's warning on the day Quintana of Charyn had entered their life. The less they knew, the better it was for them all.

"Who, if not Tariq of Lascow?" Phaedra persisted.

The princess leaned forward, pressing her lips against Phaedra's ear. Phaedra smelled the stench of hare's blood.

"Froi of Lumatere."

Phaedra stumbled back into the water, stunned. She remembered the story she had heard of the rescue in the Citavita. He had swung through the air to save Quintana. The audacity of his actions had made Phaedra like Froi even more than she had the one or two times they had met on the mountain. She knew what he meant to Lucian and Tesadora, as well as Perri, the guard who shared Tesadora's bed. Some said the queen and her consort loved the lad as if he were a brother.

And then Phaedra remembered Rafuel's strange words: *Did you mate with the last born?*

"Is he the father?" she asked, horrified. "Froi of Lumatere?"

"Don't let me have to kill you for knowing that, idiot girl," Quintana threatened. "Don't let me hear you speak it out loud to those parrots in the cave."

"Then, why tell me?" Phaedra cried, getting to her feet and following the stepping stones across the stream to get as far away from the girl as possible. She couldn't bear the idea of what the Lumateran's death would do to those on the mountain and beyond. Worse still, it would mean true war between the two kingdoms.

◆ ◆ ◆

When they returned to the cave, Phaedra heard the hushed fighting in an instant. They called it their prison. It was a small shrine house that from the outside looked like any other cave, much like those upstream, half concealed with shrubs and vines. But once inside, there were two chambers. The larger one was dedicated to the goddess Sagrami, a fact that unnerved them all. Sagrami was the goddess of blood and tears and was said to have cursed Lumatere. It was also further proof that despite Phaedra's people being allowed in the valley, the earth still belonged to their Lumateran neighbors. Through a narrow walkway, the cave opened up to another, smaller chamber. It had a wind hole that gave a view of downstream, but most of the time they kept it covered with vines and shrubs to keep out the cold. No one dared sleep in the shrine room, so here they were, living in too small a space for five women who could hardly endure one another's company.

"I can't stand this," Phaedra heard Ginny cry. "I didn't ask to save Charyn. When Rafuel returns, I'm going to ask him to tell Gies that I'm alive. I don't like being without my man."

"From the flirting I saw the fool do with those Mont girls, I dare say he'll cope," Cora said in a nasty tone.

Cora loved nothing more than riling Ginny, whose only sense of worth came from having a man. Phaedra had known girls like Ginny in Alonso. The type who rarely took the side of women in an argument. They feared it would make them unpopular in the eyes of men. She remembered Ginny in the camp and realized that most of the acquaintances the girl had struck up were with the camp leaders Gies seemed drawn to.

"You're a liar," Ginny shouted at Cora, who was still taunting her about the Mont girls.

"And you're one of the greatest idiots I've come across, and believe me when I say I've come across many."

"Enough!" Phaedra said from the entrance. "Our voices will carry upstream."

They stared over Phaedra's shoulder at the princess.

"Tell her to stay put," Cora said.

"You'll have to tell her yourself, Cora," Phaedra said firmly. "She's not deaf to your voice, you know. Now, enough of this fighting. We have a little king to protect."

"If you ask me, the only thing keeping her alive is that little king," Ginny said. "That's what my Gies would say."

"Shut it, you idiot girl," Cora said.

"You shut it. You're an ugly hag. There were women in my village just like you. Hags with nothing left to offer a man."

"Well, it's a good thing the men in the village had you," Cora said.

"Shut up, both of you," Jorja hissed. "I'd crawl through those sewers one hundred times over not to have to listen to any of you."

This was Phaedra's life now, and she wondered what she had done to the gods for them to punish her in such a way. And in the corner, Quintana of Charyn sat staring at her, shaking her head. Phaedra recognized the look directed at her. She had seen it on the mountain before she had proven her worth. It was disappointment. *You're useless, Phaedra. Useless.*

She closed her eyes and went to sleep with the sound of Florenza's retching in her ears. And a small part of her begged the gods not to let her wake.

CHAPTER 5

Froi was summoned to see the elder of the compound, Simeon of Nebia. The priest had come to visit him once when he lay injured and in pain, but Froi remembered little of that time except for the constant questions regarding Quintana's whereabouts.

But this time Froi was well enough to visit the leader's residence, and it was the first time he was able to study the underground galleries. They were unlike Tariq's compound under the Citavita. Here the ceilings were high and the rooms were wide. Froi could see that they had not always been a hiding place. The archways seemed about six feet high and large enough for a pushcart to fit through them. The walls were made of limestone, and Arjuro had mentioned that the galleries were once used to quarry chalk.

They entered a long, wide corridor with a dozen or so small alcoves on either side where the *collegiati* slept. In each cubicle was a bedroll, a stool, and books scattered around. The passageway led to another cavern, referred to as the chamber of reflection, which was much like a small godshouse where they assembled for prayer or to find solitude. Froi watched as Arjuro stood at the wall and traced his finger against the stone, as if writing a secret message that only the gods could decipher.

"What were you doing?" Froi asked quietly as they stepped out of the chamber onto a landing.

"That's between me and them."

They finally came to a vertical shaft that led down to a lower level, and it was there that Simeon lived.

"I've not been invited," Arjuro said. "So speak to him as you would the Lumateran priest-king."

"I yell at the priest-king," Froi said. "I've thrown manuscripts at him when he's forced me to read the jottings—or droppings, as I preferred to call them—of the ancients on their visit to the off lands. You do not want me speaking to the elder as I would the priest-king."

Arjuro poked him in the shoulder.

Froi entered Simeon's residence. It was covered from top to toe with brightly colored shards of clay tile. It was as if someone had smashed a plate to the ground, then gathered the pieces to stick on the wall. On the ceiling were the most magnificent frescoes he had seen, better even than De Lancey's or those in the locked wing of the Lumateran palace where Isaboe's family had been slain. Simeon the elder was shelling broad beans beside a pot of boiling water. He acknowledged Froi with a tilt of his head and beckoned him close. He pointed at Froi's cap.

"Can you remove it?"

Simeon had a cold countenance, unlike the priest-king, and it was difficult to read his thoughts. But Froi had to respect a man who had succeeded in keeping a frightened community thriving not only after the slaughter in the oracle's godshouse, but during the years since the curse in Charyn as well.

Froi did as he was told, then turned, knowing it was the lettering Simeon was interested in seeing.

"Just as confusing as the mark of the last-born women," Simeon mused. "But different."

"Can I see the markings on one of your last-born girls?" Froi asked. Because Quintana's hadn't made sense to him, he had never truly studied them. Now he had a chance to compare.

Simeon shook his head.

"Our last borns have hidden in these caves for eighteen years, so they were not marked when they were of age. But we've had visitors from outside, and I know the lettering well."

Simeon stood and shuffled toward a bench of books piled high. He retrieved a piece of parchment and held it out for Froi to study.

"Yours has stems on the round letters. Here and here," he said, pointing to the copy of the last-born girls' lettering. "I have a feeling that the idiot king's riders copied it wrong on the girls. So all these years, we've been trying to decipher words that don't exist."

"Do you think you can decipher this?" Froi said, pointing to his skull.

"Not all priests are gods' blessed, Dafar," Simeon said. "Did you know that?"

Froi felt strange hearing his true name spoken by the priest.

"Arjuro says the gods close their eyes and point, and that he just happened to be in their line of vision that day," Froi said.

Simeon didn't respond.

"Are you?" Froi asked. "Gods' blessed?"

"No," Simeon said. "I think I fooled myself as a younger man, but when you meet the likes of Arjuro of Abroi, you realize the difference between ordinary men and those the gods chose to lead us."

"It's hard to believe just by looking at Arjuro," Froi said.

Simeon's expression softened. "My grandson Rothen is

gods' blessed. He's with Rafuel of Sebastabol in the Lumateran valley. We've not heard from them. We're beginning to fear the worst."

"The Lumaterans would never harm them," Froi said.

"You don't know that."

Simeon was not the sort of man to fool others with false hope. "It's not only the Lumaterans we fear, Dafar. Arjuro mentioned Zabat of Nebia's treachery."

Froi nodded. "But your lads keep to themselves. If they're as cunning as Rafuel—"

"But they're not," Simeon said, his voice grave. "They don't have the nature of Rafuel. Rothen is . . . a dreamer."

"Is he a physician?"

A faint smile appeared on Simeon's face. "No. He's an artist." He pointed to the walls and then the roof above them.

Froi looked at him, dumbfounded. "Those were done in our time? They look as though the ancients drew them."

"My grandson's work replicating the ancients' manuscripts is humbling. I can only take responsibility for providing the seed that created his mother."

Simeon emptied the broad beans into the water.

"But we're not here to talk about Rothen and the lads in the valley. We're here to talk about the two people born last in this kingdom."

Simeon lowered his voice. "Or more important, the king and the curse breaker they may have created."

Simeon's knowledge of events may have had little to do with Arjuro. So Froi waited. Trevanion always said that silence from one party always resulted in information from another.

"Apart from the oracle's godshouse, the one here in Sebastabol was the largest and the most political of all in Charyn," Simeon said. "It sits on a cliff overlooking the vast Ocean of Skuldenore

and has not been used since we heard of the attack on the godshouse and oracle in the capital. For centuries the godshouses of
Charyn have sent their most brilliant scholars to the Citavita.
Those men and women chronicled our lives, studied the stars,
and designed the structures that have kept us in awe. The godshouse produced physicians and alchemists and nurtured genius.
Always guided by an oracle sent by the gods."

"But the oracle wasn't sent by the gods," Froi said bluntly.
"She was taken from a goatherd's family in the Turlan
Mountains."

Simeon looked away. "Regardless of how she was found, lad,
she was still sent to us by the gods."

"But why lie to the people about her origins?"

"Because people aren't interested in the truth, Dafar. They're
interested in what keeps them safe. They're interested in being
looked after. They're interested in a tale being spun. Do you
know the story they tell now in Charyn about the Lumateran
priest-king? That he sang his song, and from across the land, his
people heard his voice and followed him home to Lumatere after
ten wretched years. A better story than the truth. That he was
found wallowing in a death camp with no hope."

"He is a mighty man," Froi said, catching his breath at the
thought of the priest-king. "Don't you forget that."

"But mighty men have moments of great despair that common people do not want to know about."

Simeon's eyes were full of regret.

"The *provincari*, the priests, and the palace are rivals, and in
the new Charyn, it is best that we do away with that rivalry. So
we're going to chronicle a different tale. The people of Charyn
won't enjoy the real one. The one Arjuro told me, anyway."

Froi and Quintana were the real story. So were Gargarin,
Lirah, and Arjuro.

"And what story is that?" Froi asked, trying hard to obey Arjuro's command to behave.

"The story of the last-born lad who was left on our doorstep eighteen and a half years ago. Of the priests of Trist, who decided to keep the babe safe by taking him to Sarnak. Charyn is not going to enjoy the story of their failure. That the priests of Trist lost the last born—lost him for all those years—and that he was brought up on the filthy streets of the Sarnak capital. They're going to hate the part about the king raping the oracle and that she gave birth to the princess. So we're going to have to make up a story everyone will love, Dafar. One befitting a king."

Froi felt the tears stinging at his eyes.

"Tell me that story, then," he said, unable to keep the bitterness out of his voice.

"Oh, it's a beautiful one," Simeon said. "In which the king's daughter found love with the heir to the throne, Tariq of Lascow, despite having Lirah, the Serker whore, as a mother. Where he planned her rescue from the gallows and married her in their underground home. And he gave up his life to keep the future mother of his child safe. It's a love story, Dafar. Everyone wants to believe in one. And if we manage to keep Quintana of Charyn alive, do you know why the people will love her? Because the heir, Tariq of Lascow, loved her. The little king will mean even more to us."

Froi turned away. "I was never one for stories," he said, staring up at the frescoes.

"Do you want me to tell you another one?"

Froi didn't respond. His eyes focused on the larger-than-life image of a warrior aiming a longbow on the wall of the cave. He searched the ceiling for whatever it was the marksman was aiming at. Simeon pointed to the image of a tree whose roots stretched across all corners, as if reading his thoughts. Painted on the trunk was a decree pinned with a bronze arrow. It was the same word written three times in faint gold. *Hope. Hope. Hope.*

"I've never heard that story," Froi said softly. "About a warrior shooting messages of hope."

Simeon smiled ruefully. "Because it doesn't exist." He pointed to his bedroll, which lay directly under the three words. "My grandson's first work at the age of thirteen. He said I was a pessimist and he wanted me to stare up at it to remind me not to be. In the darkness, the gold letters are illuminated and all I can see are the words."

Charyn needed more men like Rothen, Froi thought.

"Did you know it was Arjuro who first took you to Sarnak as a babe?" Simeon asked.

Froi was stunned to hear the words. He shook his head because he could hardly speak. There were so many secrets hidden inside Gargarin and Arjuro, and he wondered if they would all ever be revealed.

"Arjuro was a broken man on the night he escaped from the palace eighteen years ago. He said there was a darkness tainting his spirit, and he had to make something right. It was his idea that we smuggle the abandoned babe out of the kingdom. He volunteered to be the one."

Simeon's stern face softened. "You spent the first month of your life in the safety of his arms. I've seen you both together these past weeks, and it is clear that the ties that bind you are still strong."

The bond was strong because Arjuro was blood kin. Froi knew that more than anything else.

"Arjuro returned from Sarnak and lived here with us. He was as wild as ever and full of rage at the world. At himself. Over the next few years, we would hear news about you from the priestess of the Sarnak godshouse. You were *Our Dafar*," he added.

"If any of us ever experienced hardship, we would say, 'At least Our Dafar is safe.'"

"But four years after we sent you to Sarnak, we received word that the godshouse of the Sarnak capital was destroyed by fire. All we knew at the time were the names of those who had perished. And that there was no child among the dead. So we sent a messenger to bring you home . . . but the messenger never reached Sarnak. Your fate was lost to us until Rafuel of Sebastabol sent word three years past that he believed he had found you in the woods on the Charyn-Osteria border."

"Rafuel was there?" Froi asked. "In the barracks when I was taken by the Charynites?"

Simeon nodded. "Rafuel ran away from his father and the palace when he was fourteen years old. When he returned to the Citavita years later to find out what he could about the last born, he was rounded up with a group of lads and put to use in the army. And as fate had it, Rafuel was at the right place at the right time. And here you are, Dafar of Abroi."

There was something about the way Simeon said his name this time that made Froi uneasy.

"What do you want from me?" Froi asked, because he knew he hadn't been summoned to listen to Simeon's stories.

"Find us the girl."

The priest's eyes were ice-cold.

"And then go back to being Froi of Lumatere. And no one need get hurt."

That night, Froi sat opposite Arjuro in silence for the most part.

"What did he say?" Arjuro asked finally when the candle between them had burned low.

"I think he threatened me."

"He sent Rafuel to find you, Froi. Rafuel is an assassin. A

well-read assassin, but one all the same. When I first lived here with these people, one of their lovers in Nebia was murdered because she would not divulge their whereabouts. The retribution was bloody."

"You never said you were the one who smuggled me out of Charyn when I was a babe," Froi said softly. "Simeon said it was your idea."

"Yes, well, that proved to be one of my better ones," Arjuro said dryly. "Because Sarnak seems to have been a wonderful experience for you."

"You blame yourself?" Froi asked.

"Well, I'm to blame for many things, so I try to make it easier on the gods and take responsibility for all of them."

"Even for the war in the kingdom of Yutlind?" Froi teased.

"Oh, yes, my fault. Shouldn't have told the northern king that he was far more handsome than his southern cousin."

But with all the jesting, they were both quite somber, and Froi knew why.

"I'm ready to go, Arjuro," he said softly. "You know that."

"You're safer with me."

"You sound like your brother."

"My brother?" Arjuro asked. "The one who happens to be your father?"

Froi thought of Simeon's story that day. "I wouldn't say that too loudly."

Arjuro's face was suddenly cold.

"If the priests and *provincari* will agree on one thing, it's Gargarin's fate," Arjuro said. "Locking him up in the palace as the next king's First Adviser."

"But he'll have Lirah by his side," Froi said. *And Quintana,* he thought. And his son.

He saw the uncertainty in Arjuro's expression.

"Do you think I should have stayed in Paladozza?" Froi asked. "That I put Quintana's life at risk?"

Arjuro studied him and shook his head.

"There are so many awful possibilities. So many. But none worse than Quintana and the babe being in the hands of the Sorellians. Wasn't that what you said Feliciano of Avanosh and his uncle planned?

"And if you had taken Gargarin with you, they would have trained their arrows on him first. Intelligence and goodwill are Bestiano's greatest enemies; he will kill my brother before he kills anyone else in this land. Gar is Bestiano's greatest competitor for a place in the palace, as reluctant as he is to return there. You did the right thing."

"But I failed," Froi said, pained to think of how much he had. "You don't know how that feels."

Arjuro's laugh was humorless. "You are saying those words to the wrong man, Froi. Failure is more of a twin to me than my own brother."

Two days later, a messenger returned from Paladozza with a letter addressed to Arjuro. Froi watched him open it and noticed that Arjuro's hands trembled.

"Read it aloud. Hurry," Froi ordered.

"What if it's private?" Arjuro argued. "It's addressed to me. See, *Arjuro*," he added, pointing to his name on the note.

"Read!"

Arjuro sighed.

"Just so you know, De Lancey always gets carried away in his letters," he muttered.

Froi tried to snatch the parchment from him, but Arjuro stepped away.

"*Dear Ari,*" he read. Arjuro cleared his voice, hesitating a moment. *"Quintana is not with us. We, too, have sent out messengers to Jidia and the Turlan Mountains, as well as Lascow, but each returns with no idea of her whereabouts. She has disappeared from existence and we hold grave fears for her life."*

Froi held his head in his hands. When Arjuro didn't read on, he looked up.

"Read," he said quietly.

Arjuro continued. *"Gargarin and Lirah have left. . . ."*

"What?" Froi demanded, reaching for the letter. "Let me read."

Arjuro held up a hand to silence him.

"Your brother has been corresponding with the Belegonians. After writing a countless number of letters to every contact he had in the palace, the Belegonians have finally responded. A messenger of the king has agreed to meet Gar at an inn on the Charyn-Osteria river border."

Froi didn't like the news at all. How could Gargarin imagine that he could protect Lirah and himself from enemies both inside and outside Charyn?

"He shouldn't have left," he raged at Arjuro. "He was supposed to stay safe in Paladozza." Froi paced the cave, fearing the absolute worst. "Doesn't he know how dangerous it is to be traveling through the kingdom these days?"

Arjuro looked just as unhappy about the news. He went back to the letter.

"You may want to know that two weeks ago, your moronic horsearse father arrived, demanding to see you and Gar. My guard had his heinous self escorted from the province, cursing you both to oblivion. As much as your leaving angers me still, I was relieved you weren't here to see him. . . ."

Arjuro stopped reading aloud.

"What?" Froi demanded. "What are you keeping from me?"

"Nothing."

51

"You're hiding something, Arjuro."

Froi snatched the letter from Arjuro, furiously pointing a finger at his face.

"You keep nothing from me, do you hear?" Froi said, his eyes fixed on the page. An instant later, he handed back the letter sheepishly. There was a hint of a smile on Arjuro's face.

"The letter was addressed to me, runt. See here," he said, pointing. *"Arjuro."*

Froi's face felt warm. "Yes, well, I thought you left on bad terms. I didn't expect him to express himself so . . . explicitly."

Arjuro folded the letter. Something told Froi that Arjuro and De Lancey expressed themselves explicitly whether they were on speaking terms or not.

"Perhaps it's best I read it in privacy," Arjuro said.

CHAPTER 6

Isaboe watched Jasmina and Vestie play among the children of the Fenton house staff. After weeks of preparation, Beatriss had finally moved into the village. The manor house was large, and the children raced from room to room, giddy with excitement. Beatriss showed Isaboe the home while Lady Abian helped Tarah in the kitchen, listing every item that had arrived to stock the larder.

In the library, there was a portrait of Lord Selric and his family, and Isaboe studied their faces somberly.

"I've decided to keep it there," Beatriss said softly. "They're as much a part of this village as we are now."

"I hardly remember them, you know," Isaboe said. "Pretty girls." She tried not to think how Lord Selric's daughters would have been a year or two younger than her own sisters when the entire family died from plague during their exile in Charyn. She reached out to touch the painting. The replicas of Isaboe's family in the palace had been desecrated during the curse by the impostor king. There was not one likeness left of them, and some days she could hardly recall their faces.

Abian called out from the kitchen, and they joined her there.

"Your husband comes to this union with one box?" she asked, glancing at Trevanion's chest sitting on the bench.

Beatriss laughed. "Two uniforms. One image of me drawn when we were first betrothed fifteen years ago; one of Finnikin's mother, Bartolina; a lock of Finnikin's hair as a child; and a fishing rod. His kingdom, his river, and his family. 'Who needs anything else?' he says."

"Where would you like them?" Abian asked.

"I'd like you to sit, Abian," Beatriss said. "We've not spoken for so long, and I just want to sit and enjoy my time with my friends."

"Yes," Isaboe said shrewdly, glancing at Abian. "So would I. At times I think you're avoiding me. Lord August, too."

"Trevanion has spoken of the same thing," Beatriss said with a meaningful look.

Abian continued her counting and recording of the grain sacks.

"Is your silence about Celie?" Isaboe asked.

Abian was not one for restraint, but finished what she was writing before giving them her full attention.

"August is livid," she said. "And I can't say I'm too happy about it, either. Our daughter spying on the Belegonians!"

"It's not spying at all," Isaboe said in a light tone with a shrug. "It's stealing mail. Jasmina steals mail all the time. She loves the colorful seals on the notes, and days later, we find the most important of letters in obscure places around the palace."

Abian seemed in no mood for humor, but Isaboe was in no mood for wasting time. "We would never put Celie's life in danger. Stealing the mail was her idea. And this anger — your anger — is not about Celie. You and August distanced yourselves from me long before Celie gave us the news from Belegonia."

Abian collected the records and placed them on a shelf built into the wall.

"This matter with Froi . . ."

Isaboe stiffened. She shook her head, not wanting to hear another word.

"Well, if you must know, it's affected us all," Abian said. "Froi's been part of our family all these years, and then suddenly he was gone, sent away on some mission to Sarnak, which we then find out is Charyn. We've waited all autumn, and it's almost winter's end and still he's not home. Now there's talk about Froi collaborating with the tyrant who was behind the slaughter in this kingdom. Talon and the boys are furious to hear those words from others. Froi is a brother to them, and it's too much to bear."

"He doesn't belong to you, Abian."

"How can you say that, my queen? Does one have to be blood kin to be considered family? We love him as a son. Celie and the boys miss him terribly. Celie's reckless actions are a reflection of how she's feeling. She wants to know where the brother of her heart is and stays in the Belegonian court for any whiff of information about Charyn."

"Celie has a reckless spirit, Abian. She inherited that from you, despite her pretty politeness and quiet ways. You should celebrate the fact that she's her mother's daughter."

But Isaboe could see Abian didn't want to hear it.

"Will it always be my children, Your Majesty? Augie's and mine? First Froi and next Celie, and then the boys. Do you know what they say in the Belegonian and Sarnak and Osterian courts? Probably in Charyn, too? That the children of a Lumateran Flatland lord are a prize in this land. Sired by the gods themselves, and the perfect marriage match. It's as close to Lumateran royalty as one can find. Are all my children going to be sacrificed for the protection of this kingdom?"

Isaboe heard a sad sigh from Beatriss, but she was too angry to care.

"Yes," she said coldly. "Your children will be used to impress our neighbors, Lady Abian," she added, stressing the formality. "And I'll watch you closely, as will Finnikin. You and Lord August will be our guides. So when the time comes for our daughter to be given to a useless son of a foreign king to keep this kingdom safe, I'll know how to hold back my tears because I will have learned from you!"

There was stone-cold silence in the room.

Jasmina and Vestie came racing back, giggling and panting with fatigue. But as they did, Jasmina tripped and fell, her head hitting the floor. Abian was closest and picked her up in her arms as they all crowded around, soothing Jasmina's cries with words and soft kisses. Finally Abian placed her in Isaboe's arms and pressed a kiss to both their cheeks.

"I spoke out of line." Abian shook her head with regret. "But promise me that Trevanion and Perri have not been sent to Charyn to—"

"Abian, enough," Beatriss said, sorrow in her voice. "Froi means everything to the Guard. To Isaboe and Finnikin and all of us. If he's done any wrong, he will be dealt with here. Fairly."

Isaboe rocked her daughter in her arms. "It always ends in tears, my love," she murmured. "All this silliness ends in tears."

When everything was calm except for Jasmina's quiet sobs, Tarah served them sweet bread and honey brew and they sat talking awhile about Beatriss and Vestie's time on the mountain.

Vestie came to stand by them, brushing Jasmina's cheek with a gentle hand until the little sobs were merely hiccups.

"Is it true I'm her aunt?" Vestie asked.

"Well, you're Finnikin's sister now, so I suppose that does make you Jasmina's aunt," Isaboe said.

"Can I look after her, then, Isaboe?"

Isaboe nodded. "Always, precious."

"I'll take her to the valley to meet my new friend."

Beatriss grimaced. "I said no more talk of that, Vestie."

Isaboe could see Beatriss was still shaken by the incident. Isaboe had heard about it from the Guard that morning, and it frightened her to think of how they almost lost Vestie.

"Do you think Millie will cheer Jasmina up?" Vestie asked, referring to her doll.

"She cheers everyone up. Go get her," Beatriss said, and Vestie skipped away as Jasmina lifted her head to peer toward where her older friend had gone.

"Are we sure she wasn't taken from her bed?" Isaboe asked quietly.

Beatriss shook her head. "Vestie went down the mountain on her own. She claimed . . . she claimed to have walked the sleep of the girl."

Isaboe felt both women's eyes on her.

"Do you think she's walking the sleep on her own?" Beatriss asked.

Isaboe had no idea how to answer that. Not after the strangeness of her own sleep. "What does Tesadora say?"

Beatriss seemed uncomfortable. "Not much, really. She was very strange. Almost . . . bewitched, if one could ever imagine Tesadora bewitched."

"Tell us about this mad girl, Beatriss," Abian said.

"She was so strange," Beatriss said with a shudder. "Tesadora was wonderful with her. She managed to disarm her. The poor girl is obviously hiding from the Charynites, and Tesadora has taken it upon herself to take care of her."

"She's seen her again?" Isaboe asked.

"As I was leaving the mountain, Tesadora was setting out for our side of the valley," Beatriss said.

Isaboe was disturbed to hear the news. She had sent message after message to Tesadora, asking her to visit. She had excused everyone's mood after Phaedra of Alonso's death, but to hear that Tesadora was back in the valley seemed wrong. Isaboe's bond with Tesadora was strong. It had grown since Isaboe first walked the sleep with Vestie and the Other while in exile. The Other had been Tesadora, their protector and the person partly responsible for breaking the curse her mother had placed on the land. Tesadora and Beatriss had once been strangers to each other, but had worked tirelessly together to protect those trapped inside the kingdom. Through the benevolence of the goddess, they had found a way to lead Isaboe home. It had been Tesadora who had nursed her back to health after Trevanion and the Guard reclaimed Lumatere.

Vestie returned with her rag doll, and Jasmina was happy to see it.

"You're a kind friend to this stranger, Vestie," Isaboe said, gathering the little girl toward her. Vestie placed her lips beside Isaboe's ear and growled in a strange, savage way, then giggled.

"Are you a little wolf, Vestie?" Isaboe asked, bemused.

"That's what she sounds like," Vestie explained. "When I walk the sleep."

Jasmina began to squirm, and Isaboe placed her back on the ground, her attention on Vestie.

"Tell me more about her," Isaboe said calmly, despite the fact that her heart was pounding. She remembered the feeling night after night of waking from the sleep.

Vestie shook her head.

"Can we guess?" Beatriss said. "Vestie so enjoys guessing games with her father."

Vestie liked the idea and nodded emphatically. "Father guesses every time. He knows everything."

"Oh, wonderful," Isaboe said, winking at Beatriss. "Another besotted child of Trevanion's."

"You'll have to give us a clue," Abian said.

Vestie hesitated, and then she took Jasmina's hand and swung it. "She's just like Jasmina."

"She's pretty?" Beatriss said.

"She's bossy?" Abian said.

"She's incorrigible?" Isaboe said.

Vestie giggled. "I don't know what that means."

Isaboe looked at her daughter, who loved nothing more than hearing her name. "Aren't you incorrigible, beloved?"

Jasmina thought about it a moment and nodded emphatically, liking the word.

"What else are you, Jasmina?" Vestie asked, excited.

Jasmina thought another moment and everyone laughed to see her pensive face.

"Pwincess."

The others laughed again at the joy of hearing her speak, and Vestie clapped with glee.

"Yes. Yes."

Isaboe froze, the hair on her arms standing tall.

"Your friend in the valley is a princess?"

Vestie put a finger to her lips to silence herself, but nodded, giggling again.

"And does this princess have a name?" Isaboe asked.

Beatriss shook her head at the same time as Vestie's nod. Beatriss stared at her daughter, surprised.

"You've not mentioned a name, Vestie," she said, worry in her voice. "You said she didn't have one."

"It's a secret."

"Whose secret?" Beatriss asked, alarmed. "Who said it's a secret?"

"She did. And so did Tesadora when I told her. Tesadora said that the Charynites have the biggest ears in the whole world and even if I told someone my secret in Lumatere, they'd hear it."

Isaboe, Abian, and Beatriss exchanged looks.

"All these secrets," Isaboe tried to jest. "Who said there were any secrets from me in Lumatere, Vestie?"

Isaboe bent down to her.

"You can whisper it to me. The Charynites will never hear. I'll make sure of that."

Vestie took the time to think and then leaned forward.

"It's a strange name, Isaboe. I can hardly say it."

"I'll help you, my sweet."

Vestie placed her lips against Isaboe's ear.

"Her name is . . . Kintana. Kintana of Charyn."

CHAPTER 7

A rjuro insisted on escorting Froi for at least part of his journey. Their exit was through the cottage of a draper wed to one of the priests. It lay on the northern outskirts of Sebastabol, and as they crept out of the cellar into the early-morning blustery wind, Froi smelled a difference in the air, one that seemed foreign, yet still strangely familiar.

"The ocean," Arjuro said. "We're not even a half day's walk from it to the east."

The map Arjuro had drawn for Froi would take him across the center of the kingdom to Charyn's border with Osteria. Froi knew they would pass Abroi in the morning and Serker later that afternoon. He thought of Finnikin and Lucian and the pride they felt in having come from the Rock and Mountain. Froi felt no such pride in the homes of his ancestors.

"Stop thinking about it," Arjuro said to Froi, who had looked back over and over again after they passed north of Abroi.

"How do you know what I'm thinking?"

"I just know," Arjuro said. "Shit to the south and killing fields ahead. You want neither in your life."

The terrain south of Serker was a slush of melted snow and dirt, and above them was a whirl of filthy clouds that lay low all the day long. A wind whistled an eerie tune, and even the horses responded to the misery, tearing across the country as if they wanted to get as far from this place as possible.

"Do you ever think of traveling through Serker?" he asked Arjuro.

"Nothing we can do," Arjuro said. "I have no chronicle of their names, so I can't sing them home. Never have been able to."

Which meant that Arjuro had tried. Froi pulled up a sleeve and rubbed his arm, shivering at the raised hair on it. Arjuro stared at him.

"The unsettled spirits are dancing on your skin."

"I thought we only danced for joy," Froi said.

"Not in Serker, they don't."

When it was time to say good-bye, they stood huddled by their mounts, fussing with reins and comforting the horses. Being with Arjuro these weeks had been Froi's only relief from the torment of Quintana's absence.

"You died twice in my arms," Arjuro said quietly.

Froi looked up at him.

"It would have been the last thing I could have endured." Arjuro said, his eyes filling with tears. "Your death would have been the very last I could have endured."

Froi thought of those strange moments after the attack outside Paladozza. When he knew he was dying, he had heard the *reginita*'s voice ordering him away.

"When I was removing those barbs," Arjuro said, "and your thoughts and words were feverish, you wept and wept from the memories . . . from the horror of your memories in Sarnak."

Froi saw the rage in Arjuro's eyes, his clenched fists.

"If I could find the men who did those things to you as a child, I would tear them limb from limb."

Froi embraced him.

"One day," Froi said, clearing his voice of emotion, "I'll introduce you to my queen and my king and my captain; and Lord August and Lady Abian, who have given me a home; and the priest-king and Perri and Tesadora and my friend Lucian; and then you'll understand that I would never have met them if you hadn't journeyed to Sarnak all those years ago, Arjuro. And if the gods were to give me a choice between living a better life, having not met them, or a wretched life with the slightest chance of crossing their path, then I'd pick the wretched life over and over again."

He kissed Arjuro's brow. Finnikin called it a blessing between two male blood kin. It always had made Froi ache seeing it between Finnikin and Trevanion.

"I'd live it again just to have crossed all of your paths. Keep safe, Arjuro. Keep safe so I can bring your brother home to you."

Froi felt an acute loneliness the moment Arjuro mounted his horse and rode away. The sleet half blinded him, and the cold brought a new sort of pain to his bones. But he traveled all day and night, not wanting to rest in a place where he couldn't shelter from the malevolence of nature. This was ancient land, filled with spirits, and apart from his journey to Hamlyn and Arna's farm, Froi hadn't been alone since his days in Sarnak. He fought the need to weep, but blamed it on his aches.

On his second day alone, he saw lights from afar and knew he had reached the Charyn River and the road south to the Osterian border. He couldn't bear another night of sitting in the saddle with only the horse and his fleece for warmth, and the lights promised everything. They delivered little but a rundown inn that was full to the brim. Froi's heartbeat quickened when he saw the sign to Alonso. How easy it would be to change direction and take the road home to Lumatere. But there was something about De Lancey's news that made him uneasy. Gargarin was no fool, yet if there was a lesson Froi had come to learn from living with Lord August's family, it was that the Belegonians could not be trusted.

So he paid a coin for a corner in a crowded stable a mile south of the inn. It was mostly filled with Citavitans who had not found refuge in Jidia and were heading upriver to Alonso. Froi knew how their journey would end. Alonso would turn these people away, forcing them to travel to the Lumateran valley. As he watched these desperate, landless people, he couldn't fight the crippling fear that Quintana was somewhere out there on her own with no coins to trade, cold to the bone.

"Any news from the Citavita?" Froi asked the couple beside him. He had watched the husband tie their pack around his waist in case someone tried to steal their possessions.

"I was there when the street lords took the palace, and fear for the lives of friends," Froi continued, eyeing the bundle of food tied up in an apron.

"Street lords are gone," the woman told him. "Nothing left to take. The gods only know who has control over the palace. Every week, a different story."

"If Bestiano's a smart man, he'll return now," a bearded man close by said. "Best thing for Charyn."

"How can you say that?" another called out from his bedroll. "He's a killer of kings."

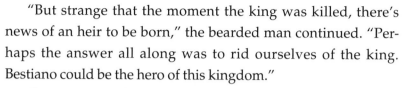

"But strange that the moment the king was killed, there's news of an heir to be born," the bearded man continued. "Perhaps the answer all along was to rid ourselves of the king. Bestiano could be the hero of this kingdom."

Count to ten, Froi. Count to ten.

"They say Bestiano is the father of the future king," a woman called out.

The bearded man made a sound of approval. "If he's smart, he'll take the poor mite out of that mad-bitch Quintana's hands the moment it's born."

Froi flew across the space, landing heavily on the man, pounding his fists wherever he could land them. He felt arms drag him away, their fingers pressing deep into his wounds, and he pulled free.

"You dare talk about the princess in such a way," he raged. "I challenge you to speak those words when the future king grows to be a man. I dare you to say that about his mother to his face!"

The bearded man cowered away. "Who are you, with your fancy talk?"

"Someone who knew them," Froi said. "Knew the heir Tariq of Lascow. Knew that he sacrificed his life to keep Quintana of Charyn safe. I defy you to dishonor his memory by claiming Bestiano a better man."

The words felt like rough parchment in Froi's mouth, but there was silence all around.

"They breed good men in Lascow," the husband from the Citavita said. His wife stared at Froi. "Tariq of Lascow would have made a just king if he had lived," she said.

Later, the wife held out a dry strip of meat to Froi, and he ate it, shamed that whether she had given it to him or not, it would have somehow ended up in his belly. She looked at him closely, confused. "You remind me of someone. I don't know who," she said quietly. She reached over and he flinched, but her hand touched his face gently.

When she was asleep, Froi felt her husband's eyes on him. "She doesn't usually take to your kind," the man said.

"My kind?" Froi said coolly. Who wasn't it safe to be now? A Lumateran assassin? A Serker lad? A defender of the princess?

"A young one," the man said. "My wife . . . she usually turns away. She bled on the day of weeping. It was close to being born, our child was. She bled it and has spent the last eighteen years turning her eyes away from last borns or the young."

The man looked down at his wife, but then back at Froi. Then he smiled. "It's not your face. It's something else. It's in your spirit. I feel it as well."

Froi relaxed for the first time since he left Arjuro, and lay down on the straw. Although he had been taught not to take chances, he had a sense that the couple beside him were not a threat.

"How many inns are on the river border across this stretch heading toward Osteria?" he asked the man softly in the darkness.

"Three. One is closed for the winter, though. You'll be lucky to get a bed. But I would not head that way, lad."

"I've no intention of returning to the Citavita," Froi said.

"It's not the Citavita you need to fear," the man said. "There's talk that the Osterians have allowed the Belegonians to camp across the river. If they decide to cross, there'll be nothing left of us. It's why we're heading toward Alonso. Don't head south, lad. Come north with us."

Froi sighed. Oh, to head north to Alonso. It would be so easy to follow these people. He was closer to Lumatere than he had been for the past five months, and all night his dreams beckoned him home.

But in the morning the reality hadn't changed. Quintana was still somewhere out there, and he needed to find Gargarin and Lirah. The three of them had a better chance of finding her if they joined forces.

When Froi walked his horse out of the stable, south to everyone else's north, he felt the wife stare at him.

"Are you gods' blessed?" she asked.

He shook his head, not meeting her eyes.

"Do you know what I dreamed last night?"

Froi didn't want to know. People's dreams frightened him. But he looked up at her all the same.

"I dreamed of my ma, who died long ago. Her words are still singing in my ears." The woman's smile was gentle. "She said, 'The half spirit of your unborn child lives in that lad.'"

CHAPTER 8

They arrived at the border of Osteria and Charyn five days after setting out from Lumatere, having stopped to meet with their ambassador in the kingdom of Osteria. Finnikin couldn't help but think of the last time they were at this exact place. Isaboe . . . Evanjalin had been out there somewhere. With Froi. She had walked away from Finnikin because he hadn't trusted her. Froi had followed. "She and me. We're the same," Froi had said. Finnikin could hardly remember the boy Froi had been, except for his ability to let fly his emotions whenever they rose to the surface. Froi as a lad was easy to control. Froi as a man threatened Finnikin. He had restraint and an ability to play with his opponents. He would make a formidable enemy.

"You've been quiet these past days," Trevanion said. "Are you going to tell me what the . . . exchange of words was about?"

"Who said there was an exchange of words?" Finnikin asked with irritation.

"When a woman says 'I hope you fall under your horse' and 'catch your death, then see if I grieve you,'" Perri said, "then there's been an exchange of words."

Finnikin glared at him.

"In my humble opinion."

"It's no one's business but ours."

"Understandable," Trevanion said. "Although the entire Guard and palace village heard it."

"Perhaps the south of the Flatlands, as well," Perri concluded.

Finnikin dismounted, and they led their horses to the river. There was little teasing here. They stayed quiet, remembering the day three and a half years ago when they faced Sefton and the village exiles held by the Charynites. They knew now that Rafuel of Sebastabol had been one of the soldiers, and if Finnikin closed his eyes, he could imagine just where Rafuel had stood. Perhaps if he had looked at the soldiers and not their leader, he'd have seen fear and shame on their faces.

"Let's go," Trevanion said quietly.

Gargarin of Abroi had instructed the Belegonians that he would be waiting in an inn five miles north of the Charynite barracks. It was the only ale house for miles upon miles and was frequented by the Charynite soldiers guarding the border, as well as people from a cluster of isolated villages. Finnikin had been advised by the ambassador that the Belegonian army was camped farther upriver on the Osterian side with Osteria's blessing, a sign of great intimidation and provocation to Charyn. Would the Belegonians be so ready for attack if they had received Gargarin of Abroi's letter asking for an alliance? Instead, that letter had been intercepted by Celie and passed on to Finnikin. In trapping the man who had planned the slaughter of Isaboe's family, had Lumatere inadvertently triggered a Belegonian invasion?

Finnikin stayed focused and thought over the instructions given by Gargarin of Abroi. The man would carry a walking stick as a means of identification. He would greet them with the words, "You're a far way from home." He would set out a treaty between Charyn and Belegonia that would acknowledge him as the one who would return the true heir to the palace. Finnikin remembered the words in the note. *The Lumaterans need not know of our alliance. We'll talk later about what to do with them. Leave it to me, for I have a plan for Lumatere that will eliminate them as a threat.*

Finnikin's blood chilled just to think of it again.

As they guided their horses through the trees, he found himself back in the past. He thought he heard a whistle, and imagined the sight of her: Evanjalin of the Monts. Her hair cropped short, her arms hacked from her need to bleed so she could walk the sleep. He cursed himself for his weakness, because what he felt for her then paled in comparison to how he felt now. Despite the fury at her speaking another man's name that carved at his insides, Finnikin had never desired his wife as much as he did this moment.

Suddenly Trevanion held up a hand and they slowed their horses. Finnikin watched his father dismount. The smell of horse shit was overwhelming. Whoever had stopped at this place had not traveled alone.

"A small army has been here, it seems," Trevanion said.

"Could the Belegonians have already crossed?" Perri asked.

Trevanion shook his head. "No. The Belegonians are on foot. This group has horses."

"The barracks are close by," Finnikin said.

"This was a rest stop for someone traveling a distance." Trevanion looked up at them. "At least twenty. Pity whoever it is they're after."

They tethered the horses and set up camp in a clearing some distance from the inn. Quietly Finnikin changed his clothing. Trevanion and Perri would wait here, concealed, until Finnikin returned with the man, but Finnikin would have to look the part convincingly. The Belegonians wore their clothing more fitted, and bolder in colors.

"Cover up, Finn," his father said, and Finnikin pulled the cap over his head, covering every strand of his berry-colored hair. If anything would give him away, it would be his coloring. He had to be careful. He had to steady his hand so Gargarin of Abroi would not see it shaking.

"When the time comes, you don't have—" his father began to say.

"It's my duty," Finnikin interrupted. "What these people did to Isaboe's family will haunt her for the rest of her life."

He walked the trail to the inn. Charyn afternoons were eaten by an early darkness, lit with a strange moonless hue. Closer, he heard the voices and knew that soon enough he'd reach the isolated inn. This is where he would kill a man tonight. He'd lead Gargarin of Abroi back to this very place and slit his throat. And regardless of everything, he'd do it for her.

There were the usual stares as he walked in. But with the threat of Belegonia invading, the inn was frequented by travelers rather than soldiers. So the stares were not for long. And then Finnikin saw a man with a walking stick enter alongside a woman of great beauty. Every man in the room stared.

"Mercy," Finnikin muttered. There was never any talk that Gargarin of Abroi would have a companion. The moment they were seated, Finnikin joined them, his eyes meeting the man's cold stare. Cold, but handsome. Gargarin of Abroi's hair was coal-black, which contrasted alarmingly with his pale skin and dark-blue eyes. There was silence, and Finnikin felt studied by both of them. For all her beauty, there was little warmth in the woman. But in their fine pelt cloaks, the two looked regal.

Apart from Trevanion and Beatriss, a more striking couple he had never seen.

"You're a far way from home," the man said in Charyn.

That I am, Finnikin wanted to say. He nodded.

"I don't trust him," the woman said to her companion.

The Charynite held up a hand to wave over the servant. When the lad arrived, Gargarin of Abroi turned to his woman.

"I'll order us food," he said quietly. Gently. He looked up at the lad. "What have you got?"

"Leftovers."

"Always a favorite," Gargarin said dryly. Finnikin watched him reach a hand over to touch the women's gaunt cheek. "I'm begging you to eat, Lirah."

"I can't stomach food. I told you."

"If he sees you like this, he'll blame me."

The woman wrapped her arms around her body miserably. "Shouldn't have let them go," she said quietly.

It was as though Finnikin didn't exist, and although he tried his hardest, he couldn't keep his eyes off them both. Before him was love and contempt and yearning, and it filled the air.

Then the food came, yet there was still no acknowledgment from the Charynites.

"Did we organize to meet so I could watch you eat?" Finnikin asked finally.

Gargarin lifted his eyes from his plate and stared. "Your army is waiting to cross the border from Osteria," he said, ice in his tone. "You have our people running scared. A strange turn of events since we exchanged letters."

"Yes, you're quite the letter writer," Finnikin said, cursing the Belegonians for persisting with their plan to invade, despite Isaboe's objections. "Give me something to offer my king, and I may be able to speak to him about his eager soldiers."

The woman spat at Finnikin.

"Offer him that," she said.

Finnikin refused to allow his anger to surface. "That's very rude," he said, wiping the spittle from his face. "Especially since, unlike you, leftovers are my least favorite."

"We promised you peace between our kingdoms, unheard of for at least thirty years," Gargarin said. "Why would Belegonia not take advantage of such a pledge?"

"But what if Bestiano is offering Belegonia the same?" Finnikin asked.

Through the information collected about Charyn, Finnikin knew that the battle for the palace would take place between two men. Bestiano of Nebia and Gargarin of Abroi.

"Bestiano was the dead king's adviser," Gargarin said. "Why would he offer Belegonia peace now when he had years to offer it while the king was alive? He wants something from you, and he'll promise you nothing but lies."

"And what do you want from us in return?"

"A powerful ally. The Osterians are weak. They'll give in to the Sorellians one day, and we will all be left unprotected. What happens when the Sorellians cross the sea to invade your kingdom?"

"We'll have the Lumaterans. They're our allies and neighbors."

Gargarin of Abroi shrugged arrogantly. "Lumatere's not a kingdom. It's a road." He smiled. "Would you not agree?"

"You're forcing words in my mouth, sir," Finnikin said, keeping his tone even. "Is this a trap by the Lumaterans to test our allegiance?"

"No, just a jest enjoyed by most Charynites and Belegonians I know."

"We must have a different sense of humor," Finnikin said, his hands clenched under the bench.

"Oh, no," the Charynite said. "Your kingdom and mine? Power and size ensure that we have the same sense of humor. We all agree that Lumatere is insignificant except when it comes to its coal."

That was all Lumatere ever was to Charyn. A road to Sarnak. A road to Belegonia and a coal mine. Murder Isaboe's family, and replace them with a puppet king who would give them a path to wherever they wanted to go. Finnikin swallowed, hardly able to speak from the fury.

"So what will we get out of acknowledging you as regent?" he asked Gargarin.

"I never claimed to be regent. I'm here to speak for Charyn until the day that someone sound of mind is placed in charge. And you need an ally. Against Sorel to your east, and those Yut madmen to your south, who are going to bring the whole of Skuldenore down. United, we could be powerful. Divided, this land does not stand a chance."

The only thing this Charynite and Finnikin had in common was the belief that Skuldenore would work better together than alone.

"Call off the army," Gargarin said. "For now, that's all we ask. Give us a chance to stand on our feet."

Finnikin stood. "I'll take you to the border. You may get the chance to call them off yourself."

"Then you accept the offer?"

"I need to speak to the king," Finnikin said. "He didn't seem to trust your letters, and he wanted some sort of certainty that this wasn't a trap."

Finnikin held out a hand to shake.

"But how do *we* know *this* isn't a trap?" Gargarin asked, not taking the hand outstretched. "That you aren't playing Bestiano against us?"

74

"You don't. But many say that Bestiano of Nebia became First Adviser because the king sent his better men to Lumatere thirteen years ago, only to have them trapped by the curse. We don't make treaties with last-resort advisers. You, however, were said to be everything a king wanted, and you walked away from it all. The Belegonian king is impressed."

"Well, there you go," Gargarin of Abroi said. "Always pleased to impress a foreign enemy. The king of Yutlind Nord remarked quite emphatically that he found me smarter than most men and expressed great pity that he could not come to our assistance, because he hated the Charynites as much as he hated his countrymen from the south."

"And how is it that you know the king of Yutlind Nord?"

"Well, you see," Gargarin said, leaning closer to feign a conspiratorial whisper, "I'm a bit of a letter writer."

Finnikin was being mocked. The only person who got away with mocking him was Froi and perhaps Perri. This man slightly intrigued him, which was unfortunate when Finnikin knew what was to take place this night. It actually made him feel sick to his stomach.

"So when do I get to meet someone more important than you?" Gargarin asked.

"More important than me?" Finnikin scoffed. "According to my wife, there is no one more important than me."

A ghost of a smile appeared on the Charynite's face.

"Keep that wife."

Finnikin stood.

"Let's go," he said.

"Hand him his staff," the woman ordered.

Finnikin stared at it.

"You need it?" he asked Gargarin.

"Yes, well, it is a walking stick, fool."

◆ ◆ ◆

Finnikin had never killed an unarmed man with a limp before. Apart from training with the Guard and an incident with drunk yokels in Sarnak the year before on palace business, he hadn't used a weapon since the battle to reclaim Lumatere. He was good with a sword. Not as good as Trevanion's Guard, but better than most men. But he had never assassinated a man. It made him think of all those times Trevanion, Perri, and Froi had done so on palace orders over the years. His and Isaboe's. Sometimes the men would return from their mission and he'd sense a change in his father. A mood so dark. Perri always disappeared for days after, and Froi . . . Froi would have a vacant look in his eye. As if he had lost a bit of himself.

Outside the inn, Finnikin watched the man and woman before him. They were of the same height. Both reed thin. And they loved each other. That was the fact Finnikin wanted to forget. That he was about to assassinate a man who loved someone. Who was gentle with her and cared whether she ate or not. But Finnikin remembered the stories of past leaders from the books of the ancients. The kindest of fathers were often the greatest butchers of innocent women and children.

When they reached the clearing, Finnikin saw Perri and his father. Unlike Gargarin of Abroi, he knew where to look for them in the shadow of the trees. And before he could change his mind, Finnikin had one arm around the Charynite's shoulders, the other hand holding a dagger at his throat. Finnikin kicked away the man's staff, and Gargarin of Abroi's body slumped against him.

He heard a sound from the woman as Perri's hand muffled her cry and pulled her away.

"Don't hurt her!" Gargarin said. Almost ordered. "Just let her go. She's of no use to Bestiano. She's suffered enough. If you have any compassion, let her go."

Finnikin tightened his grip. "I don't follow your orders, and I don't follow Bestiano's," he said. "I'm just a fool who comes from that road you call Lumatere."

He silenced the man's shout with a hand, pressing the dagger closer to his throat. But suddenly he heard the rustle of leaves underfoot behind him and felt the tip of steel pressed into his back.

"Drop the dagger," he heard a hoarse whisper say. "Drop it now!"

Gargarin of Abroi tried to turn in Finnikin's arms and Finnikin sensed his desperation. The knife he held to the Charynite's throat drew blood as Gargarin struggled. Behind Finnikin, the sword dug deeper into his back.

"I said drop it!"

Mercy!

And just when Finnikin thought the moment could get no worse, he heard his father's voice. Cold. Hard. Anguished.

"Put down the sword, Froi, or I'll slice your head clear from your body."

CHAPTER 9

Lord Tascan and his family's visit to the mountain was met with great enthusiasm. At first. Yata received them in her home and Lucian spent the afternoon showing them the dairy farms and the silo. Lucian was keen to set up an agreement between the Monts and the Flatland lords. The first of Lumatere's market days with the Belegonians and Osterians had been a success for the kingdom, but the Monts had been absent, due to Phaedra's death in the valley. Their hearts had not been in it. But Lucian believed it was time to show the rest of the kingdom that they were more than just sentinels.

And here Lord Tascan was, as keen as Lucian desired. But when the nobleman insisted he accompany Lucian alone on a tour of the stables, Lucian quickly came to understand the truth behind his visit.

"I'm not going to waste time here, Lucian," he said as they inspected the stalls. Lucian was hoping to show off the size of their boars to Lord Tascan, but he didn't seem interested.

"Since our return to Lumatere, I've watched you carefully and have been impressed with your potential, lad. But then, of course, there was the unfortunate marriage to the Charynite. All behind you now."

Lucian stiffened. When he had visited the palace village a week past, friends and acquaintances had approached, one after the other, with hearty congratulations.

"It must be a relief," the weaver had said.

Relief?

The sun appearing after days of rain or darkness was a relief. Orly and Lotte's news that Gert and Bert had finally found each other and would produce the finest calf known to the mountain was a relief. Phaedra of Alonso's death was a never-ending pain that gnawed at his insides. It made him a prisoner in his own cottage.

"Lucian, this kingdom would love nothing more than your betrothment to my daughter, Zarah."

Sweet goddess.

"It will bring opportunity to both our villages, and it will bring light back to this mountain. Isn't that what you want, Lucian? I've seen your *yata*. This marriage to the Charynite darkened her doorstep."

No, her death did, Lucian wanted to say. Yata had come to admire Phaedra. Even love her.

"Zarah's a good daughter, Lucian. The Osterian court held her in high regard when we lived there during the curse."

"I don't want to offend your daughter, sir—"

"Then, good." Lord Tascan thumped Lucian on the back heartily. "It's settled. No need to rush into anything formal just yet. But we'll expect you for supper when you visit for market day. You can stay the night in the palace. I'm sure the queen will enjoy seeing a beloved cousin. Perhaps there will be an invitation for my family to join you."

Lucian forced a smile. Lord Tascan had waited a month. Not

to talk hogs and mutton. But to talk unwed daughters. How could Lucian have been so stupid not to notice?

After a long good-bye, the guests departed, demanding promises that he would come visit them, and Lucian returned home. From where he stood outside his cottage, he could see Lord Tascan's people disappearing down the mountain trail and he felt nothing but great relief. Since Phaedra's death, his cottage had become his refuge. Sometimes he imagined her there beside him. She had once told Lucian that she liked how high his home sat on the mountain, overlooking the other cottages and farms. She had loved the dips and slopes of the land in the distance, the smoke that came from Orly's home, and the sight of Miro's herd of sheep on a neighboring property.

"It's a pity you can't see it all from inside," he heard her say. "Windows would give you the greatest view all around."

"Why would I want to see more of everyone?" he said. "Then they'd never leave me alone. The walls blocking out the mountain work just fine for me, Phaedra. It means I don't have to see the sadness of their faces now that you're gone."

He spoke aloud to her often. This is what he was reduced to. Speaking to the ghosts of his father and his wife.

He was about to walk inside his cottage when he saw the horses traveling up the trail from the village of Balconio. Was it Lord Tascan returning? Lucian would have to hide, if so. But then he realized it was the Queen's Guard, and fearing the worst, Lucian walked down the path back to Yata's compound and waited for their arrival. As they ventured closer, he saw his cousin Isaboe among them. They were usually forewarned that she would be staying so that Yata could organize her quarters. But he also knew that sometimes his cousin craved to be with her mother's kin, because no one fussed over Isaboe like Yata and the aunts. She was still their little Mont girl despite being queen of them all.

When she arrived with Jasmina and the Guard, he helped her dismount and they embraced. She seemed to want to hold on a moment longer and he let her. He took Jasmina from one of her other guards, Moss, and placed the imp on his shoulders.

"Should you be riding?" he asked Isaboe.

"I'm with child, Lucian," she said dryly, "not dying. And I'm actually on my way down to the valley."

"What?" Lucian asked, stunned, looking up at her guard Aldron, who grimaced.

"I'd appreciate your talking the queen out of doing that, Lucian," Aldron said.

"And I'd appreciate your not talking about me as if I'm invisible," she said, rolling her eyes.

"Did the queen of this kingdom just roll her eyes?"

"She's been doing it all the way up the mountain," Aldron muttered.

"And still you're talking about me as if I'm not present!" she said.

Lucian exchanged a look with Moss. No one seemed to like the idea of Isaboe traveling to the valley.

"Stop doing that! All of you," she said firmly.

Lucian held up a hand in surrender.

"If this is about your fight with Finn—"

Aldron was shaking his head at Lucian in warning.

"My conversations with your beloved friend are no one's business," she said.

"How come Finnikin's my beloved friend whenever you fight and he's your beloved husband all other times?"

Isaboe stared at him, unamused. "Take me to the valley, Lucian, or I'll have Aldron, here, relay the conversation I just had with Lord Tascan as we passed each other. The one where he suggests an invitation to the palace next time you're in town. With his daughter in attendance."

Lucian sighed. Isaboe would do it to spite him.

"Moss, can you take Jasmina to Yata and tell her we'll be staying the night?" she said, taking Jasmina's little fingers and kissing each and every one of them. "I'm off to see Tesadora. I've not seen her for such a while."

"Then, I'll send Jory to fetch her," Lucian said. Moss and Aldron nodded, liking the idea. "Tesadora can eat with us on the mountain tonight."

"No," his cousin insisted. "Tesadora's not one for fetching, and I want to surprise her."

Lucian insisted that Isaboe share his mount. Yata spoke often about the babe arriving at the end of spring. When Jasmina was born, the kingdom had been in a state of euphoria for months. Lucian couldn't bear the idea of the horses getting skittish and something happening to the queen.

They rode down the mountain with Aldron and two of the other guards. He had forgotten how much he enjoyed his cousin's company and how little time they had spent together lately. After sharing family gossip, they spoke of market day in the palace village and Lord Tascan.

"Be careful," she said. "Lady Zarah trills. Finnikin used to flirt with her when he'd visit the Osterian court during his exile."

"Yes, but that was before he met you."

"I overheard Finnikin once telling Sir Topher that Lady Zarah's voice was a soothing sound."

"Hmm, soothing voices are in decline on the mountain . . . and in the palace, the way I hear it," Lucian said. He peered over his shoulder for her reaction.

Isaboe's eyes narrowed. "If I had the power to make anyone in this kingdom mute, I'd begin with her trilling voice," she said. "Nothing soothing about it. She speaks softly so men must step closer to ask her to speak again."

"You're mean," he said with a laugh.

"It's true," she protested. "The first time Jasmina heard her voice, she held her hands to her ears and cried."

He reached back and poked her side with a finger, and they both laughed again. But the closer they came to the valley, the more silent they became. He knew he would never speak the words out loud to her, but he had been disappointed that she hadn't acknowledged Phaedra as his wife. After her death, Isaboe had sent her condolences, but Lucian wished that she had come to know Phaedra in life.

When they reached the point on the mountain where they could see the first glimpse of the Charynites in their caves, he heard her sigh.

"What are we going to do about this valley, Lucian? If it's true that Alonso has refused to send grain, I can't take food from my own people to feed an enemy."

"Perhaps . . . they could fertilize the land and grow more of their own," he said. "I've only allowed them a small patch, but they could grow much more along the stream and between the caves."

Hadn't that been Phaedra's idea?

"Do you know how we fertilized Kasabian's vegetable patch?" Phaedra had asked him with delight one time when they were traveling back up to the mountain. "We climbed to the higher caves and carved holes for the pigeons to . . . you know."

"No," he had said, pretending ignorance. "I don't."

"So they can . . . you know."

"So they can shit."

"Well, I would have put it more delicately."

"Trust me, Phaedra. There's no delicate way to shit. It evens out the entire land. Humans and other creatures. Queens and peasants."

"Then we collect the pigeon . . . droppings and mix them with the water and soil, and that's how we fertilize our garden," she said proudly.

It's what he told Isaboe, without mentioning Phaedra.

"People who plant gardens and vegetable patches become part of the land, Lucian," Isaboe said. "We can't have them forming an attachment. It means they'll never go."

At her campsite on the Lumateran side of the stream, Tesadora was boiling a broth that smelled too repulsive to be considered dinner. She was surprised to see them but held out her arms to Isaboe.

"Stomach upsets in the valley," she said. She looked suspiciously at Aldron and the Guard as they began searching the area.

"If you're so worried about the dangers, why bring her down here?" she snapped.

"Don't talk about her as if she's not here, Tesadora," Lucian said.

But no one seemed in a mood to jest.

"You know they won't risk crossing the stream," Tesadora said, irritation in her voice and still watching Aldron and the Guard. She returned her attention to Isaboe and brushed a strand of hair out of her eyes. "You look tired, beloved."

"I'm not sleeping too well these nights."

"I can imagine why," Tesadora said. "Your husband's an idiot. Have I not told you that many times?"

Isaboe laughed, but Lucian could see worry in her eyes.

"I sent for you, Tesadora, but you mustn't have received my notes."

"Circumstances have been strange here since . . ."

Tesadora sighed, looking at Lucian.

Since Phaedra. Since Vestie traveled down a mountain on her own in the early hours of the morning. Since a strange, savage girl took up residence in their valley.

"I wanted to talk to you about the sleep," Isaboe said.

Tesadora looked perplexed. "You still walk the sleep? But you've not bled. And I've not walked it with you."

"It's odd," Isaboe admitted. "Vestie walks it, too. Not alongside me. It's as if we walk our own."

Tesadora was unnerved by the news, her beautiful face creased with worry.

"I'll come up the mountain with you tonight, and we'll make a strong brew to ease those jitters," she promised.

Tesadora extinguished the fire under her pot, and Lucian helped her pack up.

"I want to meet the girl, Tesadora," Lucian heard Isaboe say. He watched Tesadora freeze.

"Vestie says she's a Charynite with no place to go," Isaboe continued. "That she's frightened of her own people."

"She's no one," Lucian said. "Just a stray who doesn't want to be in the presence of Donashe and his cutthroats, if you ask me."

Tesadora covered the pot. "They're arriving from all over these days," she said dismissively. "Ever since the events in their capital. The girl can look after herself. You three," she said to the guards, pointing to her pots and jars, "make yourselves useful and put these in my tent."

"And what if she can't look after herself, Tesadora?" Isaboe continued. "What if there's something I can do for her? All those people in the valley, waiting for my permission to climb this mountain. Perhaps she's the one. She is on her own with no kin. Take me to her, Tesadora. We'll ease her fear."

Lucian looked at Tesadora. As strange as the girl was, perhaps it was the first step. He liked the idea, but suddenly preferred that the conversation take place on the mountain and not down here in the valley.

"Let's get this over and done with," he said finally. "I want us all in Yata's house by the time the sun disappears. Lead the way, Tesadora."

Tesadora was reluctant, but finally she agreed.

"I don't want the girl frightened," she said, looking at the Guard. "Lucian and Aldron only. The others can stay here."

They traveled half a mile downstream. It made Lucian wonder how much contact Tesadora had made with the mad girl since they had encountered her the morning Vestie went missing.

"We don't even know her name, Tesadora," Aldron muttered. "If I get a blasting from Finn and Trevanion and Perri over this, I'll blame you."

"Yes, well, I'm trembling at the thought," Tesadora said, but Lucian could hear the strangeness in her voice.

They passed the tree where they had first found the girl with Vestie. Farther downstream, shafts of light forced their way between tall pines. It was here that they found the girl on her haunches, close to one of the trees, with a blanket wrapped around her body that Lucian recognized as one of Tesadora's. She was scrounging for something in the dirt, and he could see that at least she was eating well, looking rounded and full-figured. When she heard the crunch of the pine needles under their feet, she scrambled to stand, her eyes wide with alarm.

Tesadora stepped forward, holding out a hand to quell her fears, but the girl's eyes fastened on Isaboe. Lucian saw a snarl curling her lips and then heard the bloodcurdling sound. Aldron stepped forward, a hand to his sword.

"We won't hurt you," Tesadora called out meaningfully, for Aldron's ears as much as the girl's. "Step back, Aldron. You're frightening her."

Aldron refused to move. The girl seemed poised to lunge.

"Step back, Aldron," said Isaboe, repeating Tesadora's words. Reluctantly, Aldron did as he was told. Isaboe approached slowly, tentatively, and the girl stumbled back.

"Your Majesty!" Aldron warned. Isaboe held up a hand, stepping closer and closer to the girl. Neither spoke, but there was a tension in the air that unnerved Lucian. He looked at Tesadora, and when she refused to meet his eye, he knew something was wrong. And then it happened quickly, the speed of it stunning them all. Isaboe's hand snaked out and pushed the girl against the closest trunk, her fingers clenched around the Charynite's throat.

"Give me your sword, Aldron," his queen ordered, her voice so cold.

"Isaboe," Tesadora hissed. "Let her go. You're hurting her."

"Aldron," Isaboe repeated. "Give me your sword."

"What's happening here?" Lucian demanded as Aldron unsheathed his weapon and placed it in Isaboe's hand. In an instant, his cousin had the blade pressed under the girl's chin.

"Isaboe, let her go!" Tesadora cried, stepping forward, but Aldron held her back.

Lucian couldn't see Isaboe's face, but he saw the girl's expression. With the blade to her neck, she was petrified. He reached out a hand to Isaboe's shoulder, but she shrugged it away.

"I was one of five children," she said, speaking Charyn to the girl. "I want you to know that before you die. I want you to know their names. Evestalina. Rosemond. Jasmina. Balthazar. My mother's name was Tilda. My father's name was Carles. On the day he died, my brother, Balthazar, got in trouble for lying about breaking a vase in the reading room. My father said he was ashamed of him and so my brother went to his death thinking he had lost the king's respect."

Lucian heard her voice break.

"My sister Rosemond . . . We called her Rosie. She carved her name on the cherry-tree trunk in my mother's garden, declaring her love for one of my father's guards who later died in the prison mines of Sorel. I want you to think of them when you're choking on your own blood, Quintana of Charyn."

Lucian's pulse pounded to hear the name. Aldron stared at him, having no idea of the queen's plan.

"Isaboe!" Tesadora said, her voice desolate. "Do not do this. It will break your spirit."

With her hand still pressed against the girl's throat and the weapon still in place, Isaboe looked back at Tesadora.

"My spirit was broken long ago, Tesadora. And it was broken again yesterday when Vestie told me about your deceit. While I was begging you to come spend time with me, you were playing nursemaid to the daughter of the man who ordered my family's slaughter."

Isaboe turned back to the girl. "Did you think you could find refuge in my valley, filthy Charynite?"

Tesadora struggled in Aldron's arms. Lucian knew that nothing would stop the queen. Wasn't this exactly what Finnikin and Trevanion and Perri were doing in Charyn? Wasn't this something they all had sanctioned?

But it was horror Lucian felt when he saw Isaboe raise the blade to strike. The girl's scream was hoarse and full of rage and fear. The sound of it would ring in Lucian's ears for days to come.

And just as Isaboe went to use the sword, something came flying out at them from the copse of trees.

"*No!*"

The voice made his knees almost buckle.

Phaedra?

Lucian watched, stunned, as Phaedra threw herself at Isaboe. And then it all happened so fast, and he did what he was taught to do in battle . . . when his queen was under attack. He acted on instinct. Lucian didn't hesitate. Not for a single moment. His father's sword was in his hand, pressed against the throat of his wife. He knew he'd kill anyone who was a threat to his queen. He knew he would kill Phaedra of Alonso. But Phaedra was on her knees, gripping the blade of Isaboe's sword and pressing it to her own chest. Lucian could see its sharpness cutting into his wife's hands. Until they dripped with blood.

"Kill me," she pleaded, her head pressed against Isaboe's knees. "I'm begging, Your Majesty. Kill me. Please. If you want to avenge anyone, kill me. I'm a last born and daughter of a *provincaro*. Ride through Charyn and take every last-born girl to exact your revenge. But not her, Your Majesty. Charyn will cease to exist without her. We are nothing without the babe she carries."

Lucian watched Isaboe shudder. Even Tesadora was speechless at the sight of Phaedra.

"They don't stay dead, these Charynites, do they?" he heard Isaboe say, her voice so foreign to him. Compared to all the battles or deaths or sieges Lucian had ever witnessed, this was different. He swore later that the air changed, that there were spirits at play. That the Charyn gods and the goddess herself were damning Lucian for the blade he held. Damning them all. And then suddenly Isaboe stepped away, letting go of Quintana of Charyn and pulling free of Phaedra.

"Get out of my valley," Isaboe said. "Before I change my mind and slice you in half as your father's assassin did my mother!"

Lucian lowered his sword and stumbled back. Without hesitation, Phaedra gripped the girl's hand and they ran for their lives, disappearing through the trees.

For moments, all he heard was the sound of their own ragged breaths, but Lucian knew it wasn't over yet. Phaedra was alive. He had held a sword to her throat while she knelt, begging for another's mercy, her hands drenched with blood. He thought that the difference between him and Isaboe was that his love for a Charynite had sometimes made him forget. And he despised himself for it. He had forgotten the way Balthazar had died. His cousins. His aunt. His king and his father.

"You're to return home to the cloister in the forest," Isaboe ordered Tesadora. "I forbid you to come here again. I'll deal with you in my own time."

Tesadora gave a humorless laugh.

"You forbid," she mocked. "You'll deal with me? I'm not yours to deal with, little girl. You're mistaking me for someone else."

"Tesadora," Lucian warned as she walked away.

"If you return to this valley, Tesadora, you face the consequences," Isaboe said.

"I stay where I'm needed," Tesadora said.

"She'll stay with the Monts," Lucian said.

"I stay here!" Tesadora shouted, turning to face them all, eyes blazing.

Isaboe walked to her. She stood before Tesadora, shaking.

"Is it the filthy Charynite inside of you that draws you to these people?" she asked, and Lucian knew there was no turning back from those words.

"Oh, beloved," Tesadora said, both rage and sadness in her voice. "Don't force me to choose."

"Choose?" Isaboe said. "Between her and me? You'd choose her?"

Tesadora leaned forward and cupped the queen's face in both her hands.

"Blood sings to blood," Tesadora said. "And yours doesn't carry a tune."

Isaboe stumbled back as if she had been struck, and then Tesadora was gone, and Lucian could only stare at his cousin. He wished Finnikin were here, because only he could tear that look from her eyes. Lucian had seen him do it. Walk into a room when the images in her head were too powerful to bear. Finnikin would take her in his arms and whisper the words and she'd choke out a cry, but she'd breathe.

Lucian reached out to comfort her, but she stepped away. Being Evanjalin had trained her for years and years not to cry. It's how she differed from the rest of the Monts. But he could see that she was still broken inside.

"Let's go," he said quietly. "I need to get you home to Yata."

CHAPTER 10

"Froi, put down the dagger!"

"Finn first. Then we talk."

Later, Froi thought it would have looked strange to someone who stumbled across them in that clearing. Finnikin with an arm around Gargarin's neck and a dagger to his throat. Froi with a blade to Finnikin's back. Trevanion with his sword against the side of Froi's neck, ready to strike the moment he moved. Froi was dizzy from the confusion and the rage and the despair of it.

"Froi, put the dagger down!" Perri ordered.

Froi chanced a look and saw Gargarin's feet struggling to keep his body upright. Whether it was from pain or helplessness, it stirred Froi's fury even more.

"Let him go," Lirah cried, struggling in Perri's grip.

Perri was strong enough to hold Lirah as he stepped forward and pressed the tip of his sword against Froi's temple.

"Put it down, Froi. You know I'll do it," Perri threatened softly. "You know it."

Because you don't let emotion get in the way of what you're doing. Isn't that what Perri had once said?

"Froi," Gargarin said. "Put your sword down." His voice was hoarse from the pressure of Finnikin's dagger across his throat. "What good are you to us dead?"

"And what good are you to all of us dead?" Froi asked in return. Stupid, filthy tears filled his eyes, and he felt weak and helpless. He had a blade to his king's back. His king had a dagger to his father's throat. The men he respected beyond question were threatening to kill him. Here at this place, where Perri had tenderly carried Froi in his arms after they had rescued him from the Charynites more than three years ago.

"Just put the dagger down, Finn," Froi begged. "He's an architect. Nothing more."

"An architect of a path soaked in blood." Finnikin spat out the words, tightening his hold on Gargarin. "That's all Lumatere is to these people, Froi. A road."

Gargarin made a sound of regret. "I said what the Belegonians wanted to hear," he said with bitterness. "But you interfered, Lumateran. You interfered, and the blood of Charyn is on your hands the moment Belegonia crosses that river."

"What have you done to us, Finn?" Froi demanded.

Froi heard Finnikin's hiss of fury. "Us? Froi, we're not them. You're not them."

"He's not who you think, Finn. If you put down the dagger, we'll talk and you'll hear it all."

Lirah bit Perri's hand and tried to struggle free.

"Don't hurt her!" Froi shouted. He didn't know whom to protect first. Where to look.

"Do you know of this man's promise to the Belegonians in his correspondence?" Finnikin demanded. "To eliminate Lumatere. To eliminate the people who gave you a home."

"You're mistaken—"

"*Leave it to me, for I have a plan for Lumatere that will eliminate them as a threat,"* Finnikin said. "His words. Not mine. And how were you planning to do that, Charynite?" he demanded, holding Gargarin closer to him. "March an army through my kingdom and rape my wife and child? It's all Charynite men know how to do."

Froi watched Gargarin slump, his head bent in defeat.

"There are more ways than killing and maiming to eliminate a threat, Your Highness," Gargarin said, his voice low. "You misunderstood our use of weapon. Not a blade or an arrow, but Froi. We thought we could use him to eliminate Lumatere as a threat. His ties to you. His words."

How could Finnikin not have understood that? Froi begged the gods.

"We offer Lumatere peace, my lord, and you trap the man who can make it possible?" Froi asked, gutted.

Finnikin was silent. He loosened his grip on Gargarin slightly, and Froi waited, but there was nothing.

"Finn, I'm begging you. Let him free."

"We have evidence that this man was behind the plan to annihilate Lumatere all those years ago," Finnikin said.

"Never," Froi said fiercely. "I will give my life saying that. They will be the last words I speak, and they will haunt you, Finn. Never."

"Froi, step away," Gargarin said. "Put the dagger down. They won't listen to reason, and it will only get you killed. Put it down."

"You don't tell me what to do, Gargarin!"

"Can you not listen for once?" Gargarin shouted. "If you had listened . . ."

But Gargarin didn't finish his words.

"Say it!" Froi shouted over Finnikin's head, not knowing whom he hated most. "I wouldn't have lost her. That's what you wanted to say."

"Put the sword down and at least bargain for Lirah's life," Gargarin said.

Finnikin uttered a sound of disbelief.

"He thinks we'd kill his woman?" he said. "Is that what he thinks we are? Murderers?"

"You're holding a dagger to an innocent man's throat, Finn," Froi snapped. "He builds cisterns and plans water meadows and waterwheels. You collected all the information, but you got it wrong. Most times we're right, Perri once told me. This time you're wrong!"

Froi couldn't stand the silence. He couldn't stand to hear the sound of Gargarin's ragged breath and Lirah's despair. Just as he was about to lower his weapon, he watched Finnikin release both the dagger and his hold on Gargarin, who crumpled at his feet.

Froi dropped his dagger and Lirah was suddenly beside them, holding the staff, helping Gargarin to his feet. Somehow they managed to separate into two groups with space between them. Despite the lowering of swords and daggers, the atmosphere was tense. Perri's stare was fixed on Gargarin.

"Where do I know you from?" he demanded.

"You don't know him," Froi said tiredly. "Just leave it, Perri. He doesn't understand what you're saying."

Perri's hand gripped Froi by the throat, pulling him close. "Speak Lumateran, Froi! Or have you forgotten how to?"

And Froi felt a shame beyond reason. It made him despise the Charynite tongue to know it had such control. All this time, he hadn't spoken a word of Lumateran.

Perri didn't let go. "Since when do you hold a weapon to your king's throat?" he raged quietly. "Since when do you disappear for so long and take up with an enemy of Lumatere?"

Froi pulled free, viciously. "Since you sent me into Charyn to create holy hell. Isn't that what you'd call it, Perri? Because this is hell enough for me!"

He walked away, trying to think. All this meant was that he was even further away from finding Quintana and their child.

"How did you manage to get the Belegonian letters?" he demanded, swinging back to face them.

Finnikin didn't respond.

"How?"

"We have . . . a spy."

Finnikin refused to meet his eye.

"A spy? In Belegonia?" Froi was confused, and then it registered.

"Celie? Our Celie? You put her life in danger? Isaboe would never have allowed that!"

Finnikin was suddenly advancing on him. "Oh, really? You know what my wife would allow, do you? An expert on all things Isaboe?"

Finnikin was deadly in one of these moods.

"I know Isaboe well enough," Froi said. "She would—"

Finnikin flew at Froi and knocked him down. Froi shoved him back, and they wrestled, rolling in the dirt toward where the others stood.

"Are you going to stop them?" he heard Gargarin ask Trevanion and Perri.

"This has little to do with palace business," Perri responded almost politely in poor Charyn.

"Step back, madam," Trevanion ordered Lirah. "You'll get hurt."

Froi hesitated, thinking how ludicrous it all sounded. Finnikin took the opportunity to straddle him, holding him down to the ground.

"You want to ask about my wife?" Finnikin demanded.

"What would you have me tell you, Froi? You probably know more about her than I do. Her little confidant."

Froi popped him in the nose with his fist, and the next moment, he was on top and Finnikin was struggling to break free.

"It's the word *little* I take offense to, my lord," he said. "I think I'm the taller one now. Perhaps we can have Isaboe decide."

Finnikin's elbow caught Froi in the eye, and he fell back before Finnikin dived on top of him.

"What else did she tell you?" Finnikin hissed. "What else has she confided in you that she couldn't tell me?"

Froi shrugged free. "Are you insane?"

He was on his feet, shaking his head with disbelief. "What have you done, Finn?"

Finnikin leaped up seconds later, and they stood nose to nose.

"What else, apart from her time in Sorel, did she trust you with and not me?"

Finnikin shoved him hard for an answer. Froi shoved him back.

"Do you really want to know?" Froi goaded, fury lacing his voice. "She spoke to me of love and obsession and the way the goddess can weave ties between human hearts that burn with every touch."

Finnikin roared and charged for him, but Froi leaped up onto one of the branches, shoving a boot into Finnikin's face.

"She trusted me with the knowledge that loving the way she loved frightened her beyond imagining."

Finnikin gripped at his boot, and Froi tumbled, landing back on the ground with Finnikin pressing his face into the dirt. Froi crawled free.

"She trusted me with the knowledge that her people think she's the bravest queen who ever lived, but she fears she doesn't know who she is without the man she worships," Froi continued.

"She fears that if something happened to him, she'd lie in her bed and never ever get up."

Froi scrambled to his feet, and they were standing before each other, so unlike the time in training back in the meadow before Froi had traveled to Charyn.

"When she was carrying Jasmina in her belly, she trusted me with the knowledge that she feared she wouldn't love her child as much as she loved her king," Froi continued. "She told me about her slavery in Sorel, because she had to speak to someone about her shame. If anyone understood that sort of shame, it was me . . . and her king. But she couldn't tell her king because their curse was that he had to share her pain twofold and she will never forgive herself for putting him through that."

Froi threw a punch, and it knocked Finnikin down.

"And do you know what else we spoke about? Not that she doesn't believe that her consort is a man of worth because he is less titled than his wife, but that her consort doesn't believe he is worthy. You have no idea what that does to her, you fool. Because you're too busy being proud. What an indulgent luxury pride is," he raged. "I would give my life to be the consort to the woman I love. I'd give my life to be her footman! Her servant. Any chance to stand close enough to protect her. Yet your queen asks you to sit on the throne by her side and it's all too degrading for you. You fool," Froi said bitterly. "You will drive her away."

There was no satisfaction in Froi's victory. After a moment, they both looked over to where Trevanion, Perri, Gargarin, and Lirah were watching dispassionately. Froi suddenly felt like a child. Under the same stares, Finnikin fidgeted uncomfortably beside him.

"Finished?" Trevanion asked.

No one responded.

"We head home," the Captain said. "You ride with me, Froi.

And you better be speaking the truth about this man's innocence. You're going to have to face the queen about the decision we made to let him go."

They were the last words Froi wanted to hear.

"I'm staying," he said quietly.

Finnikin turned to stare at him but didn't say a word.

"Get on the horse, Froi," Perri ordered.

Froi shook his head. "Don't ask me to do that. For now, I need to stay here."

Finnikin still hadn't spoken, and Froi waited, wanting a word, a gesture. From his king. His friend.

"You're making a choice here, Froi," Trevanion said. "Charyn or Lumatere?"

Froi couldn't fight the anguish he was feeling. "Why does there have to be a choice?" he asked.

Finnikin made a sound of disbelief, and Froi felt as if he was with strangers.

"How can you even ask that?" Finnikin said, mounting his horse and riding away.

And on that night, Finnikin traveled with a heavy heart, his thoughts on his childhood friend Balthazar. Because the loyal friendship he had shared with Froi had become just as fierce over the years. Lucian would have agreed. Froi reminded them both of how they had been before Balthazar's death. They were more carefree in his presence. Content. But all that was gone now.

"They're not safe here," Trevanion muttered when they reached the border. "There's an army camped somewhere close back there. Probably for one of them."

"Not our problem," Finnikin said, steering his horse toward the river that would take them across to Osteria and then home.

"Froi made his choice. He's dead to Lumatere."

And I'm shaking with Phaedra as we climb to the cave, Froi. Our skin is still fastened by blood that is hers. And the women are stunned and all asking questions, but the fool girl just cries and lets go of my hand. And she weeps and she weeps, so I lay by her side and I whisper the order, "We'll kill them together." Phaedra reaches a hand to her cheek, and I see that it's pressed where the Mont's blade had pierced her. And I can see in her eyes that she's almost convinced. The next time we meet them, it's the bitch queen who weeps.

And sometime the next day, Isaboe returned from the mountain to the palace. She responded to the letter from the Sarnak ambassador that was waiting for her. Then she spoke to the kitchen staff about the dinner banquet for the Osterian archduke and chose the design for the garden they were building in honor of her mother. Sir Topher arrived in the residence soon after, and they put the finishing touches on the invitations for the next market day. Rhiannon came fussing with Jasmina, who wanted no one but her mother, and Isaboe rocked her daughter to a song of unicorns and rabbits and all things fluffy and white. And then the palace was quiet and she was alone for the first time in days, thinking of that hideous night of death, trying to remember with all her might what her last words to every one of her family were. Until Finnikin's hound came searching for his master and found her instead. It was only then that she felt the weary sob release. And she wept into the hound's coat until her body ached and she feared she would hurt the babe that was inside of her. Because everything was broken. Everything. And there was no design, nor treaty, nor map that could put it all back together.

part two
The Lumateran

CHAPTER 11

"S he's gone again," Cora said, shoving Phaedra awake.
Phaedra didn't want to go out in the cold. She didn't
want to move from the bedroll where she had been
huddled all day and night. But Cora shoved her again.

"Get up. I don't know what took place out there with you two
useless girls, and I don't care. But we didn't sacrifice our pathetic
half lives in the valley only to lose her."

With all the strength she could muster, Phaedra untangled
herself from her meager blanket and wearily got to her feet.

"How long has she been gone?" she asked.

"Since yesterday evening, although she did leave that," Jorja
said, indicating a dead rodent, pierced with a sharp twig through
its length, "outside the entrance this morning."

"Ready for roasting," Florenza said. "You're wrong, Cora.
She's not completely useless."

"She revolts me," Ginny muttered.

"Yes, but you'll be the first one to eat anything she hunts,"
Jorja said.

That began another round of bickering. Phaedra ignored them and walked to the entrance.

"Take a blanket," Cora said, and Phaedra heard a touch of kindness in her voice.

She knew exactly where to find her. When Phaedra had gone searching for Quintana two days past, before those terrifying moments with the queen and Lucian, she had come across a small collection of berries and nuts and a large amount of ferns and moss pulled from the ground. Phaedra imagined Quintana was planning to burrow herself into the ground like the little rat that she was.

When Phaedra reached the small clearing, she searched the area for anything that resembled a hiding place. When she saw what looked to be a shelter made of bracken and bramble, she bent to peer in and saw the princess instantly.

"You can't stay in there," Phaedra called out. "Do you want a repeat of what happened with the queen of Lumatere?"

"Well, I'm not returning to the coven," Quintana responded briskly.

Phaedra got to her knees and crawled into the space, half impressed with the underground nest Quintana had built for herself. It was a space big enough for two or three, but the princess refused to make room. Phaedra shoved the girl aside and wrapped her blanket around herself, shivering, but soon Quintana clutched at the end of blanket and they were forced to huddle together. And there they sat for a while in hostile silence.

"You need to give me most of that blanket," Quintana ordered after some time. "I'm with child, and I'm covering up for two. I don't like the cold. Did I not mention that?"

Phaedra bristled. "More than once."

The princess watched her closely.

"Are they still bickering? What are they saying back there?"

"That we have a lot in common, you and I. Both useless."

The princess curled her lip in disgust. "What does one have to do in this kingdom to be considered useful?"

Phaedra had to agree and was glad to hear that the princess recognized Phaedra's efforts.

"I don't see any of them staking rodents and catching hares," Her Royal Awfulness continued. "I think I'm the least useless Charynite in these parts, if you ask me."

"And me? I saved your life!" Phaedra said. "A thank-you would be appreciated."

A show of savage teeth this time. "Oh, you're one of those," the princess said.

"One of what?"

"One of those who need to be told their worth over and over again by others. Do you know who tells me my worth, Phaedra of Alonso?"

The princess pointed a hard finger to her own chest.

"Me. I determine my own worth. If I had to rely on others, I'd have lain down and died waiting. See this," she said, pointing to her belly. "This is Charyn. It can ill afford a curse breaker who's waiting for everyone's approval."

She studied Phaedra suspiciously. Phaedra could sense that she was not going to like the next words that came from Quintana's mouth.

"You're more useless than I am. That piece-of-nothing girl Ginny told me your Mont husband sent you back, and that ugly hag Cora mentioned it, too."

Phaedra bristled. Not only did the princess have the habit of repeating everyone's favorite description of one another, but Phaedra's marriage to Lucian was now being discussed with vigor among the women. How many of them had ridiculed her behind her back?

"Did your Mont husband not enjoying swiving you? Is that what it was?"

Phaedra was mortified to hear such filth come out of the girl's mouth. She yanked Cora's blanket away.

"If my father were here, he would wash your mouth out to hear such a word," she said.

"Well, he's not here, Phaedra of Alonso. He's too busy trying to starve the people of the valley. Do you know what Gargarin of Abroi says?"

"I don't care!"

"That it is what a man does for strangers that counts more than what he does for his family."

"Oh, really," Phaedra asked. "And what have you and your father done for strangers?"

The girl's hand suddenly gripped Phaedra's mouth.

"You'll not enjoy my response to that question," the princess said. "You don't seem the type to stomach such filth."

She shoved Phaedra away. "Leave me in peace. I'll take care of the little king on my own."

CHAPTER 12

There had been silence among the three of them for most
of the next day. Gargarin had suggested that they first
return to the inn for their horses and then head north to
the Lascow Mountains. If there were any chance of raising an
army, it would be with the people grieving the heir Tariq and
his family.

"What are your thoughts?" Gargarin asked Froi.

"Whatever you think is right," Froi replied.

When they reached the inn, however, Gargarin and Lirah's
horse was gone. Stolen. The stable boy knew little, except that out
of all the horses taking shelter, theirs was the only one gone. Froi
was suspicious.

So Lirah rode with Gargarin on Froi's horse and Froi kept
up with them on foot. Once or twice he felt Lirah's stare, but
he couldn't meet it. He thought of what he had told them in
Paladozza that last day, when he escaped with Quintana.
About who he had once been on the filthy streets of the Sarnak
capital. There were too many ugly memories. Too much
shame. He didn't want to see judgment in Lirah's eyes. Froi

didn't have to worry about seeing anything in Gargarin's eyes. Gargarin refused to look at him.

They traveled farther into the woodlands that evening. It was a peculiar place, where branches hung low and bare limbs in a blue-gray mist hovered over them like the long, thin specter of death that sometimes haunted Froi's dreams. He knew they would soon be back in the stone terrain he had become used to. But, for now, these woodlands were a strangely familiar reminder of winter in the forest of Lumatere. Rather than feeling comforted, Froi was reminded that he no longer belonged in that kingdom.

When they were deep in the heart of the woodland, Lirah stopped the horse.

"I can go on," Froi said, his voice curt. Did they think him weak? Had he shown in any way that his body didn't have the strength it once had?

"Well, I'm tired," Lirah said, dismounting. "I need to rest, so we rest."

Froi made himself scarce, collecting kindling and ignoring Gargarin, who sat hunched on a log, scribbling.

"We need to write a list of where she would have gone," Gargarin said, not looking up. "We can't leave any stone unturned. Tell me of those last moments."

Those last moments outside the province of Paladozza. When Olivier betrayed them. And Quintana cried. For Froi. And he made a promise to protect her. And failed. And the sound of arrows as they flew past his ears. The way they felt when they tore into his body time and time again. Froi had never been injured before then. He remembered the time in Yutlind Sud when he had seen Finnikin lying facedown in a filthy river with an arrow in his side. Worse still, he remembered Isaboe's despair. Is

that what Quintana thought? That he was dead? Was she afraid?

"I told her to run. . . ." He shook his head. "I lost consciousness. . . ."

Gargarin muttered something and went on scribbling. Froi despised himself for every moment of his life since he made that decision to take her from the *provincaro*'s home in Paladozza. *More than you,* he wanted to shout out to Gargarin. *I despise myself more than you.*

When it was time to sleep, Gargarin and Lirah bunked down in a hollow that seemed large enough to protect them from both the cold and rain. Froi chose to squeeze himself under two fallen logs close by, and he watched the world outside with a misery deepened by the sleet and cold. But soon after, Lirah squeezed in beside him. With a rough hand at his chin, she began to dab at the cuts on his face with some sort of sap from a plant she had picked while they had set up camp. Froi tossed his head, pulling away, but she grabbed his face again.

"Push me away and I'll hurt you more than that Lumateran ginger cat."

For an instant he imagined the amusement Finnikin would find in the description until he realized that there was nothing Froi could ever say again that Finnikin would find entertaining. He felt Lirah's stare on him the whole time as she dabbed and cleaned the wounds, and when Froi could no longer ignore her and pretend Gargarin wasn't there, his eyes clashed with hers. He was tired and bereft without his friends, and because he ached for Quintana, he spoke the words that had choked him since he awoke in Arjuro's cave.

"I couldn't protect her and I've let down my queen and her king and . . . he"—Froi pointed in Gargarin's direction—"he won't even look at me."

And this time her fingers were gentle and she pushed his cap up from his eyes.

"I've seen Gargarin weep twice in his life," she said quietly. "Once when they arrested his brother for the slaughter in the godshouse, and some weeks ago when we received word in Paladozza that a lad struck by eight arrows lay dead on the northern hills. De Lancey sent his men to retrieve your body, but it was gone and we waited a week to discover the truth. That you were with the priests of Trist in the caves, saved by Arjuro."

Froi let her clean the rest of his grazes.

"And you?" he asked. "What did you do?"

"I've wept enough in my life. I have no tears left."

Not one for great sentimentality, she finished her task and shuffled out from under the logs. "I'm not giving up the comfort of a better shelter," she said, her voice cool. "And you'd be a fool not to join us."

He watched Lirah hold a hand over her head to protect her from the rain as she made her way back to Gargarin.

It was some time before Froi joined them. Lirah made room and sat between Froi and Gargarin and he saw her lips curve into a smile. After a while, Gargarin reached across her to pass Froi his journal. Froi took it, looking at the map.

"We've sent messengers to the Turlan and Lascow Mountains. She won't go north to Satch of Desantos because of the plague," Gargarin said. "Any ideas?"

Froi pointed east on the map. "Perhaps to the ocean. On the last night we were together at De Lancey's in Paladozza, she told me that she had always wanted to see the ocean. She loved the stories of the sea sirens. Perhaps she'll go searching for the safe places from the tales she loved."

"Not much to go by," Gargarin said. Froi watched him swallow hard. "If Quintana was dead . . . we would know of it soon

enough. It's been some time now. She has the sign of a last born on her nape and a babe in her belly. A Charynite would have to be hiding under a rock not to know that a girl fitting that description is the princess."

"She's not dead," Froi said.

"How do you know that?"

Froi felt strange to say the words. "It's as if I hear her tune . . . not the words, but the beat. I've always sensed it. It strums in my blood."

They were quiet after that, except for the rustle of Gargarin removing his pelt cloak to wrap around them. Lirah tugged Froi closer and covered them all, and that night, despite the rain and cold and the cramped space of their dugout, Froi placed his head against her shoulder and slept.

Early the next morning, he left them sleeping in a bid to find anything edible. At least with the rain there'd be slugs, and that would have to do for now. He was interrupted by the faint sound of neighing, and although it could easily have been a Charynite traveling upriver, wanting to get as far from the Belegonian river crossing as possible, Froi wasn't convinced. Finding the closest sturdy tree, he climbed quickly and looked out toward the direction of the sound.

"Sagra!"

He twisted around once, twice, three times to search in every direction, his knees almost buckling from under him. The woodlands were swarming with riders, traveling toward the center. A small army was coming from three different directions to trap their prey. Froi didn't have to guess who they hunted. He scampered down and hit the ground, then ran toward the shelter and watched as they disappeared into the woods. The soldiers must have waited, finding a way to surround the three of them, ensuring they were too deep within the woods to escape.

"We've got company," he said, reaching the shelter. Lirah and Gargarin crawled out, quickly gathering their possessions.

Froi had to think fast. If he attacked from up high, he could slow down Bestiano's men. He only had one longbow with very few bolts, but it would be enough to get Lirah and Gargarin to safety. Although he sensed movement from south of the woods, those men moved stealthily, and he could barely make out their presence. He was better off attacking those who were visible.

"Get back into the shelter," he ordered. "They know exactly where we are, and they'll be pelting us with arrows in no time. When I give you the signal to take the horse and run, you do it."

"Which direction serves us better?" Gargarin asked.

"North. Those men are sluggish. There's perhaps nine or ten of them. I'll have enough barbs to slow them down. Whatever you do, don't head toward the river or cross the border. Sagra only knows what the Osterians and Belegonians have got in mind."

Froi turned, searching for the tallest tree, but Gargarin grabbed his arm.

"You know it's me they want. If I surrender —"

"It won't be a surrender!" Froi said. "It'll be a slaying. Don't even try to fool me into believing you can bargain for your life. That army is after you, Gargarin. For a kill. You're the only person who stands between Bestiano and the palace."

An arrow flew into the clearing and landed close by.

"The shelter!" Froi shouted, spinning around. He found what he was looking for and began his climb up a tree close to the fallen logs where he had first taken refuge. Although an easy climb, he tried not to look down. He was high above the ground, and he knew it would be a backbreaking fall if it was to happen.

But you won't fall, because you can climb anything, Froi. Remember the gravina.

He cursed himself for not exchanging Arjuro's coins for more weapons. He knew he could not afford to miss, not with only eight arrows in his quiver. He had to hit his marks. He reached the top branch, and a glance on all sides told him that those from the north and east had picked up speed. He couldn't see the men coming from the south but knew they were there. They were the ones to fear. They were perhaps Bestiano's best-trained men.

Froi secured himself in the crook of the tree and waited . . . waited . . . needing the riders to be within his range, fighting the urge to fire a bolt, knowing it was an arrow he could not spare. He begged himself patience, and with a steady hand, he held the bow taut. Waited. And then when those from the north were near enough for Froi to almost catch a glimpse of their faces, he took his chance and fired . . . once, twice, three times. Retreated. Waited. He quickly peered out and saw he had hit with precision, and he felt bitter satisfaction in seeing the men fall. But behind him, he heard the air whistle with arrows and prayed that Gargarin and Lirah were protected by their shelter. He retreated again, knowing he needed to clear a path for them both to the north. But when he looked in that direction, the riders were no longer there. Froi felt the hairs on his arm raise. He didn't want to be playing cat and mouse with them now. Desperate to see where they were concealed, he crawled onto the exposed tree limb, balancing himself until it afforded him a better look. He took aim. One man went down and then another. But just as he aimed for the last, he felt the sharp nip of an arrow at his thigh, causing him to lose balance. He fought to stay straddled upright but failed and toppled off the branch, his hand shooting out to grip the branch, leaving his body hanging from just one arm.

"Froi!" Gargarin's voice sounded far away.

"Stay in the shelter!" Froi shouted, beads of perspiration on

his skin as he tried with all his might to reach the tree with his other hand. That was all he needed. Two firm handholds. He dared not look down, knowing his fall would not be broken, but his body would be. With his arm so weak, Froi couldn't hold on for much longer. He heard the whistles of arrows as he hung like a well-marked target on a practice range, his body a beacon.

"Take the horse. Head north!" he called out, his voice straining.

He could hear shouting in return, but he was too high up to understand their response. Had Lirah and Gargarin already been taken? He felt his hand slipping and knew he didn't want to die this way. Not from a fall. He closed his eyes and summoned the strength to hold on, but he was too weak. His body had not yet recovered, and he couldn't save himself. And he prayed, realizing, while he hung from this tree in the kingdom of his birth, that Sagrami wasn't just a curse to him; she was his guide as well. Not Trist or any of the gods of Charyn, but Lumatere's mighty goddess. He prayed to her with all his might. *Don't let me die. Not now,* he begged.

Why? she demanded to know.

Because I deserve to live.

A hand suddenly gripped his wrist.

He wondered if the hold came from the realms of the gods. But he didn't care. All he knew was what the goddess was whispering to him, *He'll never let you go. How could you have ever doubted him?*

"I've got you, Froi."

"Finn?"

CHAPTER 13

L ucian issued the order more than once as he traveled
down the mountain. It was firm and spoken in a tone that
was not open to discussion.

"Go. Home."

His cousins Constance and Sandrine followed, all the same.
Their brothers and fathers had refused to allow them horses, so
the girls had resorted to riding on donkeys. Lucian's peace and
quiet on the mountain was all but over.

"If Tesadora has returned to her work with them, why can't
we?" Constance shouted back.

"Because it's not your work," he said. "It's not our duty or
our work to take care of them. It's Charyn's."

"But the valley dwellers are running from Charyn," Sandrine
argued. "So why would we expect that the very kingdom they're
running from will feed them?"

Lucian didn't have a response for that. He had a response for
very little these days, despite the questions that plagued him.
And the guilt. He had held a knife to his wife's throat. His wife
who had betrayed him.

What he did know for certain was that there was talk of starvation in the valley and it was his duty, not as a Lumateran but as a man, to see how the valley dwellers were faring. He watched them for a while across the stream. They looked frail, older than the last time he had seen them. Harker was working with Kasabian on the vegetable patch that was yielding very little. Harker's movements were furious as he hacked at the earth. After all they had done to get to this valley, he had lost a wife and daughter to plague. But had he? If Phaedra was alive, it could mean the others lived as well. Cora, too. And the other girl whose name he could not remember. He crossed the stream, and within moments Constance and Sandrine were hurrying ahead toward Tesadora, who was on the rock face of one of the higher caves. He was about to follow but stopped at the sight of Rafuel sitting outside one of the lower caves with Donashe and his men.

Weeks before the supposed death of Phaedra and the women, Rafuel had been a prisoner of Lumatere. Circumstances had changed Lucian's mind about the Charynite, and a trust had built between them. Lucian and the Queen's Guard had agreed to send Rafuel down to the valley as a spy for both Lumatere and the Charynite priests Rafuel answered to. Men who were desperate for peace in their kingdom. Within days, Rafuel, taking the name Matteo, had established a place alongside Donashe, the leader of a group of cutthroats who had slaughtered seven unarmed supposed Charynite traitors. Donashe answered to those who had taken control of Charyn's army, and Lucian knew that the people of the valley feared for their lives. But they had nowhere else to go, and Lucian had no way of getting rid of Donashe and his men without involving Lumatere in a war.

Since Phaedra's "death," Lucian had no idea who Rafuel was aligned with. All he knew was that Rafuel had been the one to remove the five women from the caves and had lied about

Phaedra's death. What else had he lied about?

Lucian wanted answers. He made his way toward the group, his eyes meeting Rafuel's the moment the Charynite looked up. Rafuel stood, and as soon as he was close, Lucian's fist connected with Rafuel's face. He watched the Charynite's head snap back as he stumbled to the ground. Suddenly the murderer Donashe was up on his feet, furious.

"It's nothing," Rafuel said, fighting to regain his breath, wiping blood from his mouth. "Leave it, Donashe. These Monts cannot control their emotions."

"You are a lying traitor—"

"Lucian!" Tesadora shouted, and Lucian heard the warning in her voice as she scrambled down the rock steps followed by his cousins and Japhra. "This is my fight," she said, pulling him away. "Japhra is one of my girls." Tesadora gripped Lucian's arm, her fingernails deep in his flesh. She was protecting Rafuel, making it seem as if Lucian's fury was about Rafuel sharing a bed with a Lumateran girl.

"Is this about one of their women?" Donashe asked, laughing. He held a hand out to Rafuel, lifting him to his feet, patting him on the back.

Lucian pointed a finger at Rafuel.

"I want a word in private."

"Perhaps our Matteo is a man much like yourself, friend," Donashe said to Lucian. "Perhaps he enjoys pounding into women of foreign blood."

Lucian flew at Donashe, and it took Rafuel, Tesadora, and Japhra to hold him back. Kasabian rushed toward them and stood between Lucian and the camp leader.

"We don't pound into our women like you Charynite rapists!" Lucian shouted.

"What are you doing, lad?" Kasabian asked, trying to push

him back. "Ignore him, Lucian. Come now."

Lucian's blood boiled, and his gaze fixed on Donashe, who had the smarts to look afraid.

"Call me friend again, and I'll cut out your tongue," Lucian threatened before he looked at Rafuel. "I said I want a word."

"Go with him," Donashe said to Rafuel, relishing the control he believed he had in the valley. Lucian gripped Rafuel and pushed him forward as they walked back toward the stream. Rafuel stumbled.

When they were at a distance, Lucian flew at the Charynite again.

"Lucian!" Tesadora shouted. "What's gotten into you?"

"What's gotten into me, Tesadora?" he shot back. "What's gotten into you? Choosing that mad-bitch daughter of our enemy over our queen?"

Rafuel closed his eyes, shaking his head. "You've seen her?"

Lucian's fist connected again, and when Rafuel was down, he pushed the Charynite's face into the ground. Tesadora and Japhra pulled him away.

"Colluding with this traitor, Tesadora?" Lucian asked, staring down at Rafuel.

"Traitor to whom?" Rafuel hissed, pushing him. "I'm not working for you, Mont. I'm not working for him," he added, pointing back to Donashe, who was watching. "I'm here for my people. I'm a traitor to no one."

"Talk," Lucian ordered. "We don't have time, so if you have something to hide from your friends, talk to me now, Rafuel. Or that princess you have hidden may not be hiding too much longer."

Rafuel's eyes met Tesadora's with regret.

"How did you find her?" he asked.

"My queen almost took a dagger to her throat," Tesadora

said. "Who is taking care of things out there, Rafuel? She's running around like a savage."

"*Gods!*" Rafuel cursed. "Who else knows?"

Lucian watched Kasabian approach.

"Not a word," Rafuel whispered hoarsely. "Not a word, I'm begging you." His eyes found Japhra's. "I need to see the woman, and at least Donashe won't question why I'm not in the camp if I'm with you, Japhra."

"No," Lucian said.

"Enough!" Japhra said firmly, and Lucian saw the surprise on everyone's faces. "I answer for myself," Japhra said. She looked at Rafuel and nodded, and he walked back toward Donashe and his men. Lucian watched them surround Rafuel, clapping him on the back. It made Lucian's blood boil again. They were congratulating him on having a Lumateran woman.

"Do you feel no shame?" he said to Tesadora and Japhra.

"Only for you," Tesadora said, her voice cold.

Harker was there before him.

"You've been a stranger to us, Mont."

"I've been a stranger to myself, Harker," he said. "What goes on here?"

Harker shook his head. "Nothing good. You've heard about Alonso and how they've stopped the grain wagons? Donashe and his pigs consume any food we do get. These people are starving, Lucian. And just up there," Harker said, pointing to Lucian's mountain, "your people are filling their bellies. *Just up there.*"

Lucian didn't know what to say. He could have convinced himself that these people were not Lumatere's responsibility, but how could they not be?

"Come," Tesadora said to Lucian quietly. Reluctantly, he followed her up into the caves. She wanted him to see firsthand, but he didn't have to. What was he expected to do? Defy Isaboe?

The valley dwellers were listless, worse than they were in the days Phaedra had kept their spirits high. There was barely any talk among them, and the only emotion they seemed to show was a pitiful flare of hope at the return of Tesadora and the girls. Later, they entered a cave where a handful of the men sat miserably. One man clutched Tesadora's arm.

"Can you see to my wife?" he asked her. "They won't let us share the same cave, and I know she's not herself here," he said, pointing to his heart.

"Does she suffer from melancholy?" Tesadora asked.

"I've not seen her in such a way since . . . since a long time ago. Since the first day of weeping eighteen years past."

Lucian saw sorrow on Tesadora's face. "You lost a babe?" she asked huskily.

The man nodded. "It was so close to being birthed," he said. "And then it was gone. But we learned to live with our pain, and my wife swallowed her grief. Until now. Until all those weeks ago . . . on our journey here to the valley. We came across a girl . . . a mad-looking girl, who begged us for a ride. From the first moment my wife . . . even myself . . . from the first moment we saw her, there was a bond I cannot explain."

Tesadora looked up at Lucian, who said, "Repeat his words in case there are some I don't understand." She looked at the man. "Speak."

The man smiled at the memory. "It was as though I could look into the girl's eyes and see a spirit I knew. My wife felt the same." The man shook his head. "And then she was gone."

"Gone where?" Lucian asked.

"Dead. From the plague. She was one of the younger women who took ill."

The man's face was pained. "And for my wife, it was as though we lost our unborn babe again."

Lucian heard the intake of Tesadora's breath. She bent forward and cupped the man's face in her hands.

"I'll go see your wife," she said.

Lucian followed Tesadora out of the cave.

"Is it her?" he asked quietly. "The girl he was speaking of? Is it that . . . princess?"

"Shh. And don't speak of her again," Tesadora warned. "Don't you risk her life, Lucian. Enough has been lost. Do you understand? Enough."

There was more than a warning in her voice. And Lucian remembered the day they had first interrogated Rafuel in the prison on the mountain. "Have you noticed anything strange in the valley?" the Charynite had asked. Lucian remembered how Tesadora had been the one to guess that day. There were no children in the valley. They had bled from the loins of the women. Tesadora had left the prison shattered. Lucian knew she was half Charynite. She claimed it was her Charyn blood that called her to this valley.

"You lost a babe?" Lucian said. "Eighteen years past?"

Tesadora stared up at him and continued to walk, but Lucian gripped her hand.

"On the day of their weeping, you bled, didn't you, Tesadora?"

Tesadora pulled away, and Lucian saw the tears that refused to fall.

"Mind your business, Lucian," she said, her voice cold. "And feed these people, or may the food you put into your own mouth turn to parchment."

Late that night, Phaedra heard a sound outside their cave.

"Did you hear that?" Cora asked.

"Shh."

There was silence. Nothing but the sound of the malevolent wind. And then Phaedra heard it again. Three short whistles. Rafuel.

They hadn't seen Rafuel for weeks, and something inside Phaedra made her feel uneasy. She held a finger to her lips to signal the others to stay silent. Until she saw Tesadora and Japhra and the Mont girls, Constance and Sandrine. The Mont girls gaped when they saw Phaedra.

"How . . . how could you do that to us?" Constance said. "After we gave you a home. How could you do that to Lucian?"

"I warned you not to make a fuss," Tesadora told Constance. "If you can't keep silent, go back to the camp."

Sandrine began to weep, while Constance stared at Phaedra with anger. And hurt.

Meanwhile, Phaedra's companions were as furious as the Monts, turning on Rafuel.

"Why trust Lumaterans over Gies and our men?" Ginny cried.

"You need to tell Harker," Jorja said.

"Father will know what to do," Florenza added.

"If you can trust anyone, it's Kasabian," Cora snapped.

Tesadora threw them a scathing look.

"You'd think death would have silenced you all," she muttered. She knelt beside Quintana, and Phaedra saw the beauty of Tesadora's face now more than ever. Her eyes, normally so hostile, danced with joy and life, with an almost purple hue to them. Her hair looked silver in the light of the moon. Phaedra had only seen Tesadora this animated once before. When the queen of Lumatere had sat in her tent with Princess Jasmina on her lap, laughing with the women of her kingdom. And now, here, with Quintana. Deep down, Phaedra had wanted Tesadora's laughter and warmth herself.

The princess responded to Tesadora's presence with a show of savage teeth, the closest thing she had to a smile.

"Are you going to let Japhra see to you?" Tesadora asked Quintana, her Charyn still weak.

"I'll translate if you want," Phaedra said.

Tesadora waved her away. "Oh, we understand each other, don't we, my little savage?"

Quintana looked almost haughty with such attention, her smile now wolfish. Tesadora laughed and held a gentle hand to her cheek.

"Japhra is the best midwife we have. More than a midwife. Gifted beyond imagining." Tesadora gently lay Quintana down. "It will seem as if she's doing strange things, but it's only to ensure the babe is safe."

They lifted Quintana's shift and Phaedra wanted to look away. The belly frightened her, but she didn't want them to think she was a coward.

Quintana flinched at whatever Japhra was doing.

"I'll hold your hand," Tesadora reassured.

"I can hold it," Phaedra said. "She's beginning to trust me."

"She snarls at you all day long," Florenza said.

Tesadora turned to them, annoyed.

"Go away. Both of you. Go speak to Rafuel. He has news from the camp."

Phaedra stood and walked outside onto the rock face, where Rafuel was speaking to Cora and Jorja.

"What is the news, Rafuel?" Phaedra said, her voice weary.

"Not good. Your father has stopped the grain, Phaedra. The older valley dwellers aren't faring well. Donashe and his men are the lowest of dogs, and they are growing in numbers. There is also one who watches me. As if he suspects. You all need to be careful. How could you have allowed the princess out of your sight?" he said, anger in his voice. "Her throat was almost slit by Isaboe of Lumatere. What were you thinking, Phaedra?"

But I begged the Queen Isaboe not to, Phaedra wanted to cry. *And she let us go.* Didn't that say something of her worth?

"How are the men?" Jorja asked. "How is my Harker?"

Rafuel shook his head. "Angry. I fear he will do something foolish and get himself killed for it. Donashe's men don't have the discipline of an army. They don't have a bond to anything or anyone, including one another." Rafuel's eyes met Ginny's. "Your husband and some of the other men in the valley have taken to being Donashe's lackeys. It means their bellies are better taken care of than the rest, but they have sold their honor."

"Well, that's your fault," Ginny said spitefully. "Gies is despairing without me." She looked at the other women, nodding in satisfaction. "He's smart to have aligned himself with those in power."

"Those in power, you stupid girl, slaughtered seven innocent men," Cora said.

Ginny looked away. "Well, my Gies and me, we weren't here to have seen that, and according to Gies, those scholar lads were traitors."

Rafuel's stare was murderous. The seven scholars had been his men, and Phaedra knew he would never forgive himself for not dying alongside them. By the look on his face, she thought he'd strike out at Ginny. She was relieved when Tesadora and Japhra were finished with the princess and joined them.

"Will you come again soon, Matteo?" Cora said.

Rafuel didn't correct her.

"Now that Donashe and his men believe that I've taken to Japhra, they may not question me slipping away more often," Rafuel said.

"The princess is fine for now," Japhra said in Lumateran. "The babe will be born in the spring."

And then Tesadora, Rafuel, and the girls were gone, and Phaedra stood on the rock face watching until the last flicker of their lamps disappeared. Back inside, she lay beside the princess, turning away from her. But then she felt Quintana lean over her, her lips close to Phaedra's ear.

"I do believe we're going to have to kill that piece-of-nothing girl Ginny."

Phaedra's heart thumped to hear the words. She turned to face Quintana.

"Are you mad?"

"A knife to her side and a slit ear to ear. It'll take us less than five seconds."

"That's evil."

Her Royal Awfulness gave a laugh.

"Can you honestly say with the clearest conviction that Ginny will not betray us the first chance she is given?"

No, Phaedra thought. She couldn't honestly say that. But nor could she sanction anything this mad girl suggested.

"Find a better way of securing Ginny's trust," Phaedra said. "It would help if you were nicer to your own people . . . and not just the Lumaterans."

"Well, only one Lumateran has tried to kill me so far, as opposed to the number of Charynites who have attempted."

What kind of a girl was this who would speak of taking another's life so freely?

"I think—"

"Go to sleep," Quintana said dismissively. "You're useless to me when you feel sorry for yourself."

CHapteR 14

roi woke to see five faces staring down at him.

"You fainted," Lirah said.

"No, I didn't."

"Yes, you did," Gargarin argued.

"You climbed down well enough, but the moment we touched the ground, you fainted," Finnikin said.

"I've never fainted a day in my life."

"Well, you fainted today," Finnikin said, leaning closer, "and you're going to really upset Perri and my father if you don't speak Lumateran," he added, feigning a whisper.

Froi's eyes met Perri's and then Trevanion's. Neither looked happy.

"Reckon I stumbled. Hit my head on a rock," he said in Lumateran. It felt so strange on his tongue now.

"You fainted," Perri said, his voice flat.

If Froi had fainted in front of Gargarin, he wouldn't have cared, but it was different in front of his captain and Perri and Finnikin. Warriors didn't faint. Froi was shamed.

"If you like, I can tell you in Sarnak or perhaps a bit of Yut, and then we would have made it clear in quite a few languages that you fainted," Finnikin said with a grin.

"I fainted," he concluded miserably.

Lirah made a sound of disgust. "I can't understand a word anyone's saying," she said, walking away.

Froi watched Finnikin stare after Lirah, shaking his head. "Rude, rude woman," Finnikin muttered. "She spat at me, you know."

Froi wanted to sink into the earth beneath him. He sighed and sat up, but the movement was too abrupt and he found himself lying back down again, his head spinning.

"Slowly," Finnikin said, holding out a hand for a second time that day. "We're going to have to move from here. There are still some riders out in the woods."

"From which direction did you come?" Froi asked.

"South."

"We head east," Perri said.

"There's no path east through these woods," Froi said.

"Perri's found one," Finnikin said. "Come."

Gargarin and Lirah were looking at each other as Froi approached them, and they grabbed their packs, ready to follow the others.

"Perri's found a path east," Froi explained, leading his horse along.

"Well, thank the gods for Perri," Gargarin muttered, following.

Perri stopped and turned to face Gargarin, his stare deadly. But Froi stood between them, giving Gargarin a warning look.

Perri's path was unmarked, and they followed him into a thicket of trees that joined overhead, shielding them from all sides. The horses were there and Perri tended to them. Trevanion collected kindling and tried to nurture a flame, but the twigs were too damp and it took some time for the smallest of fires.

"For warmth, not food. We can't draw attention," Trevanion said.

Froi watched them all. Strangely, Lirah and Gargarin looked like nobility, with their cold haughty stares and dressed in the best De Lancey had to offer. They all continued to study one another with suspicion.

"Take him," Gargarin finally said to Finnikin, pointing at Froi. "No matter what he says, take him with you."

Froi shook his head with fury.

"We're traveling together whether you like it or not."

Gargarin still refused to look at him. "I don't need him."

"You're just as helpless on your own!" Froi said. "You were moments from death yesterday before I turned up."

"And you weren't today?" Gargarin shouted. "You're still injured."

"Tell them to lower their voices," Trevanion said to Finnikin.

"I think Froi can understand you just fine," Finnikin said to his father.

"I'm not leaving you behind," Froi said to Gargarin and Lirah. For a minute there was only the sound of twigs snapping in the flames. He turned to Finnikin and spoke in Lumateran. "He's useless on his own. Both of them are. Twice this year he's trusted the wrong people."

"Well, it's sort of been us both times," Finnikin said. "Rafuel tricked him into believing you were Olivier of Sebastabol, and we tricked him with the Belegonians."

"I thought he was supposed to be brilliant," Trevanion said, stoking the fire.

Perri's stare was still fixed on Gargarin. "You know me," Perri said.

"What's he talking about?" Froi asked Finnikin with frustration.

"Why are you asking me? Perri can understand you!"

It was silent again, miserably so.

"It's best my way," Gargarin tried again. "You go back with them—"

"You are useless on your own, and you're going to get Lirah killed!" Froi shouted again.

Trevanion was staring from Gargarin to Froi.

"Well, he is," Froi said to Trevanion. "I'm not being disrespectful to the old, Captain. Every time I turn around, someone's trying to shove him off a balcony or beat him black and blue. She even knifed him," he said, pointing to Lirah.

"What's he saying?" she asked Gargarin.

"We're old, I think," he muttered.

"He's useless," Froi repeated to Trevanion.

Trevanion was still looking at them, and this time he included Lirah in his study.

"Try not to remind him of that too often, Froi," the captain said quietly. "When a son knows more than a father, it makes us feel very useless."

Froi's eyes smarted, and he looked away. He felt Perri's stare burn into them all. They knew.

"His father?" Finnikin asked, stunned.

Except for Finn. Sometimes Froi thought that Finn truly believed that Froi was a Lumateran. His king had always refused to take part in any conversation that suggested otherwise.

"Not much of a father," Trevanion continued coldly to Gargarin. "Can't truly understand how our boy found himself in those wretched streets of Sarnak on his own if not for a father who didn't care."

"What did he say?" Gargarin demanded to know, his voice deadly.

Froi closed his eyes. He didn't want to be here doing this.

"Froi?" Gargarin questioned.

It was Finnikin who repeated the words, and Froi saw the hard line of Gargarin's mouth. Lirah was still. A serpent waiting to strike.

"Circumstances, Captain," Gargarin said, his tone ice-cold. "You understand circumstances, don't you? Those strange little occurrences that ensure that you're separated from your son for more years than you want to think of. Count your blessings that yours ended up with Kristofer of the Flatlands and leave us with the misery of what happened to ours."

Finnikin translated, still stunned.

"His father?" Finnikin continued, trying to register the information. He took in Gargarin's slight build. "Froi comes from warrior stock. There's no doubt of that."

"Serker," Perri muttered, staring at Lirah. "The mother's a Serker."

Finnikin looked agog, and if it was under different circumstances Froi would have mimicked him and they would have both laughed.

"You have a mother?"

Froi stole a look at Lirah.

"Her name is Lirah," he said, his tone husky.

Finnikin held a hand to his head, as if trying to clear it.

"Lirah of Serker? The king's whore?"

Perri nudged Finnikin, his eyes flicking toward Lirah.

"Mercy!"

Froi could see Gargarin bristling. His only relief was that a fire separated Lirah and Finnikin. Any closer and she would have struck him, for sure. Or spat.

"Anything else you'd like to tell us, Froi?" Finnikin demanded.

Lirah and Gargarin and Froi looked away.

"A double mercy! They've got something else to tell us."

"Finn, leave it," Froi said. "It's a long story."

"Then it's a good thing we're not leaving until morning."

Froi and Finnikin sat away from the others, talking half the day and night. The more Froi spoke of the events since he had left Lumatere, the more relentless Finnikin's questions were, his reactions ranging from shock to horror to disbelief.

"If I didn't know you better, I'd swear you were lying to me, Froi."

"Yes, well, you know me better," Froi said. "What are they doing now?"

Finn peered over Froi's shoulder to where the others were sitting in two separate pairs.

"Same as what they were doing an hour ago. Staring at each other. She's going to win, you know. I think she'll outstare them all."

"No," Froi said, shaking his head. "She can't outstare him. No one can. Not even Perri."

Then it was silent between them, and Froi thought he wouldn't be able to bear another moment of this. It was as if three years hadn't existed and they didn't know who he was anymore.

"I . . ." Finnikin began.

Froi looked up. Waited.

"What?"

"I almost slit your father's throat," Finnikin said.

Froi swallowed. He didn't want to think of what would have happened yesterday if he had come across them all too late.

Finnikin moved in closer to whisper.

"Do you want to know the truth? He actually intrigued me."

That was Gargarin's gift and curse. To unintentionally intrigue people, even those who wanted to slit his throat. Finnikin peered over Froi's shoulder again.

"They're obscenely attractive people," Finnikin said politely. Froi couldn't help but laugh.

"And I'm not?" he asked.

"Well, no . . . I didn't say that. But really, Froi. Look at them."

Froi twisted around. Perri hadn't stopped staring at Gargarin, and Gargarin chose to deal with it by returning the stare. Froi turned back to Finnikin and for the first time in hours, the truth registered.

"You returned for me, Finn. After everything you said."

Finnikin's eyes were fierce with emotion.

"Do you honestly think I would have left you out here, knowing there was a small army in the vicinity?"

"I'm surprised you were able to convince Perri and your father to return."

Finnikin laughed. "All I had to do was stop the horse and say, 'I think . . .' and they were racing back into the woods to you."

Froi laughed and it felt good. Real.

"Can I tell you something without you beating me up?" he asked.

Finnikin nodded.

"Isaboe . . . she told me about her time as a slave because we were speaking of shame. She had seen awful things. What men did to their slaves and what some of the other girls had done to keep her safe. I told her worse things . . . what I'd done and what I'd allowed others to do to me."

Froi shook his head, wanting to clear his mind of it all.

"She said that she couldn't bear sharing more of her misery with you, Finn. She'll never forget her curse and that you suffer everything she feels when she walks the sleep. She couldn't add more suffering to someone she adores with every ounce of her being. Her words."

Froi looked up, feeling wonder. "You're loved with every ounce of another's being, Finn. How could you doubt her?"

Finnikin grimaced, shook his head.

"You have a strong bond with Isaboe, Froi," he said uneasily. "Don't deny it."

"I have an equally strong bond with you, my friend," Froi said. "It's not that I desire one of you over the other. It's that I want what you have together. I know that despite everything . . . it must eat at your heart that you're her consort and not her king. . . ."

Finnikin shook his head again.

"It's not about having power over her," Finnikin explained. "If I was the king, I could take care of her. I could keep her free from the troubles of Lumatere, which seem endless. And so trite. Honestly, Froi, ours are such ungrateful people at times. Despite our hard work, all we hear are complaints and woe and who suffered most and whose soil deserves more. Why can't they just be happy with what we've got? We have our kingdom back, but no one seems truly happy, and I'm frightened that it's now in our blood. That we'll pass on that dissatisfaction to our children and our children's children and that we'll be the ancients one day and our descendants will say, 'Ah, yes, a melancholy, dour lot.'"

Froi let him speak. He knew Finnikin would never express these feelings to others.

"And if I was the king, she could spend afternoons making friends and having them over for sweet cakes and hot brew. Do you know her greatest sadness? That she may have Beatriss and Lady Abian and Tesadora, but she would love friends her own age. She could have had Celie, but Isaboe made a sacrifice allowing Celie a life in Belegonia, and Isaboe hangs on every word of Celie's adventures with the young people of the Belegonian court. She's a queen and a mother, but I think she grieves the young girl she never got to be."

Froi couldn't help thinking of Quintana. Of the girl she never got to be. Isaboe and Quintana had more in common than anyone chose to believe.

Finnikin sighed and stood, looking over Froi's shoulder at the others. "What are we going to do about them? Your Gargarin is going to provoke Perri into beating him to a pulp."

Froi looked back at Gargarin, who was still exchanging stares with Perri.

"Could you just tell Perri to ignore him?" Froi said. He could protect Gargarin from the enemy, but not these men.

Finnikin gave a short laugh.

"You know what Perri's like. He's not going to stop until he works out where he knows him from."

"He doesn't know him," Froi insisted.

Froi couldn't bear an entire night of this silence.

"Do something, Finn. Talk to them. You're good at making conversation."

Finnikin stood, and Froi followed him back to the others. He stoked the fire, although it was fine as it was. An owl hooted, and Froi wished that everyone would just turn in.

"Perhaps we can have a word, sir?" Finnikin said to Gargarin.

Froi shook his head in warning. First mistake.

"I'm not a sir," Gargarin snapped.

"Can I draw you something?" Finnikin said, retrieving parchment from his pack. "An idea I have for a drainage system I want to introduce to the Flatlands in my kingdom."

Gargarin didn't respond. Finnikin glanced at Froi, who

nodded. A lack of response from Gargarin was not a bad thing, all things considered. Especially when someone was speaking about drainage.

Finnikin sketched for some time and then handed the parchment to Gargarin. Lirah looked over Gargarin's shoulder to study what was there.

"Where did you get the idea from?" Gargarin asked. Froi could see he was impressed.

"The ancient Haladyans," Finnikin replied.

"Those goat swivers," Lirah said.

Gargarin chuckled. "I've never quite believed those tales. Remember, they were written by Aristos, Lirah. Not much of a fan of the Haladyans."

"Aristos was jealous," Finnikin said, glaring at Lirah, and Froi could see he was bristling on behalf of the Haladyans.

"I've always said that those who underestimate the worth of the Haladyans are fools indeed," Gargarin said.

Finnikin made a sound of satisfaction and looked at Trevanion. "Have I not always said that?"

"Are they the ones who lost?" Trevanion asked.

"Not quite lost. It was all about the surrender," Gargarin said.

"A surrender for a surrender," Finnikin confirmed, and Gargarin nodded.

They seemed to be the only two interested in a Haladyan battle that ended when two sides surrendered to each other.

"Ridiculous," Perri muttered, walking away.

Finnikin turned back to Gargarin. "My wife claims the Haladyans were a bunch of men in skirts who made too many mistakes," he said. "And that the surrender-for-surrender battle is a myth made up by men who enjoy crying over campfires and telling battle stories."

Gargarin made a hissing sound of irritation. "Ah, yes, that wife."

But the conversation had broken the ice, and the two spoke well into the night while Froi penned a letter to the priest-king and to Lord August, laughing when Lirah said something to irritate Finnikin. Froi had always respected his king's intelligence but had never appreciated it as much as on this night. He hadn't seen Gargarin so relaxed in conversation before. There was nothing forced between these two men. In another life, they would have been friends.

"Can you sketch something else, Finn? And take it back to the priest-king with this letter?" Froi asked.

Finnikin nodded, quill poised to begin.

"This," Froi said, removing his cap and showing them the markings on his skull.

He heard Lirah's gasp, and suddenly they were all around him, tracing the lettering with inquisitive fingers.

"You've been injured," Perri said, not the least bit interested in the lettering. Froi felt Perri's fingers on the dent caused by the arrow.

"I ran into a bit of trouble weeks ago. All good now," Froi said.

He watched Finnikin copy the lettering.

"How did you possibly catch a bolt to the head?" Trevanion asked.

"It was an ambush," Gargarin said. Regardless of how little Lumateran Gargarin understood, it was clear what was being asked.

Finnikin looked at Gargarin. "What's he not telling us?" he demanded. "About this ambush?"

"There's more," Gargarin said. Froi grimaced, shaking his head.

"It's finished," Froi said. "I'm cured. Leave it."

"I told you," Perri said to Trevanion. "He never favors his left from right, and there was no reason for him not to have held on to the branch."

The five waited, and Froi reluctantly removed his tunic and undershirt. They stared in horror.

Gargarin reached over and traced his hand gently across the scar on Froi's chest.

"He sewed you."

"He thinks he's a genius," Froi said, and laughed reluctantly. There was a pained smile on Gargarin's face.

"Gargarin has a brother who is a physician," Froi explained to the others. "They look the same, you know," he couldn't help adding. "Twins. I'd never seen twins before."

"We have a pair on the Rock," Finnikin said.

"You should never have trusted anyone," Trevanion said.

Froi covered up quickly, shivering. He noticed that Perri's stare was back on Gargarin.

"How is Lucian faring?" Froi asked, trying to take Perri's attention away from whatever it was that seemed to irritate him about Gargarin.

He noticed the uneasy look between Trevanion and Perri.

"Finn?" Froi asked, praying that nothing had happened to Yata or any of Lucian's lads.

"Lucian lost Phaedra of Alonso," Finnikin said. "They were close to reconciling, and he lost her."

"She went home to her father?" Froi asked.

Finn shook his head, and suddenly Froi knew the truth.

"Dead? *Dead?* How?"

"The plague in the north. It's been a bleak time in the valley for the Charynites."

And still Perri stared at Gargarin, and Froi knew that if Perri wanted to strike, there would be no stopping him.

"He's not a threat, Perri," Froi said, a plea in his voice. "On my life, he's not a threat!"

Perri's stare didn't waver until he turned to Froi.

"My Charyn is weak. Can you fill in my words?"

Froi was confused by the request but nodded.

"In the first days after we took back Lumatere," Perri began, "I escorted the impostor king and his men to the dungeons. Inside one of the cells was a Charynite, half-starved and mad, and I thought nothing of it and locked them up together. Later it occurred to me that if the man was in the dungeons, the impostor king must have placed him there. So I returned to the dungeon and moved the Charynite into another cell, intending to come back the next day to find out why he was imprisoned.

"But one morning, as we know, the impostor and his men were poisoned."

"By whom?" Gargarin asked, listening to the translation.

"Not your concern," Finnikin responded.

There was an uncomfortable silence.

"I discovered that the Charynite was innocent of any crime against Lumatere," Perri said. "So thankfully he escaped death."

Froi couldn't understand why Perri was telling this story, but he realized how much he missed the blunt way Perri spoke.

"I sent for the priest-king, and he and this man spoke for hours. The Charynite had a strange tale to tell about a child long ago smuggled out of Charyn, and how this man had been traveling through Lumatere to Sarnak to retrieve the boy, who was then five." Perri looked up. Suddenly, he had the audience he deserved. Gargarin and Lirah exchanged glances, and Froi's heart was hammering.

"The prisoner had taken that journey thirteen years ago."

Froi was beginning to understand. The Charynite was the

messenger Simeon had spoken about, who had never arrived in Sarnak to retrieve Dafar of Abroi. Froi realized why.

"He became trapped by the curse?" Froi asked.

Perri nodded. "In the early days of the curse, the Charynite prisoner had hidden in the forest between the borders of Sendecane and Sarnak. He even made Tesadora's acquaintance and was one of two men who hid the novices of Lagrami. Remember, the novices were smuggled out of the palace village one night and Tesadora hid them with the novices of Sagrami. The prisoner was found by the impostor king's men and arrested, mistaken for a traitor back in Charyn. They placed him in the palace dungeon, and he stayed there for ten years. The second man, a young soldier named John, who helped the prisoner save the novices, was hanged."

Finnikin was intrigued. "I remember this. The priest-king petitioned Isaboe to have a prisoner released on religious grounds. He was the first Charynite we sent home."

Froi remembered Tesadora telling him the story.

Perri pointed at Gargarin. "He had your face."

Froi stared at Gargarin, speechless.

"What did he say, Froi?" Gargarin demanded. "What?"

Froi couldn't respond. He thought of the fury Gargarin and De Lancey had felt for all those years they were unable to find Arjuro. He thought of the Charyn word for *traitor* scorched on Arjuro's back.

"Froi!" Gargarin asked. "What did he say?"

"Arjuro," Froi whispered. "Arjuro was trapped in Lumatere for ten years in a bid to bring me home, and the impostor king and his men imprisoned him for all of that time . . . because they thought he was you."

Lirah covered her face with her hands. Gargarin stumbled to his feet, staring at Perri, stunned. Then he turned and walked away. Moments later, they heard the roar of fury and the sound of Gargarin's staff striking the tree. Froi turned to see the splintered pieces and heard Gargarin's grunt of rage with every blow. Froi started to stand but felt Lirah's firm grip on his wrist.

"Leave him."

Finnikin watched Gargarin. "Well, that makes better sense. Now I see the resemblance."

The next morning, Perri handed Froi the reins of his horse, Beast.

"Don't be ridiculous, Perri. He's yours."

"I'll be home in three days. You won't." Perri said. "I'll ride with Finn."

"No, you'll—"

"Take it," Lirah said, and when Froi didn't, she reached for the reins. "It's a Serker horse—did you know that? The king ordered the slaughter of the Serker people, and the army took the horses. The king's army invaded Lumatere on these horses as a show of strength."

Froi stared at the reins, and before he could speak, Perri walked away and mounted Finn's horse.

Overwhelmed and unable to speak, Froi handed Finn three letters. They embraced quickly. Finn held out a straight hand to Gargarin, and Froi wanted to laugh at how rigid it seemed.

"Sir Topher of the Flatlands is the smartest man I know," Finnikin said. "And Froi seems to think you're a smart one yourself. One would like to think that a collection of smart people can put their heads together and do something right for once in this cursed land. Not just for their own kingdom but for the whole of Skuldenore."

Gargarin was silent. He had said very little since the news of Arjuro, but Froi could see the strength of the handshake between the two men.

"Walk with us, Froi," Trevanion said, and Froi obeyed, feeling the captain's hand on his shoulder. At first he believed the captain wanted to speak, but as always with Trevanion, his silence spoke loudly. At his horse, Trevanion handed him a quiver of arrows.

"You know where your home is," the captain said, mounting his horse, and then they were gone.

Yet Froi didn't know where home was anymore. He wanted to return to Lumatere, and he wanted to stay in Charyn. What strangeness was that? To belong in two kingdoms. He felt a sob rise within him that he swallowed hard the moment he felt Lirah and Gargarin at his shoulders.

"They think they own you," Lirah said.

They do, he wanted to shout. Half of his heart.

"Where to?" he asked instead.

"We go to the priests of Trist," Gargarin said. "I need to see my brother."

CHAPTER 15

They reached Sebastabol two days later, and Froi felt as if he had been gone for an eternity rather than merely a week. Although he had a fair idea where he and Arjuro had exited the underground community of Trist, it was Gargarin who led them to the entrance on the outskirts of the province, knowing the exact words to speak to the Sebastabolian who lived in a cottage above it. The woman signaled for them to follow with their horses to the stable outside. When the horses were settled, she showed them back inside wordlessly and led them down into the basement.

"Something's wrong," Froi whispered to Gargarin and Lirah as they climbed down the shaft. Gargarin didn't respond. Froi glanced at him, wondering what his relationship with the hidden priests was. A fury remained in Gargarin after his reaction to Arjuro's imprisonment in Lumatere. Froi had no idea when it was going to unleash itself.

Froi knew exactly where to find Arjuro's cavern, hurrying through the strangely quiet passageways that he had last seen bustling with voices and life. But Arjuro's chamber lay empty.

His books and surgical instruments were still there, but Froi sensed that the room hadn't been inhabited for days. He wondered if Arjuro had returned from accompanying him, or had the priestling met foul play somewhere on that ghostly road that cut across the kingdom?

Froi watched Gargarin pick up one of Arjuro's medical chronicles. They heard a sound behind them and Marte was there. She beckoned with a hand but didn't speak.

"Marte, what's happened here?" Froi asked as they followed her down the passageway. But she didn't respond. "Marte, speak to me!"

Gargarin placed a finger to his own lips to quiet Froi. He pointed to the inside of one of the caverns they passed, and Froi saw a couple huddled together, weeping quietly.

"They're in mourning," Gargarin whispered. "It's forbidden to speak outside a private chamber."

Although Froi could see no sign of destruction, his memory of Tariq's compound made him fear the worst. They reached the residence of the *collegiati*, where the young men and women were huddled in individual cubicles, heads down solemnly. One looked up, curious to see Gargarin. Marte hurried along, and they followed her to the tunnel that Froi knew would lead them to Simeon's chamber, down in the next level.

The girl left them there, and Froi climbed down before helping Lirah and Gargarin.

Simeon was seated at his desk, head bent over his correspondence. He continued with his work, not indicating whether he even knew they were there.

"Where's my brother?" Gargarin demanded, his voice abrupt.

Simeon finished what he was writing, and only then did he put down his quill.

"What's happened here, Simeon?" Froi asked, giving Gargarin a warning look. "Why the silence?"

The Head Priest finally stood up, and Froi saw emptiness in the man's stare.

"Gargarin says you're in a state of mourning."

Simeon glanced at Gargarin, ignoring Lirah completely.

"Who's dead, Simeon?" Froi asked. "Where's Arjuro?"

"Arjuro has gone to sing home the spirits of the dead. I don't know when he'll be back. Last time he was sent on a mission, he didn't return for ten years."

Before Froi could speak another word, Gargarin hobbled to Simeon and pressed the Trist leader to the wall of the cave.

"I came here and begged to know where my brother was," Gargarin hissed, close to Simeon's ear. "And all those years, you told me nothing. *Nothing.*"

Froi stood between them, shoving Gargarin away gently. After months of contained silence, suddenly Gargarin had turned into a madman.

Simeon pushed past them and walked back to his stool.

"You were last seen in the palace throwing the oracle and a child to their deaths, Gargarin," the priest said calmly. "Witnessed by your brother. Regardless of what I know now, how could I possibly have trusted you when you came searching for Arjuro?"

"Because he was my brother and I had the right to know he was trapped in Lumatere."

Simeon rubbed at his jaw and poured water from the pitcher.

"Ten years ago when you came searching for him, we had no idea where Arjuro was. We suspected he had reached Sarnak and that he had been forced to travel the long way home back to Charyn because of the Lumateran curse."

He took a sip of his water, and Froi noticed his trembling hands.

"We never imagined that Arjuro was trapped inside Lumatere, let alone imprisoned. Most of us hoped he had found the boy and kept him safe all that time. We were shocked when he returned as skin and bones with no idea of Dafar's whereabouts."

But Gargarin was shaking his head, and Froi knew that if it wasn't for Lirah's hand on his shoulder, he would have attacked Simeon again.

"You know what I think frightened you, Priest?" Gargarin spat. "That I would have searched and found him. That I would have convinced him to stay away from this cesspit of a kingdom. You priests were no better than the palace. You wanted to own the most powerful spirits in this kingdom, and you weren't willing to let Arjuro go."

Simeon's stare stayed impassive.

"We see events in different ways, Gargarin," he said. "You say we wanted to own, and we say we wanted to protect. From the very beginning, the palace wanted what the godshouse nurtured. And what they couldn't possess, they destroyed. There's nothing more frightening to those in charge than learned people; it's why the palace always strikes at brilliant young minds and those who teach them."

Gargarin made a sound of disgust.

"Your weakness, Gargarin, was your ambition. Did you know the oracle didn't trust you and would have done everything to keep Arjuro away from his brother in the palace?"

"Oh, she told you that, did she? After your elders snatched her from her people when she was thirteen? Don't talk to me about ambition, old man."

Gargarin's eyes blazed with emotion. "My weakness was my brother," he continued, "and nothing awed me more than his blessings. My ambition sprung from wanting his respect. And you didn't trust me with the truth of where he was because you would have done anything to sever the tie between us."

Simeon waved away Gargarin's words.

"All the same, we've finally found a use for you."

Froi bristled at Simeon's tone and words. He had never seen Gargarin as the lesser brother, but until Gargarin's time in the palace as a young man, it seemed he had always come second to Arjuro. Especially in the eyes of those in the godshouse.

"The *provincari* are meeting in Sebastabol city as we speak," Simeon said. "To decide the fate of the kingdom and to determine if there is truth in the mad Quintana's words. Yet there was no invitation to those of us who represent the godshouse."

Simeon's lips thinned with displeasure. "Charyn cannot start anew without the blessing of the godshouse. It's a good thing you've arrived at this time, Gargarin. The *provincari* will listen to you. If you want a place for those like your brother in the new Charyn, you go and see them. Talk on our behalf."

Gargarin shook his head. "I'm here to collect Arjuro, not to be sent on a fool's errand for the godshouse. Haven't my brother and I given enough for Charyn?"

"We all have," Simeon said, and Froi saw a flare of pain in the old man's eyes.

"You priests all hid the moment you could and let this kingdom go to ruin," Gargarin said.

"Yet you trusted us with the last born all those years ago," Simeon reminded him. "We must have been worth something once, Gargarin."

"Necessity. Nothing else."

Simeon nodded, his eyes suddenly on Froi.

"It's a good thing, then. Because despite everything, our last born was clever enough to stay alive. And if we are to believe Arjuro, Dafar has done more than stay alive. He's fathered a curse breaker."

"So you'll take credit for that now?" Gargarin asked. "Are you writing your letters to priests across the kingdom, Simeon?" he added, looking at the quill and parchment on Simeon's desk. "Congratulating yourself?"

"No, not at all," Simeon said. "I'm writing a letter to my daughter to advise that the corpse of her son is lying in the grasslands beyond Serker with his eyes gouged out by vultures. His spirit perhaps lost for eternity. You see, my grandson Rothen was a dreamer, Gargarin. He dreamed of a Charyn for smart men and women who didn't live like rats underground. He dreamed of his paintings adorning city walls. He dreamed of a godshouse that would become a school to educate men and women about the glory of Charyn's past. All under the eye of a benevolent future king."

Froi's eyes went to the three words written in gold on the ceiling.

"Don't talk to me about sacrifice," Simeon said, his voice pained. "Eight scholars left this cave in search of hope, and the bodies of seven have returned."

"Rafuel?" Froi asked, heavy with the grief for seven men he never knew.

Simeon looked away. "Arjuro has traveled with one of the priests who knew the lads, in an attempt to work out who is not accounted for. Arjuro hopes to sing them home. Perhaps a spirit has strayed behind, lost. We know for certain they did not die where they lay and that it may have been some weeks back, perhaps months."

"Is Arjuro powerful enough to bring home their spirits if their deaths are not recent?" Froi asked.

"Who knows what he can do?" Simeon said. "He's there more for our peace of mind."

Froi couldn't help thinking that the scholars had been forced to stay in the Lumateran valley because of him. Finnikin and Isaboe had insisted that Rafuel was not to be released until Froi returned from his mission. Rafuel's companions had refused to leave without him.

"Rafuel was held captive by my people because of an incident with one of our women," Froi said quietly. "Perhaps it saved his life."

But Simeon's attention was on Gargarin. "What have the *provincari* sacrificed for Charyn?" Simeon asked him bitterly. "Nothing. If anyone buried their heads in the ground, it was them, and now they join to take control of this kingdom. If you love your brother, Gargarin, give the godshouse a voice in the new Charyn."

"I came here for my brother. Nothing more."

Gargarin turned and walked away from the chamber. Froi could see that he was shaken by the news of the seven deaths, despite his anger.

Lirah began to follow Gargarin.

"Talk to him," Simeon said to Froi.

"I can't control Gargarin," Froi said.

"But she can," Simeon said, acknowledging Lirah for the first time. Lirah turned back with the disdain she showed most people.

"You don't know Gargarin of Abroi if you think he can be controlled by another," she said. "Any more than the priests or the oracle could control Arjuro."

Lirah left, but Froi stayed. He was worried for the old man. Despite his cold nature, Simeon had softened each time he spoke about his grandson Rothen.

"Your loss is felt," Froi said, "but the brothers have given enough for this kingdom. Leave them to their peace."

"Do you know how Charyn will have peace, Dafar? With

one of the brothers in the palace, and the other in the godshouse. Without that sort of peace, the little king she claims to carry will not survive. That mad girl's son will not stand a chance."

"That mad girl has a name," Froi said. "It's Quintana, and soon she'll be the mother of a king or curse breaker. If you want honor in this kingdom, Simeon, preach to the people of Charyn that the mother of their king endured everything to break their curse."

Simeon shook his head disbelievingly.

"Sometimes you sound like a simpleton," the priest said, his voice scathing.

"Then, so be it," Froi said. "The father of your future king is a simpleton, and the mother is mad. But Charyn has a better chance with whatever Quintana and I created together than with any other."

In Arjuro's cave, Gargarin was surrounded by the *collegiati* who had once tended to Froi, their voices hushed.

"Your face is thinner," one said to Gargarin, reaching out to touch it. Gargarin flinched and moved away.

One young man, Corris, showed Gargarin pages of drawings.

"For the godshouse," Corris said, excited. "Arjuro promised that if there's peace in Charyn, he will return to the oracle's godshouse and bring it back to what it once was. The most powerful place of learning in this entire land."

"Yes, well, the Belegonians will love to hear that," Gargarin said. "They believe they're the smartest."

"And the Osterians?" Marte said.

There were snorts. "Their godlings know nothing compared to us priestlings," one pompous lad said.

"Who says you're a priestling, anyway?" Corris asked.

"Hush. We grieve the lads," another said.

"Rothen and the lads would be the first to agree," Corris said. "The Osterians are idiots."

Marte was the only one to notice Froi. "Did you see the way he sewed up the Lumateran?" she asked Gargarin. There were glances from the other *collegiati*, but Froi was unimportant to them in the scheme of things.

Corris showed Gargarin another sketch. "For the godshouse walls."

Gargarin took it and studied the drawing. "You have a gift," he acknowledged.

"But I am not gods' touched," the young man said. "Sir, my talents lie in drawing bridges and ditches. I've heard of your work. Take me to the palace with you and I'll create the greatest—"

"And who says I'm going to the palace?" Gargarin said.

The young men and women exchanged looks.

"Simeon says there's no one better than Arjuro's brother to guide the future king," Marte said. "We look forward to living in a world beyond these cave walls."

There were sounds of agreement, and for the first time, Froi saw a beauty in their hopeful, pale faces.

"How can one draw without having seen the true shadings of the land?" Corris argued. "See this," he added, pointing to one of his sketches. "I'm not good with light and color because I've not had a chance to truly study it. But I want to see it. They say the colors over Paladozza will take my breath away. That the light illuminating the north inspires awe."

Corris glanced at Lirah. "Can I draw you?" he asked, his cheeks reddening. "Your face seems to have been sculpted by the gods."

"Yes, well, I should thank them for that when I see them," she said coolly. "Because such a gift has afforded me so much joy in my life."

But somehow the passion of these scholars had softened both Gargarin and Lirah.

"Can you draw him?" Lirah asked, pointing at Froi.

The young man looked taken aback, then studied Froi's face. Froi didn't enjoy the attention. If it wasn't his wounds being examined, it was now his face, as if they hadn't noticed it before.

"Your eyes have a touch of Serker," one of the girls said to Froi.

"According to the chronicles of Trist, the seed of Serker has been scattered far and wide in the land," Marte said.

"Even in Lumatere?" one asked.

"Especially in Lumatere. They were our neighbors—are our neighbors."

Corris continued to study Froi. "The Lumateran has the sort of face that only a mother could love," he joked.

"Draw him," Lirah ordered.

Gargarin was quiet that night after the *collegiati* left.

"What are your thoughts?" he finally asked Froi.

"What are yours?" Froi asked in return.

Froi heard a sound of irritation come from Gargarin. He wondered if it was weariness but sensed it was something more.

"We're too close to Sebastabol city to walk away," Gargarin said. "I say we listen to what the *provincari* have to suggest. If they combine an army to search for Quintana, then they may have a chance to return her and the babe to the palace."

"Will you speak for the priests?" Froi asked.

Gargarin hesitated.

"A man's losing his grandson doesn't make him a man you can trust," he said. "But he does have a point. The godshouse needs to exist, and that won't be the priority of the *provincari* once things have settled. The priests can't afford to be left behind in talks of the new Charyn."

"Then, why your doubt?" Froi asked.

"Because I don't trust them," Gargarin said flatly. "There is no denying that the people loved the godshouse before the curse. If Charyn begins again and the priests find themselves an oracle from the gods know where, then the priests may take control."

"And how is that any worse than the *provincari*?"

"At least the *provincari* keep one another honest to a certain degree," Gargarin said. "Remember, it was the priests who sent out Rafuel in search of a king killer. Who is to say that they don't have an entire army hiding somewhere? I don't want Simeon's people finding Quintana first. I don't want any of them finding Quintana, except for a combined army. There must be a balance of power, Froi. For Charyn to survive, there must."

CHAPTER 16

It rained for days and days, and Phaedra could have endured
the damp if it weren't for the company of the other women.
Strange that she had liked them well enough in the Charynite
camp, but confinement had turned them into bitter cell mates.

In their boredom, they spoke of every person with ugly
words, judgment in each breath. Jorja and her daughter had
learned to gossip with the nobility of Nebia. Cora never ever had
anything good to say about anyone but her brother, and Ginny
had praise for no one but men. By the third day of rain, they had
covered every camp dweller's life and had no choice but to start
on the Lumaterans, beginning with Tesadora. Ginny believed she
was a witch and the others half agreed.

"I saw her once," Phaedra said, her cheeks flushed. "With her
scarred lover."

"You saw them?" Cora asked.

"I saw them."

Cora looked annoyed. "I have no idea what you're talking
about, Phaedra. I'm sure many people have seen them. It's no
secret she has a lover."

"No," Phaedra said, feeling her face become even warmer. "I saw them." She put her hands together. "Together. Naked. No . . . not naked. I don't think they even took the time to remove their clothing. It was out in the woods. I heard them first. . . ."

She regretted the words the moment she spoke them.

Enough, Phaedra.

"And then you *saw* them," Ginny mocked, looking for the others to join in, but no one in the cave was interested in Ginny. Phaedra didn't care to elaborate and hoped that very soon one of the women would find the next victim to scrutinize.

"Swiving," Quintana finally announced. She never joined in, not having known the camp dwellers. She just watched with disdain. "That's what she means."

Ginny choked out a laugh, and the others flinched to hear the word. It was the second time Phaedra had heard the princess use it. She had only heard the word spoken by one of her father's guards once, never out of the mouth of a woman. Matters of the body and the mysteries of what men and women did behind closed doors were not spoken about in such crude terms.

"You saw them mating?" Cora asked.

Phaedra looked away, nodding. She caught Quintana's stare. It was almost curious. She heard an ugly laugh from Ginny.

"You're not still intact, are you, Phaedra?" she mocked. When Phaedra didn't respond, Ginny snorted. "But you are!"

The women were suddenly interested in what Ginny had to say. They waited for Phaedra's response.

Phaedra's face was burning now. "Of course I'm not," she mumbled. "I was married."

"Well, I heard . . ." Ginny shrugged and Phaedra saw spite in her face. "I heard the Mont sent you back because you didn't satisfy him."

Quintana stared at Phaedra with an I-told-you-so look in her eyes. She was the last person Phaedra wanted commiserating with her about spousal life.

"I've seen the Mont," Ginny continued, relishing the attention of an audience. "If he was sharing my bed"—she shrugged—"there would be no sending me back."

"You're an idiot of a girl," Cora said.

"There's nothing wrong with enjoying it," Ginny snapped. "There's nothing wrong with bringing a man pleasure."

Florenza looked at her mother. "Is that true?"

Jorja looked pensive and then brushed a lock of hair from Florenza's pretty face.

"Of course, my princess. Don't let anyone ever convince you otherwise. But we have to find you the right man first."

"See?" Ginny said spitefully to Cora. "Even Lady Muck of the Sewers agrees."

There was an exchange among them all, and the words *hag* and *slut* bounced off the cave walls. Quintana was strangely quiet, and Phaedra caught her staring at Jorja.

"She's not a princess," Quintana said, her voice cold. "Your daughter. Why is it that so many girls in this land presume to be one?"

"It's just a word of endearment, Princess," Jorja said disdainfully.

"Funny that when you use it to address me, it's not endearing at all, Jorja of Nebia. And it's *Your Majesty*, if you please. I was married to King Tariq. The title of *Queen* is mine."

The mood in the cave changed, and Jorja had the good sense to look fearful. Quintana was a mystery to them still. They had no idea whom she was aligned to, or what lay behind the madness. Was it a façade? Worse still, they had no idea what she was capable of. But people like Jorja knew exactly what Quintana's father had been capable of. Harker, Jorja, and their daughter had escaped a province aligned with the dead king. They had heard stories from the surviving Serkers. As much as Phaedra didn't like the air of superiority enjoyed by Jorja and Florenza, she understood that they had a strong sense of right and wrong. They had given up everything for it. A place in the Nebian *provincaro*'s court. Land. Privilege. Everything Harker and Jorja had worked for all their lives. As hard as life in the valley seemed, Jorja was there because she had two weaknesses. Her husband and her daughter.

"I want to hear about Phaedra and her Mont," Ginny said, and Phaedra didn't know what was worse: the idea of what the queen of Charyn would do to Jorja or listening to more talk about her failure with Lucian.

"There's nothing to say," Phaedra mumbled.

"Did you at least enjoy it?" Florenza asked, curious.

Phaedra was silent.

"She didn't enjoy it, poor girl," Ginny continued. Ginny only came to life when talking about keeping a man happy.

"You don't have to be embarrassed, Phaedra," Florenza said, all too eager to hear the woes of Phaedra's life. "Tell us more. It's just certain words that we don't use."

Florenza sent a quick look at Quintana.

"Such as *swiving*?" Quintana asked bluntly, and Phaedra knew she was taunting the girl. She was like a cat Phaedra had once seen, playing with a mouse. Jorja nudged her daughter into silence.

"Well, if you must know, such things were never spoken about in my home," Phaedra said. "My father would not have dreamed of mentioning it, and my mother . . . she died when I was ten. So let us say . . . it was quite a shock." Phaedra hoped the discussion was now well and truly over.

"What was a shock?" Jorja asked.

Phaedra looked away. "It was. We're no different from animals when you think of it."

Cora rolled her eyes.

"Ah . . . *it*," Ginny said.

Phaedra felt Quintana's scrutiny. The princess had grown more savage-looking as the days had passed; her face was thinner, the untamed nature of her eyes more prominent. Sometimes when Quintana was consumed by her demons, she just sat in the corner of the cave and rocked with fury. There was no warning, not even weeping. Just pure unadulterated fury and pain. The fury was there now, accompanied by clenching of her fists. Phaedra thought it best to take Quintana outside, now that the rain was dwindling.

"We'll go for a walk, Your Majesty," she suggested. "You seem to be the only one of us who knows how to hunt, and we could do with something to fill our bellies."

Phaedra held out a hand to Quintana.

And surprisingly, the princess took it, but by the time they were climbing down the rock face, Phaedra felt the nails of Quintana's fingers digging into her skin.

"Did he ask first?"

Phaedra looked confused. "Who?"

"The Mont. Or was it force he used?"

"No! No, of course not," Phaedra said, shuddering at the thought of any man taking a woman by force. "It may have been awful and primitive, but there was no force."

Quintana let go of her hand and raced toward the stream.

"Where are you going?" Phaedra called out, catching her on the other side. She grasped her arm. "Don't go too close to the Lumateran camp. It can be seen from the Charynite side."

"Tesadora's moved downstream," Quintana said, satisfaction in her voice. "For me."

They reached a small gully, and Phaedra smelled the cabbage first and then heard Tesadora's voice. The novices and Tesadora were scrounging for roots and seeds while one of the

Mont girls was stirring the pot.

Quintana tossed a stone toward them.

"Don't!" Phaedra whispered, gripping her hand and pulling her down.

They waited, concealed behind a fallen log. Then they both peered into the place where Tesadora and her girls were glancing in their direction. Tesadora approached, and Phaedra saw a look of satisfaction on Quintana's face.

"I hope you're being careful, my little savage," Tesadora said.

Quintana chuckled. *Chuckled?* All sharp teeth and wolfish smile. Tesadora didn't seem afraid and held out a hand, which Quintana took. Phaedra followed them into the clearing and stopped short, stunned. Lucian was there, his back to them, studying the fetlock of his horse.

Tesadora held out a bowl of hot stew, and Quintana sat beside her, eating it up like the piglets Phaedra had seen on Orly of the Mont's farm.

"Are they not feeding you?" Tesadora asked, looking at Phaedra with disapproval. "She needs to eat more, Phaedra."

Lucian swung around, his eyes dark and hostile, surprised to hear her name.

"It's not safe for us to be out here," Phaedra said quietly, looking at everyone but her husband.

"Then don't venture out of your cave," Tesadora said. "For now you're fine, though. Donashe and his men know Lucian is here checking up on us, and they won't dare cross the stream. Come and eat, Phaedra. You look like the walking dead." Tesadora's tone was one of irritation, and Phaedra grieved for the days when they had befriended each other, short as they were.

It was silent. There was much staring at both Quintana and Phaedra. Scowls from the Mont girls. Phaedra opened her mouth to speak a number of times, but had nothing substantial to say.

Then the silence became ridiculous.

"She saw you swive," Quintana said to Tesadora, pointing at Phaedra. "With a scarred man."

Phaedra closed her eyes, wanting the earth to shake and swallow her whole.

"*Swive?*" Constance asked, looking at Lucian. "I've not heard that word."

Lucian bluntly interpreted. The girls gasped, giggling. Tesadora's eyes met Phaedra's.

"Did you enjoy yourself?" Tesadora asked coolly. "Watching us . . . swive?"

Phaedra didn't respond, the dirty strands of hair covering her face.

"She said it was quite primitive," Quintana continued.

Phaedra could see that Quintana was going to speak again and she shook her head emphatically, with a look of warning. The moment she saw Quintana's attention turn toward Lucian, Phaedra almost leaped over to gag her.

"You may not use force, but you rut like an animal," Quintana said to Lucian coldly.

The Mont girls were agog, staring at Phaedra. They'd hate her even more for this. Feigning her death was one thing, but insulting a Mont lad in such a way?

"Have I not said that over and over again?" Constance said to anyone who would listen. "A few more tender words and a slower pace would work a treat, we Mont girls say."

"All true," Sandrine reassured Tesadora's novices, who seemed most interested. "If you want to find a Lumateran man who takes the time for pleasantries, then go to the Rock," she added, nodding with certainty. "And then perhaps the River."

Tesadora made a rude sound. "The men from the Rock are useless."

"A man has to pleasure you here, here, and here," Constance said knowingly, pointing to her head, heart, and the place between her thighs. "It's what my *yata* told me. Pity she didn't tell you, cousin," she teased Lucian.

Phaedra wondered for the umpteenth time what she could have possibly done to the gods to deserve the life she was living.

"Excuse me," Lucian said calmly and politely. "I have an appointment in the palace village and need to be off." He walked away, but then turned back, and Phaedra could see his rage. "I'm courting—did I mention that? A true Lumateran rose. A lady of discretion!"

Phaedra was stunned. Courting? Another woman? She must have made a sound, because suddenly everyone was staring at her.

"Well, it's your fault for pretending you were dead and all, Phaedra," Constance said. "We were all speaking of how hopeful things seemed to be between you and Lucian until you died of plague."

Phaedra scrambled to her feet, her whole being trembling. Courting another woman.

"It's getting dark now," she managed to say. "It's best we go. Come, Your Majesty," she said briskly. She stared down at Quintana, cursing the awfulness this creature was able to cause merely by opening her mouth. Quintana didn't take her hand. She wasn't going anywhere by the look of things. Unable to bear being there another moment, Phaedra brushed down her skirt, to avoid giving the impression that she desperately wanted to cry. But then she could stand it no longer and rushed away, running through the undergrowth, wanting to get far away from them all. Behind her, she heard someone following, and suddenly her arm was seized and she knew it wasn't the princess.

"Is that what you do with your people?" Lucian snapped. "Do you sit around and ridicule me? Call me an animal? Tell them I can't pleasure my own wife?"

Phaedra looked away, shamed again.

"I said no such thing."

"Then, what did you say?"

"Not the truth," she cried. "I didn't tell them the worst parts. That when we mated, you didn't look at me. You didn't say a word. Not once. And then you discarded me and lay with your Mont girls. So I'd have to hear the women in your village speak of how the Charynite girl was useless in all things."

He pointed a finger at her face. "I don't break bonds! I lay with no woman until you left. *You.* All this talk of the wife I sent back when it was your tears that begged me to send you back. Preferring to live in those filthy caves rather than share my home . . . my bed. Because I'm some animal."

She stared at him through hot tears.

"That's not what I—"

"And then you came back, and I thought things were different." Lucian walked away, but then swung back around and she could see the hurt in his eyes.

"I grieved for you," he blurted out, as if it was the last thing he wanted to admit. And Phaedra stepped back from him, frightened by the emotion of his words. She tripped on a raised tree root, and suddenly Quintana was there, flying at Lucian, a fist to his temple.

Tesadora reached them, trying to pull Quintana away. "Lower your voices," Tesadora hissed. "We're still close enough to Charyn for your words to be heard."

Quintana's other fist landed on Lucian's arm.

"Stop!" Phaedra cried, gripping both of Quintana's hands. "Stop," she cried again. "All of you."

She dared to glance up at Lucian, and he pointed at them both.

"Keep out of my sight," he said, with such hatred in his voice, Phaedra had no idea whether he was speaking about her or Quintana. "Keep her out of my sight, or I don't know what I'll do."

CHAPTER 17

The ocean was a strange thing to Froi. He wasn't much of an adventurer; he had discovered that about himself only after he was settled in Lumatere. He would have been happy to stay and never leave the confines of Lord August's farm if he'd had the choice. Finnikin and Isaboe were different. Despite how ugly the world had been to them, they had both experienced the freedom of an open road for most of their life in exile. If his queen and her king had the chance, he knew they'd escape together to see the land on their terms.

The Ocean of Skuldenore would have made their heads spin.

They arrived late afternoon, and Froi had been surprised at just how close the underground community of Trist was to the port capital. Not even half a day's ride. He thought of the *collegiati* and the feast of sights that would meet them once they escaped the confines of their safe prison.

Gargarin found them a room in a sea merchant's cottage high above the city. The town steps down to the port of Sebastabol lay outside their lodging, and Froi questioned whether it was a good idea for Gargarin to attempt the steep climb.

"We're better off at an inn down below," Froi said.

Gargarin shook his head. "I want Lirah to have the view."

Their room was on the top floor, and it had a balcony that indeed afforded them a spectacular view over the rooftops, the bustling port, and the ocean beyond. It seemed to stretch out forever and Froi heard Lirah's gasp as she stared out at it. Gargarin stood behind her, his good arm around her body, his head close to hers.

"Did I not promise to show you the ocean one day?" he said softly, tenderly.

"Nineteen years is worth the wait," she responded, her voice filled with emotion.

It only served to remind Froi that Lirah and Gargarin had been imprisoned a long time and most of their hopes of freedom had come from books. *Stories*, he thought. All they created was a yearning for faraway places.

He stayed inside, not wanting to intrude. Watching their intimacy made him feel awkward. He was born out of that intimacy, and all Froi's life he had believed he'd come from something sordid. He had greater difficulty understanding the reality of this strange love than accepting the nightmare he had grown up believing to be truth.

"Don't you want to see it?" Gargarin said, stepping aside to make room. So Froi joined them, because he wanted to be part of the contentment between the two. He could see that, much like in Paladozza, the townspeople of the port city of Sebastabol lived in dwellings built from quarried stone rather than carved out of caves. But he could also see that they were being spied on by at least one man disguised as a peddler, and another two outside a baker's house.

"We have company," he said.

Gargarin sighed. "People can't seem to keep away from us," he said. "How many are we talking about?"

"Three. Not in uniform, but definitely soldiers. What's the *provincaro*'s security like?"

"Extensive. I'd be surprised if he hadn't sent out a welcoming party." Gargarin sounded more bored than annoyed. "The *provincaro* was always torn between thinking I was a spy for the king and wanting to move me into the residence as his adviser." Gargarin stepped inside, and Froi followed.

"We're going to have to pay a visit," Gargarin said.

"Whatever you say."

Now Gargarin looked truly irritated.

"No, I mean it," Froi said. "I'm not trying to challenge you. Whatever you say."

Lirah joined them inside, and Froi watched Gargarin send her a look that he couldn't quite work out.

"What?" Froi asked, angry.

Gargarin didn't respond. He collected his cloak and staff. "Lirah, you stay here," he said. "Froi will come with me. Don't let anyone in. If we fail to return, you wait a day and then make your way back to the priests and find Arjuro."

"Why wouldn't you return?" she asked sharply.

"Because this is Charyn," Gargarin said, bitterness lacing his words. "People go and buy a loaf of bread and don't come back." He pressed a kiss to her mouth.

"If he returns wounded, I won't be happy," Lirah said, and Froi didn't know whether she was speaking of him or Gargarin.

If not for the annoyance of being followed, Froi would have enjoyed Gargarin's lessons about tacking and winds and the moon and the sun and the spring tide.

"Can you just hold that thought?" he told Gargarin, pushing him into an alleyway and waiting for the right time before his hand shot out to grab the throat of their pursuer, pressing the man against the stone wall beside Gargarin.

"Is there something we can help you with?" Froi asked politely.

"The *provincaro* requests your presence," the man wheezed.

"Well, what a coincidence," Gargarin said. "We were just going to visit him."

"Yes," Froi said. "Tell your friends to come along and join us. The more, the merrier."

The *provincaro*'s man hesitated, opened his mouth to deny the presence of the others, but then seemed to change his mind and made a signal. In no time, four other men joined them.

"Five of them?" Gargarin asked Froi. "You said there were only three. You're slipping in your old age."

Froi shrugged, and they continued walking.

"Where was I?"

"Neap tides."

"Ah, yes, the neap tides . . ."

The *provincaro*'s fort was perched at the end of a long stone pier that jutted out to sea. Froi could see it was a treacherous coastline and could not understand anyone's desire to leave dry land.

"Sagra! You'd be a fool to sail out there," he said.

"It's a life of uncertainty for the sailors," Gargarin said. "There's been many a wreck against those rocks."

A good deterrent for those planning to attack Sebastabol from sea.

By the time Froi and Gargarin reached the entrance, a welcoming party that included De Lancey and his guards was waiting there for them.

"Any news?" De Lancey asked urgently. "Do you know where she is?" he demanded of Froi. Was there accusation in his voice?

Froi looked away. He had been dreading this meeting and

hadn't expected to see the *provincaro* of Paladozza so soon.

"We'll find her," Gargarin said. He eyed De Lancey suspiciously. "You made no mention of this meeting with the *provincari* when I was in Paladozza."

De Lancey waved a hand of irritation. "Gargarin, don't pick a fight. I'm annoyed enough with all of you," he said. "How did you know I was here, anyway?" he added.

"We're not in Sebastabol for you, De Lancey. We're here to pass on a message from the priests of Trist, who aren't too happy about such a gathering taking place without them."

De Lancey ushered them in, and they followed him up a set of winding steps.

"This is a *provincari*'s meeting, last I was told," De Lancey argued. "Since when do the priests make decisions in this kingdom, Gargarin?"

"Since when do the *provincari*?" Gargarin responded.

De Lancey reached the top of the steps, staring down at them both. "Since we don't have a king and our princess has disappeared, carrying the possible heir!"

Froi stiffened, knowing he wasn't mistaken in hearing an accusation.

"I hope this means you're combining your armies," Gargarin said.

De Lancey hesitated and shook his head.

"It just means we're finding common ground," he replied. "And you're here at the right time. They were overjoyed to hear you had been sighted."

They walked down a long torchlit passageway, from which Froi could see a short walkway leading into another section of the residence.

"Just agree to everything they say, Gargarin," De Lancey said softly. "We need to be unanimous about matters, and you seem to be the only thing we agree upon."

"Is Grij here with you?" Froi asked quietly.

De Lancey shook his head. "I've sent him and Tippideaux to . . . a safe house. We're going to ground in Paladozza. Bestiano is desperate to find Quintana, and with the help of Nebia's army, he may just do so." De Lancey's expression was bleak. "Did you know the Belegonians are on our doorstep, Gar? I thought you were traveling to the border to strike up a deal."

"Things changed," Gargarin said. "But for now, Lumatere, at least, is not a threat to us. I can't speak for the future, but their immediate plan is not to invade from the north."

They stepped inside a large hall that afforded them a view of the ocean from three sides of the room. In its center was a long bench that sat at least eight people. The individual guards of each province stood close to their *provincaro,* watching suspiciously for any threat from another. At the head of the table was an older man, with skin weathered by the sea, who was presumably the *provincaro* of Sebastabol. He stood and walked toward them, extending a hand to Gargarin.

"It's as if we conjured you up, Gargarin," he said. The man's eyes rested on Froi.

"Is this the Lumateran impostor?" the man asked. "How could he have ever passed as a Sebastabolian?"

"How could a Sebastabolian last born betray the mother of our curse breaker?" Gargarin asked in return.

The *provincaro*'s mouth was a thin line of anger.

"Olivier no longer exists for us. He will never have a place here again, and his entire family has been banished. He has a price on his head, and if he shows his face, there'll be a noose to greet him."

Froi wasn't expecting to hear such a definitive punishment. It made his stomach lurch regardless of how he felt about Olivier of Sebastabol.

"Who is he really?" the *provincaro* asked Gargarin, indicating Froi with a toss of his head.

"Froi of the Lumateran Flatlands," Gargarin replied without missing a beat. "He's my personal guard, if you must know. But from a Lumateran perspective, he was sent as a spy, so until we can get him back to his people, we're going to have to keep him safe."

Part of it was truth and part a lie. Gargarin's purpose, however, was unclear. Why was it so important to Gargarin that the *provincari* knew Froi was a Lumateran?

The *provincaro* was studying Gargarin suspiciously. "And you trust him?"

"He does me a favor. I do him a favor," Gargarin said. "It's a good arrangement."

The *provincaro* indicated the room. Froi recognized one or two faces, and then he froze at the same time Gargarin spoke.

"What's he doing here?" Gargarin demanded. "He's not a *provincaro*."

Vinzenzo of Avanosh was sitting smugly beside Orlanda of Jidia. Froi had met him in Paladozza and hadn't trusted him from the moment the man arrived with his family and nephew, Feliciano. Avanosh was an island off Charyn and Sorel, considered neutral despite being part of Charyn long ago. When the Avanosh lot had come with talk of Feliciano being Quintana's consort and rumors the island was aligned with the kingdom of Sorel, Froi had decided to escape with Quintana.

"In these times of turmoil, we all agree that Avanosh has much to offer Charyn," Vinzenzo of Avanosh said. "I'm afraid we didn't get to meet in Paladozza, Gargarin. You were ill, I hear."

Vinzenzo looked around the table. "Yes, I do recall the dead king's Serker whore mentioned it."

There was whispering among those sitting around the table, and Froi watched Gargarin's hand clench his staff.

"Sit, Gargarin," De Lancey ordered.

Froi wasn't invited to sit, so he waited for a signal from Gargarin, who merely handed him the staff. Froi took it and went to stand beside one of De Lancey's guards by the entrance.

"We're here to make decisions about the new Charyn," the *provincaro* of Sebastabol said, once he was seated again. "A new Charyn that will exist, both if a king is born and if she gives birth to a girl child—"

"Her Majesty Quintana of Charyn," Gargarin interrupted.

They all looked at him questioningly.

"She is the queen," Gargarin continued. "She was married to Tariq of Lascow, the heir. So it's best that we refer to her as the queen of Charyn. I stressed that to Orlanda and De Lancey when we were guests in their provinces."

The *provincari* looked uncomfortable, and Froi watched them find each other's eyes across the table.

The *provincaro* of Sebastabol cleared his throat. "What's important is that we decide—"

"What's important," Gargarin interrupted again, "is that Quintana of Charyn is acknowledged as the queen. She is carrying the curse breaker and possibly our future king."

"Regardless of her title, she has no power," Orlanda of Jidia said.

"Move on," one of the other men ordered gruffly. It could only have been the *provincaro* of Alonso. Phaedra's father. Grief-stricken and bitter.

Froi watched Gargarin push back his chair and stand, slightly unbalanced on his feet. Froi reached him and handed him his staff.

"Then my time here is wasted," Gargarin said.

There was dismay from most occupants of the room.

"What are you doing, Gargarin?"

"Sit, sit."

Gargarin shook his head. "I'm here to pass on a message from the priests of Trist, who believe that they have a role in the new Charyn. It would be to your best advantage to include them. The people of Charyn will want the oracle's godshouse reopened and working alongside whoever is in the palace. That is my duty done. But if you would like me to stay to discuss the new Charyn, which will exist after the queen of Charyn gives birth to the curse breaker, then I will stay."

Everyone nodded, except Vinzenzo of Avanosh.

"But only if Quintana of Charyn is acknowledged as the queen," Gargarin continued. "Are you writing that down, scribe? We have a queen, and regardless of how powerless she is, that is her title. It will be the title her people will become used to, and a strange thing happens when people become used to good things. They forget who she was in the past and get used to who she will be in the future. The mother of the king. The first mother of Charyn. Trust me, gentlemen, and Orlanda, if Quintana of Charyn survives, she will be the new Charyn. She will have the people of the Citavita eating out of her hands. One hand, anyway. The other will be holding the curse breaker, a reminder that he or she has ended eighteen years of barren misery."

He swayed, not having taken his staff, and Froi placed Gargarin's arm around his shoulder to prop him up.

"You want to make a good king?" Gargarin asked. "One of sound mind? One who knows he was loved so he can love his people in return? One who understands justice and the sacrifice of those who came before him? Then treat his mother as a queen."

Froi watched the others, his heart pounding with a truth he had never acknowledged before.

He loved Gargarin of Abroi. Never more than this moment.

No one spoke.

The *provincaro* of Sebastabol cleared his throat. "I want us to make a good king."

"As do I," De Lancey said.

"As we all do," Orlanda said.

Gargarin waited for everyone's agreement.

"Then allow Quintana of Charyn to raise her child. Acknowledge her as the queen until her son takes a bride. Teach the people of Charyn that there is order in that palace—not what we have experienced for the last three generations, where kings either refused to wed the mother of their children or did as they pleased. We need Belegonia and Osteria and Lumatere and every other kingdom to look up to our throne and see dignity and a new order."

Gargarin held out his hand for his staff, and Froi gave it to him.

"When you have something to offer the future of this kingdom," Gargarin said, "I may just agree to be who you want me to be."

"What are you truly hoping to achieve here?" Froi asked quietly as they made their way out of the residence.

"That they give us an army to go search for her," Gargarin said. "What are your thoughts?"

"You're right," Froi said.

Gargarin stopped, his stare hard. "Why am I right all of a sudden, Froi?"

Froi didn't know how to respond.

"What now?" he mumbled instead.

"Let's take Lirah out for a treat."

◆ ◆ ◆

Sebastabol wasn't as pretty a city as Paladozza. It was seedier and filthier in parts, but Froi liked the winding cobblestoned paths and the liveliness of it all. Despite the blistering cold, the sea breeze was invigorating, and he could almost taste the salt on his tongue as they walked along the shore. The port was bustling as men lugged merchandise off ships.

"We were obsessed," Gargarin said, holding Lirah close to him for warmth as they sat on the shore. "Arjuro and I. We were convinced we'd live a life at sea. We'd build ourselves a boat and head off into the beyond." He grinned at them. "The closest we came was Arjuro drawing it all on the walls of our hovel."

"I was on a boat on the straits once," Froi said, looking out to where men were carrying willow pots of strange-looking orange sea creatures from one of the barges.

Lirah and Gargarin seemed surprised.

"Yes, yes. Good times, indeed. I spent most of the trip with my head over the side, vomiting." Froi nodded. "True. And then we came around the straits and traveled upriver into Yutlind Sud, and the spirit warriors attacked and killed our crew and wounded Finn, who would have died if it wasn't for Isaboe . . . well, Evanjalin. She begged for his life." Froi sighed. "I miss those days."

"What a ridiculous story," Lirah said.

"It's true!" He laughed.

They stood among the fishermen, watching them store the writhing eels in barrels of salt. One of the men held out a basket of strange shells to them, and Gargarin took a handful and broke one open, slurping the sluglike substance down his throat. Froi nearly gagged to watch him. Gargarin offered one to Lirah, who seemed just as disgusted.

"It's an ormer," he said, laughing. "The look on both your faces is priceless. Go on," he said, offering one to Froi.

172

"I'd rather eat dirt."

Gargarin laughed again, and there was something so normal about them all being together.

They arrived back at their inn early that evening, still laughing about the strength of Gargarin's stomach after his consumption of some of the vilest food Froi had ever seen.

"Morsels," Gargarin corrected as they climbed the steps to their room. Froi stopped suddenly, holding up a hand to silence them both. They waited and heard the creak of the floorboards above. Theirs was the only room up these final steps, and Froi silently retrieved a dagger and crept up to the top, where the door of their room was ajar. He turned back to the others, holding up his hand again to still them, and seconds later, he kicked open the door and came face-to-face with De Lancey, the *provincaro* of Sebastabol, and their guards.

"Bit dramatic, these Lumaterans," De Lancey murmured, getting to his feet. "Gar!" he called out.

Gargarin and Lirah appeared at the top of the steps, looking hesitant. De Lancey stepped out onto the landing to greet them. "Promise you'll agree to everything, Gar," he said quietly.

"I won't promise anything at all until I hear what you have to offer and you agree to what I want," Gargarin replied.

Inside the room, the *provincaro* of Sebastabol looked slightly uncomfortable in so small a space.

"We'll make this brief, Gargarin," he said.

"Please do."

"Quintana of Charyn will be referred to as the queen and will raise her child in the palace."

Froi felt hopeful, but when his eyes caught De Lancey's, the *provincaro* looked away.

"She will hold no power, of course," the *provincaro* of Sebastabol said. "And she will be wed to the right consort when she's settled in the palace with the child. A man of title, but not a Charynite. We must let nothing divide the provinces, and there must not be an imbalance of power in the palace. This consort will provide guidance and stability in the life of the king, if it's a boy she births. If it's a girl, let's hope that if she succeeded the first time, she — the queen — can do it again with the man she is wed to."

Froi could hardly breathe. He always knew it would come to this, but it shattered him to hear the words that some other man would raise his son and father another child of Quintana's.

"The little king, if one is to be born, will be instructed by a regent until the age of fifteen. A regent unaffiliated to any province. When he comes of age, the little king will take control of Charyn. Until that time, decisions on how to run this kingdom will be made by the *provincari* together. They will each have an ambassador living in the palace . . . to keep an eye on things."

De Lancey still refused to meet any of their eyes, and Froi knew the worst was yet to come.

"We will have no control over the oracle's godshouse, but hope that the union between the palace and the godshouse will be strong," the *provincaro* of Sebastabol continued. "We believe this is possible if Arjuro of Abroi is made head priest of the godshouse and you, Gargarin, are the regent of the little king."

Gargarin was silent.

"Take time to think it over," the *provincaro* of Sebastabol said. "You'll be staying awhile, I presume."

Gargarin nodded. "We'll speak soon, then."

The *provincaro* shook Gargarin's hand and walked to the door.

"One more thing," the man said.

"There's always one more thing," Gargarin muttered, and they waited.

"Most agreed . . . that the Serker whore is prohibited from

living in the palace, regardless of her motherly ties to the queen."

The only relief Froi felt at the *provincaro*'s words was that no one suspected the strange circumstances of Quintana's and Froi's births. As far as the kingdom was concerned, Lirah had birthed Quintana, not the oracle queen.

"It was you who gave us that idea, Gargarin," the *provincaro* said. "We will be teaching our people new ways, and it's best that we teach them that a whore did not beget their queen. We will show our neighboring kingdoms that our palace is not a place of ill repute. So that one day they'll forget. A whore has no place in a palace."

Froi flew at the man but was pulled away and held down by the guards. The room was silent except for the sound of Froi's own breathing, rasping with fury.

"You take back calling Lirah a whore," Gargarin said, his tone ice-cold.

"They were not my words," the *provincaro* said. "I was merely repeating—"

"Then use your own words, coward," Gargarin said.

The *provincaro* of Sebastabol shook his head with regret. "Lirah of Serker will not live in the palace. I've said my piece."

He walked out with his guard. De Lancey looked at his men and signaled for them to wait outside. He closed the door behind them and turned to face the others. At least he looked contrite.

"Gargarin, take the deal or they'll give it to the next man."

"There is no next—" Gargarin stared at De Lancey, and Froi saw the *provincaro* of Paladozza look away uncomfortably.

"What?" Froi asked, looking from one to the other. "Who's the next man?"

De Lancey winced. "We have no choice if Gargarin says no. Avanosh is neutral, and whoever acts as regent cannot have ties to any of the provinces."

"Vinzenzo of Avanosh?" Gargarin asked.

"What?" Froi shouted, looking at De Lancey for confirmation. But the *provincaro*'s silence said it all. *"No,"* Froi shouted. "Never."

"They are even willing to make an agreement with Bestiano, to keep Charyn stable and safe from Belegonia and any other kingdom ready to cross our borders."

"You'd agree to any of those *pigs* raising the boy, De Lancey?" Gargarin asked.

"Careful, Gargarin," the *provincaro* of Paladozza warned, his eyes flickering to Froi. "You're sounding like the future king's grandfather. His *shalamon.*"

Gargarin's stare was deadly.

"That type of talk is dangerous, De Lancey."

"Is that a threat?"

"Not a threat, but say it out loud again and I may have to turn it into one."

"Take the deal, Gargarin," De Lancey said, his voice tired. "I'll make provisions for Lirah. She'll have a home in Paladozza. She'll want for nothing."

"I'll want for everything," Lirah cried out with bitterness, speaking for the first time. "And what will I have to give you in return, De Lancey? Will I be a gift to visiting *provincari* and their sons?"

De Lancey was taken aback by the words, and Froi saw fury in his expression.

"You're getting older, Lirah," he said cruelly. "You may not be what they want anymore."

Gargarin shoved him, and although Froi wanted to beat De Lancey black and blue, he knew the *provincaro* had spoken the words out of hurt. Froi didn't know how he came to that realization. All he knew was that pain placed the wrong words into their mouths. All of them. Forces outside their control had destroyed the lives and friendships and loves of De Lancey and Lirah and Arjuro and Gargarin long ago, and now even the future would keep them apart.

"You never trusted me, Gar," De Lancey accused. "I was never good enough for the brothers from Abroi."

"You were the first person I went to upon my release. The first," Gargarin said.

"And what did you tell me?" De Lancey asked. "Half-truths. About a dead child, but you made no mention of the living. Was that punishment, Gargarin? For betraying Ari all those years ago?"

"You mistake me for another, De Lancey," Gargarin shouted. "You mistake me for yourself. You're the one who never forgave yourself. That was your weakness, and that was why I couldn't trust you with the truth of the last born. Because as long as you live, you will never, ever forgive yourself."

"I curse the day you and your brother came into my life," De Lancey said. "I curse it. Go hide in your caves and punish anyone who cares for you. It's what Arjuro's done all these years. You care about no one but yourselves."

"He wasn't hiding!" Gargarin said.

"Gargarin," Froi warned, standing between the two men, knowing this was not the time for De Lancey to know the truth.

"Arjuro was trapped inside Lumatere, De Lancey," Gargarin said, pushing Froi out of the way. "That's what he hid from us. Nothing else. Arrested by our army, who mistook him for me. A traitor. The word carved on his body as if he was a rump of mutton. Chained in a Lumateran prison for ten years, believing he was forsaken."

Froi was tired of seeing the broken spirits of men and women. He finally understood the curse of Isaboe and Finn, weighed down by the grief of their people. It wasn't a curse that belonged just to his queen. It was Froi's curse to feel the sorrow of these people. Blood sings to blood, he had been told all that time ago by Rafuel. Charyn blood sang to Froi, but it was Charynites' pain that gnawed at him. He saw it on De Lancey's face now. It was as though he had aged in seconds, and Froi wished Grij were here to take care of his father. Grij and Tippideaux would know what to do.

He saw regret appear briefly on Gargarin's face. "Let's talk in the morning," he said quietly. "When our words aren't dipped in poison."

De Lancey nodded listlessly. "Yes," he said, opening the door and stumbling out to where his men stood. "We'll talk in the morning."

Froi woke to murmuring. He was used to Gargarin and Lirah's murmuring. These past few nights it had lulled him into a strange, peaceful sort of sleep—the first he had had since he lost Quintana.

". . . I don't know, but he's hiding something," he heard Gargarin say. "I know De Lancey."

"You think he can't be trusted?" Lirah asked.

"I didn't say that. But what if it's not in his power to support us, Lirah? Regardless of how strong Paladozza is and how quickly they can go to ground, they've not had an army ever. I respected his decision for so long, but not these past months. He should have raised an army the moment those street lords took the Citavita, but he didn't. That was weakness and a mistake, and we can't trust ourselves with a man who makes mistakes."

Lirah sighed. "That may be, but only you can take Quintana and the babe safely back to the palace."

"Do you honestly think I'm going to let you go?" he whispered, and Froi heard pain in his voice.

"Listen to me," she said firmly. "We may doubt and question

178

the truth, and entertain the horror that Quintana's child may belong to Bestiano, but you know the gods have done something right here. That babe belongs to Dafar. And if you allow another man to raise our blood, I will never forgive you."

And at that moment, Froi was never so sure. Regardless of his constant fury at Gargarin, there was no other man he wanted taking care of Quintana and the little king.

"You're the smartest man I know," Lirah said fiercely. "If you can't find a way of placing my grandson in my arms or sharing my bed without the *provincari* knowing, then you are as big an idiot as the rest of them."

Gargarin made a sound of frustration. "I'm not agreeing to anything . . . yet. If I never have to step inside the palace again, I'll be the happiest man alive. But I'll meet De Lancey in the morning to see if we can come to an agreement."

Lirah was silent a moment.

"Ask the boy what he thinks when he wakes."

"He'll only say yes to anything I suggest!" Froi heard the irritation in Gargarin's voice. "I need him to be sure. Not compliant. He's lost faith in himself, Lirah."

Froi froze. Despite his attempt to stay quiet, he was desperate to get out of the room because he needed to breathe. He stumbled to his feet, tripping over his bedroll, and climbed onto the balcony. Despite the icy wind from the ocean, he sat down, smarting at the words he had just heard.

A short while later, he heard a sound behind him and Gargarin was there.

"Lirah said to go back inside," he said. They both had a habit of doing that. Saying *Lirah said . . . Gargarin said . . .*

Froi didn't respond.

"We thought you were asleep, Froi—"

"I don't want to hear it," Froi snapped.

There was silence, and he wasn't sure whether Gargarin was still there.

"If you had stayed in Paladozza, the Avanosh lot would have taken her. She would have ended up in Sorel. Or being used as some bargaining tool."

"Why are you telling me this?" Froi asked, looking back at him angrily. "To make me feel better about my *lack of faith* in myself?"

Gargarin rubbed a palm over his eyes with frustration.

"I'm telling you because you're punishing yourself over and over again. You caught eight barbs in your body to keep her safe, Froi. That's enough."

"*I lost her.*" Froi was on his feet. "Do you understand? I lost her. Tariq would never have lost her."

"Tariq would never have left that cave in the Citavita. You take chances, Froi. When you were five years old, you went out into that filthy Sarnak capital and survived. Let's pray to the gods that Quintana listened to everything you had to teach her."

Froi shook his head with frustration.

"We could look at the side of wonder," Gargarin said.

"What?" Froi asked, as if Gargarin had gone insane.

"Well, let's say that instead of losing her, you gave her a chance to escape," Gargarin explained. "That's the side of wonder."

Froi heard a sound behind them, and Lirah was there.

"Since when do you look at the side of wonder?" Froi asked.

"I'm trying very hard," Gargarin said, scowling. "It's irritating me, but I'm not giving up. I try to think of a wondrous thought every day when I wake, if you'd really like to know."

"Yes, it's very annoying, but slightly contagious," Lirah said.

Froi couldn't believe what he was hearing.

"It's true," Gargarin said. "And now even Lirah is saying, 'Let's look at the side of wonder as opposed to the disastrous.'"

Froi wondered if they were mocking him.

"Lirah?" he asked, looking up at her. "You are the least wondrous-thinking person I've ever met."

Lirah looked irritated. "Well, if you'd really like to know, I used to skip as a child and collect poppies. Sometimes I think that deep down there's an idiot inside of me who wants to laugh."

For some ridiculous reason, Froi wanted to laugh now.

"Do you want to know this morning's wondrous thought according to Gargarin?" she asked. Gargarin looked uncomfortable.

Lirah stood before Froi and held a hand to his face. "He said, 'Well, at least the three of us are together.'"

Froi was silent and then gazed at Gargarin, who merely shrugged as if to admit guilt at such a ridiculous thought. *Hope. Hope. Hope.* Rothen of Nebia had written it on his grandfather's ceiling. Froi saw the hope in Gargarin's eyes. He imagined a time when Arjuro would be with them. And Quintana. And the babe. Could they endure anything if they were together?

"You want a decision?" Froi asked.

Gargarin's mood changed in an instant. He nodded solemnly. "Yes, I do."

"We're nothing without an army. The queen of Lumatere's greatest accomplishment in exile was reuniting Trevanion with Finn and his men to take back Lumatere. I saw it. We walked into death camps and exile camps, and the moment the Lumaterans saw Trevanion and the Guard, they'd follow us in an instant. I say we go to Serker."

Lirah looked surprised.

"When I was with Tariq, he spoke of an army in the center of the land," Froi said. "I've dreamed of him often these nights. It's a sign."

"I'll speak to De Lancey—"

"De Lancey's a weakness," Froi said flatly. "Your news about Arjuro's imprisonment will slow him down. We go now."

CHAPTER 18

Isaboe heard the sound of the horses and knew Finnikin had returned.

"My queen," Rhiannon said, and there was a reprimand in her lady's-maid's voice. "You know it's best to come out here. They're approaching . . . and he's sneezing."

Finnikin and Isaboe had observed a ritual ever since they moved into the palace. She'd wait in the courtyard to welcome him if he had been away for more than a day or two. He said it was the first thing he looked for. It meant he was truly home.

Isaboe finished the document she was preparing for the Sarnaks and put down her quill, joining Rhiannon on the balcony. And there he was and her heart pounded. All of these years and her heart still pounded out of control at the sight of him. She had felt it that day in Sendecane almost four years past when she first saw him in the cloister. He had an irritated expression on his face when he discovered she was a girl. Even as a child, when her brother and cousin would insist on dragging her around to be part of their mischief, her heart would beat hard at the sight of Finnikin of the Rock.

Today she watched him hunched over his horse, sneezing into his kerchief.

"He looks quite ill," Rhiannon said. "He's always so . . . needy when he's ill."

"Pitifully so."

"It's a trait of the Rock people, I'm afraid," Rhiannon said. She was from the Rock herself and was the best authority to say so.

"Could you prepare a bath, Rhiannon? I'll take care of the rest."

Isaboe watched as he glanced up, not quite as sheepishly as she would have liked, but she did see his shoulders relax at the sight of her. It had been weeks since he left in rage, and she still felt raw from the accusation he had made before they parted. She felt raw from everything. She remembered the time she had carried Jasmina in her belly, when the future had felt promising. But this time was different, and she didn't know how to put it into words. This fear. This premonition of doom.

She went back inside to where Rhiannon was pouring water into the tub and waited. She knew him well. Now that his father no longer lived in the palace, they would speak for some time at the stables about the outcome of their travels.

A short while later, he shuffled into the chamber, and she could see his relief that the tub was filled. She imagined he was cold to the bone. His clothing seemed to weigh him down. Wordlessly she approached him and unhooked his fleece cloak, pushing it from his shoulders and dropping it to the ground, and then she pulled free his shirt. He held up his arms as she dragged it over his head, his eyes on her the whole time. Her hands went to the fastening of his trousers and his head bent toward hers, but she turned her face away, though not before she caught the flash in his eyes. Then he stepped out of his clothing and climbed into the steaming water with a deep sigh of pleasure. Isaboe crouched beside him, and her hand tugged his hair back.

"If you ever walk out of this palace accusing me of disloyalty to our spousal bed again, I'll tear you apart, piece by piece."

A hand as quick as hers gripped her face. "And if you wake with another man's name on your lips again, I'll tear him apart, piece by piece." His mouth was hard on hers but she matched his force and then he let go, lifting a hand to trace her lips with his thumb. She gently pushed him back and tended to him, and she could see his eyes on the opening of her shift that allowed him a glimpse of the curve of her body, ripe with their child. He reached to clench her garment in a fist. "Take it off," he begged hoarsely. "Please." And she lifted it over her head and climbed into the tub, straddling his thighs as his hands wandered over her swollen belly. He pressed a kiss against it before taking her face between his hands, his mouth back on hers. She felt a hunger from him like never before, their mouths greedy for anything they could take, and when she moved above him, he thrust into her and she covered his mouth with her hand to stop his cries echoing across the quiet chamber to where their guard stood outside.

Later, they lay in each other's arms in their bed. She pressed her lips against his pale chest, tracing a finger across a new bruise or two.

"My queen . . ."

"Yes, my king?"

"I'm dying," he groaned.

She laughed.

"You've caught a chill because you weren't wearing an undershirt, and every year you catch a chill for the same reason and you believe you're dying. It's a common cold, my love. The type that men catch. The one they believe is killing them."

"I'm speaking the truth. I am dying. My nose is red raw and

my throat . . ." He made a choking sound. "It hurts," he said hoarsely. "And you mock me when all I need is your tender care."

"I'm surprised you didn't go home with your father and have Beatriss fuss over you."

His arms bound tightly around her. "If I spent one more night away from my wife, I would have just laid down and died."

She chuckled. "Ah, you're a clever man for saying all the right things."

She covered them both with a blanket, and he tucked her in the crook of his arm.

"Tell me everything," she said quietly.

"From the sounds of things, you've got as much to tell me."

She tried to find the words, but still hadn't spoken them aloud.

"Tesadora . . . and I are no longer on speaking terms," she finally said.

"Because she's befriended a strange Charynite in the valley? That doesn't sound enough of a reason for you to break with someone you love as dearly as you do that hostile woman." He peered down at her. "Why are there so many hostile women in this land?"

"You're not very good with women, Finnikin. Your father, on the other hand, has them eating out of his hands, but you're just hopeless."

"I am not."

"This is how my Mont womenfolk refer to you," she said, doing an exaggerated movement with her eyes and mouth. *"Finnikin!"*

He laughed. "You are ridiculous, and we're digressing from Tesadora's strange friend."

Isaboe turned to face him.

"Are you ready for this?" she asked.

"After the tales I've heard in Charyn, I'm ready for anything," he said.

"Tesadora is hiding the princess of Charyn from the Charynites."

"Mercy!" Finnikin sat up, stunned.

She nodded.

"You mean Quintana of Charyn has been here all along?" he asked.

Isaboe looked at him, confused and irritated.

"That wasn't quite the response I was expecting," she said.

Finnikin sighed. "We found Froi. With Gargarin of Abroi, who isn't exactly the man we thought he was."

"And how certain are we of that?" she asked.

"Quite certain. All three of us agree that we could have made a catastrophic error."

"I wouldn't exactly call killing a Charynite a catastrophic error," she said.

"Are you ready for this?" he asked.

"I'm ready for anything," she said, but she felt the doubt of her own words. When it came to Froi, she wasn't quite sure.

"Gargarin of Abroi is not just a Charynite, Isaboe. He's Froi's father."

"What?" She sat up instantly.

"I met the mother as well."

"Froi has a mother?"

"Awful woman. Beautiful beyond comprehension, but awful. Spat at me. Granted, I was about to kill her lover, but still . . . she hated me at first sight. But beautiful. Achingly beautiful."

"Yes, I do think I've got the point about her being beautiful," Isaboe said. "But tell me of Froi. How would he know such a thing?"

Finnikin slipped out of bed to get to his pack, and she watched him shiver as he riffled through his belongings. Holding up a letter, he sprinted back to her and settled himself under the comfort of the blankets.

"He's written to you and Augie and the priest-king. It's all strange. Lettering scorched into his head, hidden all this time. Wording on his back, only visible to the gods' touched. That's what they call their gifted. He's been wounded and sewn up and he's confused, and I'm sure I saw a tear or two, and Perri hasn't coped with any of it. Deep down I think Perri thought Froi was his. And the father . . . Gargarin. An intellect? Froi's father an intellect? His body all mangled from palace beatings. The father's, not Froi's. And the father has a twin with the same face, who was trapped in Lumatere for ten years and was almost poisoned by you and Tesadora with the rest of them."

"Finnikin, be serious."

"That was serious," he protested. "And they're angry at each other, Froi and the father. And the mother is just cold."

Isaboe studied Finnikin's face for the truth and saw it there.

"Poor Froi," she said, heartbroken for their friend. "Why didn't you bring him home instead of leaving him with those hideous people?"

"Because I think Froi loves those hideous people."

Isaboe's head was spinning from everything she was hearing.

"It was strange . . . but he looked so foreign," Finnikin said.

"Gargarin of Abroi?"

"No. Froi. I'd never noticed before. Perhaps it was hearing him speak Charyn. His manner with the father and the awful . . . but beautiful mother — ouch, that hurt."

"I'll pinch you harder the next time." She reached for the letter.

"Have you read it?" she asked.

"Over and over again. It's a fantastical tragedy . . . and you're going to have to prepare yourself."

"I think I know a thing or two about fantastical tragedies," she said.

He shook his head. "No. It's the mad princess you'll have to prepare yourself for. She's with child."

Isaboe sighed. "I know. It was the only thing that stopped me from slitting her throat."

"Yes, we'll talk later about your running savage in the valley with a dagger," he said, and she could hear the anger in his voice. "But read the letter and you'll understand."

She felt him watching her as she read and she felt sick from dread as she took in the details before her. She read it twice. Three times. Then she looked at Finnikin with disbelief, and he nodded because he knew it all well.

"What are your thoughts?" he asked quietly.

She didn't respond. She couldn't. Then she'd have to feel anger . . . and regret. Guilt, perhaps. But she didn't want to. She had every right to despise Quintana of Charyn.

"You think it's his?" she asked quietly.

"Yes, I do."

"What a mess," she said. "I hope Froi doesn't think they'll let him raise that child alongside her."

"He's not thinking that far ahead. He's desperate to know she's alive, and here she is in our valley. If you want to know the truth . . . I believe that the Charynites want her dead more than we do."

"Well, I'm not protecting her, regardless of who the father of her child is."

She thought about it a little longer, and the more she did, the angrier she grew.

"Don't tell me he's in love with her, Finnikin. You've got to see her. She's . . . this vicious cold-looking viper. All small and round, much the same as Lucian's supposedly dead wife. Little people irritate me. I felt like this monstrous giant alongside them."

"Well, it's not as if we're letting her up the mountain," Finnikin said. "That's all we need. More of our people killed to protect a mad princess, regardless of what she means to Froi."

They stayed in bed, sorting through correspondence.

"Nothing from Jehr?" he asked, and it pained her to hear the sadness in his voice. In exile, they had taken refuge in Yutlind, a kingdom that had been at war with itself for as long as anyone could remember. Finnikin, Isaboe, and Froi had all struck up a profound bond with the heir of the southern throne, Jehr, and they all despaired at not having heard from the southern Yuts for at least two winters now.

"I think those northerners have done something to Jehr. It's been too long. I think we're going to have to accept that Yutlind Sud is gone," Finnikin said.

They heard a sound in the hallway and then Jasmina's chatter, and Isaboe saw Finnikin's face soften. Her heart sang to see his smile. Sometimes she was frightened that Finnikin would never understand their daughter, in the way he didn't understand most women. Jasmina ran into the room, eyes wandering, searching, then lighting up with joy when she saw her father. Finnikin leaped out of bed and held out his arms, and she ran to him. "Fa," she said with delight, and he pretended to collapse from the weight of her until they were lying beside Isaboe.

"I like the sound of *Fa*," he said.

"She's copying Vestie."

"Tell me again why she has to call us Isaboe and Finnikin?" he asked.

Jasmina was smothering them both with kisses.

"In case anything happens to us," Isaboe replied. "I read it in one of the chronicles of the ancients to do with child-rearing. The more a child gets used to comfort terms such as *Fa* and *Mumma*, the more they will grieve if something happens to them. It's the words they miss using."

Jasmina squeezed them all together, her little arms around both their necks, and she practiced her counting with a kiss to each cheek.

"Yes, I can see it working," Finnikin said dryly. "Can we rid ourselves of the child-rearing books and let her call us whatever she wants?"

Isaboe laughed at Jasmina's antics and he kissed them both. Suddenly the three of them were knocked aside by a force beyond reckoning, and she knew by the thunderous look on Finnikin's face that she'd have to explain the hound's presence on the bed.

"We were all so sad, and he cried and cried for you," she explained. "We all did."

She patted the dog.

"He's only slept with us when he's cold and lonely," she said.

Finnikin stared at her with disbelief.

"Isaboe, he is a hound. He will feign loneliness for the rest of his life just to lie on this bed. My bed. I was the king of this bed."

He was woeful, but at the sound of the dog snoring, Isaboe could see a ghost of a smile on his face.

She could already hear the world they had to tend to outside calling to them, but for now it was just the three of them . . . and the hound, and Isaboe understood that happiness came in such moments and she savored it.

CHAPTER 19

I see Tesadora in the woods, scraping sap from the trees. She knows I am there and she turns, holds my stare. She knows me, she knows me, she can see deep within.

"Is it true that you love me more than the Lumateran queen?" I ask.

It's the news that I've heard. It makes my blood sing. She walks to me, smiling, takes my face in her hands. But standing so closely, I see the truth in her eyes.

"I love Isaboe of Lumatere with all my heart."

I pull free from her grip, and I clench both my fists.

"Do you love her more than the scarred one?" I demand.

"His name is Perri and he doesn't like to be reminded of his scar. So don't mention it," she adds with a mocking whisper.

"Would he be handsome to you without it?"

"I was the one who put it there," she says with a shrug. "And he's handsome enough with it."

"Do you love your Perri more than the queen of Lumatere?" I ask again.

"If I love him less, does that make it less than love?"

"But if you had to choose between them?"

"I don't want to live in a world where I have to choose," she says, and I hear fury in her voice and I dance on its embers. It's for the other, that bitch queen who dared threaten my life. I'll kill her for that; I'll slice her to pieces. A jab to the side and a blade ear to ear.

"And if your scarred lover doesn't come down the mountain because she forbids him?" I ask. "What then?"

"Then so be it," Tesadora says. "They'll both lose me."

"And it will just be you and me," I say. "That's why you stayed in the valley. For me."

And she looks at me sadly, and I see tears pool in her eyes.

"I stayed here because Isaboe can live without me. You can't. You're a pathetic lost spirit with no one."

And I hold back my hurt, Froi. The hurt that you've seen.

"Put away those savage teeth," she says with a laugh. "They don't scare me the slightest."

And she grips my chin so I cannot break free.

"Do you know what I just did, my broken little savage?" she asks. "I told a truth. Do you understand the power truth has to hurt? Ask me again why I stay, and I'll find better words."

If it was you, would you ask, Froi, or would you just walk away? But I'm desperate to know, and I wait for the strength.

"Is it true that you love me more than the queen?" I say, and my voice is small and frightened. I don't want to hear this truth twice.

"I love the queen with all my heart," she says. "But, for now, my place is here, because I'll do anything to protect you. I can't explain why. You're on your own, and I can't bear the idea of someone hurting you."

I unclench my fists. I like her new words.

"Better?" she asks, and I nod in relief.

"Understand what your truth does to others," she says. "Others such as Phaedra, my savage cat. Think for a moment. Not every thought in your head has to come out of your mouth."

I don't understand.

"Learn to cloak your words, Quintana. Not with lies, but without so much truth. Do you want everyone like Phaedra to walk away from you, bleeding in spirit?"

I stay next to her and I work alongside her, watching the way she tears the bark into strips, and when everything's silent, she looks deep in my eyes.

"Who else is in there with you? Who else, my noble little savage?"

And I feel the tears in my eyes, but I don't let them fall.

But she takes my hand and presses it to her cheek, and I speak words I've never said aloud.

"Sometimes . . . sometimes . . . it seems I'm bits and pieces and she—my sister, the *reginita*—she was able to make sense of it all. I'd say, 'Look after them! I don't have the time,' and she'd say, 'They're part of us now. Not whole beings, but part of you. They want to go home, but they can't. Because they're not complete.'"

Tesadora stares at me, her face pale.

"And I don't understand her," I say. "So don't ask me more."

"What are you hiding from me?" Tesadora asks.

And I place my head against her heart. "Tesadora," I say. "I think the half-dead spirit of your child lives within me."

CHAPTER 20

Phaedra heard the crunch of leaves coming closer and closer and hid deeper inside the shelter, praying it wasn't Donashe or one of his men. No matter how hard she tried to convince herself that the camp leaders would not venture so far downstream, she had no trust in Donashe's vow to the Monts that he would not cross. These men were opportunists of the worst kind, and she feared what would happen if they ever found out the truth of who Phaedra and the women were hiding.

She saw two pairs of feet and caught her breath until Tesadora squatted down to stare inside.

"We've been looking for you," Tesadora said, none too pleased. "She's refused to return to the cave, and we can't have her running around without anyone keeping an eye on her."

She appeared a moment later, to peer into the shelter.

"And this belongs to me," Quintana said coldly, annoyed. "If you want to use it, Phaedra, ask me in the future."

"Well, if you must know, it belongs to the Lumaterans," Phaedra said. "Perhaps we can travel to the palace and ask Isaboe of Lumatere for permission, so we can both use it. What say you?

She seemed to have taken a shine to you last time we all met."

Quintana crawled in beside Phaedra, who shoved her hard out of the way.

The princess hissed. "You could have harmed the little king."

"I shoved you in the arm, not the belly," Phaedra said. "And I was here first."

She heard Tesadora's sound of annoyance.

"Are you sulking?" Tesadora asked.

"She is," Quintana said. "About the Mont."

Phaedra ignored them, not wanting to give Quintana the satisfaction of reacting. She was going to hold her tongue if it was the last thing she'd do.

"You have no idea what it felt like that everyone knew the business of my spousal home!" she cried out, because Phaedra failed at most instructions to herself.

Quintana stared at her with disdain. "No idea? What a thing to say." She waved Phaedra off, as if an irritant. "One gets used to the whole kingdom knowing when you're swiving," she said to Tesadora as if Phaedra weren't present. "If that's the worst thing that's going to happen to her, she's fortunate indeed."

"Just go away, Your Majesty. Tesadora is right. You're safer in the cave with Cora and the others."

Quintana's lip curled with distaste. "I can't bear another day with them. The hag was already at it with the slut this morning."

"Can she at least try to remember their names?" Phaedra said to Tesadora.

"I remember their names perfectly well." The princess sent her a look of irritation. "Have I not told you about my memory for detail?"

Phaedra wanted to scream with frustration. The delusion would have been amusing if she wasn't speaking to the future heir's mother.

"No? Well, I should have mentioned it." Quintana spoke as though Phaedra had responded. "I know all their names. I know the name of every woman who slighted Ginny in her village and every lad who has so much as winked at Florenza and every person in the valley who irritates Cora. It's all they speak of day in and day out."

"You do not," Phaedra said.

"Oh, I do."

Phaedra looked out to where Tesadora was still crouched. "She does not."

"I think she does," Tesadora said with a sigh. "She's quite extraordinary."

Phaedra bit her tongue, well and truly sick of Tesadora's awe of the Queen of Uselessness.

"Go on," Tesadora said to Quintana. "Let's get this over and done with. Prove her wrong. Florenza's suitors to begin with."

"Josslyn, Kent, Freshier, Arns, Mitcheloi, Samule, Talbot, Patroy, Idiotjoy."

Tesadora gave Phaedra a meaningful look. "Don't get her started on how many bricks held up her chamber in the palace of the Citavita, or how many steps there are in the second tower, or how many leaves with a red-gold tinge there are in this forest."

"She made up that last name. Florenza has never mentioned an Idiotjoy."

Tesadora laughed and finally stood.

"Look after each other, you silly fools. All this running around will end with someone getting caught. Rafuel insists that one of those men is on to him."

"Which one?" Phaedra asked, her stomach twisting at the thought of being captured.

"The squat one with fair hair," Quintana responded. "The hangman."

They both stared at her. Phaedra shivered to see the look of terror on Quintana's face.

Phaedra knew exactly whom she was referring to. He was the one always whispering in Donashe's ear.

"He wants to impress Donashe and seems to resent our Matteo," Tesadora said. "You'll protect yourselves in numbers. Not on your own."

With that, she walked away.

Phaedra felt Quintana studying her.

"We're going to need weapons," Quintana said.

"And where will we get these weapons?"

"I watched Froi." Quintana crawled outside. "We're going to have to be practical. Come."

Phaedra followed reluctantly and watched the princess collect sturdy tree limbs and scrounge for stone.

"We can't survive with only a dagger and bare hands to find us food," the now Princess of Practicality said. "We're going to have to make spears. That way we can better catch the trout. Farther downstream I saw an elk, too."

"Spears? An elk? You'll never catch an elk," Phaedra said.

"I'm hungry." There was the cold determination again. "If I'm hungry, so is this child, and if I have to catch an elk to feed it, I'll do it."

She ordered Phaedra to collect a certain type of stone, describing its features. Phaedra collected anything she could find, holding them up in her skirt to show her. Quintana chose carefully and made rude sounds of annoyance if Phaedra had collected one not to her liking.

"It's for a purpose, fool. We need to make a flint fuse. This," Quintana said, selecting a stone, "will not do. And we need a hammer stone to shape it."

Then they collected more branches, and Quintana measured two to both their heights. And the more Phaedra watched the

certainty in her movements, the more she found herself respond-
ing to the princess's orders.

Once they were ready, they sat in the shelter, working at creating a spearhead out of flint, using the hammer stone. Phaedra
enjoyed hearing nothing but the sounds of their labor.

Once or twice she felt Quintana's eyes on her, but she didn't
want to look up. It was too small a space to endure her stare, so
Phaedra kept her head down.

"I only enjoyed it with the Lumateran . . . Froi," Quintana
said quietly.

"What?"

"It."

Phaedra's peace was over. She felt an anger rise up inside her
at the memory of her humiliation that day with Lucian and the
Lumaterans.

"You're mocking me."

"I'm not at all."

Phaedra studied her suspiciously, hoping that any conversation about mating would not take place again. She was happy
when they continued their work in silence. But not for long.

"Even if he did live," Quintana said, her hands clenched
fiercely around the hammer stone and flint spearhead, "there's
no life for us together."

Don't let me want to like her, Phaedra pleaded with the gods. *Don't
let her bewitch me like she's bewitched Vestie of the Flatlands and Tesadora.*

The princess glanced down at her belly. "One of the many
blessings of this is that I don't ever have to lie with a man again.
If they don't kill me, they'll wed me to some idiot nobleman, and
do you know what I'll say on my wedding night? I'll say, 'Charyn
already has an heir and curse breaker. Leave me to my peace.'"

Quintana sounded weary of the world, and her focus was
back on her task.

"How did you learn to do that?" Phaedra asked quietly, watching her shape the stone.

"I have a good head for detail. I watch. I learn."

There was arrogance in her voice, as if everyone else was a total fool.

"Then, if you watch and learn, why is it that you can't do your hair? Something so simple?" Phaedra tried to lighten the mood.

Quintana looked up questioningly.

"I think you're being mean."

"No, actually I spoke in jest," Phaedra said.

"Well, you're not very good at being funny, Phaedra. Don't try it again."

And they left it at that.

They worked for the rest of the afternoon, scraping stone against stone, sharpening the flint on each side. By the time the sky began to darken, Phaedra's hands were bloody, every line and crevice filled with filth. Quintana stood, handed Phaedra the tree limb of her length, and they both forced the stone into the end of the branch until it was secure. Quintana gripped the branch at its center and made a move to jab at Phaedra, her savage teeth showing a hint of glee. Phaedra stumbled back, her throat constricting. Their very mad princess was now armed. Apart from Donashe and his men finding them, Phaedra couldn't think of anything more frightening.

"You try," Quintana said, and Phaedra held the weapon. Quintana adjusted Phaedra's hand until her grip on the spear was firm.

"If the Mont holds a dagger to your throat again," the princess promised coldly, "I'll rip him from crown to heel."

Phaedra shivered. She saw the vicious teeth appear again in a smile of satisfaction.

"Let's go slaughter something," Quintana said. "We'll see if they call me useless with their bellies filled."

"You've got to stop saying that," Phaedra said quietly. "About the women thinking you're useless."

"You're the one who's said it yourself about both of us," Quintana taunted. "And I'm sure you and the women have called me other names. An abomination? A whore? Have I missed anything? Go on! Speak the truth."

Phaedra swallowed hard. Oh, all those words and more. Mad. Indulged. Delusional. Cold. Vicious. Broken.

"It doesn't matter what we've said in the past; you need to endear yourself to your people, Your Majesty," Phaedra said.

Quintana leaned forward conspiratorially, as if someone were close by. "I'm not too fussed about that title, really, Phaedra. It's what they used to call my father, and I only stress the use of it when I'm dealing with the likes of those fishwives in the cave. You may refer to me as . . ."

She thought for a moment, her brow creased in thought.

"You may refer to me as Your Highness instead."

Phaedra couldn't stop a laugh.

"I think I'm going to call you Quintana, actually."

Quintana's eyes narrowed.

"Only because the queen of Lumatere is referred to as Isaboe by those close to her." Phaedra nodded, enjoying herself. "Froi called her Isaboe as well. If the queen of Lumatere discovers that those close to the queen of Charyn use such a formal title . . . well, she'll think that the queen of Charyn can't make friends."

Quintana's contemplation was thorough.

"She's not as beautiful as people say, you know," Quintana said. "But the little person Vistie was."

"Vestie."

"The little person has a voice . . . much like someone I once knew . . . my sister, if you'd like to know."

Phaedra was surprised. "I didn't realize you had a sister."

"In here, I did," Quintana said, pointing to herself.

Phaedra thought a moment. "I understand about Vestie. The little ones on the mountain—they made me feel a joy and sadness beyond reckoning."

"Is that how you feel about your Mont?"

"I don't want to talk about him," Phaedra said quietly.

"He's very handsome."

Phaedra had to agree, and glancing at Quintana, she thought that perhaps the princess wasn't so bad, after all.

"It's a pity about his swiving, though."

And Phaedra saw her smile, with a hint of mischief in it, and she couldn't help smiling herself and then she was laughing. They both were, and the savage teeth were the most joyous sight Phaedra had seen for a long time. It was as if they were dancing. There it was. Suddenly the strangeness of Quintana of Charyn's face made sense. Because it was a face meant for laughing, but it had never been given a chance. It robbed Phaedra of her breath.

In the palace village, Lucian said his good-byes to Lord Tascan. He had come to the capital for discussion with Finnikin and Sir Topher that had been a great success. Finnikin's market day would be open to other kingdoms for the first time since the end of the curse. It would bring to Lumatere cloth merchants from Belegonia, drapers from Osteria, weavers from Sarnak. All interested in Mont fleece, which every Mont knew was second to none in the kingdom, even the land. Added to that was Lord Tascan's suggestion of a possible exchange of goods. His villagers grew sugar beet and barley.

"We'll talk on market day. I'm to judge the barley," Lucian said. "A neutral eye is required, according to our consort."

Suddenly Lady Zarah was there beside her father.

"What a surprise to see you here, Father," she trilled softly.

She said something to Lucian, but he could hardly hear and was forced to move closer. There was too much noise in the palace village today.

"Just saying my good-byes to the lad here," Lord Tascan said, handing Lucian a flask.

"The best wine this land has to offer," he promised. "A gift from the king of Osteria for my service to him."

Lucian thanked him and placed the wine in his pack.

"I'll walk you to your horse," Lady Zarah said. She held a hand to his sleeve, and Lucian instantly felt every pair of eyes in the palace village on them.

"Will you always live in your dark little cottage?" she asked as they reached his mount. "It's sweetly quaint."

"It suits me," he said. "And I love my *yata*, but I wouldn't want to be living with her and the aunts in the big house." He chuckled at the thought.

Lady Zarah laughed, too, but it seemed forced. She was a pretty girl, and he could grow to love her. He knew that. She was a Lumateran, and he could grow to love any Lumateran girl. But he was already imagining himself trapped inside his cottage with no room to breathe and having to stand so close just to hear her voice. Sweet as it was.

He saw Finnikin with Perri at the tannery and took Zarah's hand.

"I see my cousin," he said, kissing her hand gently because the Mont girls had taught him that a lady liked to have her hand kissed. "I'll come visit the next time I'm in the village."

"I'll look forward to that, Lucian," she said.

Not *Luc-ien*.

"Sweet, sweet girl," Finnikin said politely when Lucian reached him. They watched as Zarah walked away, whispering to her father.

"Oh, yes, the sweetest."

"Yes, yes. Very sweet. I say it all the time. What a sweet girl."

"Hmm."

And then the discussion of Zarah was complete because there wasn't much else to say and Finnikin mentioned a hunt and Lucian was relieved to speak of something that had his heart racing. Close by, Perri was saddling a horse that wasn't his own.

"He's been strangely wounded in spirit since we returned," Finnikin said quietly about the guard. "First this thing with Froi, and then returning to find out about Tesadora's estrangement from Isaboe. Why didn't you put a stop to it, Lucian?"

Lucian couldn't believe what he was hearing.

"There were daggers, Finn. Women with daggers. Not just any women. Your wife. Tesadora."

They watched Perri walk the horse toward them, stopping to speak to the priestess of the Lagrami novices. Through his ties with Tesadora, Perri had a friendship with the novices and the priestess, and it was known that he visited both cloisters in the village and forest on occasion. It was strange to think of Perri sitting and drinking tea and eating cake with such women, as though he were civilized. But Perri had always been difficult to work out.

"He's on his way to the valley to see Tesadora, so finish your business and go with him," Finnikin whispered quickly as Perri approached. "It will be good for him not to be on his own."

As much as Lucian enjoyed Perri's company, he had wanted serenity on his journey home. He desired nothing more than silence as a companion and truly hoped Perri wanted the same. Trips home to the mountain were long, and there was nothing worse than someone chewing at his ears with words.

". . . and then, not only am I dealing with the fact that she feigned her own death," he said to Perri as they passed the inn of Balconio hours later, "I also find out that she discusses our marriage with her companions. Our spousal bed. And do you want to know the truth, Perri? Without going into infinite detail about what took place between us those nights — two nights — did I mention that it was only two times? Have you seen how small she is? She reaches here," Lucian said, pointing to his chest. "What was I to do? The first time, she cried, and the second time, I know I hurt her. No woman had ever wept in my bed, so I spent some nights at Yata's to relieve her of the fear, and now I discover that she believed I was lying with one of the Mont girls. . . ."

When they reached the mountain, all seemed calm among the Monts, so Lucian decided to accompany Perri down to the valley.

"No, you stay. It's fine," Perri said, and Lucian heard weariness in his voice.

"No, no. I'll travel with you. It's a good thing, because you seem quite drowsy."

"Pity . . . because I believe you're needed on this mountain, Lucian," Perri said. "Here comes Potts."

"Ignore him."

They took the path down to the valley.

"Anyway, what I was saying," Lucian continued, "is that this business with Lord Tascan's family has now become an issue because when I started seeing his daughter Zarah, I believed that my wife was dead and now she's not, and although I know that all I need to do is see my cousin Isaboe to speak of the marriage with the Charynite . . . do you notice how I say that now? How I don't refer to her by her name? Well, I know that Cousin Isaboe can sever this marriage based on the grounds of our separation and the fact that the union brought no peace between our kingdoms."

"Then why don't you do that?" Perri finally spoke bluntly.

"Do what?"

"Have the marriage severed?"

Lucian stared at him, stunned. "With . . ."

"With the Charynite," Perri said. "Have the marriage with the Charynite severed."

"Phaedra?"

"I'd hate to refer to her by name, Lucian. Isn't that what you want?"

Lucian bristled. "I think you should keep silent now, Perri. You've said too much."

Lucian didn't speak for the rest of the journey into the valley until they saw Tesadora's tent in the hollow and he thought it wise to warn Perri.

"She's angry and she's hurt," he said. "She'll be very frosty in her response to you because of your duty to the queen, and you might just find yourself back up that mountain, because when Tesadora's furious, you have to give her space."

Perri stared at Lucian impassively.

"Yes, we've actually become friends . . . almost," Lucian continued, "and I think she's beginning to trust me. She's not going to want to talk about what happened with the queen, and she's especially not going to like the fact that you've come down this mountain with not so much as a note from Isaboe. So let me do the talking, Perri. This may not end well for you if you act too prematurely."

Lucian watched as Tesadora stepped out of her tent, having heard their horses. Perri leaped off his horse, and a moment later, she was in his arms and they were kissing in a way that had even the horses tossing their manes in surprise.

"Where's Beast?" she asked, staring at the strange horse.

"A very long story," Perri said.

They walked into the tent, perhaps to talk about the queen or where Beast was.

Lucian thought it best not to follow.

CHapteR 21

Serker was a wasteland. Cracked earth, dead stumps of
trees, and not a speck of fertile land as far north as the eye
could see. Worse still were the piercing shrieks that sliced
at Froi's ears.

"Can you hear that?" he shouted to Gargarin, who rode with
him that day. Lirah was riding ahead on Beast. It was only fitting
that she entered her province on a Serkan horse.

"The wind has a bite in these parts," Gargarin said.

"It's not the wind I hear."

Froi dismounted, his knees buckling, fatigued by the sounds
of the damned that called to him. He took in his surroundings,
unable to fathom the horror of what had taken place in Serker
nineteen years past. Low ruins of cottages burned to the ground.
Other dwellings so intact—an even crueler reminder that a people
once existed here. Skeletal remains lay where people had been
slaughtered. The once-thriving town void of breath. Even the air
seemed to have stilled to nothing.

"The land is so flat," Froi said, looking up at Gargarin. "How
can an army possibly be hiding here?"

"You know better than to ask that when you've spent so much time living as a trog these past months," Gargarin said.

But there was doubt even in Gargarin's voice. What were the chances of an army and their horses hiding in this strange place? The only army Froi knew of was the one he had glimpsed in a valley between Sebastabol and Serker earlier that morning. He hadn't told Gargarin and Lirah. He saw no reason to alarm them.

"How could they not have seen the king's army coming?" Froi asked.

Gargarin didn't respond, and Froi could see he was watching Lirah up ahead as she followed the road to the colossal theater they had glimpsed the moment they entered Serker.

"The Serker army was too busy attacking up north," Gargarin said. "They were lied to and misinformed by a spy that the northern province of Desantos was set to invade. That was Serker's weakness. They'd fly into any skirmish at a moment's notice, always to prove their power. Later, when the people saw the horses approaching from the north, they believed them to be their own returning soldiers. They didn't realize it was the king's men who had circled the province. And by the time the real Serkan army returned home, they didn't realize they were walking into a trap and that most of their people were already slaughtered."

Froi continued to walk alongside Gargarin in silence. He tried to remember Arjuro's song calling the dead so he could sing it in his heart and perhaps stop the shrieks of the spirits that only he could hear, but it would not come to mind. And then finally they reached the place once called Il Centro, an open-air stage surrounded by tiered steps reaching so high that they disappeared beneath the low, filthy clouds. It was as if Serker had built a way to touch the gods.

"I've never seen anything so mighty before," Froi said.

"As young men, Arjuro, De Lancey, and I traveled here to

listen to great lectures about the planets and the philosophy of the ancients," Gargarin said. "It wasn't rare to meet a Lumateran here, and if you ask your priest-king and the priestesses of your cloisters, you'll find they'll all have visited Serker in their day."

Froi wondered if Tesadora's mother, Seranonna, had come to this place and lain with a Serkan.

"It's where most of the people of this province died," Gargarin said.

"How did they all come to be there?" Froi asked.

Gargarin put a finger to his lips as they approached Lirah and Beast. She had slowed down and seemed in her own world.

"The census," Gargarin said quietly. "The *provincaro* called one, which meant that every Serkan had to travel to Il Centro. The seneschal had recorded the name of every soldier who had gone off to fight, so what better time to complete the task of a province-wide reckoning? The people of Serker were all assembled in this great place of learning, waiting to have their names recorded. But it never happened, and those names are lost. Almost the entire population was annihilated. It's been said that those who survived later crawled out from under the bodies of their loved ones and have been hiding ever since."

They listened to Lirah crooning to Beast.

"Nineteen years ago, we had children and babes in Charyn," Gargarin said.

Froi wanted to smash his head with a fist to keep the images from entering his mind.

"It's what happened in Sarnak to the River people of Lumatere," he said quietly.

"We heard the stories of the Sarnak slaughter," Gargarin said. "Is it true that your queen bore witness and demands that the Sarnak king arrest the men responsible?"

Froi nodded. "Those River folk belonged to Trevanion. He and

Lady Abian are the last of their village. Only now have the queen and Finnikin allowed others to live in Tressor. The land is too fertile to waste, but there is a signpost with the name of every man, woman, and child who ever lived there. When Princess Jasmina was born, the queen and Finnikin had her blessed and titled Jasmina of the River in honor of her *pardu*. Her grandfather."

But Gargarin's attention was again drawn ahead to Lirah. "See to her, Froi," he said, his voice low.

"She'll not want me there."

Lirah was weeping. It twisted Froi up inside to see Lirah the strong, Lirah the fierce and cold and unbreakable, weeping.

"Go," Gargarin said.

Froi hurried to catch up with her, but the moment she saw him, Lirah wiped her tears fiercely, her attention on the bridle of Beast. Froi didn't know what to say. He glanced around, trying to think of something. Everything was dead. Or so it seemed at first. But what he had come to understand in his travels with the Lumaterans and Charynites was that nature chose to defy man's will to destroy. Close by, wild pink and purple flowers peppered the landscape on the road beside them.

"Let me up," he said.

Lirah made room, and Froi climbed onto Beast behind her. He pointed over her shoulder. *"Bronshoi."*

She looked up and then nodded. Then she pointed to another. *"Sajarai."*

And Froi understood Lirah's passion for her prison garden. She had planted the Serker that she couldn't forget.

They continued riding through the province, mostly in silence. Froi couldn't help but think of Lumatere. It was less than a day's ride from Isaboe's palace to Lucian's mountain. Here, it was more than a day's ride from one end of Serker to the other.

Lumatere had never seemed so vulnerable.

When they reached another barren settlement of half-standing cottages, a murder of crows swooped close by. Froi dismounted and walked toward whatever had drawn them to the ground.

"What is it?" Gargarin asked, pulling up beside Lirah's horse.

"Someone's here," Froi said. "Those birds would have nothing else to scavenge otherwise."

Gargarin looked around and then struggled off his horse.

"We're out here in the open," Gargarin said. "If they want me dead, they'd have killed me by now. Let's set up camp and wait for whoever it is to politely come calling."

"I haven't exactly been trained to wait for attackers to reveal themselves," Froi said, irritated.

"Wait, I say."

The three of them found refuge in a half-standing cottage that at least protected them from the wind. Gargarin built a small fire, and Froi watched him cover Lirah with the robe he had borrowed from De Lancey, and for a short while at least, she slept.

"You asked before about the sound," Gargarin said later. "If it's not the wind, what is it?"

Froi shook his head. He didn't want to say the words.

"You've got some of my brother's gifts. That I'm certain of," Gargarin said. "Do you hear the Serkan dead?"

Froi felt Lirah's eyes piercing into him.

"I sense nothing," he lied. Because the truth was that he sensed agony and despair and unrest.

Something moved outside the shelter, and Froi crept toward the sound. Gargarin gripped his arm, held him back.

"Wait until he chooses to reveal himself."

"No," Froi said firmly. "We do this my way."

He stepped outside and stared into the darkness. He could

hear the sound of shallow breathing. It was a human sound, unlike the shrill whistle of the dead that he couldn't block out. Froi knew they weren't dealing with an army. It was one person, perhaps two. Good at staying concealed, but not good enough. Or perhaps their intruder wanted to be found.

Froi retrieved his dagger. "Reveal yourself!" he called out. There was no response, and he called out again.

"Are you armed?" came the response.

Froi recognized the voice and sighed with relief, regardless of its hostility.

"Of course I'm armed," he said, irritated.

Gargarin was suddenly at Froi's side.

"Get back inside," Froi ordered.

"Perabo?" Gargarin called out. "Is that you?"

Froi heard the sound of something being lit, and then a flicker of light appeared as a figure with a large bulk and craggy face and oil lamp in hand crawled out of the shadows.

"You know each other?" Froi asked. Perabo ignored him and held out a hand to Gargarin.

"It's been a long time," the keeper of the caves said as the two men shook hands.

"And sad days in between," Gargarin responded. "Our boy always spoke highly of you."

Froi was confused. He had never mentioned Perabo at all, but then he realized with a wave of gut-deep envy that Gargarin was referring to Tariq. He felt Perabo's accusing stare on him. Even after everything that had happened in the Citavita with Quintana's rescue, Perabo would never forgive him for not getting her out sooner.

"What are you doing here in Serker, Perabo?" Gargarin asked. "On your own, at that?"

"Waiting and hoping," Perabo said. "And here you are."

Gargarin ushered Perabo into the shelter.

"Tell me there's an army here," Gargarin said. "One gathered in Tariq's name."

Perabo shook his head. "I've found nothing here but old ledgers hidden by a moneylender, and the town gossip's chronicles."

"You have them?" Lirah spoke up.

Perabo looked beyond Froi and Gargarin and stared at her, his expression showing appreciation at what he was seeing. He retrieved the chronicles from his pack and reached out to give them to her.

"Lirah of Serker," he said, not needing to be told who she was. "This must cause you great pain."

"What in Charyn doesn't?" she said in a flat tone.

Perabo's attention was back on Froi. "I heard it was you who lost her," the keeper of the caves said bluntly.

Froi bristled but didn't respond.

"You're being followed," Perabo finally said. Froi nodded, glancing at Lirah and Gargarin with a shrug.

"I saw something when we rested in the valley of Sebastabol," he said.

"Can you keep us informed of the 'somethings'?" Gargarin said sharply.

"I reveal information when it needs to be revealed," Froi responded.

"There is no army for us here," Perabo said, and Gargarin gave a sound of frustration. "But I can take you to one."

"Where?"

"North," Perabo answered. "Two days' ride beyond the great lake of Charyn."

CHAPTER 22

When five sacks of barley arrived on the mountain, on a horse and cart from Lord Tascan's river village, it caused more interest than Lucian cared for. At first, one or two of the Monts stopped their midday work to watch the sacks being offloaded outside Yata's residence, but then Lucian's kin began arriving in clusters of interest and intrigue, and by midafternoon there was no more work to be done on the mountain, just a whole lot of observations and opinions and rubbish.

"Enough now. Back to work," Lucian ordered.

"It's a dowry," Jory said.

"A what?" Potts asked.

"A dowry."

Everyone turned to look at Jory, who was nodding with certainty, his stare fixed on Lucian.

"Lord Tascan is offering you five sacks of grain as a dowry for Lady Zarah. That's what this is."

"And what do you know about a dowry?" Lucian asked, irritated because suddenly everyone was fascinated by what Jory had to say.

"Phaedra," Jory said. "She explained them to me. The way I understand it is that if I want to betroth myself to a girl, her family will offer me something to take her off their hands."

Lotte sniffed. "Oh, sweet Phaedra," she lamented.

"Which I didn't understand really, Lucian," Jory continued, "because wouldn't Phaedra have been enough of a gift?"

Was there a challenge in his young cousin's stance? Had Lucian been as obnoxious and bursting with all that thumping boy-blood energy when he was fifteen? He was sure he hadn't. All that pent-up emotion that pointed down to one area of a lad's body. Thankfully spring was coming. The Mont boys had been confined too long.

"He's right," Cousin Alda said.

"I'm going to have to agree," Lucian's uncle said.

Hmm. Yes, yes. Everyone had to agree. *Everyone*. Nothing better than a good death to create such affection for a Charynite.

"Enough," Lucian snapped, well and truly sick and tired of it. All this talk of Lady Zarah and the two visits she had paid to the mountain had driven him to madness. Or was it Phaedra in the valley who had driven him to madness?

"Let's just agree that Phaedra was a gift and maybe I could have treated her better and kept her on this mountain and taken care of her as she deserved to be taken care of, the way men take care of women in all . . . ways, but the past is the past and we move forward!"

The Monts were gaping. Even Yata. Had he revealed too much?

"No, I mean I agree about the fact that the sacks of barley are Tascan's attempt at a dowry," Alda said.

Lucian watched Jory hide a smirk.

"You can't accept the barley, Lucian," Yata said practically. "Finnikin has chosen you as judge of the crop for market day,

214

and to accept five bushels of barley at this point from one lord over another will cause a feud."

Wonderful. Now Lucian was going to be responsible for civil war in Lumatere.

"But sending it back will seem an insult," Potts pointed out. Potts always pointed out facts with no good solutions.

"A humiliation of Lord Tascan," one of the aunts said. "Imagine the sacks arriving back on his doorstep for the whole kingdom to see. The river lot don't know how to keep their mouths shut."

"True, true," Lucian said, "and the gossip will spread like plague."

"Sweet Phaedra," Lotte cried. "Taken from us by a plague."

"Lucian! Respect."

Perhaps a wrong choice of word.

"If Lord Tascan is insulted, there goes our exchange of pigs for crops," Alda said, irritated. "Don't ruin this, Lucian!"

Everyone agreed that Lucian would ruin this.

"Diplomacy is needed," Jory said.

"You know what that means, do you?" Lucian demanded. It was Jory who had started all this talk of dowries.

"I didn't," his young cousin said, "until Phaedra told me about it. 'Diplomacy is better than war,' she would say."

"Phaedra's not here!" Lucian shouted.

Lotte cried into her apron, and Lucian was the target of much head shaking and disgust.

The sacks of barley and Lotte's crying and Jory's smugness haunted Lucian all the night long.

"So what would you do?" he demanded out loud, as if Phaedra were in the room.

I'd be diplomatic, Luc-ien. And I'd do the right thing.

He fell asleep to those words and woke to them the next

215

morning and found himself at Yata's, where the sacks of grain were exactly where he had left them in the courtyard. He fought himself not to kick them hard for being the cause of a sleepless night.

From her kitchen, Yata knocked at the window and beckoned him in.

"You are so hard on yourself, lad," she said when he was seated at her table, drinking warm tea.

He could see outside the window, where the mountain looked sublime with its crawling fog. On the slope close to his cousin Morrie's home, Lucian saw a goat's black face among the sheep. Beyond that were Leon and Pena's vineyards. Sometimes Lucian forgot the beauty of his mountain, but here in Yata's kitchen he truly understood why his ancestors had built the compound on this slope. So they could see their people.

"Every decision I want to make hurts someone I love," he said. "Every decision I don't make hurts someone I love. Fa never had doubt. *Never.*"

Yata sat before him. "On the day Saro decided to take us down that mountain and outside the kingdom walls during the five days of the unspeakable, he wept at this very same place you're sitting now. Some of the Monts were furious. They weren't going to leave their homes, and Saro had to decide whether to stay or leave them behind. I asked him what his heart said, and he didn't hesitate. 'Keep the Monts together, regardless of anger and resentment. Keep them together.'"

And his father did just that.

"What does your heart say, Lucian?" Yata asked. "You're not torn about the barley. It's more than that."

Lucian and Isaboe and any of the cousins would agree, they could hide little from Yata. He sighed.

"Half of my heart says it would be so simple to share what

we've got here with the Charynites in the valley. But the other half of me says I don't want to share it with the enemy, and then I have to work out who the enemy is. I mean, look at what we have," he said, pointing outside at the lushness of their mountainside, even in this winter haze. "And look at how little they have down there. And why don't I care?"

Yata laughed. "Well, from where I'm sitting, it looks as if you do care, Lucian," she said. "Too much in one place, not enough in another, and wouldn't it be simple if we shared? It's that way across this land, and it's been that way since the beginning of time. Yes, it would be so simple to share. But there's no place for being simple when blood has been shed and the people we love have been torn from us." She took his hand across the table. "But forgiveness has to start somewhere, Lucian. It *did* start somewhere. It started with Phaedra. The Monts learned not to hate all of the Charynites because of her. I learned." Yata had tears in her eyes. "Because you may not have seen it, my darling boy, but I hated with a fierceness I can't describe. And do you want to hear something that was breaking my heart, day after day? I forgot the faces of my granddaughters in all that hatred. Hatred smothers all beauty. Beloved Isaboe has little resemblance to her older sisters, but your Phaedra—she made me remember those precious, precious girls, and I wasn't angry anymore. I just missed them, and it's the beauty in here," she said, pointing to her chest, "that made me remember them. Her beauty."

He could see the truth in her words.

"You know she lives," he said softly.

Yata nodded. "Constance and Sandrine have sworn me to secrecy."

He felt the strength of her hands.

"I don't want you to take those sacks of grain," she said firmly. "They'll tie you to someone who will bring you regret and dissatisfaction all your life. It's not what your father would have wanted for you."

He swallowed hard. "I've made my decision."

She made a sound of frustration, shaking her head, but he held up a hand to stop her. "I'm going to write a note to Lord Tascan and thank him for the grain, but explain that to accept it will compromise my role as a judge at the fair. I'm going to emphasize just how humiliating it may feel to him if anyone in the kingdom sees that I returned the grain, in case he doesn't realize it's humiliation he should be feeling, and then I'm going to suggest that I send the grain down to the valley where the Charynites are in need of it. I'll promise him that no one in Lumatere will ever be able to say that flatland or river barley was consumed by a Mont judge, nor will they be able to prove that the grain existed in the first place."

Yata smiled. "Oh, you're a clever boy."

"It's not enough, of course," he said. "The grain will run out eventually."

"Then, we have weeks to think up another plan."

He traveled to the valley with Jory, who insisted on coming along.

"Do you want to know what I think?" his cousin asked as they passed one of the farms midway down the mountain.

"No, I don't actually, Jory. I want peace and quiet."

"I don't think Phaedra's dead," Jory replied. "And you know she isn't."

"Really."

"Yes, really," Jory said, imitating his tone. "'Cause sometimes I come up to your cottage, you know, Lucian. You hide up there, all closed up, and everyone wishes you didn't. At first, I'd see that small shrine you had to blessed Lagrami and how you'd lay petalbane beside it every day. For Phaedra. Because petalbane

218

is the flower for grieving the dead. But then weeks ago, after Cousin Isaboe left the mountain, you stopped. So the way I see it, something happened in the valley that day and you know she's alive and you know that it's bad luck to bring petalbane to the living, and you don't want to curse Phaedra."

"It's been some weeks since her death, Jory," Lucian said, his voice practical. "We all have to move on. That's why I stopped laying the petalbane."

"The mourning season for Phaedra ends midspring. I know that because Cousin Cece was seen drinking ale and Alda, well, she blasted him. 'How dare you?' she shouted."

"Funny that all of a sudden Alda cares for Phaedra," Lucian said.

Jory looked surprised. "I don't think Alda cares that much for Phaedra. She hardly knew her. But Alda, she said to Cousin Cece, 'You show respect for Lucian. He's our leader.'"

Lucian had never heard one of the Monts acknowledge that before.

"You know what my father says?" Jory said. "He says you weren't born to lead, Lucian. That you were made to. But regardless, Fa says Monts couldn't have asked for a better man to get us through this time."

Lucian stared at him, overwhelmed. "What are you all of a sudden?" he demanded gruffly. "An ancient wiseman?"

Jory pointed to himself.

"Look at me, cousin. Did ancient wisemen have shoulders like mine?"

The valley dwellers wept when they were told about the barley and crowded around Lucian and Jory as if they were gods. Lucian's attention was on Harker and Kasabian. The men cut a sad picture working on the vegetable patch that Cora had planted.

Jory worked alongside them for a while, and Lucian couldn't stay angry at his young cousin for too long. Then they followed Kasabian to his cave, and Lucian saw Rafuel and Donashe watching carefully from their place by the rock face, Rafuel's expression tense and questioning. Inside the cave, Lucian removed the bottle of ale Lord Tascan had given him from his pack and handed it to Harker to take a swig.

"To my wife and my daughter," Harker said, his voice a hoarse whisper. Lucian winced to think of what he kept from him. Harker handed the bottle to Kasabian.

"To my sister Cora."

The flask was back with Lucian, and the men waited. Lucian realized he was to drink to the memory of his wife. Jory watched him questioningly.

"To Phaedra," Lucian said.

Jory held out a hand, and Lucian reluctantly gave it to him. The lad took a confident swig, but then choked, not so grown-up after all.

"Arm us," Harker said quietly.

Lucian sighed.

"I can't do that, Harker. You know that. Whatever happened to the women was not at the hands of Donashe."

Harker's stare was hard. Lucian had come to realize that this man would have been a leader much like his own father. The type of man born for it.

"My actions are not determined just by my sorrow," Harker said. "Donashe and his murderers are going to bring a bloodbath to this valley. I've seen this before."

As if they knew they were being spoken of, Rafuel and Donashe and a third man entered the cave. There was an arrogance in the way they stood in Harker and Kasabian's dwelling, but Lucian and the others refused to acknowledge their presence.

"I mentioned to Donashe that I didn't trust you here, Mont," Rafuel finally said. "And that I'd question what you were doing."

"My valley. My cave," Lucian said with a shrug. He knew Rafuel feared what Lucian knew about the fate of the women.

"I was hoping to convince Harker and Kasabian to go hunting with me," he added. "As well as this grain, I'm willing to allow one or two of you on my side of the stream to catch an elk."

"I'd say it's a better idea if you take Matteo," Donashe said. Lucian noticed the bitter jealousy in the expression of the third man watching the exchange between Donashe and Rafuel. "These two are useless old men," Donashe added, dismissing Harker and Kasabian with a sneer.

"Get out of my cave," Harker said.

"This moping and silence of yours are dampening camp spirits."

Harker leaped to his feet, and it took Lucian and Jory and Kasabian to hold him back.

"We don't need lessons on how to move on," Harker cried. "Those lads you slaughtered and the deaths of our women have crushed this camp's spirit."

Rafuel stood between Donashe and Harker, pushing Harker back.

"Let's accept the offer to hunt for elk, Donashe. Before these fools force the Mont to take back his words. It will feed us for days."

Donashe kept his stare on Harker, but Harker was not a man to look away.

"When it's time for the hunt, Mont," Donashe said, "Matteo here will accompany you across the stream." Donashe clasped Rafuel's arm before leaving the cave, his lapdog following.

Lucian felt the full force of Rafuel's stare.

"You've turned into a hard man, Rafuel," Jory said. "Don't you trust us anymore?'

"Rafuel?" Harker's head shot up in surprise.

Lucian sent Jory a warning look.

"Matteo," Jory muttered.

"Rafuel was the name of the leader of those poor slaughtered lads," Harker said.

A muscle in Rafuel's cheek twitched with emotion.

"You have a good memory for names, Harker," Jory said.

"And you have a tongue that needs to be cut off," Lucian said to his cousin.

Lucian could see the confusion on Kasabian's and Harker's faces. Jory held the bottle out to Rafuel, who hesitated, but then took a swig and passed it on.

"Phaedra's alive, isn't she?" Jory asked, barely able to contain his excitement.

Rafuel stepped closer to them all. "Quintana of Charyn is hiding downstream," he whispered.

Kasabian and Harker stared at him, stunned. Lucian could tell even Jory couldn't believe what he was hearing.

Harker gripped Rafuel's coat, his fists clenched and trembling.

"Did my wife and daughter die to keep the spawn of that wretched king alive?" he asked.

"Well, the spawn of our wretched king is going to spawn another hopefully not-so-wretched king in less than three months. . . ."

Lucian heard their intake of breath. He could see that Kasabian and Harker didn't seem to know what to believe. He took the flask from Rafuel and raised it.

"To the women . . . and whoever it is they're protecting."

"Yes!" Jory hissed, lifting Rafuel off his feet.

"My sister Cora is alive?" Kasabian asked, tears in his eyes.

Lucian nodded.

Kasabian clenched a fist and pressed a kiss to it, a thanks to the gods.

Rafuel shoved Jory away with affectionate irritation.

"And this is why they couldn't know," he said, pointing to Harker and Kasabian. "Look at them. Do they look like grieving men?"

Harker caught Rafuel in an embrace and Lucian watched as Rafuel held the older man in his arms, tenderly. "I've lost them twice," Harker wept. "I sometimes wake in the night and can barely breathe."

"We'll have to tell that idiot Gies," Kasabian said. "He'll want to know that his Ginny is alive."

Rafuel shook his head emphatically.

"Gies has become one of Donashe's men. We cannot trust him. I need to go now. Trust no one."

The men embraced again.

"It may be some time before you see the women," Rafuel said. "I beg your patience, friends. Nothing gets in the way of Quintana of Charyn's safety. She is the only hope we have left in this kingdom, and she is as helpless as the babe she carries."

Phaedra watched as Quintana waited and then pounced, saw the satisfaction on their strange princess's face as she removed the writhing trout from her spear and tossed it onto the ground. Phaedra tried next and almost succeeded, but it was always Quintana who caught them.

"I almost had it," Phaedra said.

"Almost isn't enough, Phaedra," Quintana said.

The women had joined them today, much to Quintana's annoyance, but all seemed well behaved. Florenza showed a great talent for trout spearing, and by the end of the afternoon, she was looking as savage as Quintana. Ginny, on the other hand, did little to help.

"Is there anything you're good at except for complaining and pining for men?" Cora asked Ginny as she scaled the fish with one of Quintana's sharp stones.

"Well, if you really must know, I'm a great seamstress," Ginny said.

"Oh, good, good. Much needed at the moment," Jorja said. "When we get invited to that feast at the Nebian ambassador's home, you'll be the first person we have in mind, Ginny."

"Why would you move from your village if you had such a talent?" Phaedra asked, trying to grip a wriggling fish in both hands and failing. It hit the water with a plonk, and she dared not look at Quintana.

"Because I'm not privileged or born last, Phaedra," Ginny said, spite in her voice, as if speaking to a fool. "I had the misfortune of living in a village where the girls closest to me in age were last borns. Five of them. Five!" she said, as if the disbelief of it all was still raw. "Most villages had one, maybe two. But *five*?"

"Five, you say?" Quintana murmured, not looking up. Phaedra hid a smile.

"If you weren't a last-born girl in my village, you were nothing," Ginny continued, oblivious to Quintana's mockery. "They were given gifts all the year long. Even the privy cleaner's daughter was considered better than me. *The privy cleaner's daughter!* When they turned ten, the village threw the grandest of celebrations. I played with the last borns every day of my life and was given nothing."

Quintana seemed genuinely confused.

"I'm not quite sure what your point is, Ginny," she said. "Were you poisoned? Were you pinned under the heaving body of a man who smelled of pig fat and onions? Was your head held under water so the half dead could clamber for your spirit?"

They stared at Quintana, horrified. Was she speaking of her experiences or those of others?

"It's very easy for you to be so offhand, Your Majesty," Ginny said. "When there were those of us in Charyn who truly suffered while you enjoyed a privileged life in the Citavita."

"But you haven't actually come to the point where you've suffered yet," Quintana said. "Apart from not getting as many presents when you turned ten. So I'm getting quite bored, Ginny, and I'm going to be tempted to slice off your tongue any moment now."

Quintana was gutting the fish with savagery, and Phaedra thought she would surely carry out her threat.

"I was good with dyes, if you must know," Ginny continued. "What I could do with fabric was a gift from the gods. My mother was an alchemist who worked with colors, and one time I made a dress of indigo."

Florenza, who loved pretty things, seemed the only one interested.

"What color is that?" she asked.

"A much richer shade than the sky. The darkest of blue."

Florenza liked the idea of it.

"If we ever attend a feast again, Mother, I'll have Ginny make me a gown."

"You crawled through shit, Florenza," Ginny said, her voice nasty. "Do you honestly think the nobility is going to invite you anywhere ever again?"

Florenza began to gag, and they all sent Ginny scathing looks. Apart from what the memory of the sewers did to Florenza, it was a sickening sound to listen to. Jorja placed an arm around her daughter, fussing quietly.

"You have the prettiest face in Charyn," she reassured Florenza. "The Lumateran nobility won't be able to resist you when they let us in." But Florenza began to retch again, and Jorja held her daughter's hair from her brow. Phaedra wondered how long it would take Jorja to accept that the queen of Lumatere was never going to allow any of them into her kingdom.

"You people of privilege understand nothing," Ginny said.

"I thought last borns understood nothing," Quintana said, but her attention was on Florenza, who was still retching.

"All of them. The privileged. The last borns. The hags who could never get a man," Ginny added, looking at Cora.

"Yes, well, I curse the gods every day for that one," Cora said, her tone dry.

"The tailor's sister was a hag," Ginny continued. "When the day came for the tailor to choose his apprentices, guess whom he chose. A last-born girl. *Our precious ones*," she mimicked. "I hardly existed until Gies came traveling through the village last autumn. Some men don't care whether you're last borns or not." Ginny looked smug. "Not when they enjoy the pleasure you can bring to them. If you ever get the Mont back, Phaedra, I'll teach you a thing or two about how to hold on to him."

Phaedra's face smarted, but she watched Quintana get to her feet, one hand on her belly, the other on her back. The princess walked to where Florenza was still retching and weeping. When Jorja noticed Quintana approaching her daughter with the spear, she put a shaking hand on Florenza's shoulder to quiet her. No one spoke as Quintana bent before Florenza, gripping the girl's face with one hand, studying it hard.

"Our spirit is mightier than the filth of our memories, Florenza of Nebia. Remember that, or you'll be vomiting for the rest of your life."

Florenza stared up at Quintana, and something passed between them as she nodded solemnly and wiped her mouth with the back of her hand.

"And Tippideaux of Paladozza, the *provincaro* De Lancey's daughter, has the prettiest face in Charyn," she continued to inform them all. "Not you. So don't believe a word your mother says."

She stood up and looked down at their bounty of fish, satisfied.

"If we can build a fire tonight, we'll eat well," she said. "Phaedra and I will collect the kindling."

"Do you think that's wise?" Cora asked. "You're beginning to waddle with that load."

"Waddling helps me clear my head of your voices," Quintana responded. "It lessens my need to kill you all."

"Then, off you go," Cora muttered. "Keep an eye on her, Phaedra."

Quintana was up to something. That Phaedra knew. All the same, she followed her into the undergrowth, picking up anything that could pass as kindling. There was plenty to choose from, and Phaedra hummed as she worked, pleased with what she was able to collect.

"I'm getting good at this," she said to Quintana, holding up her bundle of twigs for emphasis.

They reached a steep slope that afforded them a view of a lower clearing.

"Put it down," Quintana ordered. "Let's go."

Phaedra stared at her stash. "Go where?" she asked.

Quintana was already gripping a vine and half sliding down the incline. Phaedra dropped the kindling and quickly followed.

"You're going to hurt yourself!"

"He's down there," Quintana whispered when Phaedra caught up with her, both of them hiding behind a waterberry tree.

"Who?"

"He'll arm us. I know he will."

"*Who?*"

Quintana pointed down. In a deep, narrow gully, Tesadora was bent over, tugging at the exposed roots of plants growing around its edges. But it was her lover, Perri, that Quintana was pointing at. He sat with his back against a tree, in some sort of contemplation. Quintana started to step out, but Phaedra dragged her back.

"If you dare mention what I saw them do, I will—"

They both heard a sound and looked up to see the Lumateran on his feet, alerted to their presence.

Tesadora noticed them as well and climbed to where her lover stood, whispering to him, her eyes on Quintana with unbridled love.

"You there, Lumateran," Quintana called out. "You're to make me a few scabbards." Phaedra cringed, listening to the demand spoken in Charyn as if the queen's guard would understand every word.

Quintana walked closer, handing Phaedra her spear to hold.

"Like the ones you made him. Here. Here. And here." She pointed to both wrists and her shoulders. "So when they come to attack, I'll . . ."

And then she did a quick show of what she'd do. Phaedra was quite enthralled. Perri studied Quintana, and then a chuckle escaped from his lips. Quintana reached him, and he held out a hand to gently touch her face. "What have we got here?" he said in strange wonder.

Tesadora's eyes filled with tears. "Tell her," she urged her lover. "Tell her about Froi. She'll want to know."

Quintana heard the name and clenched her fists so tight that Phaedra found herself dropping the spear and gripping both the girl's hands, loosening her fingers.

"You're going to draw blood. Stop it."

And blood she drew, but not her own. Quintana's nails dug deep into Phaedra's hands.

"Let Phaedra go," Tesadora ordered gently. "You're hurting her, Quintana."

But she didn't let go, and Phaedra fought hard not to cry out in pain. And then Quintana was a heap on the ground before them as if she had willed the breath inside her to stop. Tesadora and Phaedra fell beside her. Perri didn't speak, but when Quintana looked up to him, his smile was bittersweet.

"So you're the one Froi is running around Charyn searching for?"

"Did he say my name?" she asked, her voice cold. But Phaedra had learned to listen to the words and not the voice. The words craved love. The words were those that Phaedra thought over and over again at night. Did Lucian say her name? Did he think it or murmur it in his sleep like she did his?

Phaedra translated the queen's words, but Perri understood them well enough.

"Did he have to?" he asked Quintana. "When your name is written all over his heart?"

A smile appeared on Tesadora's face. "Ah, you're getting soft in your old age," she said to him, pressing a kiss to his shoulder. Perri held out a hand to Quintana and helped her to her feet, inspecting her wrists, as if measuring them for the scabbards.

"You too, Phaedra," Perri said, and her face flushed at the sound of his saying her name. She hadn't even realized he knew who she was, despite the nights he had come up to the mountain and shared her table with Lucian.

He made a gesture with his hand, asking them to turn around.

"I don't know how to use a weapon," Phaedra said over her shoulder.

"You're a Mont's wife," he said gruffly. "So you better learn."

She heard an intake of breath and turned to watch as he traced a finger along the lettering on Quintana's nape. He then traced along the marks on Phaedra's.

"What's this?" he asked.

"The mark of the last borns," Quintana said.

"I thought they were supposed to be exactly the same," he said to Tesadora in Lumateran.

Phaedra felt Tesadora's coarse fingers on her neck.

"They got it wrong," Tesadora insisted, surprise in her voice. "Those fools copied the same lettering onto every last born, but it's different from yours, Quintana. Yours has stems on some of the letters. And a strange mark or two that seems nothing more than a dot."

Phaedra thought of all those years when the priests and her father's advisers had tried to work out the meaning of the strange lettering. "It makes no sense," they'd say. To think that Quintana's differed from hers and those of the rest of the last borns frightened her. It made the princess seem even less of this world.

"On my thirteenth day of weeping, when they grabbed me and tried to keep me down to copy the lettering, I was a snake," Quintana said. "I squirmed and I squirmed and I bit any man who dared come close." There was glee in her voice at the memory, her sharp little teeth showing. "I knew what they'd do to the last-born girls, so I made a decree."

Her stare was suddenly on Phaedra, blazing fiercely

"Did I keep old men from your bed of innocence, Phaedra of Alonso?"

Phaedra couldn't speak. She remembered the women in her father's residence. How they wept and wept at the thought of what would happen to her after she was marked. She shivered just to think of those awful days.

"I remember it well," Phaedra said. "And then it was decreed that you and only you would give birth to the first and that any man or last-born girl who tried would be punished by the gods. The women in my father's residence thanked the gods that you were delusional."

But there was nothing delusional about her. Phaedra stared at her in wonder. Quintana of Charyn had insisted on the decree to protect the last-born girls. And in return, they mocked her madness.

"You're not going to start crying, are you, fool?" Quintana asked bluntly. "It irritates me."

Tesadora made a clucking sound of annoyance.

"What did I tell you?" she said to Quintana in a reprimanding voice.

Tesadora's lover continued to study Quintana, and in return, she appraised him with arrogant curiosity, except for the flash of pain that crossed her face.

"Did I imagine Froi's arrows?" she asked quietly. "I dream of them every night. I feel them."

"Where do you feel them in your dreams?" he asked gently.

Quintana touched her head, her arm, her belly, her side, her shoulder, her thigh, her breast, and her ankle.

Perri exchanged a look with Tesadora.

"You remember exactly where they struck him?" he asked, surprised.

Quintana didn't respond, and Phaedra caught her shudder.

"She has a very good memory for detail," Phaedra said.

CHAPTER 23

The great ice lake of Charyn lay beyond Serker, and once crossed, it would mark the entrance into north country. Froi could have imagined it glistening white under the spell of a blue sky during the winter months. But spring was creeping over the land, and the snow that had covered the lake had melted, leaving the ice below exposed. Froi could see that parts of the lake were darker already from the first signs of the thaw.

"Black ice," Perabo muttered, pointing. "Not a good sign for crossing."

Gargarin dismounted. "Off the horses," he ordered. "We don't want to be tangled up with these animals if the ground breaks beneath our feet."

And so their journey across the lake began with caution and not a word spoken among them for most of that day, every step taken with the fear of it being the one that would crack the ice and break the lake's surface in its entirety. The sound of the wind was their greatest foe. Froi was coming to hate its taunting whistle. If it wasn't mingled with the cries of the Serkan slaughtered, it was warning them of its power. How insignificant they must have looked in the eyes of the gods. Not even when he had climbed the *gravina* had Froi felt so vulnerable to the elements.

The dying light of the day faded, and Froi watched until Gargarin and Lirah and Perabo were merely shapes around him.

Darkness brought with it new fears, and its only benefit was that it blinded them to the vastness of the lake. More than anything, they were weary, and Froi knew he would never take the feel of solid ground beneath his feet for granted again.

"Look," Gargarin said, sometime deep into the night. He pointed, and they looked up to see a spectacular sky, the stars so low that Froi felt he only had to hold up a hand to touch them. He'd never seen a night sky so perfect, so milky and magical.

But what sunrise had to offer was worse than they could have imagined. In the far distance behind them, they saw riders beginning their journey across the lake. Bestiano's army was closer than they had thought.

"It's best not to run," Froi said. They still hadn't reached land, and he didn't want to take a chance. "This ice won't hold us all if they give chase."

"They'll attack," Lirah said.

"They're out of range, so we just need to make sure that we keep up this pace."

"Can *you* attack from here?" Gargarin asked.

Froi shook his head. "Too far and too many. I could wait for them to get closer, but unless Perabo can strike from this distance, I'll be outnumbered."

They turned to Perabo, but the keeper of the cave shook his head. "Only if they were closer, and we don't want that. So we do as the lad says and we keep this distance between us. They could be travelers, for all we know."

But no one believed that the men on horseback weren't soldiers. These were Bestiano's scouts, sent out to assess and report back to their leader and the Nebian army. Froi tried to count their number. Perhaps eighteen or nineteen in total. Too many to fight on his own, even with Perabo's help. Too many to stand on thin ice.

"Keep walking," he ordered the others. They had to get off this lake soon. But before they could take another step north, two of Bestiano's horsemen broke free and came riding toward them. Froi retrieved his bow and took aim.

"Go," Froi shouted to the others.

"They're holding flags," Gargarin said.

"They can't be trusted," Perabo argued.

"Go," Froi shouted again, but he felt Gargarin's hand on his shoulder.

"Don't shoot, Froi. Perhaps they come in peace."

They watched and waited, Froi's fingers clenched on the bow. At the halfway point between both parties, the two horsemen stopped. The first dismounted, but Froi could see there was another astride his horse.

"There're three of them, not two," Froi said.

Froi watched the first rider as he plunged a flag into the ice. They heard the moan of the ground beneath their feet, and before Froi could issue an order to keep on moving, the man on the second horse came riding toward them, leaving his two companions behind.

Froi knelt, his aim on the target.

"Wait, Froi. Wait," Gargarin said.

Froi's fingers ached from the hold he had on the longbow. Closer and closer the rider came until his face was recognizable.

Dorcas.

The king's rider approached, the flag in his hand still raised. His face was drawn, his eyes almost void of emotion. Almost, except for a flash of fear when Froi retrieved his sword and stepped forward to press the point of the blade against Dorcas's cheek.

"A message, sir," Dorcas said to Gargarin. "From Lord Bestiano."

"Oh, a lord now," Gargarin said.

"A message, sir," Dorcas repeated. Dorcas never steered far from the script he was given to follow.

"Yes, we heard you the first time, idiot," Froi snapped. "Do you want to know why they've sent you, Dorcas? Because they know I can easily kill you and they don't care if you live or you die."

Dorcas kept his attention on Gargarin, despite the pressure of the blade on his face.

"If you would please surrender, Sir Gargarin. Only you. We have no need for the others."

"Just like that?" Froi scoffed. "You ride over here and politely ask Gargarin to follow you? And he's going to obey Bestiano's wishes. Just like that?"

Dorcas swallowed this time. "No," he said, clearing his throat. "Our Nebian friends are approaching. Four hundred men. They should arrive soon. If Gargarin of Abroi chooses not to surrender before their arrival, the captain of the Nebian army will be forced into the uncomfortable position of . . . having to do something drastic and—"

Froi removed his sword and shook his head, turning away. "Let's go," he called out to the others. "He's too useless to be a threat, and he'll be too easy a kill. See, Dorcas, you're not even worth my time to kill."

"And your brother dies."

Froi froze. Gargarin made a sound, stumbling toward the rider. Dorcas pointed to a now-solitary man standing at the place where the flag was pitched into the ice. Although it was too far to see Arjuro's face, Froi knew it was him. Dorcas raised his flag and waved it, and in the far distance beyond Arjuro, where the group of riders sat astride their horses, an arrow was lobbed into the air and landed within an inch of where Arjuro stood. Gargarin may have been out of attacking distance, but Arjuro wasn't.

"Regardless of what you do to me, sir," Dorcas continued, "your brother will die if you choose not to surrender. The moment the army arrives, every soldier has been instructed to fire a bolt. Unless you surrender. No one wants the priestling hurt, sir, but an order is an order. You can avoid the death of your friends here, but if you choose not to surrender, we cannot protect them."

Dorcas turned his horse and galloped toward his men, leaving Froi and Gargarin in stunned silence. When Dorcas rode past Arjuro, Froi saw a movement from the priestling and he imagined he spat at the guard.

Gargarin began to limp toward his brother, but Froi grabbed him.

"They might not be able to shoot from where they stand, but we don't take chances."

Gargarin wasn't listening. He shrugged free and continued to walk. Froi dragged him back again.

"Gargarin, I must suggest that we continue," Perabo pleaded. "They want you so that Bestiano has no one stopping him from taking the princess and her child back to the palace. If that happens to Charyn . . . then Tariq of Lascow died in vain."

Gargarin's eyes were still fixed on Arjuro as if he could see into his eyes. And for the longest time, no one spoke. All around them, the cracking and rumbling of the thawing ice rang in their ears, and Froi knew that nature would be crueler than an approaching army.

"Gargarin," Perabo prompted softly.

"No," Gargarin said. "I won't walk away from my brother."

"You're making a mistake," Perabo insisted. "You're placing your emotions before this kingdom."

"This kingdom has taken my lifeblood!" Gargarin shouted. "I've given it everything! What else does it want from me?"

Perabo turned to Lirah.

"Talk to him, Miss Lirah. Is this what you want for him?"

"What I want for him is peace," she said, her voice low. "And if he walks away from his brother, he will never find it."

"His brother is a dead man standing," Perabo said. "You'll lose them both. This kingdom will lose them both."

Gargarin's stare had not strayed from where Arjuro stood, and Froi knew Gargarin would not turn his back on his brother. Not after Arjuro had spent ten years in a Lumateran dungeon for him.

"Give me your robe," Froi ordered. "And your staff."

Gargarin turned to him questioningly.

"The moment I give the signal, you get on the horse and you ride and you don't stop riding," Froi said, walking behind Beast, who would shield him from the eyes of the riders. He removed his own cloak and cap.

"Perabo, you stay, and when all hell breaks loose, you wait for Arjuro and then you follow them and don't stop until you're off the lake."

"What are you planning, Froi?" Lirah demanded to know.

"Give me your robe, Gargarin," he said again. "You want me to make decisions, then trust me."

"Why would I trade one misery for another?" Gargarin demanded, but Froi heard sorrow in his voice.

"Because the misery standing behind this horse has a better chance of surviving than Arjuro."

"No," Lirah said. "*No!*"

"These are the options," Froi said. "Gargarin walks to his

death. Arjuro is torn to pieces by four hundred flying arrows. Or else we all live and later speak about looking on the side of wonder!"

"Take Froi's offer, Gargarin," Perabo begged. "Let's fight them on our terms."

Still Gargarin refused to move.

"Don't you trust me?" Froi asked.

Gargarin stared at him over Beast's head and then wordlessly stepped behind the horse, hidden from the riders. He removed his robe with trembling hands and placed it around Froi, covering his head with the hood.

"Remember," Froi said, taking the staff, "don't let them suspect anything. Let them think we're all watching Gargarin walk away. Don't get on your horse until I give the signal."

Froi handed his longbow to Perabo and heard the protests.

"All I need is your ax," he told the keeper of the cave.

He didn't dare look at Lirah. He didn't wait for good-byes or arguing. Instead, he began to limp toward Arjuro. From this distance, Dorcas and the riders would not suspect, but Froi could not be so certain once he reached midway. All he prayed for was that the riders didn't move within striking distance before he reached Arjuro.

The ax felt heavy on his shoulder, and somehow he was back on Lord August's farm and they were walking home from felling timber. He remembered that day well because he was happy, because Lord August had put his arm around both Froi and the boys. "My lads did well today," he had said, and as Froi crossed this icy tomb, it occurred to him that he might never see Lord August and Lady Abian again. That he had never told them the truth. Finn and Isaboe had taught him to love, but the village of Sayles had taught him to belong.

Let this work, he begged silently. *Let this work.* Because he wanted to see all their faces again.

When he reached Arjuro, his teeth were chattering through blue lips as the wind tore through the priestling's robe. Arjuro was muttering a prayer to the gods, his eyes watering from the cruel wind.

Before Arjuro could speak a word in surprise, Froi embraced him.

Over Arjuro's shoulder, he saw Dorcas and the riders already advancing toward them.

"Will you trust me and do as I say?" Froi asked.

"What could you possibly say that would have me leave you here alone?" Arjuro asked, his voice broken.

"Your brother is waiting for you, Arjuro. I can protect myself, but I can't protect you at the same time." Froi watched as the riders gained ground on horseback. He was running out of time.

"So will you trust me and do as I say?" he asked again.

Arjuro's arms tightened a moment and then let go. His eyes met Froi's. And then Arjuro nodded.

"Go!"

Arjuro ran and within seconds the first of the arrows flew past Froi. He swung around to signal Gargarin and Lirah to mount their horse, and then he began hacking relentlessly at the ice with his ax. When the surface broke beneath him, it sounded like the demons of young Froi's dreams, devouring the earth and swallowing him whole. He heard the roar of men's voices, and he stumbled as the world tilted and he plunged through the ice, escaping the sharp tip of an enemy's weapon, but finding himself falling into a freezing abyss.

Froi tried to make his way to the surface, but solid ice surrounded him and he struggled to break free of the tomb he had created for himself. No matter how hard he tried, he could not find an opening that would let him out. He felt a sob rise in him from pure fear and panic, and he pounded a clenched fist at the ice, his knuckles burning and his chest tightening. He thought he heard words from far away say, "Retreat! Retreat!" and his only comfort was that it meant Bestiano's men were turning back and Gargarin and Lirah and Arjuro would be safe. He couldn't think, and he couldn't breathe; his head, his chest, everything felt as if it would explode, and he tried to count, tried to remember anything. . . . Think of her name. Think . . . nothing . . . someone's there . . . name . . . name . . . you know his name . . .

Don't close your eyes, Froi.

Tariq!

How can you find her with your eyes closed, Froi?

Reginita.

But he had nothing left inside him to keep him awake, and he was scared and he wanted to be with them because Tariq and the *reginita* were safe and they'd take care of him.

Go back, Froi. Go back.

And suddenly he was someplace else . . . on the streets of the Sarnak capital . . . and he could see himself tossing and turning on his bed of lice and hay in that sewer he shared with the rats, awoken by a voice . . . how could he have forgotten that voice . . . the voice . . . it sang . . . *Sprie.* One word promised him a life he hadn't dared to imagine, and so he traveled from the Sarnak capital to the town of Sprie, where he stole a ring from Evanjalin of the Monts . . . *she and me? We're the same . . . we live . . . we do anything to make that happen . . . that's the difference between us and the others. . . .*

He opened his eyes and saw a face.

Tariq!

Hurry, Froi. Those from the lake of the dead are coming for your spirit.

Suddenly the ice broke above him and Froi swam up toward the blinding light. Later, he couldn't say how he climbed out of that hole, but Beast was there, pounding at the ice with his hoof, his teeth pulling at the shirt on Froi's back until he was lying on the ice, Beast down beside him, the hot air of his breath warming Froi's face. And with the last strength he had left in his numb body, Froi crawled onto the saddle, and then they were flying across that fractured lake. A Serker lad on his Serker horse.

And as the world behind them caved in, Froi wrote his bond. The one to live by. The one that would keep him on Beast as they raced to a place where the earth beneath their feet was solid. He wrote his bond with a name. And then another and another and another. Of every person he loved and would be condemned to never see again if he let go. He didn't know how long it took, but the list was long and it kept him warm and clinging to life.

And later, in his half-conscious state, he felt hands grab him and drag him from the horse, but he needed to burrow, he needed to keep warm, and he heard the sobs and his clothes were ripped from him and he was numb again and Tariq was there once more and so was the *reginita*'s voice, telling him to stay away.

She's not here, Froi! She needs you there.

He thought he heard Arjuro's voice. "Keep him warm — his body is letting go," and then Froi felt the heat as they held on to him tight, until he drifted off to a sleep where he could find her, where he could hold her in his arms and feel the roundness of her belly between them.

"We'll be his cocoon," she said, *her voice always cold, but her words flaming with the heat of emotion, "and he'll never doubt that he was loved, regardless of everything."*

CHAPTER 24

Finnikin spent the day with Isaboe and Jasmina, visiting the Flatlands. There had been much change these past months, with Beatriss's people moving to Fenton and the priest-king opening a shrine house in her old village of Sennington. Who would have believed contentment could come to the area after so much upheaval?

"August and Abian are meeting us in Sennington for supper with blessed Barakah," Isaboe said to Beatriss. "Why don't you join us?"

Beatriss's smile was bittersweet.

"Trevanion's home tonight and Vestie does love our nights together, so perhaps another time."

Finnikin could see his father from the window. "There are a lot of hardworking lads out there, Beatriss," he said, watching Perri and Trevanion working with the Fenton lot in the fields. The younger lads were full of vigor.

Beatriss peered over his shoulder. "Well, the fact is that the lads do work hard, but not as much as when Trevanion's home. Then every young man seems to break their back for his attention. As though he's recruiting for the Guard."

"And how is life with my father?" he teased.

"What I've seen of him?" she said, returning to fuss over Isaboe with currant cake. Everyone in the Flatlands felt a great need to feed his wife today. *For the baby,* they'd whispered to him.

"Your father instructs the Guard, and they do what he says," Beatriss said. "He instructs Vestie, and she wants an explanation of the why and the why not. They love each other dearly, but he's not used to having to explain his instructions."

Finnikin laughed. "My father was never good at the why and the why not."

"And how is Vestie faring?" Isaboe asked. Finnikin could see Beatriss's daughter carrying Jasmina on her back around the fields, always staying close to Trevanion.

Beatriss grimaced. "I can't lie. She asks at every single opportunity if she can go to Lucian's mountain and down that valley. I asked her the other day if it was Tesadora she missed and she said . . ."

Beatriss hesitated.

"What?" Isaboe asked.

"She said, 'I miss them both. I miss her, and I miss my friend Kintana.'"

Soon after, Trevanion entered the kitchen with Vestie and Jasmina, to find some string to mark out the rose garden he had promised to plant with the little girls in remembrance of Lord Selric's daughters who once lived there.

"I thought you were on leave, Trevanion," Isaboe said. "You're supposed to rest."

"There's too much work to be done," he said, reaching over Beatriss's shoulder for a slice of cake. "Some wives buy trinkets and cloth. Mine buys a village."

Beatriss laughed. She looked tired from the responsibility, but happy, and Finnikin knew that she would enjoy a reprieve these next few days with Trevanion home. By the entrance, Perri hovered. He was more agitated since they had arrived back from Charyn. No, perhaps not agitated, but withdrawn. Today he was Jasmina's guard, and he watched her like a hawk. Fenton was a beehive of activity, with villagers coming and going, and the guard was at times overly cautious.

Beatriss's bailiff came to the door soon after, and she disappeared for a while, to sort out an issue with one of the cottagers, while Trevanion took the two little girls with him to plant the rose garden.

"Come and sit, Perri," Isaboe said when it was just the three of them left in the room. She had a strange relationship with Trevanion's second-in-charge. In those months they were all together in exile, Perri had doubted her the most, but once she had proven her worth, he was steadfast in his allegiance to her. She had once told Finnikin that no guard made her feel safer. But perhaps the situation between Tesadora and Isaboe had altered things between them both.

"You want to speak to me," she said. It was a statement rather than a question.

"What makes you think that, Your Majesty?" Perri asked quietly.

"You hover whenever you want to speak to me, and then you wait until everyone is gone and you speak. Even if it's about the weather. Or your concern about Jasmina's safety. Or about an idea you have to include the Forest Dwellers in the Flatland villages' harvesttime."

Perri didn't respond.

"Am I not right?" she asked.

There was a ghost of a smile on Perri's face. "You're always right, my queen."

"See there," Isaboe said, looking at Finnikin and pointing at Perri. "There is a clever, clever man."

Perri sat down, but still didn't speak until finally Finnikin stood, knowing there would be no talk today in his presence.

"I'll see what my father's doing," he said with a sigh.

"No. Stay, Finn," Perri said.

Finnikin was glad to, and he caught the quick flash of concern in Isaboe's eyes.

Perri swallowed hard. "I feel as if I'm breaking a confidence here, but she never quite confided in me, so perhaps it's my truth I speak of today as well."

Finnikin somehow knew Perri was speaking of Tesadora.

"We were enemies all our young lives . . . Tesadora and I," Perri said, "and then when we reached fifteen . . . well, you can imagine. We still hated each other and hardly ever exchanged a word, but I'd know where to find her in the forest and she'd know what I was there for." He shook his head. "It was madness, and regardless of what we got up to out there among that bracken, we were both filled with hate for each other and everyone else in this kingdom. Until the day I came across Trevanion. You were newly born, Finn, and your father had lost your mother, Bartolina. And he put all his trust in me." Perri looked away. "Me." He shook his head. "You both do it now with the little princess, and sometimes I want to warn you that there's something base inside of me. How could you trust me with that precious creature?"

"You never need ask that, Perri," Isaboe said, reaching out to take his hand. He moved it away. Perri wasn't much for touching and emotions.

"Were you still with Tesadora when my father made Trevanion captain?" Isaboe asked.

Perri nodded. "We were aged twenty at the time. I lived in the barracks with the rest of the Guard, and when I was on leave, I'd ride out to the forest and share her bed. It was nothing more than that, I'd tell myself. Tesadora would say it as well. 'Don't read more into this than what it is.' Through Trevanion and my place in the Guard, I'd been introduced to respectable women, but I was always drawn back to her. We'd do cruel things to each other, but she reminded me of your father, Finn. She knew exactly what I was, but still saw some good. I began to see my worth through both their eyes."

He looked at Isaboe. "I'm breaking an unspoken confidence here, Your Majesty."

"There are many unspokens between you and Tesadora, Perri," she said firmly. "I'd advise you one day to speak them."

He sighed, and for a moment, Finnikin believed Perri wouldn't continue. But they waited.

"Almost nineteen years ago, she was with child."

Finnikin heard the sharp intake of Isaboe's breath.

Perri nodded. "So we played a game of pretense that we lived a normal life. I spent every spare day with Tesadora in the forest. We started planting gardens and building a cottage. She told no one about the babe, of course. At that time, she was estranged from her mother and from every Forest Dweller. They did hate Tesadora for her mixed blood."

"Why estranged from her mother?" Isaboe asked.

He looked up at her, a rueful expression on his face. "Because Tesadora believed Seranonna loved the royal children more than her own half-Charynite bastard. They had a strange relationship, Tesadora and Seranonna, but she still grieves her mother today. That I know."

"And the babe?" Isaboe asked quietly, her hand absently going to her swollen belly.

"I came home to Tesadora one time nearing her ninth month and she told me there was no babe. She had bled and it was gone." He shook his head bitterly. "And I . . . I accused her of killing the child. The only thing that stopped me from harming her was a promise I made to the captain that I would never strike a woman. I felt it so strongly. In my heart she hadn't killed just our babe; she had killed the life I wanted with her. So I made sure I never crossed her path again . . . until six years later."

The days of the unspeakable.

"After the deaths of your family, my queen."

Perri seemed to be in another place. Every Lumateran had his or her own horror-filled memory of that time.

"Regardless of what I thought Tesadora had done, I couldn't bear the idea of watching her burn like her mother, so I traveled out to the forest and found her in a hiding place. One known only to us. She had gone searching for any survivors and found the helpless novices of Sagrami."

Perri had hidden them across the kingdom and close to the Sendecane border, the first of many to keep them safe.

"We spent another ten years apart during the curse, and for all that time, I still believed she had done something to that babe. That she didn't want a child with my savage blood. But when we all returned here with Froi, the strangest thought occurred to me. It was during those times I'd take Froi out to the Forest Dwellers. His bond with Tesadora was strong, in a strange way. He had the same shaped eyes. More than anything, I . . . I felt something strong toward him and I knew she felt it as well and I started to believe . . ."

"That he was yours?" Finnikin asked.

Perri nodded. "Strange, but yes. I convinced myself that all those years ago, she had given birth to a child and perhaps passed it on to a traveler. Eighteen years ago in this kingdom, it wasn't rare for the forest to be a path for foreigners. I didn't know what to think with Froi, except I honestly believed he was ours."

"Until we interrogated Rafuel of Sebastabol in the spring?" Finnikin asked.

Perri nodded. "When he told the story of their day of weeping."

There was bitterness and self-disgust in his expression.

"Tesadora had spoken the truth. And, of course, meeting Gargarin of Abroi and Lirah of Serker confirmed that Froi didn't belong to us."

"And when you finally spoke of it, what did she say?" Isaboe asked.

He shook his head with regret. "We never spoke of it. Now all I feel is shame and confusion. She would have been . . . broken after the loss, and I broke her even more. At the time she lost the child, she had no one. I try hard not to speak ill of the Forest Dwellers. Most of them are dead, and I'll never forget the way they died. It took me a long while to get the stench of burnt flesh out of my head. But they treated her poorly all her life. Even before we were at war with Charyn, they hated the idea of tainted blood. Her mother made no apology about the foreigner she had taken as a lover. The way the Forest Dwellers saw it, Tesadora didn't belong to them. . . . She still feels it, and it pains me."

He looked up at Isaboe. "I want her to be happy . . . yet I've never known her to be so confused and sad . . . and euphoric at the same time as she is now. And it's all about you . . . and the Other."

Isaboe stiffened. "You met her?" she asked. "Quintana of Charyn?"

He nodded.

"And?"

Perri retrieved an envelope from his pocket.

"It's for the priest-king . . . from Tesadora. It speaks of strange things."

Isaboe stared at it and then retrieved an envelope from her pocket.

"It's the letter Finnikin gave me from Froi to the priest-king. I'm presuming no less strange."

Perri handed his letter to Isaboe, and she placed the two together.

"Describe it," she said quietly. "You feel it as well. Whatever Tesadora feels for the girl, you do as well."

Perri looked away.

"I won't judge you," Isaboe said.

He grimaced. "It's a recognition of—I can't explain. It's as if I know her, not in the realness of our world, but in here," he said, pointing to his chest. "The way I believed I knew Froi."

Isaboe stared at the letters, her fingers tracing the writing on both envelopes.

She looked up, and Finnikin saw tears in her eyes. He knew she missed both Froi and Tesadora.

"I get a sense that the priest-king knows more than he's let on," she said. "It may be quite a supper we have tonight."

It was late in the night when Isaboe retrieved the two letters and handed them to the priest-king. They had enjoyed a simple meal with Abian and August, and Finnikin was grateful for their presence in his family's life. With them, he and Isaboe weren't the consort or queen. They were the children of people once loved by these friends. Tonight there had been talk of the dead king and queen that brought a laugh, instead of tears.

"We should go," Abian said, understanding that the letters meant palace business.

"No," Isaboe said. "Stay. This concerns Froi . . . and Froi concerns you."

The priest-king spent some time reading the letters while Jasmina slept in Abian's arms and Perri and August found more candles to light the room.

Finnikin took the time to look around the house that once belonged to Beatriss. It was as if it was always meant to be a house of learning. Once or twice he had attended a lecture here with Sir Topher on rhetoric and dialectics. When Celie of the Flatlands was home weeks ago, Finnikin had accompanied her to an Osterian godling's lecture on philosophy. But they had a long way to go in their plan to create lessons for the young. Their greatest obstacle was convincing Lumaterans of the worth of their children learning when they believed they were better put to use on the farm or in the quarry on the Rock. Neither Finnikin nor Isaboe wanted the school filled only with the children of nobility. It was not what they wanted for Jasmina.

Back in the solar, the priest-king spread out the parchments on the bench. Finnikin could see the markings copied from Quintana of Charyn's neck and those from Froi's skull. The words differed, but the lettering style was similar. They belonged together in a way that the lettering on Phaedra and the Charyn princess's nape didn't.

"Here are the similarities in Tesadora's account and Froi's," the priest-king finally said. "A woman traveling the same road as Froi tells him that the spirit of her half-dead child lives within him. Her husband makes mention that she bled a child on the day of their weeping."

He pointed to Tesadora's letter. "A woman in our valley is suffering melancholy because her connection with a young girl who traveled to the valley has been severed. We assume the girl was Quintana of Charyn. The woman, according to her husband, bled a child on the day of weeping."

He looked at Perri. "Tesadora is told by Quintana of Charyn that the half-dead spirit of Tesadora's child lives within her. Tesadora bled a child on the day of their weeping."

Abian's reaction was much the same as Isaboe's. A sorrow for Tesadora beyond words.

"Are they possessed?" Abian asked when she was composed. "Tesadora and the women?"

The priest-king shook his head. "I need to look into this more, but no. I don't think so. And it's not just the women. It's the men as well. Perri?"

Perri hesitated and then nodded.

"But what do these shared experiences have to do with Froi's lettering and the Charyn princess?" Finnikin asked.

"Well, you gave me the letters just after supper, Finnikin," the priest-king said, his eyes twinkling with laughter. "Do you expect me to have worked it out that fast?"

Finnikin laughed with him. "Yes, actually I do."

"Did you know?" Isaboe asked the priest-king quietly.

The old man looked up at her, and Finnikin saw the tremble in his shoulders. Finnikin wasn't quite sure what Isaboe was asking, but the priest-king seemed to realize exactly what it was.

"Why do you ask?" the priest-king said.

"Because of the markings on Froi's back that only the gifted such as you can see. Different from the visible ones on his skull."

The priest-king smiled. "Well, let's not pretend that you don't have a gift, Your Majesty. Did *you* know?" he asked.

Isaboe looked at Finnikin and shook her head. "Froi was naked that time in Sorel when he was to be sold as a slave. I saw nothing written on his back."

"Nothing at all?" the priest-king asked.

"I knew where to find him," Isaboe said. "I always seemed to know where to find Froi, but never realized I was looking. So he was a beacon of some sort. But I don't have the power of this second sight."

They waited for the priest-king to speak.

"And from the very moment you met him, you began to teach him," she said, after he remained silent. "Even in exile. As if you were preparing him for something."

"I never saw the writing," the priest-king said. "He worked my garden enough times without a shirt on his back, but I saw nothing. I'm not as powerful as the priestling Arjuro. But I knew there was something about Froi."

The priest-king's smile was gentle. "Sometimes . . . sometimes, I can see the essence of the gods in another. Rich or poor. Man or woman. Lumateran or Charynite. I've seen yours, Isaboe. Its power matched by only a few. That doesn't make you or me or Froi better or worse than others. It just means the gods have marked us for a journey, regardless of whether we want to take it."

"Who else?" Finnikin asked. "Who else is marked by the gods?" He prayed it wasn't his daughter. He didn't want Jasmina to walk a path without them. He could see Isaboe's hand pressed against her belly.

"Who?" Isaboe asked, but the priest-king shook his head.

"If I tell you that, my queen, you'll do all you can to alter their path. The gods don't like that."

The priest-king sighed, tapping at the pages before him. "But we're not here to discuss the essence of the gods. We're here to talk about spirits."

"Wonderful," August muttered. "I was just getting to understand all the essence talk."

"We're born with a spirit," the priest-king said. "It exists before we are shaped by time and place and wealth or poverty or circumstance. The lives we live tame and shape our spirits."

Finnikin watched the various expressions around the room. He was glad to see that most were as confused as he was.

"I think it's quite clear that Froi and the Charyn princess have acquired more than one spirit," the priest-king said.

He was pensive for some time. "I remember long ago when I was a child, my *pardu* died. We were very close. Around that time, my sister's child was born, and I could have sworn I sensed the spirit of my grandfather in that babe. Soon after, my *pardu*'s spirit left the boy. Once the departed rest in peace, most of their spirit settles with them. But they do leave some of it behind and it becomes part of another's traits."

"So Froi and the Charyn princess . . ."

"Unfortunately for now are a mystery." The priest-king smiled. "But what this enemy girl has to offer Froi and Tesadora and Perri is a thing of beauty rather than malice, my queen."

"Then why do I want to kill her?" she said coldly.

"Because you're human and she shares the blood of a hateful man who tried to destroy our lives," Abian said.

The priest-king took Isaboe's hand.

"This will take me time. I don't recognize the strange lettering on Froi's scalp and Quintana's nape. It's not of the ancients. Whoever, or whatever, placed it there may have cursed Charyn. It might not be ours to solve, but it threads through the lives of those in Lumatere just as much."

"Then how do we solve it?" Finnikin asked.

"I'll see what we can find in our library, but our neighbors, the Belegonians and Osterians, are the greatest pilferers of the sacred mysteries from all over this land."

"Perhaps Celie can—" Finnikin felt a kick under the table

from Isaboe and remembered August and Abian's presence "—ask a few questions. She's so very good at that."

August looked at him suspiciously. "I don't want my daughter embroiled in this."

Finnikin nodded. "Yes, yes. Women asking questions never ends well."

He felt another kick. It was best to keep his mouth shut now.

The priest-king studied Froi's note, and then he smiled.

"Beautiful penmanship. And who would have thought he could express himself so eloquently? What a waste that all he wants to do is be a soldier and a farmer."

He looked at Perri and August. "No offense."

"None taken . . . I think. Is it true that the . . . father is clever?" August stumbled on the words.

"Very," Finnikin said, nodding, "and the uncle is apparently a gods' touched genius. And the mother . . ."

"Have you gone on about the mother's beauty as well?" Isaboe asked Perri.

Perri pulled up the sleeve of his shirt and displayed a bruise. "Twice. Tesadora's fist."

"That would be interesting." Abian smiled at the thought. "Pitting the mother and Tesadora up against each other. Placing them in a room and seeing them fight it out."

"Mercy," Finnikin said.

"Yes, I'd pay all the gold in the land to see that," Perri agreed. All the men agreed with gusto. Isaboe and Abian exchanged a look, and Finnikin saw a gleam of cynical humor in their eyes.

"Too predictable," Isaboe said. "You men are too predictable."

CHAPTER 25

We'll be his cocoon, and he'll never doubt that he was loved, regardless of everything."

Froi woke lying between Lirah and Gargarin and wondered if he had heard those words out loud or in his dreams.

Arjuro crouched beside them and handed Froi a cup of something hot. He took a sip and tasted the bitter herbs, made a face, but took another sip. Arjuro held the back of his hand to Froi's brow.

"You've got your color back, at least."

"Why? Where did it go?" Froi joked, because Arjuro looked so serious.

"It went to that place you seem drawn to," Arjuro said. "The dead are greedy for you!"

Arjuro's eyes blazed with fury. Gargarin sat up, and Arjuro handed him a brew.

"I'll say this once, and if you don't honor my wishes, I'll find a way of making your lives unpleasant," Arjuro said to them all. "You never attempt to sacrifice your life for me again. No matter what they threaten me with, you move forward. You don't look back!"

Gargarin's response was a slurp. He passed the brew to Lirah, who was staring at Froi.

"I dreamed you died."

"I'm here, Lirah."

"Those at the lake of the half dead will never let me be," she said.

Lirah would always be haunted by her attempt to end her life and Quintana's, all those years ago.

"They trapped me in my dreams and I saw you there."

"I'm here, Lirah," he repeated. "Being threatened by Arjuro, who obviously woke up in a bad mood."

Arjuro scowled. Froi smiled. Perhaps he was just relieved to be back with them.

"I wasn't actually sacrificing myself," Froi explained. "I came up with a plan and the plan went accordingly. Why would I sacrifice myself for any of you?"

"It wasn't a plan, though," Gargarin said, suddenly angry at Froi. "You didn't talk it over with us. You just said, 'Give me your cloak and your staff,' and then you started walking away."

"You would have talked me out of it," Froi said.

"How do you know that?"

"I would have," Lirah said. "I would have said, 'What a stupid idea. You're sacrificing yourself for Arjuro.'"

She handed the brew back to Arjuro. "Despite the fact that he lost ten years of his life searching for you, trapped in that hellhole Lumatere," she added.

Froi couldn't help thinking how much smarter Lirah was than the rest of them. Everyone else would have danced around the truth for too long a time. Lirah was able to slap them in the face with it until it could be avoided no longer.

Arjuro was even more furious.

"Who told you that?" he demanded of Gargarin.

"The Lumaterans."

"What?"

"Yes, yes. You've missed out on some great excitement," Gargarin said, waving him off as if it was old news.

"The ginger king tried to kill Froi," Lirah said.

Arjuro seemed to think they were playing with him and started to stalk away in disgust, but Gargarin gripped his robe and pulled Arjuro toward him.

"We're even, brother," Gargarin said, their faces so close and alike.

Arjuro grimaced with anguish.

"We'll never be even," Arjuro said. "You didn't plan Lumatere's curse, so my imprisonment was not your doing. But on the night of the oracle's death, I planned exactly what I'd do to you and it became your prison for all those years. So we will never be even."

And Froi heard the self-hatred in Arjuro's voice, but Gargarin didn't let go. Instead he held a hand to Arjuro's face.

"I want my brother back. So I say we are even."

Arjuro didn't speak, and it was too strange for them all.

"Tell him about looking at the side of wonder," Froi said to Gargarin.

Gargarin seemed irritated. "Am I going to have to do that again and again?"

"Already he's sick of it," Lirah muttered.

Froi laughed. They were the maddest people he knew, and he laughed until his side hurt.

"What's the side of wonder?" Arjuro asked, confused. "Why is he laughing like a fool?"

"Because there are two sides of a day, according to Gargarin,"

Froi explained. "The side of despair and the side of wonder. On the side of despair, we're freezing half to death. On the side of wonder, the four of us are together."

The words lay unspoken among them. One was missing.

And all that time, Perabo wordlessly watched them. Froi didn't want to know what the keeper of the caves was thinking.

He slept and woke again, heard Gargarin and Arjuro murmuring beside him. They didn't speak of their time in the dungeons of two rival palaces and they didn't speak of love, either, but it was all there in their voices. The brothers were talkers, after all. They were different from Trevanion and Perri in that way. In his time since Sarnak, Froi had come to learn as much about the power of silence as the power of words.

He slept on and off, but always woke to the sound of their voices.

"Who knows? But there's talk that the street lords are in the valley and that they murdered those lads. . . ."

"The Avanosh uncle? That idiot?"

"You shouldn't have spoken to him that way. You know what De Lancey's like. . . ."

"It's the star of the north, and it's only seen when the land is ready to thaw. . . ."

"I'm telling you. They want me to set up a school in the gods-house, and you have no idea how annoying those *collegiati* are. . . ."

"Did you see his hideous self?"

Froi was wide awake. He knew they were speaking of their father, the man Froi resembled.

Gargarin was silent.

"In his letter, De Lancey said you refused to speak to him," Arjuro said.

"But I saw him," Gargarin said. "I saw that wretched piece

of shit. And I wanted to step outside and look him in the eye and say, 'You don't scare us anymore. You can't hurt us anymore. Because you don't exist to us anymore.'"

Froi sat up and Gargarin's eyes were on him.

"I wanted to say, 'Your face has been taken by another, so I've forgotten the malice in your eyes and the bitterness of your mouth.'"

"Why can't you just kill him?" Lirah said, her voice hard. "It's easy. You wouldn't think twice about killing an enemy. He was your enemy."

"I'd do it for you," Froi said quietly. "I'd do a good job."

If there was contemplation, it was only brief.

"No," Arjuro said. "Let Quintana bring our little one into this world without his spirit being stained by blood on our hands."

"Anyway," Gargarin said, his voice ragged, "I've seen you kill, Froi. You're too quick and clean, and I saw his hideous self close enough to know the truth. That he's dying. Of the same disease that took the stonemason in Paladozza, Arjuro. Do you remember?"

"Oh, yes. Slow and painful. Good. Good."

And all the while, Perabo still watched them.

"Who are you people?" he finally asked. "You're no stranger to them, Lumateran."

Froi stayed silent.

"If we tell you the truth, we'll have to kill you, Perabo," Gargarin said, getting to his feet.

Sometimes . . . sometimes Froi wondered how far Gargarin would go to hide the truth. Was it jest in his voice, or a warning?

"Then answer me this. Is Quintana of Charyn carrying Tariq's child?" Perabo demanded. "Or another's?" His eyes were fixed on Froi.

"Does it matter?" Gargarin asked.

"It does to those of Lascow!" Perabo said.

"Then, we give the people what they want to hear, Perabo," Gargarin said with a sigh. "And if the people want to hear that the child she's carrying belongs to Tariq of Lascow, then we tell them that the babe belongs to Tariq."

Gargarin stood before the man. "What did Tariq always say? Anything for Charyn. Anything for peace."

Perabo was silent.

"So it's your choice. Take us to the Lasconian army or we continue this journey without you, as we have since he"—Gargarin pointed down at Froi—"flew through the air and snatched the future mother of our king from death. No one else did that, Perabo. They planned it, they started it, but they did not see it through, and he did." Gargarin pointed at Froi again, just in case Perabo forgot who "he" was. "So do you travel to the Lasconians and tell them that perhaps Tariq's queen doesn't carry his child? And do they turn their back on saving a king because they believe his mother is a whore? Does the cycle of shit in our lives continue, Perabo? Or do we give Charyn a fighting chance?"

Perabo extinguished the fire with the brew from his mug.

"We don't want to be traveling through the woods in the dark" was all he said.

Froi rode with Lirah that day.

"Tell me again," she said, asking him to replay every conversation that had taken place between Froi and Quintana on their final night together. Lirah believed the answer to Quintana's whereabouts lay in those words. "You're leaving something out."

"Well . . . there are certain things that are . . . private," he mumbled, aware that Gargarin and Arjuro were riding beside them.

"You little beasts," Arjuro said. "I thought it was only the once."

Froi seethed. "Yes, well . . . it's none of your business . . . and it was a very long and stressful night in Paladozza and we woke up quite a few times . . . and one thing led to another."

"What? With the belly in between?" Arjuro continued.

"I'm not going to have this conversation," Froi muttered, trying to take the reins from Lirah so they could ride ahead. She pushed his hands away.

"Then, what did you speak about that night?" she asked.

"Lists. Of people we trusted. Hers was short. Mine wasn't. End of conversation."

The next day, they reached what was known as the little woods of Charyn. There in the middle of the kingdom sat a tiny piece of Lumatere, teasing Froi. It was as if one of the gods had picked up Lumatere's trees and moss and flown it to the neighboring kingdom. Beyond the woods were the three hills of the north that led to the province of Desantos. But north wasn't Perabo's destination for the time being. West of the woods, the Lasconians had taken up residence in a fortress that once belonged to a Serkan lord. They were planning to head south to confront the Nebian army. But from what had taken place at the lake, Froi was certain that the Nebian army would be traveling into these very same woods.

Soon after, Perabo steered his horse off the track and they followed him out of the little woods to a clearing of neglected grazing land. In the distance was a heavily guarded wall that surrounded a castle, round in shape and imposing in height. Whoever had constructed it had been interested in impressing as much as defending, and Gargarin's admiration of the structure was clear. They followed Perabo to the gates, and he waved up to the guards on the battlements. Soon enough, the portcullis was raised and they rode into the outer bailey, where men were practicing swordplay and hitting targets. Froi noticed that their skills weren't of the highest standard, and his heart sank at the idea of this being the army that would defend Quintana against Bestiano and Nebia. The lads' banter stopped when they noticed Froi watching.

Perabo dismounted first and whistled to one of the men, who came to take their horses.

Inside the castle, the keep was bustling with the business of the day. There was a fireplace on both the north and south walls and an impressive water-carrying system. Arjuro nudged Froi and indicated Gargarin with a toss of his head and a roll of his eyes.

"That's where I went wrong," Gargarin muttered.

"What?"

"The well shaft. Look. Accessible at all six levels. Imagine all the to-ing and fro-ing I could have saved the servants in the palace."

"We're about to be attacked, and he's thinking of design," Arjuro said.

But Gargarin wasn't listening. His eyes studied every detail of the castle hungrily.

"It once belonged to the *provincaro* of Serker's cousin as a means of keeping an eye on the north," Perabo said. "He liked his creature comforts."

They followed Perabo up a set of winding steps that circled the entire keep, and Froi counted up to seventy archways that afforded a view of what was taking place down below.

"Don't look down," Perabo warned them when they almost reached the top and the view from the archways became imposing. Froi sensed that Perabo was instructing himself more than the others.

"You obviously haven't been imprisoned on the roof of a castle in the Citavita, Perabo," Lirah said.

"Or hung upside down over a balconette, staring down into the *gravina,* waiting to die," Gargarin added.

"Nothing worse than being chained to the balconette with your head facing down over that abyss," Arjuro joined in, not one to be outdone in the misery stakes.

"Try balancing on a piece of granite between the godshouse and the palace with nothing beneath you but air," Froi said.

Perabo stopped and took a deep breath and looked as if he was going to be sick.

"Don't look down, Perabo," Froi advised.

In a chamber at the top of the keep, they were introduced to Dolyn of Lascow. He was a great-uncle of Tariq on his mother's side and now led the Lasconians.

"How long have you and your men been here, Dolyn?" Gargarin asked, shaking his hand.

"Too long. We first settled in Serker, believing it could be a larger training ground for the army, but the lads were spooked. We're getting restless here and are about to head south."

"Bestiano and the Nebians are on our doorstep," Gargarin said. "Heading north."

Dolyn was disturbed by the news. "Do you think they'll try to take this garrison?"

"I doubt they'll take the chance just yet," Perabo said, having recovered from his dizziness. "I'm thinking that they'll settle an army of that size in one of the valleys among those hills."

"We could follow them," Arjuro said. "They may have a better idea of where Quintana of Charyn is."

Dolyn noticed Arjuro and held out a hand.

"It's an honor to have you here, Priestling. We need all the blessings we can get."

The Lasconian leader beckoned one of the soldiers over.

"Find a chamber for the brothers to share," he said.

Froi watched Gargarin move a fraction so that his shoulder pressed against Lirah. Gargarin's eyes fixed on Dolyn. And then he waited.

"Perhaps two rooms for the brothers," the leader of the Lasconians murmured, not acknowledging Lirah. "The lad can bunk with our young men. They'll be pleased to see a new face."

"He can stay with me," Arjuro said, and it was left at that for the time being. But soon, Perabo took them aside.

"It's best that he bunks down with the lads," he said, referring to Froi. "They'll understand your attachment to each other, but not to him."

Gargarin dismissed him with an irritated hand. "It's not an issue."

"No," Perabo said firmly. "It's there in every unspoken word between you. The way you walk alongside each other. In your silence. You don't see, but it speaks loudly that the Lumateran belongs to you all. Make things simple, Gargarin. In the new Charyn, we do not want complications."

Froi shrugged, but he felt his face redden. He was once able to hide anything from anyone, but his emotions had made him dependent on Gargarin, Lirah, and Arjuro.

"I don't care where I sleep," Froi said. "A bed is a bed."

Judging from the stares when Froi introduced himself to the Lasconian lads, he was going to regret those words.

CHAPTER 26

T he Lasconian lads bunked in the great hall each night after
the supper tables were cleared. In those first days with
them, Froi came to understand that they respected Gargarin and Arjuro, lusted after Lirah, but despised him.

He knew that because they spoke it with their fists. Because
if he rounded a blind corner, he'd feel a blow to his stomach. Or
if he waited in line for whatever scraps were available for supper, his plate became the plate of those who surrounded him.
The Lasconian lads worked in numbers, never on their own. The
leader, named Florik, rarely got his hands dirty. It was what Froi
didn't like about him. In Froi's first encounter with Grij and the
last borns, he had understood that their anger came from the fury
and frustration of not having freed Quintana. With these lads, he
suspected it came from envy and dissatisfaction. There seemed
no group with more to prove than those born a year or two before
the last born. They had come second to Tariq all their lives. Worse
still, the heir had died in exile before these lads could get to know
him and prove their worth. And with Froi, it was personal. He
hadn't just lost Tariq's supposed unborn child; he had befriended

the heir. Perabo had spoken of this to the Lasconians. That despite everything, Tariq's last message had been to the Lumateran, Froi of the Flatlands. The heir had written part of Froi's name in his own blood on the cold stone as he lay dying.

Regardless of their treatment, Froi silently pledged his bond to Tariq. He would endure anything from the Lasconians and never raise his fists against Tariq's people. That wasn't to say that Froi's fists weren't clenched the whole day long in fury, or that he was to do more counting to control his temper than he ever had. Even when he woke with a sack pressed over his face, threats in his ears, and the humiliation of untangling himself from the thick cloth, only to find them gone, Froi kept his bond. He missed Finn and Lucian. He missed Grij and Olivier. No, never Olivier. Not the traitor.

So he spent his days on the wall-walk, searching the trees that lined the little woods. Each day, he recorded the facts with precision, and when he was certain of movement in the woods, he called for Perabo.

"There," he said. "See that rustle of shrubs? It means the army Dorcas spoke of is now passing through. They're heading north. There," he said, pointing to one of the trees, "someone's watching us from up in the branches. More than one, but they take turns. They know we're here, but they don't seem interested in doing anything about it for the time being."

Perabo nodded. "Good. I'll let the others know."

"Perhaps I can share a word with Gargarin, Perabo."

The keeper of the caves waved Froi off and walked away, and the moment Perabo disappeared down the steps of the wall, Florik and two of his companions gripped Froi by the arms.

"Perabo, perhaps I can share a word with Gargarin," Florik mimicked. "You're a lord, aren't you, with your fancy talk?"

Froi marveled bitterly at how strange life was. After being
told all his young life that he was nothing but street filth, here he
was, taunted for the way he spoke.

He struggled and pulled free. He didn't want to lose control.
Tariq was the first person ever to show kindness to Quintana. He
saved her life, and Froi would never betray the memory of him.

"You think you're better than us," Florik sneered. "Just
because we live on the mountain and belong to no province or
precious flatland."

"No, Florik, I think I'm better than you because you're stupid
and I'm not. Has nothing to do with provinces and flatlands and
mountains, my friend. It's all about up here," Froi said, pointing to his head. It was a mistake, of course, but Froi knew he'd
make plenty of mistakes in the days to come. He wanted to say
more. That the lads followed Florik not because they believed
him to be a leader, but because they hadn't a thought of their
own. They followed him because of their weakness, not Florik's
strength. But most days, Froi kept quiet and spent his time alone
on watch, despairing at the weakness of this army. These lads
had never seen battle. Tariq's decision to go underground in the
Citavita had kept war away from his people. They had experienced loss from afar. But they had never been forced to defend or
be the sentinels of their kingdom as Lucian of the Monts had. So
it made them lazy and proud of achievements that were small in
comparison to those experienced in greater Charyn or Lumatere.
Trevanion said often that there were some who shone brightly in
a crowd of five, but very few could do so in a group of thousands.
Froi imagined that Florik was one of the bright stars in a small
crowd and somehow he had chosen Froi as the one he needed to
pound into the ground to win. No one else around the Lasconian
tried to compete. Florik, he learned, was betrothed to the prettiest girl on the mountain. And Florik, he learned, was the best

archer on the mountain. And Florik was the mountain's messenger because of his speed. Froi found that out every time Florik's fist caught him in the face, as two of his lackeys held Froi down.

But what he could endure the least was being kept out of the talks held in the great hall between Gargarin and the elders of Lascow during the day. He knew Gargarin was appeasing them and they were working on a treaty that would have a Lascow elder represented among the *provincari*. Since Froi's time in Charyn, he had always been part of the decision making, but here among the Lasconians, his opinion was not required. He especially felt the sting of Arjuro and Gargarin spending all their free time together, leaving him to his own devices. From the entrance of the great hall that day, Froi could see the two brothers surrounded by the Lasconians and answering questions thrown at them from all corners of the room.

"Back outside," a guard ordered when Froi tried to step inside the hall.

"I'm with Gargarin and Arjuro of Abroi."

"You will be told what you need to be told. Run along."

He went to find Lirah, who was at a desk in the room she shared with Gargarin. The chronicles Perabo had given her from Serker were spread before her.

"They wouldn't let me in," he said, furious, sitting on the corner of her desk. "I couldn't even step inside to listen."

"Yes, well, try being me," she said, not looking up. Pushing the chronicles aside, she reached for her own journal. "I need you to go through that conversation you had with Quintana about whom she trusted."

Froi was sick and tired of Lirah's questions. When he didn't speak, she looked up, her eyes narrowing. "What's happened to your face?" she asked, reaching out a hand. Froi pushed it away.

"It's nothing," he muttered.

"No, it's not."

"Enough, Lirah," he said, irritated. "It's nothing."

She stood up. "Well, I'm going down to the bailey to have a word with this 'nothing.'"

Froi stared at her, horrified. "Lirah, are you insane? You'll ruin my life."

"I ruined it long ago," she said. "Come on. Take me to him. Point him out."

Froi responded with a stony silence, and she sighed, pointing to a stool beside her desk. "Sit. We can't spend all our time here idle. Tell me everything you spoke to Quintana about."

"Lirah, how many times do I have to repeat myself?" he shouted with frustration at her. At everyone.

"As many times as it takes us to work out where she is, Froi! Do you think you're going to discover the truth in a crowded room with a bunch of men who will spend days quibbling about what your son should be named?"

Froi froze. He saw her regret, and she looked back down.

He gritted his teeth with frustration. "This is what Quintana spoke about. She trusts me, you, Gargarin, and Arjuro. Remember how I said that yesterday and the day before and the day before that? You should find something better to do with your time, Lirah."

This time when she looked up, her eyes were fierce. "Well, let me see, Froi. I could walk down to the barracks and hear one of the lads point out that 'she was the king's whore,'" Lirah said, feigning a whisper. "Or I could walk through the crowd you're so desperate to be part of and have one of the elders order me to his room because, 'If Gargarin of Abroi is having her, why can't anyone else?' Or perhaps I can sit here and write out a list of all my options of where to live if Quintana is ever returned to the palace with the little king. I'm actually thinking of the soothsayer's cave. No? How about the Crow's Inn near the bridge? I think the landlady took a liking to me."

She didn't speak after that, and it was shame that made him walk out of her chamber.

As he descended the stairs and reached the landing, Gargarin was there with Perabo and Dolyn and another elder, still arguing.

"You know that if any of the *provincaro*'s armies are the first to get to her, they will claim it as a victory for years to come," Dolyn argued. "They will have the greatest favor with the new king. So I say it's my men who return Quintana of Charyn to the palace. No one else."

"We'll speak of this later, Dolyn," Gargarin said. "The safety of Quintana and her child is more important than who will have the greatest favor with the new king in years to come. For now we pray that she's kept herself alive."

CHAPTER 27

I keep my eyes shut, surrounded by fear, and I know what to do. You taught me that time, and I know what you'd say if you were here by my side: "Five seconds, Quintana, just as I taught you" . . . but it's the man with the noose and I forget to be brave. . . . He's here in the cave, Froi, and I'm scared for our lives. . . . Keep shouting your words . . . *"Plunge it into the side"* . . . Don't leave me alone . . . *"from one ear to the other"* . . . I hear you, I hear you, but it's the man with the noose! . . . I'm frightened to death, Froi, he's here for our son. If I can open my eyes I'll tear him to pieces . . . but when I open my eyes, gods! Why so much blood?

The corpse in their cave had lain uncovered for most of the day.

No one had spoken yet. No one could find it within themselves to get close enough to cover the mangled flesh of the intruder. Instead, fussing wordlessly over Florenza gave them all something to do. The intruder had used his fists on her because Florenza had been outside the cave when he snuck up on them. She had fought like a demon trying to stop him from entering, and her pretty face was all bruised, her nose broken.

Jorja rocked her daughter in her arms the whole day, and finally Phaedra heard a sob escape her. It was the first show of emotion since the screaming and crying that had taken place when the man first entered. Ginny began to blubber then, and even Cora's ragged breathing joined in with the rest. While Jorja cried and clutched her daughter, Quintana raised her head. She had spent the day curled up in a ball, her hands tight around her belly.

"You can call her your princess, Jorja," Quintana said quietly. "I'll let you."

It only made Jorja cry even more. But her tears had awakened their cold, strange princess, who crawled on all fours to be beside Jorja and Florenza.

"You tell Florenza that she'll be rewarded one day for trying to save the little king."

Phaedra trembled to see the sorrow in Jorja's eyes.

"And what of your life, Princess? What is the reward for saving the life of the little king's mother?"

Quintana was confused by the question, almost scornful.

"You'd barely get a piece of silver for that, Jorja," she said. "It's better to ask for more in this life."

Phaedra watched Quintana struggle to her feet, her belly so round and ripe.

"Where are you going?" Cora asked. "Lie down, you silly girl." There was a gentleness in her voice that Phaedra hadn't heard before.

"To find Tesadora," the princess said. "She'll know what to do." Quintana held out a hand to Phaedra. "Come, Phaedra, we can't stare at a corpse all night. It's dark now, and no one will see us. We'll take the weapons."

The idea of holding a weapon made Phaedra sick to her stomach. She shook her head, refusing to move.

"Don't go out there, Your Majesty," Jorja said. "Another could be watching."

"Why would you think that?" Ginny asked with a cry. She had been the most hysterical of them all.

"You stay," Cora said quietly to Quintana. "Ginny, come with me."

And then they were gone and Phaedra dared to look at what lay in the center of the room and her eyes found Quintana's and there it was. The savage satisfaction in her eyes, a glimpse of pleased little teeth showing through her lips.

Much later, they heard a sound and Florenza whimpered. Jorja was on her feet in an instant, the spear in her hands. She looked like one of those crazed women who lived by the swamp in Phaedra's province. They all did. They were all filthy and wild, and Phaedra hardly recognized what they had become.

Cora and Ginny entered first and then Tesadora, Japhra, Rafuel. And Lucian.

Tesadora walked to the corpse, and Phaedra saw her flinch at the state of the body. It had taken strike after strike to stop the intruder from coming toward Quintana. Fifteen strikes—Phaedra had counted. Quintana had told her just the other day that counting kept Froi focused, so Phaedra had counted the blows.

The man had known exactly who he was looking for. He had grabbed Quintana by the hair and pulled her to her feet. The viciousness of his movements had awakened something in all of them.

"What will we do with it?" Cora asked.

Lucian stepped forward to study the corpse.

"Bury him," he said.

The women gasped.

"It's not the Charynite way," Phaedra said quietly.

"When you're hiding a corpse, it's the only way."

With Rafuel's help, Lucian lifted the body and carried it away, and when Phaedra saw the blood on the stone, she took the bucket and traveled down to the stream in the dark once, twice, three times. More. She wanted the blood gone. She wanted to scrub it from existence.

The men returned, and Phaedra couldn't bear to look at them. She knew Lucian was watching her. She felt it. If she had imagined herself to be in love with him during those last days on the mountain before Quintana's arrival, now it made her ache. Once, she believed misery was a half-dead kingdom, or living among hostile people. Now she knew it also included loving a man who she'd never have.

She felt Quintana's hand on her shoulder, but Phaedra shrugged it free.

"Just go rest, Your Majesty," she said, unable to look her in the eye. "All this can't be good for the babe."

When Phaedra was a child, she had watched her father and his men drag home the carcass of a boar. They hadn't killed it for sport but because it had raced toward them and attacked a young cousin. Upon seeing the lad's mangled body, her father and his men had leaped off their horses and clubbed the boar in fury. "So it will never do harm again," her father had said. But later she heard him speak to her mother, his voice soft. Telling her that killing the boar required no thought, no logic, just instinct. "In the end, we're just animals ourselves," he said.

Kneeling on the cold, blood-soaked stone, Phaedra had never understood her father's words so much.

Lucian studied the women carefully. He was still unsure of what he had walked into. A last-minute trip down the mountain to see that all was well with his two cousins and Tesadora's girls had led to this. He watched Rafuel crouch before Quintana of Charyn and hold out a hand to her. She gripped his fingers and drew him close.

"Did they tell you what I did?" Quintana said. "I couldn't move."

Rafuel nodded. "Everything will be fine, Your Majesty. As long as you're not hurt, everything will turn out fine. You know what they're whispering about? Armies. Not just one, but many. For you and the little king."

Lucian studied her face. He had never looked at her closely. She was strangely fascinating, all cold suspicion with a quick flash of fear thrown in once in a while. Suddenly her attention was on Lucian.

"I froze," she said again. "Don't tell Froi I did. He'll be disappointed. I promised I'd stay alive, that I'd protect the little king. But it was the hangman from the Citavita. He had put a noose over my head, and when I saw his face, I froze."

Lucian glanced at Rafuel, confused.

"They tried to hang her in the Citavita. Galvin was the hangman."

Lucian remembered the story from Phaedra's excited whispers that time on the mountain. Hearing adventurous stories about Froi saving princesses was one thing, but this was different. There was nothing exhilarating about a girl with a noose around her neck.

"Then, if he was the one who put the noose over your head, it's only right that he lies in the ground," Lucian said. He stole a look at Phaedra, who was scrubbing the ground and refusing to look at him.

"Tell her to stop," he said to Tesadora softly.

Tesadora was pale. Saddened.

"There's no more blood left, Phaedra," Tesadora said, firmly but gently. "He's gone."

"Do you think he recognized Her Majesty from the time she arrived in the valley?" Cora asked Rafuel.

"It doesn't make sense," Jorja said. "Why wait all this time to act?"

"Could he have followed you, Rafuel?" Cora suggested.

Rafuel nodded. "Perhaps. Galvin wanted to prove his worth to Donashe. Let's pray he kept all this to himself with the hope of dragging Her Majesty back to the valley tonight and declaring himself the mightier of us both. Let's hope he didn't tell Gies. All we need is for the fool to come sniffing around searching for his friend."

"Gies!" Ginny cried out. "Does he know I'm here? Why hasn't he come for me?"

Lucian and Rafuel exchanged a look. "All your men have been instructed to keep away," Rafuel lied. Only Harker and Kasabian had been told to keep away. Rafuel had kept to their decision not to tell Gies about the women.

They traveled through the woods in silence. Rafuel stayed ahead for most of their journey. Lucian had a strange feeling that Tesadora and Rafuel were keeping something from him. About the bloodied scene they had come across.

"Doesn't it concern you that the mother of your heir is so savage?" Lucian asked just before they reached Tesadora's camp.

Rafuel stopped. He glanced at Tesadora, who looked away, her expression closed.

"Handy, of course," Lucian mused. "But her actions were savage and not at all princesslike. I'm not condemning, by the way. Just remarking that she's certainly her father's daughter."

"That's condemning," Rafuel bit out. "If you're comparing her to the dead king, in my eyes that's condemning!"

"Leave it," Tesadora said. "Go back and find out if Galvin was working alone, Rafuel."

Rafuel swallowed hard, and Lucian saw the despair in his expression.

The Charynite walked away but then turned back.

"Thank you," he said to Lucian. "You didn't have to be there tonight, Mont, but we were fortunate that you were in the valley all the same." He held out a hand, and Lucian knew to shake it. Rafuel still didn't walk away.

"She recognized him as the hangman, and she froze from the shock of it," he said.

"Regardless, you saw what she did to him," Lucian countered. "As I said, your princess knows how to look after herself."

Rafuel and Tesadora exchanged another look, and then the Charynite was gone.

They reached the camp where Tesadora's girls slept. Tesadora walked Lucian to his horse and waited as he mounted. Usually there were no good-byes, but tonight he sensed that she wanted to speak. He embraced her quickly.

"Lucian," she said quietly as he mounted his horse.

When he looked down, he saw tears in her eyes.

"Quintana of Charyn didn't kill the man," she said. "Phaedra did."

CHAPTER 28

The days were long, and the boredom turned the Lasconian lads restless.

"We'll run a race to see who's fastest," one of Florik's lads said. "No one on the mountain has been able to beat Florik. So we choose him to race you, Lumateran."

"What's the prize?" Froi asked.

The lad who spoke for Florik shrugged. "There's no need for a prize. It's a friendly competition."

"We run this wall," Florik said. "Stand with your back to me, and then we're off. Whoever returns to this point first is hailed the winner."

It seemed too easy and didn't involve a beating, and Froi could think of no better way to relieve the tedium on the watch at this time of the day.

"Count of three," Florik's lad said.

Florik was off at the count of two. Froi bolted in the opposite direction, and the more ground he covered, the more his pride demanded this victory. The only way to win against these lads was to show that their numbers weren't enough to break him.

His was a straight run to begin with, but then parts of the route plunged down steep spiral steps and up again, and Froi took them, two at a time, heart hammering until its beat was a song that spurred him on, forcing him to fly the confines of this prison he had found himself in. He heard them chanting, "Florik! Florik! Florik!" and he shut his ears and kept his pace, stealing a look below to the flicker of movement in the bailey where he suspected the lads and the older men had come from the keep to watch the race. But Froi blocked their voices from his mind and reached the second turret, where he and Florik passed each other. Florik's hand snaked out to hold him back, but Froi swiped at it with such force that he heard a grunt from the Lasconian as he pulled himself free, racing through a section of the walkway concealed from the grounds below. Froi raced through its tunnel, heard the sound of his own breathing, grunting, echoing harshly, then came out into the light again as if he were flying straight into the blue of this early spring sky. He could smell his victory. But suddenly as he rounded the final turret, he tripped over something wedged between the stone of the inner and outer wall. It was a short sword, there to do exactly what it had done, placed on so blind a corner that Froi could never have seen it coming. As he stumbled to his feet, he knew he had lost.

He heard the cheers for Florik as he neared the finishing place. Down below in the bailey, Dolyn and the elders were beckoning Florik to join them. Gargarin signaled, and Froi knew he was being instructed to come down and stand beside the winner.

"No man can outrun a Lasconian," the elder said as Froi reached them. He and Florik stood side by side, Florik's arm raised in victory. "The little king's blood runs from our spring."

Gargarin and Arjuro came to find Froi on watch late that night.

"Are you sulking because he won a race?" Gargarin asked.

Froi didn't respond. He preferred not to see it as sulking.

"When you accomplish something, it should be for no one but yourself," Arjuro said.

"Yes, yes. If we could all be as wise as both of you," Froi said.

"Gods," Arjuro muttered. "I wish I could go back to my youth and slap myself hard across the face for being as snarky as you are at times, Froi."

"You were very annoying," Gargarin said to his brother.

"You equally so."

Arjuro held out his ration of food to Froi, who stared at the dry horse meat.

"If they go anywhere near Beast, I'll kill them all."

"They need to feed themselves," Gargarin said.

"They should have thought of that before they holed themselves up in this place," he hissed.

A shrill cry came from the darkness of the woodlands.

"Something's happening out there," Froi told them. "I've heard cries through the night. Humans and horses. Most of Bestiano's army would have passed by now, heading north, but something in that woodlands is finishing off Nebia's flanks."

"Yes, but who?" Gargarin asked.

They were eerie sounds, eaten up by the space between the little woods and where they stood. By the time the sound reached them, all that remained was a distant echo.

"The sentinel in the tree hasn't been there the whole day, and that could only mean there's been some sort of attack," Froi said. "I can take advantage of it. Venture out and see what's happening."

Gargarin shook his head. "I don't want to take the chance," he said. "Just say they're lying in hiding, waiting for us to do just that. It could be a trap."

"But we can't stay here," Froi said quietly, in case one of the

Lasconians was listening. "Tariq's people are idiots. They picked the worse place to set up camp. We might be protected by these walls, but we're trapped and Bestiano knows we're here. He wants you dead. For all he knows, Quintana is with us, and he wants her. We need to move."

"But where?" Gargarin asked. "We'll only end up wandering aimlessly, searching for her, Froi. We have no idea which direction to turn."

"We've run out of chances, Froi," Arjuro said. "We've escaped death too many times. Gargarin. Me. You. I agree that we stay put. The next time, it could cost us our lives. Maybe Lirah's."

Froi looked away.

"Did you have an argument with her?" Gargarin asked quietly. "Lirah?"

"Why?"

"She doesn't seem herself. She was angry and distant—"

"That is herself," Froi interrupted.

"And hurt."

Fine, now he was also to blame for Lirah's feelings.

"If you really want to know," Froi said, "the matter of not living in the palace has gotten to her. Where will her home be, Gargarin?"

"*What?*" Arjuro asked, hearing it for the first time. "Why wouldn't Lirah live in the palace? She's Quintana's mother in the eyes of Charyn."

Froi waited for Gargarin to explain, but he was silent, so Froi spoke.

"According to the *provincari*, she's part of Charyn's shameful past," he said. "They want Gargarin in the palace but not her, and Gargarin threatened to not take up the position of the little king's regent. They, of course, have a second and even third option."

Arjuro looked at Gargarin.

"There is no other," Arjuro said, fury in his voice. "And since when do the *provincari* make all the decisions? Is that what took place in Sebastabol?"

"Among other things, which is why it would help us to have the Lasconians in our favor," Gargarin said.

Arjuro shook his head incredulously. "Those damned *provincari*. They have no right to tell Lirah she can't live in the palace, and if they even try to take control of the godshouse, I'll curse every single one of them. Hypocrites. Bastards."

"And I think some of the lads and men here have said something to her," Froi said quietly.

Arjuro's eyes met Gargarin's.

"I don't like these people."

"Oh, don't you start, Arjuro!" Gargarin snapped. "First Froi, now you. What do you want me to do? Run a race around this wall and compete with them? They're all we have. If we find Quintana, at least we have the numbers to get her into the palace safely. We need an army. This is the only one we have!"

"And De Lancey promised you no army?"

"Nothing," Gargarin said with frustration. "Do you think we'd be here with this lot if we had Paladozza behind us? De Lancey was all secretive, and then he got on the defensive about both of us always ganging up on him."

"Well, we actually did," Arjuro said with a sigh.

"You know him better than anyone, Arjuro," Froi said. "What could he be hiding?"

Arjuro shrugged. "I don't know him anymore, despite our history. Before the day of weeping, he was a *provincaro*'s indulged son, bored and waiting to take over one day, so we were allowed to be as decadent and wild as we wanted to be. But he's different now, and the De Lancey I got a glimpse of in both the Citavita and Paladozza is the type to have more than one plan up his sleeve."

They heard more cries and shouting come from the little woods, and even the Lasconian lads gathered close by.

"What do you think's going on out there, sir?" one of them asked Gargarin. As if he would know and not Froi.

"Either Bestiano's army is killing one another or we have more visitors."

Froi spent the rest of the night on watch with Perabo. The keeper of the caves had a disturbing way of staring at Froi and Gargarin and Arjuro as if he was going to reveal the truth about who he believed they all were to the Lasconians.

"Nothing good will come of this for you," Perabo said quietly as the sun began to creep above the trees before them.

"What?"

"Regardless of our hope that she carries the first, and that she's somehow safe, nothing good will come of this for you . . . personally . . . and you seem the person to take things personally."

"You don't know me, Perabo."

"I saw it the first time in the caves in the Citavita, and then again the next two times. You want her. Not like other men want to control her, but you want to take care of her. Love her. Make her happy." Perabo shook his head sadly. "And that will not happen. They will never give you an opportunity to be that man. The *provincari* and even Dolyn's people will want a lord, a man of title. Quintana's consort will be our showpiece to the rest of the land. 'See. Look what we got. We might have a history of shame, but look what we managed to snare for our mad princess.'"

"Always pleasant to be on watch with you, Perabo."

But all the keeper's words did was make Froi yearn for her more. He missed Quintana's voice in his ear. Sometimes he tried to recall those early months in the palace with her and the indignant *reginita*. But it wasn't her voice he remembered. It was the clipped, cold voice of his ice princess. The one that could tear layers of skin from him by merely speaking. He had become used to listening to her words and not judging them by her tone.

"I wonder what I'll say to the little king first," she had murmured that last night in Paladozza.

"Maybe you should tell him you love him."

"But what if I don't?" she argued. "I don't know him. How can I love one that I don't know? I'm frightened to see him. I've never seen a little creature. How will I know he's not all wrong?"

"And if he is all wrong, what will you do?" Froi had asked.

She thought for a moment. "I'll hold him tight and tell him that we'll be wrong for this world together."

Perabo shoved Froi out of his memories and pointed. As early light began to stretch across the sky, they could see more movement through the trees of the little woods. During the night, whatever had taken place out there had inched closer to them. Froi heard Perabo's intake of breath. Behind them, the first of the Lasconians were beginning to wake, but for now, only Perabo and Froi waited for whatever lay ahead to unleash itself.

And unleash itself it did. Horsemen appeared out of the little woods before Froi's very eyes. What they lacked in numbers they made up for in strength and speed. If he didn't know better, Froi would have sworn it was Trevanion leading them. No man looked more powerful than his captain on a horse.

"If this is part of the Nebian army, we don't stand a chance," he warned Perabo.

Perabo shouted out a command, and the Lasconian lads on the wall were suddenly awake.

"We're under attack!"

Men scrambled for their weapons, and orders were bellowed from all corners of the bailey. Froi looked back at the battlements of the keep and saw Dolyn's men ready with longbows.

"Take aim!" Perabo shouted.

Froi heard the order repeated over and over again until it reached the keep. He took aim. More and more men climbed up to the wall to stand beside them, watching the force approaching. The horsemen gained ground, their powerful mounts punishing the earth beneath them, riding at a speed beyond reckoning.

"Give the order!" one of the Lasconians shouted.

"Give the order," a voice rang out again, but Perabo waited, and Froi's hand shook to keep the bow so taut. He felt the perspiration trickle down his temple, but he kept his focus on the horsemen in the lead. Not one of the riders had raised a weapon, but their intent was obvious. They were going to enter the fortress regardless of how many soldiers stood on both battlements.

"Perabo! Give the order!" someone shouted.

And then, as the sun illuminated the clearing, Froi saw the truth.

"Stop!" he shouted. "Wait."

"Wait!"

"Wait!"

He heard the order passed back to the battlements.

Yes, the voice inside him hissed. Or perhaps he did shout it aloud, because Perabo stared at him questioningly. Froi's prayers had been answered in more ways than one.

"Who are they?" Perabo asked, as the horsemen reached the gates.

"You mean *what* are they," a lad beside them muttered.

Froi grinned. He looked at where Florik stood and felt a gleeful vengeance in his heart. The Lasconian lads were going to get a beating.

"Turlans."

◆ ◆ ◆

The Turlans rode into the fortress, splattered with blood, every fiber of their being pulsing with battle rage. Ariston gave his men the order to dismount, and they did so just as Gargarin entered the courtyard with Lirah and Arjuro. The Lasconians studied the Turlans, and they were studied in return. Two mountain clans, but different in so many ways.

Ariston and Gargarin embraced, and then the leader of the Turlans turned to Lirah and bowed.

Ariston then held out a hand to Arjuro. Froi remembered the tension between the men when they had first met and was relieved to see it all but gone.

"I thought you vowed you'd never come down that mountain," Gargarin said.

Ariston grimaced. "My woman discovered that I failed to provide a safe place for our Quintana when we had the chance," he said. "I've been banished from the bed until I find the girl."

"Smart woman," Gargarin said. He looked beyond Ariston and his men to where the Lasconians were watching carefully. "Does your wife know?" he added quietly. "About the oracle being a Turlan girl and the mother of the princess?"

Ariston nodded. "I don't keep secrets from my woman. The Lascow lot may claim the future curse breaker as theirs, but we know that babe will belong to Turla on his mother's side."

Froi wanted to say more. That the future king belonged to Abroi. To Serker. To him.

"And your men?" Froi asked. "Do they know the truth? That Quintana belonged to a Turlan woman?"

Ariston shook his head regretfully.

"They follow me regardless of whom the little king belongs to."

One of the Turlan lads approached and lifted Froi off the ground. Froi couldn't help but laugh. He understood these lads, with their grunts and strutting about, more than he did the Lasconians. They reminded him of the Monts.

"My mob took a liking to our Quintana's protector," Ariston said, glancing at Froi.

The Turlan lads were invited to share the great hall with the Lasconians but chose the stables instead. Froi figured he'd endure the smell of horse shit rather than spend another night with Florik and his lot, and joined the Turlans.

Florik and the other Lasconians cautiously retrieved their horses to make more room for the newcomers.

"Why staring?" one of the Turlans demanded of Froi. When they spoke among one another, it was in the Turlan dialect, but with Froi they used a broken Charyn.

"Because they are desperate to compete with you," Froi whispered the lie. "It's all they've spoken about since you arrived."

The Turlan lads exchanged a look.

"Tomorrow," Mort, the leader of the lads said. "We show 'em who stronger mountain men."

Tomorrow was a good day for Froi. The Turlans had an energy that was awe-inspiring, and Froi enjoyed keeping up with them. They wrestled. Jousted. Fought with practice swords. Hit targets. Grunted. Grunted some more. By the end of the day, the Lasconian lads were decimated.

"He's on our team," Florik argued, pointing to Froi just before the second round was to commence. "You Turlans can't just come in and take him!"

Mort placed a sweaty arm around Froi's neck.

"I fight you for 'im." Mort kissed the air in the direction of the Lasconians. Florik bristled. Froi laughed.

"Turla saw him first," one of the Turlans said.

◆ ◆ ◆

Gargarin and Lirah watched from the sidelines alongside Ariston and Dolyn. Froi saw irritation on Gargarin's face, satisfaction on Lirah's.

"What is it with you and these lads?" Gargarin demanded when Froi joined them for no other reason than to show them the ocher markings on his arm that displayed every win. "You turn primitive when you're around them!"

Ariston ruffled Froi's capped head. "We'll take this one back to the mountain. He's one of us, I tell you."

"The Lumaterans won't be happy to hear that," Gargarin said pointedly. "Froi belongs to them. We don't want to be waging a war with them over one of their Flatland sons."

"Flatlander," Dolyn said, impressed. "Doesn't get better than that in Lumatere."

Froi caught Gargarin's eye. He would never know what this man was playing at. Sometimes he believed it was flippancy. Other times he could see a plan brewing in Gargarin's head. Whatever it was, Froi never felt satisfied.

That night, Perabo gathered everyone in the keep. Lasconians and Turlans stood at every level looking down from the archways to where their leaders and Gargarin stood at its center below. Everyone jostled for space, and Froi squeezed himself beside Arjuro on a level close to the floor of the keep, watching Gargarin raise a hand for silence.

"I'll have Ariston speak soon about what takes place beyond the little woods," Gargarin said. "But for now, I want to talk about the return of Quintana of Charyn."

"Our Quintana!" one of the Turlans shouted from above, until they all joined in, and it became a chant that made the hair on Froi's arms stand tall.

Gargarin held up a hand again and there was silence.

"Yes. Our Quintana," he said. "The moment we know where she is, Ariston and his men will bring her and the child home to the Citavita."

There was instant outrage from the Lasconians.

"The heir belongs to us!" one shouted.

"It's our right to place him on the throne," an elder argued. "On behalf of his father, Tariq of Lascow."

Froi saw the quick flicker of Gargarin's eyes toward him, not realizing that Gargarin had known exactly where Froi stood among the crowd of men.

"The Turlans are stronger warriors," Gargarin said. "When it comes to returning Quintana and her child to the palace, there will be no room for failure. We send in our best."

Froi felt Arjuro lean close to him. "My brother's a smart man," he whispered.

Froi had to agree. If the babe was a boy, the Turlans would be remembered for placing the king on the throne for as long as they lived. It was the closest Ariston and the Turlans would get to being respected in Charyn. Although they would never be acknowledged as kin, the little king would be brought up knowing he owed much to these feral mountain people. Perhaps when the boy was older, he would understand who they were to his mother.

Ariston's head was bent in acknowledgment, and Froi could see he was moved by the honor given to his people.

"Perabo," Gargarin called out to where the man was standing at a higher archway opposite Froi's. "You were once the keeper of the caves below the Citavita, and soon you'll be the keeper of the keys to the palace. The constable. You choose your men well."

Perabo was surprised to hear the words. "I've despised the

palace most of my life," he shouted back down at Gargarin. "I've always worked against it."

"You've been working to secure the safety of Tariq and Quintana for many years. For now, Quintana *is* the palace. Would you forsake her your protection?" Gargarin asked.

Perabo shook his head reluctantly.

"What of the *provincari*?" Dolyn of Lascow asked from where he stood. "For too long they've kept both our clans out of province affairs. Will they agree to your decisions, Gargarin?"

"They may make the decisions on how to run the kingdom, but the safety of the little king will be in the hands of us all, and it begins now. Later, when we have Quintana of Charyn and her child secure in the palace, the riders will be made up of ten of the best of each province, including both mountain clans."

"But where is she?" someone called out.

There was silence before Gargarin spoke.

"We will find her. The best news we've had so far is no news. No news means no corpse."

"She's simple. She's not capable—"

"Simple?" Gargarin laughed sharply, searching for the speaker of the words. "She fooled the king and his men with stories to protect your last born girls. She survived the attack on Tariq's compound. She helped secure an escape from Bestiano's armed men at the bottom of the *gravina* by concealing weapons at her wrists and on her back. She traveled from Jidia to Turla to Paladozza with a babe in her belly and not so much as a whimper. And as we speak, she's hiding in this kingdom, keeping our king safe. She's not simple. Anything but simple."

Arjuro moved closer to Froi. "Not to mention her ability to kill a king in five seconds," he whispered.

Gargarin stepped aside, and Ariston spoke next about what had taken place in the little woods.

"Bestiano ordered the flanks of his army to guard the entrance to the woodlands."

Ariston was quiet a moment.

"They were young men. Strong lads. He's sending them out to fight like lambs to slaughter," Ariston said, his voice full of sorrow. "Bestiano and his generals are camped between the first two hills of Charyn, but they send out their youngest and strongest to fight their own people, and Charyn loses more of its lifeblood."

"How is it you came this way?" Dolyn asked.

"There's talk throughout Charyn of what took place on the lake," Ariston said, looking up at the elder. Froi heard anger in his voice. "That Bestiano was willing to sacrifice the last priestling. We also knew Lasconians were taking refuge in this fortress and that Bestiano's army was heading north. The slaughter of Tariq of Lascow's compound was felt by us all. We fight to avenge your kinsmen, Dolyn. We fight to avenge the young King Tariq who never had a chance to prove his worth."

And they fight to protect their own, Froi thought. Ariston was here for the oracle, Solange of Turla's daughter and grandchild.

"I say we get a look at what's happening between those two hills and decide on the chances we'll take," Ariston continued. "We need to find out what they know and what they think we know before we slaughter each other for no reason."

"Have you seen their sentinels?" Froi called out. "Those in the tree?"

Ariston nodded. "One saw us coming and left his post. For the time being, they are there to keep an eye on this fortress. But after last night's events, things may change."

"So we attack?" Dolyn asked.

Ariston shook his head. "We need to see what takes place between those hills and how big that army truly is. I'm presuming that they know as little as we do about our Quintana. So for now, they watch us, and we need to do the same to them." He looked at Gargarin. "We have to find a way to blind the sentinel."

Froi bunked down with his horse in the stables with the rest of the Turlans. One of the lads, called Joyner, whose upper body was covered with etchings, was marking another lad, using a bone needle and ocher mixed with earth. Froi had heard the Lasconians scornfully say that etchings were only for slaves and last-born girls, but the Turlan lads were neither.

"What have you chosen?" Froi asked the Turlan, who winced with pain each time the needle channeled the ink into his flesh.

"First time kill beyond little woods," the lad said quietly. "Mine a tainted spirit now. Keep it safe with name of my girl."

"Ariston'll kill you," Mort said. He looked at Froi, shaking his head. "His girl Ariston's niece."

"Most beautiful girl on Turla. And strongest. She beat any Lasconian today."

The lad winced again.

Mort showed Froi his etching. Froi saw the name Jocasta.

"My mother. Most beautiful woman on Turla," he boasted.

"There must be a lot of beautiful women on the mountain," Froi said.

There was a chorus from all the Turlan lads in agreement.

He watched the etching and thought of what Quintana had told him once. That Lirah was marked with the name of the man who owned her.

Later, Froi went to visit Arjuro in his chamber.

"Can you write these names in the language of the ancients?" Froi asked quietly.

Arjuro wrote them neatly, and Froi marveled at how powerful the ancient words looked compared to those in Charyn and Lumateran.

"What are they for?" Arjuro asked.

Froi patted his arm. Arjuro grimaced.

"It can't be removed," Arjuro said. "You know that. The stigma stays with you."

"My feelings will never change," Froi said. He started to walk away but turned back.

"Where did you see the writing that time? On my back?"

Arjuro traced a finger across where the writing had started just below Froi's shoulder blade.

Froi returned to the stables, where he was next in line. He handed Joyner the parchment.

"What say it?" Joyner said out of curiosity.

"Doesn't matter," Froi said. "Here. Here. And here." He pointed to the exact place he wanted each individual word to be. Both arms and across his shoulders. "But don't go here," he said, indicating where Arjuro had once seen the message from the gods.

"Goin' to hurt," Joyner said.

Joyner worked well into the night. He was precise and had the steadiest of hands. Despite the pain, Froi was pleased with what he saw on both his arms. Like the lettering on his scalp and on his back, he would never see the name across his shoulders, but he'd feel it. He'd know what it meant. He knew it linked him to her.

The Turlan lads looked impressed the next morning.

"Joyner says you gods' blessed," Mort said quietly, away from the others.

Froi shook his head. "What would make him say that?"

"Bit of a gift himself, our Joyner. He say your back was aflame. Was something there not of this world."

The other lads suddenly looked up, and Froi followed their gaze to where Lirah stood at the entrance. He saw the fury on her

293

face before she turned and walked away. Froi followed her out into the courtyard. He kicked at the dirt on the ground, waiting for whatever it was she had to say.

"Are you a slave?" she asked harshly. "In Serker, only slaves are etched."

"With the names of the men that own them," he said, his eyes meeting hers. It sickened him to think of Lirah being owned by anyone.

"I'm a Serker, Lirah," he said softly. "My body is etched with the names of the three women who own me. My queen. My mother. My woman."

He took Lirah's hand and placed it where Joyner had written her name on his arm, and he saw tears in her eyes. She traced the lettering with a finger, then quickly pressed a kiss against it and hurried away.

Froi smiled to himself and was about to climb up to his watch when Perabo called from above.

"Get Gargarin."

Moments later, Froi stood on the wall, looking out into the little woods with Gargarin, Ariston, Perabo, and Dolyn.

"It's too far away to see anything but movement," Perabo said. "But I've noticed a difference in the changeover of the guards. There are three of them. Guard one takes the day post. Guard two arrives in the evening to replace him for the night. The next morning, guard three fails to turn up on time. Every day since we've arrived. So guard two, after spending a whole night in the tree, always leaves his post and returns to camp instead of waiting. I presume he is forced to wake guard three. Or perhaps by the time he reaches the camp, guard three is on his way and they pass by each other. Any which way, for a short time early each morning, we have no one watching us."

Ariston looked out toward the little woods. "So we can take advantage of those moments? We can send out a scout, the fastest lad we have, to see what is taking place between the two hills, where Bestiano is camped."

Gargarin shook his head. "I don't like it. It's too much of a risk. We can't guarantee that tomorrow will be the same as today. If Bestiano's men capture whoever we send out, they'll use torture to find out what our lad knows."

"He's right," Dolyn said. "It's too much of a chance. We may lose our scout at the hands of one of those guards, or, worse still, at the hands of Bestiano and his riders."

"And if we don't, her life stays in danger," Froi said. "The captain of the Lumateran Guard would never question which of his men would be tortured or captured when it came to keeping the queen safe."

Ariston barked out a laugh of disbelief. "From what I've heard of Trevanion of Lumatere, I doubt he'd send out his son, the consort."

"Well, it's a good thing we have no sons among us to send out," Dolyn said.

Perabo gathered everyone in the great hall and spoke of what he had seen.

"All we need is to work out what takes place between those hills. Whether they have Quintana of Charyn. Whether they have an army as powerful as we fear."

He turned to Ariston. "Who is fastest of your lads?"

Ariston shook his head. "They're built to defend, but not for speed, I'm afraid, and for this task speed is everything."

"The Lumateran is fast," one of the Lasconians called out.

Froi heard Arjuro's sharp intake of breath beside him.

"The lad from Lascow is the fastest," Lirah's voice rang out.

Everyone stared at her. "Him," she said, pointing at Florik. "He beat Froi in the race around the wall. The lad who won the prize is the perfect soldier for the task."

Froi's eyes met Florik's across the way. Mort nudged Froi. "If come tomorrow the Lasconian sees the gods," he whispered, "pray it's a sentinel's arrow and not Nebian torture."

No one spoke. Froi could see that the Lasconians didn't want to give up their own. Perhaps they had good reason. They had lost Tariq's compound in the Citavita and couldn't afford to lose others. Finally, Dolyn nodded.

"Good. Then that's decided," Gargarin said. "We'll try for the morning." He walked away before another word was spoken.

CHAPTER 29

E arly the next day, Froi woke and made his way up to the great hall, where the Lasconian lads slept. They were all awake, standing around Florik while Dolyn and Ariston fitted him with his weaponry, speaking to him in low, calm voices.

"You've got the speed, Florik," Dolyn reassured. "Just stay focused and get to that lookout and take in everything, every single detail, and then you run for your life. Don't let them see you. We'll want this chance again, but for now, all we need to know is the strength of their army and what lies between those hills."

Florik nodded. His elder had a hand to his shoulder. "How many times have you run the mountain, Florik? How many times?"

Florik followed Ariston and Dolyn as if he were a prisoner walking to the gallows. When the Lasconian lads tried to follow, Ariston ordered them back.

"He needs to empty his head of all your talk."

But Froi followed Florik into the bailey, to the fortress gate. Up above, Perabo was in the gatehouse, watching the little woods for the departure of the guard from the tree. Ariston gave the order to raise the gate.

Froi could see the tremble in Florik's hand.

"Now!" Perabo shouted out.

Florik hesitated.

"*Now*."

One moment. Two. Three. Three too many.

Froi's fist caught Florik in the face. He bolted before any of them could stop him. He ran with the shrill wind in his ears, the little woods before him. He tried to prepare himself for the worst, although Perri always said that if you had an objective, think of nothing but getting there. Anything else would slow you down. But from the moment Froi knew that Bestiano was between those hills, he had wondered if Quintana was held captive in the camp. Knew there was nothing he could do if she was. Him up against an army? He stumbled at the thought. *See?* Perri's voice shouted in his ear. *It'll slow you down, Froi, and what good will you be to her then?*

He reached the woods, tree limbs flying in his face and half-concealed burrows catching him unaware. He remembered the time Finnikin and Isaboe freed him from the slave traders in that forest in the town of Speranza, how they had sprinted through its half-hidden trails, desperate to reach the valley that would lead them to Trevanion and Sir Topher. Finnikin's coat had been secure around Froi's otherwise naked body. They had come back for him, and the memory of it spurred him on as he untangled himself from vines that clung, leaped over fallen logs, and caught his first glimpse of the hill beyond the copse of trees. Froi clambered up the hill's unmarked track, praying that no soldier was on the path back to the lookout tree, desperate to catch his breath and find answers to what lay beyond.

Hundreds upon hundreds of tents crowded the small valley between the two hills, outnumbering those in the Lasconians' fortress ten to one. Soldiers were everywhere, huddled before campfires, dragging on their clothing and preparing for the day, and Froi wondered if there were any men left in the province of Nebia. He watched their morning drills, so much like those of the Lumateran Queen's Guard in the palace. These men were professional. Not a lazy or sloppy soldier among them, except for their late sentinel, who was now climbing the hill toward where Froi was lying behind a boulder. He had only moments to get back to the concealment of the woods and then to the fortress before the sentinel was back up in the lookout. But Froi needed more. He needed to get closer, to see if she was there. So he stayed pressed against the stone until the soldier passed him. He recognized the man. Fekra from the palace? Was that his name?

When the man had disappeared into the little woods, Froi moved from where he was hiding and climbed back to the top of the hill. Spotting a well shaft closer to the camp, he took a chance and crawled on his belly toward it, curling himself behind the stonework to stay hidden. At the foot of the hill was the largest of the tents, surrounded by four guards. Was it to protect Bestiano and the *provincaro* of Nebia? Or was it to hide Quintana?

In the distance, Froi saw a horseman ride down into the valley from the second hill. And so he waited. He couldn't go back with so little. Something was bound to reveal itself if he stayed here longer, and then he would have to work out a way to get past Fekra. Closer and closer, the horseman rode through the camp, and it wasn't until he stopped at a water barrel that Froi saw who it was. Olivier. The traitor dismounted, placed his hands in the barrel, and then pressed them against his face before walking toward the grand tent. Froi watched him exchange a word with one of the guards, who then disappeared inside, leaving

Olivier to wait. A short time later, Bestiano emerged to speak to the last born of Sebastabol, and it took all of Froi's might to stop himself from flying down the hill and tearing them both apart. How could he have forgotten the hate he felt for Bestiano? Or that smug repulsive smirk Bestiano wore as he had greeted Gargarin and Froi on the drawbridge when they first arrived in the Citavita? Or his grip around Quintana's hair as he dragged her out of the great hall that heinous day when Froi witnessed Bestiano's attack on her body and spirit?

Do it, he begged himself. *Forget the plan and kill them both now. It would be so easy.*

But he hesitated too long, and suddenly there was shouting and much pointing north. Bestiano was issuing orders, and soldiers were mounting their horses. Something was definitely happening beyond the second hill.

Froi turned and crawled back to the little woods. Gargarin and Ariston and Perabo would have to understand that the plan had changed. Froi wanted answers, and they weren't going to come from his surveillance on the hill. Perhaps he needed answers from a lazy sentinel, who for years had been easily bribed by Quintana and Lirah to be their go-between. In the little woods, he crept toward the lookout tree and saw that Fekra was settled comfortably. Froi picked up a stone and hurled it into the distance. Instantly, Fekra was alert, standing between two limbs, staring in the direction of where the stone had landed. Froi crept to the bottom of the tree and looked up, waiting for him to settle himself again.

"Fekra!" he finally called out.

The dead king's former house guard almost fell out of the tree in shock, his hands fumbling for his crossbow.

"It's Froi . . . actually, Olivier. You wouldn't know me as Froi. I'm the Olivier who lived in the palace. Remember?" Froi needed to unnerve the sentinel. He was matter-of-fact, as if he were reintroducing himself to one of Isaboe's kin.

Silence followed. Then a gruff, "I know who you are."

"Good. Good. I thought I'd have to explain my lineage. Ah, Fekra, I can't begin to tell you how complicated it all is."

Silence again.

"I don't have a weapon, Fekra. It means that I'm probably going to have to climb up and kill you with my bare hands, which may be drawn out and painful. I'm quicker with a weapon, but still thorough without. I'd say our best scenario would be if you came down and we made some sort of arrangement."

"I'm the one with the weapon," Fekra reminded him.

"Yes, but I'm not the only one down here," Froi lied. "During your tardy exchange with the other guard, at least a dozen of us made our way from the fortress into the little woods, and the only reason they sent me was because I assured them I had a better chance of making an arrangement with you. They're Lasconians. Tariq of Lascow's people. You're a member of the former king's army. They'll want you dead immediately, and I think Gargarin would prefer you alive."

"I don't believe a word you're saying. Why would they allow you to come out here unarmed?" Fekra asked, his voice flat and controlled.

Good question.

"Well, you have me: I'm lying. Because they didn't ask me to come along," Froi said, almost truthfully. "I just took a chance, hardly dressed for the day, really. But I knew the moment they came across you, they'd kill you, and to tell you the gods' honest truth, Fekra, I don't want you to die. I need information from you. So if you trust me and surrender, I'll do all I can to keep you alive."

"And you expect me to believe you?"

"Fekra, trust me when I say that if I wanted you dead, you'd be dead by now."

Froi heard a grunt of irritation.

"You're a bit of a gnat in the arse, Froi . . . or Olivier, or whoever you choose to be today," Fekra said. "It's what they call you in the barracks. That gnat in the arse that won't go away. The lads are feeling a bit of an attachment."

"Fekra, stop the flattery now, or you'll have me weeping by the time I get you to that gate."

Fekra didn't challenge Froi's lies about a dozen men in the little woods. Instead he stayed quiet as they crossed the clearing toward the fortress, shrugging himself once or twice from Froi's grip. When they were close enough to see the faces of everyone staring down at them from the outer wall, Fekra stopped. The Lasconians and Turlans aimed.

"We don't know what we're fighting for anymore," Fekra said quietly to Froi. "Do you?"

"Oh, I've always known what I'm fighting for," Froi replied. "Quintana of Charyn and her child. Nothing else matters, Fekra."

The portcullis was raised, and Froi wasn't surprised to see the bailey filled with almost everyone from inside the castle. Gargarin was limping toward them, fury in his expression. Lirah's eyes were swollen with tears.

"Did we not have a plan?" Gargarin shouted at Froi.

"I thought a hostage would give us more accurate information," Froi said, deciding to be the calm one. He looked beyond them to where Florik stood.

"I'm sorry I took away your glory, Florik. I wanted the task for myself and never gave you the chance. It's in my nature to compete and win."

Florik didn't respond. His lads glowered at Froi instead.

"Where's our girl?" Gargarin demanded of Fekra, his expression cold and hard.

"We were hoping she was with you, sir."

"Really? Bestiano was hoping she was with me?"

Fekra shook his head. "No, sir."

"So there's more than one 'we'?" Gargarin asked.

Fekra shrugged free of Froi. "We're being attacked from the north, sir," he reported to Gargarin, chatty all of a sudden. "It can't be from the provinces, because Alonso has no army and Desantos has plague. Bestiano believes that the Sarnaks and Lumaterans are advancing toward us."

Froi saw the horror on everyone's face. He knew it could not possibly be Lumatere. But Sarnak, yes.

"Which means, sir, that the Belegonians may have taken the south."

CHAPTER 30

The memory of what he saw in the cave with the women haunted Lucian all week. Phaedra scrubbing blood off stone. Harker's daughter sobbing against her mother, the girl's face battered by a man's fist. Worse still was Quintana's look of despair. Lucian knew that her body had swung its way close to oblivion months ago in the Charyn capital. What terror and madness went through the mind of one who knew she was moments from death? Had she ever imagined that Froi would save her? And with those thoughts, Lucian felt contempt for himself. He should have been able to protect his own wife, and he didn't. When he first saw Phaedra in the woods with the princess, he should have dragged her kicking and screaming up the mountain, but he allowed his pride to get in the way.

Days later, when he found time to escape, he traveled down to the valley. Tesadora and the girls were across the stream, and he joined them as they were about to enter the cave of a dying man. He noticed even more fear among the Charynites, and Tesadora glanced up high and then back to Lucian as a warning. On one of the rock ledges above, he could see a furious exchange between Donashe and his men. Rafuel was with them. When they noticed Lucian, Donashe climbed down to where he stood.

"One of my men seems to have disappeared, Mont. Galvin of Jidia. You would have seen him with me."

"And that fool Gies insists on searching for him," Tesadora said as Rafuel and the rest of Donashe's men joined them.

Lucian kept his expression impassive. He knew Tesadora was warning him that Gies had crossed the stream.

"This man who's disappeared?" Lucian demanded. "Let's hope he doesn't think he has a chance of getting up my mountain. He'll pay with his life."

"I heard Galvin's grumbling from time to time, Donashe," Rafuel said. "And he's a lazy one. If he's chosen to run off, we're better without him. I'd go through all your things to make sure he didn't take any with him."

Donashe thought for a moment.

"He has challenged me from time to time. Even in the Citavita, he wanted all the control."

"Why would he leave?" one of Donashe's men asked.

"Why wouldn't he?" Rafuel said. "It's a large reward the First Adviser Bestiano is paying for the return of Quintana of Charyn. Perhaps Galvin realized he was wasting his time in these parts and has been given an inkling of where she is in the north country."

Lucian secretly applauded Rafuel for the doubt he was planting in the camp leader's head. He hoped it worked. It meant that Donashe would steer the search for Galvin the hangman far from the women.

He spent the rest of his time in the valley with Kasabian and Harker. The men had learned half the facts of what had taken place in the cave.

"Arm us," Harker begged. "The people here are frightened. Donashe has become even more violent since Galvin disappeared. He says he trusts no one. And there's talk that an army is two days' ride from here, among the three hills of Charyn. Along with hundreds of men much like Donashe, who answer to no captain but the promise of gold. It will end in this valley, Lucian. I feel it in my bones. Arm us, so we can better protect the princess and our women."

Lucian shook his head, frustrated.

"Don't ask me to do that, Harker. That decision belongs to my queen and her consort."

Instead of returning home, Lucian found himself riding away from the mountain. It was close to her cave that he found Phaedra, not realizing that he had gone searching. He was on higher ground and could see her below in the gully. And when Phaedra heard the horse, she cried out in alarm, dropping the bucket of water she was carrying. Lucian dismounted and slid down the slope toward her, and they stood apart, facing each other, neither speaking. Once, when Lucian had returned from Alonso to argue the so-called promise between his father and the *provincaro,* a cousin had asked him to describe Phaedra. He had shrugged. "There's nothing about her to remember." Looking at his wife now, there was so much about her he couldn't forget. Her soulful eyes. The roundness of her face. The pinch of red on her cheeks. Lucian wanted nothing more than to take her home.

It was Phaedra who walked to him, and Lucian lifted her with an arm around her waist, so they were eye to eye. He wanted to go back to the first time they met. He wanted to change that one night in Alonso when he was expected to take the rights of a husband. He knew he hadn't used force. Was careful not to. But he hadn't acknowledged her fear of being alone with a man for the first time in her life. She was no Mont girl, unabashed and earthy and used to swimming naked in the river with the lads. He had mistaken so much for weakness, yet there was nothing weak about Phaedra of Alonso.

"Why are you here?" she asked quietly in Lumateran.

"Because I couldn't keep away," he replied in Charyn.

Lucian felt her study him.

"You have a scar," Phaedra said. "On the lid of your eye. It looks as if it's been there some time, but I never noticed." There was a sadness to her words. "Did you receive it at the hands of a Charynite?"

"I received it at the hands of my cousin Balthazar when we were children," he said. "Or one of his ideas, anyway. He decided that we'd swing from one tree to another to save Isaboe and Celie of the Flatlands from the silver wolf we imagined in the forest." He chuckled. "It didn't end well."

He watched a smile appear on her face. "Silly boys," she said. "Brave, silly boys."

She shrugged out of his arms, took his hand, and drew him away, and Lucian let himself be led until they reached a small shelter made of ferns. She crawled inside first, and then he followed.

"Is this yours?" he asked as they knelt before each other in the small space.

"I share it with Her Majesty," she said, as if it was the most natural thing to do with the strange princess.

Lucian waited, thinking that perhaps he'd like to speak. To tell Phaedra that he loved her, because it didn't seem so hard to think the words.

"Do you love me?" he asked instead. "Because if you don't, I'd wait until you did. I'd wait weeks and months and years."

Phaedra traced his jaw with a finger, then his cheeks,

the space around his eyes, the lump in his throat.

"No need to wait," she said. "Perhaps I've loved you for weeks and months and years. When I was a young girl in Alonso, my father told me about a Lumateran lad who would keep me safe, and perhaps I loved you then."

She reached for the frayed edges of his tunic, and when it was removed, she traced a finger against the scars: some from the battle to take back Lumatere, some from the skirmishes with his cousins.

"The gods drew you well," she said.

He chuckled softly.

"Can I be reminded of how the gods drew you?" he said. She nodded and he slowly fumbled with her clothing and she was naked before him and suddenly it all felt new. He copied her actions, tracing her body with a shaky finger. No scars but a small purple birthmark on her breast. A bruise or two on her body.

"I've made windows in the cottage so we can see the entire mountain," he murmured. "For you."

"Speak Lumateran," she said. "When you speak Charyn, you sound so strangely distant. Our voices sound kinder in the skin of our own language."

He cupped her face in his hands and he kissed her open-mouthed and he imagined that she had never been kissed before, but they kissed all the same until their lips felt bruised and swollen and then she lay back and his hand found its place between their bodies and she gasped, and Lucian thought he'd never heard a sound so promising.

Later, they lay talking, her head on his shoulder. They spoke all day and night as if they didn't have time left in the world. About the cottage and its views and Orly and Lotte's pregnant cow and of Yata, who was excited about his cousin Isaboe's decision

to birth the babe on the mountain soon, as she had done with Jasmina. They spoke of the valley, and Harker's and Kasabian's sadness and joy, and of her father's fury and whether Lucian could find a way to send word to the *provincaro* that Phaedra was still alive without putting her life or that of the women at risk. She spoke of the women, and he could hear in her voice that she had grown to love them in a way. And they spoke of Quintana of Charyn and of every scar on her body, and of the hangman who twice tried to take her life.

"I'm no better than an animal," Phaedra said after talking about the man's death.

"And no worse," he said. "It's what I've always liked about our four-legged friends. They act on what's inside here." He placed her hand against his heart. "It's their instinct and their need to survive. No malice, nothing."

He brushed the back of his finger across her cheek.

"I didn't kill my first man until the battle to take back Lumatere. All those years of practice and my father's pride in the great warrior I was." Lucian shook his head. "But nothing prepares you for the real thing. In practice, there was no blood spraying into my eye and blinding me, and there were no sounds quite like an ax wedging itself into a man's flesh. And in practice, there was no rage for—"

He bit his tongue to stop himself from saying the word.

"For Charynites?" she asked.

He took her hand. "For the Charynite king. For his family. I wanted all of them dead. And four years on . . . I'm protecting her in this valley."

"Despite everything, *Luc-ien*," Phaedra said softly, "she is worth protecting."

"Is she as mad as she seems?" he asked.

"Oh, not at all," Phaedra said. "Which doesn't mean she's

not the strangest person I've ever met, but those deemed mad in Alonso have no control over their minds. Quintana of Charyn has total control over everything she does." He noticed the smile on Phaedra's lips.

"I told her once that I constantly hear my mother speaking to me. Guiding me. In my head, I ask her questions all the time. Quintana understood perfectly what I was talking about. 'Oh, yes,' she said, 'They're most helpful, the half-dead spirits are. I only wish I knew where mine came from.'"

"Half-dead?" Lucian asked, thinking of his own conversations with his dead father.

"Well, Quintana says they can't be completely dead if they live inside of you."

Light pierced through the branches shrouding them, and he held both their hands up to its illumination.

"We're such different shades, you and I," Phaedra said. "Strangely, you could belong to the Paladozzans and Nebians of my kingdom. You have their coloring."

"I belong to you and you belong to me. That's all that counts."

She pressed her lips to his shoulder.

"I can take you away," he whispered. "Hide you on the mountain. You don't have to stay here, Phaedra. I can look after you."

She made a sound of regret. "We come second, you and I, Luc-ien," she said. "Our allegiance is always to our kingdoms. Without that allegiance, our people would fall."

She placed her head back against his chest, and he felt her tears. "This is not our time."

"But that will never mean I love you less," he said.

They slept awhile, and when he woke, he kissed her brow. He wanted to stay, but there was too much happening on the mountain. Isaboe would soon come for her birthing, and his village would be swarming with her guards and those wanting to visit her.

He crawled out of their resting place and faced the spear first. Then he looked up and saw the strange Quintana of Charyn staring down at him, with her rounded belly and savage snarl. Harker's daughter, Florenza, was there as well, her face battered but her eyes defiant as she gripped her own weapon.

"I was just with Phaedra," he mumbled as a means of explanation.

"Really," the princess said coolly. "You don't think the whole valley heard the caterwauling?"

Lucian felt his face flush as he stood. Quintana of Charyn pressed the spear to his chest.

"Phaedra," he called out softly. "Can you come out here . . . now?"

Phaedra heard the voices and was wide awake in an instant.

"Your Highness," she said, crawling out and getting to her feet. "You shouldn't be out here."

"Come now, Phaedra," Quintana said briskly. "We've got to go home."

She sounded like Cora, and Phaedra wondered if she was mimicking her.

Phaedra stole a look at Lucian, who bent to kiss her good-bye but changed his mind.

"We'll speak later, *Luc-ien*," she said.

He stared down at Quintana's belly. "You should be resting, Your Highness. Your birthing time will come soon."

"And you'd know that because you've birthed a child before?" Quintana asked.

"No," Lucian said politely. "I know that because I live on a mountain with many women. I've seen enough of those," he said, pointing to her belly. "And you don't have much time to go."

Quintana rolled her eyes. Lucian narrowed his.

"Queens and princesses should show more restraint in eye-rolling," he muttered. He stepped forward again to kiss Phaedra, but Quintana tugged her hand and dragged her away. Phaedra turned to see him, still standing by the shelter. Lucian held up a hand and waved, then disappeared between the trees.

She looked at her two companions, feeling lighthearted despite Quintana's fingers digging into her hand.

"You were away too long," Quintana said accusingly.

"What have I missed?" Phaedra asked.

"Oh, the usual," Florenza said.

"Cora says no one will marry Florenza now with a broken nose," Quintana said.

"Cora is playing with you," Phaedra said.

"And Ginny is acting strange, sniveling in a corner one moment, disappearing the next," Florenza said.

"You'd think she had never seen a corpse before the hang-man's," Quintana said.

"We've all had a shock," Phaedra said. "Florenza could have been killed, and the hangman could have taken you, Quintana. We've just got to be patient with everyone's moods."

She felt the princess studying her.

"What were you doing all that time, Phaedra? Swiving doesn't take so long."

"We were talking, Your Majesty," Phaedra said, ignoring the word, knowing quite well that Quintana was only using it to irritate her. "We had much to say to each other."

Quintana was silent for some time.

"On my last night in Paladozza, I lay with Froi and we spoke of everything," she said. Phaedra wondered if she was trying to compete.

"And in the end, he asked me who I trusted most in the world and I told him the names of four people and then I asked him who he trusted most in the world and he told me the names of thirty."

"It's a Lumateran thing," Phaedra said absently, the memory of Lucian's hands on her body." They travel in packs and trust one another with all their hearts. It doesn't mean that they have the capacity to love more than us, but they do know how to trust. It's because of their queen and her father before her and his father before him. The trust of a people comes from the goodness of their leaders."

Quintana stopped. "Are you questioning my family's failure to rule, Phaedra?"

Phaedra wanted to be mean-spirited. She wanted to hurt Quintana because so much was broken due to her. Phaedra wanted to hide on the mountain with Lucian, but this girl and Charyn's unborn child stopped her.

"Your father and the house of Charyn didn't fail as rulers," Phaedra said boldly. "They failed as leaders."

Quintana's stare was fierce, and Phaedra shivered at its force.

"Well, now you've gone and offended me, Phaedra, and I'm not going to tell you what I meant to tell you."

Phaedra sighed. "I haven't offended you," she said, trying to keep a patient tone, because she knew that Quintana had nothing to tell her. It was just a ploy so that Phaedra would be forced to beg Quintana for the news. "I offended your father and the house of Charyn."

"I am the house of Charyn. This," Quintana said, pointing to her belly, "is the house of Charyn. And you didn't just mean my father, Phaedra; you meant to insult the whole bloodline."

"Your Highness, she didn't mean—" Florenza began.

"*Didn't you?*" Quintana demanded.

Phaedra stared at her. "Yes," she said truthfully. "I meant

your father and his father and his father before him. My own father says that Charyn's royal bloodline is tainted."

"And your father thinks that women don't have courage," Quintana said, "and that his grief is mightier than his duty to feed a people. So perhaps you should question what your father has to say about the bloodline of Charyn's first child."

"I didn't mean to insult your child," Phaedra said. "Come, now," she added gently. "What were you going to tell me?"

Quintana looked away with an arrogant toss of her head. "You're humoring me now, Phaedra. Placating me like I'm some stupid hound who will be satisfied with a bone. When you learn to respect me, I will speak to you as an equal."

CHAPTER 31

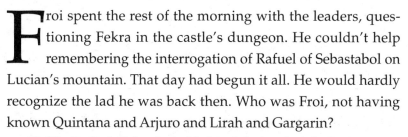

Froi spent the rest of the morning with the leaders, questioning Fekra in the castle's dungeon. He couldn't help remembering the interrogation of Rafuel of Sebastabol on Lucian's mountain. That day had begun it all. He would hardly recognize the lad he was back then. Who was Froi, not having known Quintana and Arjuro and Lirah and Gargarin?

Unlike Rafuel, Fekra kept his head down the whole time.

"Were you there?" Dolyn of Lascow repeated. He had insisted on joining them all for the interrogation. "When Tariq and our kinspeople were slaughtered?"

Fekra finally looked up, and Froi saw the bleakness in his eyes.

"No. But I was there when the men returned. They had lost their spirit."

"And that is supposed to appease my people?" Dolyn asked with anger.

Fekra shook his head.

"You're not a soldier," he said. "You don't understand orders."

"Ah, the defense of all great men. I was ordered to do it," Perabo said, looking away with disgust.

"At first we were told that Tariq of Lascow and his people had planned the murder of the king," Fekra said. "Months later, a different story emerged."

"The true assassin?" Froi asked cautiously.

Fekra nodded. "In a way. Whispers suggested that Bestiano ordered the killings of Tariq of Lascow's compound because he wanted Charyn's heir dead. That it had been Bestiano who did indeed kill the king because he had discovered that Quintana of Charyn was with child and he wanted more control over the kingdom. What better way than being regent to a helpless little king?"

Fekra shook his head. "Bestiano and those he paid to be his advisers said it was only talk, but a handful of the palace riders began to question the truth, including our captain."

"Oh, the noble palace riders," Gargarin said with sarcasm.

"Upon accepting the rumors, our captain attempted to desert but was betrayed," Fekra said, and Froi heard anger in his voice. In spite of everything, Fekra was still loyal to the riders. "When my captain was dragged back to the camp, Bestiano decreed him a traitor, to be punished by death. And not just the captain. Bestiano ordered him to choose ten riders to die alongside him as a warning to anyone else who would defy him again. It was the longest night of our lives." Tears welled up in Fekra's eyes. "Thirty men deciding who would live. Finally, those who had been sent into Tariq of Lascow's compound volunteered to die alongside their captain, as did some of the older riders who had been present as young men at the slaughter of Serker. They said they lived with shame and they would die for Charyn."

No one spoke for such a time. Fekra's tardiness each day to reach the sentinel's tree wasn't about laziness. He had given up.

They heard a sound at the entrance, and Lirah entered with Arjuro, her eyes on the soldier. Gargarin had asked her to be present. Regardless of everything, Fekra knew her.

"What can you tell us, Fekra?" Gargarin said.

"I've told you enough."

"No. You've told us about the past. What can you tell us about what's taking place over the hill now?"

Fekra's eyes met Lirah's. Froi saw his regret and knew Gargarin had made the right choice asking Lirah here.

"One hears things," he said.

"From whom?"

Froi shrugged bitterly. "Friends . . . the surviving riders . . . those who are in Bestiano's service."

They waited.

"Bestiano is paying lowlifes across the kingdom to keep an eye out for the princess. At every border, every outpost. There's an army of scum out there, sir. Made up of men who have lost their souls. Soldiers follow orders. These men don't. They want the gold in return for . . ."

"For what?" Gargarin asked.

"For the babe. At all costs. No stone is to be left unturned. If one is even suspected of hiding Quintana of Charyn, the punishment is death."

Lirah gripped Froi's arm, and her nails sank deep into his flesh.

"And they just accept this order?" Gargarin asked. "These men?"

Fekra shook his head. "You don't understand. These men are brigands. Murderers. Street lords. You saw firsthand what they did in the palace after the king's death."

"After Bestiano and the riders deserted it, you mean?" Gargarin asked.

"These brigands . . . all of them can be bribed," Fekra contin-ued, ignoring the taunt. "Whoever delivers Quintana of Charyn's babe to Bestiano has been promised a . . . king's ransom."

"Where would you hear that talk?" Froi asked angrily. "I saw how protected Bestiano's tent was. You're a sentinel who spends his day in a tree, Fekra. So why would a messenger know about such an order?"

"Friends . . . they talk," Fekra responded. "Friends who work close to Bestiano. They hear the truth."

"And this friend?" Arjuro asked. "Can you trust him? Is he merely close to Bestiano, or is he forced to work close to him?"

Fekra shook his head.

"I don't know," he said, frustration in his voice. "The riders no longer talk about trust. Trust is dead. My . . . friend follows orders. He knows no other way. Sometimes he tells me what he's heard, but do I trust him? I trust no one!"

"Dorcas," Lirah said.

Fekra didn't respond.

"He's Bestiano's messenger, so he would hear a thing or two. And he told you," she said. "Because you've been palace soldiers together since you were fourteen."

Fekra went back to his stubborn silence.

"Your shift will be over soon, Fekra," Gargarin said. "So here's what you're going to do. Return to the sentinel's tree and when you get replaced, return to camp and find out everything you can and report back to us tomorrow."

"And what makes you think you can trust me?" Fekra asked.

"Because you were the only person in the palace who made it possible for Quintana to see me," Lirah said. "That wasn't just about a bit of extra food and ale, Fekra. That was about compas-sion. What if you could be the one to keep her safe now?"

"And the way I see it, there's no way for you to betray us,"

Gargarin said. "We're in this fortress. There are about one hundred and twenty soldiers here. If you're going to betray us, Fekra, there's not much you've got. They want me. At the moment, they're not attacking because they know exactly where I am. In a way, we're already their prisoners. So what are you going to do? Go back and say, 'You'll never believe what happened. Gargarin of Abroi took me hostage, but he let me go.' They'd question why. Rest assured it would not end well for you, Fekra."

"Or else you can return to your camp and do something right for Charyn," Arjuro said quietly.

"And what if I choose to stay here a prisoner?"

"Then I'll suggest that you're put into the barracks with Tariq's kinsmen," Dolyn said. "I'll tell them you were once a palace rider and they'll know exactly what that means."

After more silence, Fekra looked up at Froi.

"I need to get back to the post, then," he said.

"Find a way to meet Dorcas tonight," Gargarin ordered. "See what he can tell you, but whatever you do, don't tell him the truth."

Later, Froi climbed the steps up to the wall and watched as Fekra walked back across the field toward the woodlands, as if he had the weight of the kingdom on his shoulders. Perhaps he did.

"It's ridiculous, really," Gargarin said behind him. "We're all camped in the middle of Charyn waiting to see which direction she appears from, and meanwhile we're all being attacked from the north and possibly the south, by foreigners."

"If you're suggesting we need Bestiano and Nebia's help, I'll walk away now," Froi threatened.

"Why would you think I'd suggest that?" Gargarin asked.

"Because they're the sort of deals that get made in desperate times. Someone as base as Bestiano gets spared as a favor. He needs to die," Froi said. He hadn't thought of anything else since catching a glimpse of the man outside his tent. "Because he loved sitting at the head of the table in the absence of the king, lording over everyone, while people starved. Nothing worse than a weak man with ambition, who gains power because those before him died rather than because his ideals were grand. Promise me she didn't suffer for nothing. If men like Bestiano get to live, then Quintana's pain was for nothing!"

Gargarin settled himself down with his back against the wall. "I can't promise that at all. Not if your life or Lirah's and Arjuro's and Quintana's are there to be bargained with."

Froi sat with him. It reminded him of the days in the palace at the Citavita when Gargarin would wait for a glimpse of Lirah. It was the first time they had been alone since their time in Sebastabol. Froi missed him. Gargarin seemed to belong to everyone now. Froi studied his features, wondering about all the layers that made up this man. His father.

Gargarin looked at him questioningly. "What?"

"It suits you," Froi said quietly. "Power."

"This isn't power," Gargarin said.

"Call it what you will," Froi said. "It suits you. They hang off every word you speak."

Gargarin didn't respond. Froi shrugged.

"It suits you," Gargarin said.

"What?"

"Idiocy."

Froi laughed.

Gargarin glanced at him. "Courage," he continued. "You hit the Lasconian lad because you saw his fear and rather than show him up in front of his kin, you made it seem as if you did it for yourself. You'll probably get a beating from them because of it."

Froi was overwhelmed, and his eyes smarted as he looked away.

"I did it for myself," he said. "I can't breathe at the thought of her being hurt. So I did it for me and her. No one else."

"And almost sacrificing yourself for me and Arjuro at the lake? Was that for you and her?"

Froi didn't respond.

"Listen," Gargarin said gently. "I want you to promise me something."

Froi nodded. He realized that he didn't even need to ask. That he'd promise Gargarin anything without knowing what it was.

"Be patient. Don't give up on me. I'll find a way."

It was a strange plea.

"That's all?" Froi asked.

"When the time comes, you won't think it's nothing at all, Froi," Gargarin said sadly.

Before Froi could ask another question, they heard a shout and he scrambled to his feet, looking out toward the little woods, pulling Gargarin up with him.

"Sagra!"

"Gods almighty!"

Gargarin swung around. "Ariston!" he shouted down into the bailey. "Perabo! We're under attack!"

An army was thundering toward them from south of the little woods, hundreds of riders galloping at full speed toward the fortress. By the time the horsemen had closed the distance by half, every Lasconian and Turlan was on the wall, weapons in hand. Froi felt Ariston at his shoulder.

"Are they Belegonians?" Ariston asked.

"It's too far to tell," Froi said.

"There's no flag. Nothing. Do I give the order?" Ariston asked Gargarin.

"If they're the enemy, give the order," Gargarin replied.

"Get out of here, now," Ariston ordered Gargarin. "Hide Lirah and your brother and yourself."

Gargarin started to protest.

"Just do it!" Froi said, keeping his eyes on the approaching army.

"It has to be the Belegonians," someone shouted from the flanks of the wall.

"Belegonians!"

"We don't know that!" another called out.

"Hold," Perabo shouted in return. "Ariston, tell them to hold."

"Hold until I give the order!"

The late-afternoon light revealed little, and they waited, the pounding of the horses sounding closer and closer.

Froi's fingers pulled the string of his bow taut, and he waited.

Suddenly, an arrow from the keep's battlement whistled past him and moments later he saw the horseman in the lead fall forward on his mount.

"Idiot!" Ariston roared to those around him. "Who fired?"

"*Hold. Hold!*"

Froi and Ariston stared at each other, shocked. The shout had come from the approaching horsemen.

"Did you hear that?" Froi asked.

"They're not firing back," Perabo said.

Which could only mean one thing. The horsemen belonged to them.

"No one move!" Ariston bellowed. "No one!"

Froi kept his stance, his aim focused, but his heart was beating fast. *It's a trap. It's a trap.* This army was going to fool them into letting them in. *It's a trap.* They could trust no one. Until Froi saw one of the horsemen.

"Grij!" he shouted. Froi shoved the others aside. "Hold your weapons. *Hold!"* He flew down the gatehouse steps that had never seemed so never-ending, fearing that some other idiot would fire a bolt. *"It's Paladozza,"* he called out to those guarding the entrance. "Raise the gate. Do not attack."

By the time he reached the gate, one of the Turlans had raised it, and soon enough, the riders entered. Froi saw Grijio first. The last born leaped from his mount.

"My father!" Grij cried, rushing to the horse with the injured rider.

And Froi realized with horror that De Lancey had been hit by one of their own arrows.

Amid shouting and threats from De Lancey's guards, they lay him down on a cot in a chamber on the first level of the keep. And then Arjuro arrived, pushing the Paladozzans out of the way. Froi stood beside Grijio, his eyes glued to the arrow lodged in the *provincaro's* chest. Too close to his heart.

"Arjuro, I'm begging you," Grij wept.

De Lancey opened his eyes wearily at the sound of Arjuro's name. The look that passed between the two former lovers was powerful and Froi saw the paleness of Arjuro's face as he studied the wound. De Lancey's guards jostled around the bed, hissing and cursing any time De Lancey so much as moaned.

"De Lancey," Arjuro said quietly.

"Yes, Arjuro. Am I dying?"

"Your guards may," Arjuro said, pressing his fingers against the pulse at De Lancey's wrist. "Die, I mean. Very soon. They're getting on my nerves and I want to kill someone at the moment. Tell them to go away."

There were furious objections from De Lancey's guards.

De Lancey opened an eye, then feebly pointed a thumb to the door.

"Am I going to die?" he asked Arjuro again.

"Perhaps of stupidity. What possessed you to come galloping north?" Arjuro asked, his hands pressing the swell surrounding the stalk of the arrow. De Lancey winced at the pain.

"Did you honestly think I'd stay in Paladozza knowing they were using you as bait?" the *provincaro* still managed to snap.

"An army just for me," Arjuro murmured, lifting De Lancey so he was sitting up. "You could have gotten yourself killed, you fool."

Their eyes met and Arjuro held a hand to the other man's face and bent to press his lips against De Lancey's, and the kiss made Froi feel as if something inside of him was breaking. Most times he knew there was no hope for Arjuro and Gargarin and Lirah and De Lancey. Too much pain in the past, too much power working against them in the present day. But as he watched Arjuro prop De Lancey up to better remove the arrow, Froi saw the foolishness of dreamers, and he decided he'd like to die so foolish. With a dream in his heart about the possibilities, rather than a chain of hopelessness. Finnikin had once said it was the only way to live. That he wanted to drown in hope rather than wallow in despair.

"Grij, it hasn't pierced his heart," Arjuro said, "but I could do damage removing the bolt if I'm distracted. It's going to hurt you more than it'll hurt him. So that's why Froi is going to take you for a little tour around our fortress."

Grij shook his head defiantly.

"I'm not a child, Arjuro."

"No, you're not," Arjuro agreed. "But you're his son, and I know him. He's not going to want you to see him cry."

"I'm not going to cry," De Lancey protested feebly.

"You're going to cry," Arjuro said.

"You're going to cry," Froi agreed. "I did." He dragged Grijio away. "So how about I introduce you to Tariq's people first, Grij? They'll like you. They hate me. And then I'll introduce you to the Turlans. We can get you etched."

He heard De Lancey's groan as they walked out.

Outside the door, they walked into Gargarin, who was pushing through De Lancey's men.

"He'll live," Grijio said when he saw the worry on Gargarin's face. "Arjuro said it's best I don't stay for the painful part."

Gargarin embraced the last born. "I would never have forgiven myself if the last words we spoke were in anger," he said.

"Father says you never trust him, sir," Grij said, with no censure in his voice. "He was broken when he returned from Sebastabol. He told me about Arjuro and Lumatere. And then when we received word about Arjuro having been taken hostage and Bestiano ordering a trade with you. . . ." Grij shook his head. "I've never seen him like that. Never. I think the library is still in splinters."

They heard a roar of pain from behind the door, and Grij paled.

"Take him," Gargarin said, and Froi dragged Grij away.

They spent the afternoon on the battlements of the keep, looking out toward the little woods.

"Is it true you had eight barbs removed?" Grij asked quietly. Froi nodded.

"It makes no difference to you, I'm sure . . . but it was Olivier," Grij said.

"It makes all the difference that it was Olivier that led us to the trap," Froi said angrily.

"No, I mean . . . it was Olivier who took you to the priests."

Froi stared at him in disbelief.

Grijio nodded. "He told Bestiano's men you were dead. Well, you were in a way. And they left your corpse there, and he returned for it later, not knowing whether you would live or die."

Froi didn't speak for a moment. And then he grew angry.

"How would you know that?" he asked coldly. "Back in the fold, is he? Last borns stick together no matter whom they betray?"

Grij didn't respond. Froi jumped to his feet. "I lost her because of him," he raged. "Don't ask me to forgive a traitor just because he took me to the priests. Those barbs were in my body because of him."

Grijio shook his head. "I'm not asking you to forgive him. None of us have. The correspondence between us is terse."

"I saw him with Bestiano, just two days past," Froi said. "Why would you be in contact with him, Grij? Why?"

"Because he's our spy, Froi," Grijio said quietly. "He came to us. We knew about what took place at the lake with you and Arjuro because of him. We've been able to build an army in the north because of Olivier, and although Tippideaux will never speak to him again and my father promises never to have him in Paladozza, and Sebastabol has expelled him and his family, Olivier fights for Charyn. Not for Bestiano."

"You're telling me this because you want me to forgive him," Froi accused.

Grijio shook his head. "No, I'm telling you because I know you'll kill him the moment you cross each other's paths, and although he doesn't deserve our friendship, I'd hate you to have his death on your conscience. I've come to know you, Froi. Despite all appearances, you wear your guilt like a smothering blanket. You don't need Olivier's death on your conscience."

◆ ◆ ◆

They returned to the chamber where Gargarin and Arjuro were sitting with a belligerent De Lancey, who was already on his feet. Lirah had joined them and was scribbling away in a corner.

"Is it bad?" Grij asked, embracing his father gently.

"No, just annoying," the *provincaro* responded.

"The word *rest* made him turn purple," Gargarin said.

"Yes, let's all rest in the middle of a war," De Lancey muttered when Arjuro pointed to the bed.

"Unlike me, he was never known as a responsible young man," Arjuro said to Grijio and Froi. "It takes getting used to."

"You, Arjuro? Responsible?" Froi asked. "I thought you were breaking all the rules and creating havoc in the godshouse."

"He's gods' blessed," Gargarin said. "He can do more than one thing at once. Be an idiot and be responsible. He has these multiple skills."

"Much like women, but they're not called gods' blessed," Lirah called out without looking up from her work. "They're just called women."

"Ah, all the envy in this room," Arjuro mused, but there was a smile on his face and Froi enjoyed hearing their banter.

But outside, a war was brewing and all too soon the humor was lost.

"How did you raise an army so quickly?" Gargarin asked De Lancey quietly.

"Not so quickly," De Lancey said. "It's been in the planning for a while. I told you in the Citavita that I was going to return home and raise an army. Does anyone ever listen to me?"

"I listen to you, Father," Grij teased, trying to break the tension.

"No, you don't. If you got yourself etched, I'll tell Tippideaux."

"But where did you train an army?" Gargarin asked.

Grij and De Lancey exchanged a look.

"Desantos," Grij said.

"Plague-ridden Desantos?" Gargarin asked, confused. "Why would you raise an army there?"

"No plague," De Lancey said. "Just a very smart plan. Bestiano would never come near Desantos if he thought there was a plague there. No one would. So we've used it as a training ground for a combined army."

"When was this planned?" Gargarin asked.

"It was a jest between Satch and me and . . . Olivier," Grijio said. "When we were together in the Citavita. But we didn't know that Satch suggested it to his *provincaro* when he returned to Desantos."

"These last months I've sent them at least two hundred men through the tunnels to the north," De Lancey said. "It's where Tippideaux is now."

"And you couldn't tell me this," Gargarin demanded.

"I was going to in Sebastabol," De Lancey said, "but you disappeared, after offending me, of course. Well, Lirah offended me, anyway."

Lirah didn't rise to the bait. She didn't involve herself in any of the conversation. As the days passed, she had become more fixated on discovering Quintana's whereabouts and scribbling from the books Perabo had given her in Serker. Today, as every other day, she sat reading over Froi's words concerning his last hours with Quintana.

"How strong is this army?" Gargarin asked.

"They're not all soldiers, but they've been training for months now. Every able man and woman has been taught to use the bow, and those who have shown great promise have been trained with swords and horses."

"You're sure about this?" Gargarin asked. "We have an army as powerful as Nebia's in the north? You're serious?"

De Lancey's stare was hard. "Gargarin, I took my son into battle with me. How serious does that seem?"

"I can't believe you didn't tell me," Gargarin said. "First you side with the *provincari*—"

"I am the *provincari*!" De Lancey shouted.

"The *provincari*'s plan leaves the palace with no power."

"No," De Lancey argued. "Our plan gives the palace limited power. Our plan gives the *provincari* limited power. It gives the godshouse limited power. And all that limited power combined may just work a spell and produce a good king and a balanced kingdom."

Gargarin's mouth was a thin line.

De Lancey shook his head with a grimace. "This can work, Gargarin."

"Yes, of course," Gargarin retorted. "It could work perfectly with that arse from Avanosh."

"You know we don't want him." De Lancey was frustrated, and Froi could see this conversation soon ending badly. "But for our plan to work, we can't have one of the *provincari*'s men as regent. If you refuse—"

"He won't refuse," Lirah said as she stood and gathered her books. Gargarin's eyes followed her across the room.

"Is this about Lirah?" De Lancey asked. "I said it in Sebastabol, and I'll say it again: you have a home with me, Lirah. You will be treated with the same respect my family receives and when Gargarin and Arjuro and Quintana and the babe come to visit, you'll see them in my home. The other *provincari* don't have control over that. Some of the *provincari* may not want you in the palace, Lirah, but there's nothing to say that you can't see your loved ones elsewhere."

Froi knew that De Lancey's heart was in the offer, and it made him like the man even more. But it would never be enough for Lirah. Froi knew that for certain, because it would never be enough for him.

"Lirah will live with me."

Everyone stared at Arjuro.

"In the Oracle's godshouse," he said firmly. "She's smarter and better read than any of the *collegiati* so I'll put her to good use. She'll be across the *gravina* from Quintana and the babe and Gargarin. You'll see them every day, Lirah. I defy anyone who says Quintana and her babe and Gargarin cannot visit the godshouse."

Arjuro's eyes met Gargarin's. "And of course we have the palace architect here, so if he can't find a way of getting you into the palace some nights without the useless *provincari* nobility's spies watching, well, he can't exactly be labeled the smartest man in the Citavita, can he?"

They all turned to Lirah, waiting.

"We'll kill each other, Priestling," she said softly, but her eyes were bright.

"I'll win most arguments, but you'll get used to it," he said.

She came to him and pressed a kiss to his cheek. "Thank you." She kissed De Lancey as well. "And thank you."

Gargarin took her hand. "And what about mine?" he asked. "I'm the brilliant architect."

They spent the rest of the evening together, and with all the turmoil awaiting them beyond the first hill, Froi was surprised at how normal life could seem with their door closed to the rest of the fortress. They spoke of all things, including the girls.

"At least you know where Tippideaux is," Gargarin said. "Olivier of Sebastabol's actions placed Quintana in grave danger."

"Yes, well, it's not that cut and dry," De Lancey said. "He has become more of a help than a hindrance."

"I don't care what part Olivier's played in helping," Gargarin said. "He gets tried as a traitor. The kingdom is going to be full of men and women who turned sides, and the palace is going to have to make decisions about what to do with them."

"Yes, but still, our runt of the litter would be dead if the lad hadn't acted," Arjuro said.

There was more arguing. Froi suddenly heard a gasp from Lirah. She looked up from her page, her eyes on Froi's, blazing with excitement. Froi stood and walked toward her. She gripped his hand.

"How did Phaedra of Alonso die of a plague that doesn't exist?"

Froi shook his head, confused, and Lirah pointed to her page where she had recorded every word Froi spoke, after weeks and weeks of her questioning.

And there he saw Phaedra's name.

"We keep asking the wrong question," she said.

By now the others had heard and were crowded around her work.

"What is it, Lirah?" Gargarin asked.

"We keep asking where Quintana would go. She had nowhere to go. She knows no one. But you, Froi, trusted how many? Thirty? It's what you spoke of that last night together."

She pointed to Phaedra's name. "You trusted Phaedra of Alonso because of her kindness."

Froi's heart began to hammer inside of him and Lirah saw his realization and nodded.

"We keep asking where she would go. Our girl is a mimic. What we should be asking is where would you go, Froi?"

"I'd go west," Froi said. "You know that."

Lirah nodded.

"I think our Quintana's gone to Lumatere, and Phaedra of Alonso is hiding her."

CHAPTER 32

Isaboe woke with a start. She had felt her again. She knew it was Quintana of Charyn who crept into her dreams.

I know you're there!

Keep away from my son!

She had no idea which were her own words and which belonged to that insidious intruder. At times it seemed as if they were one.

Isaboe heard a sound. Thought she imagined it. But then Finnikin was out of bed, placing a dagger in her hand.

"Stay," he whispered. "I'm going out onto the balconette. Someone's in the courtyard. The moment you hear my shout, take Jasmina and hide."

They were expecting no one tonight. Trevanion was in Fenton and Perri was on duty, and only Lucian and Yata had the authority to be in the courtyard outside the residence. But before Isaboe could imagine the death of any of her beloveds on the mountain or an assassin in their garden, Finnikin was back at the bed, relief in his expression.

"It's the priest-king and Celie."

"At this hour of the night?"

"Sefton let them in at the gatehouse, and they took a wrong turn and ended up in the garden, facing the end of Perri's sword. They're on their way up."

She groaned, holding out a hand to him. "I need a catapult to get me out of this bed."

The priest-king and Celie entered the residence, lugging chronicles in their arms, all apologies but flushed with excitement.

"How long have you been home without seeing me, Celie?" Isaboe asked, embracing her.

"I arrived not even two days past and have spent the whole time with blessed Barakah. Not even Mama or Father or the boys have seen me."

"Blessed Barakah, you shouldn't be out at this time of the night," Isaboe said.

"Sit, sit," the priest-king said. "We've worked it out." His voice was full of emotion.

Perri joined them and then Sir Topher entered and they all sat around the long bench. The priest-king held a parchment out to Isaboe. Finnikin reached over to steady the old man's hand. But it was excitement more than age that caused his trembling.

"The markings on the nape and skull are written in a language very few know about," he said. "I searched everywhere. Had chronicles sent from Osteria and Sarnak, and Celie agreed to . . . deliver one home from Belegonia."

"Deliver?" Isaboe asked Celie.

Celie and the priest-king were silent for a moment.

"Perhaps . . . smuggle would be the correct word," Celie said.

Sir Topher buried his head in his hands, and Isaboe heard him mutter, "Augie."

"And no one suspected?" Isaboe asked.

"Well . . . the castellan of the palace searched my room. He's very suspicious. But I was clever. And I wept, of course. You see, he accused me of theft in front of the king's men." Celie looked pleased with herself. "My tears are very convincing. There was some quite pathetic sniveling."

"Oh, so underrated, the sob and the snivel," Isaboe said. "I wish I had been taught. I would have used them more often in exile."

"If you had sobbed and sniveled when Sir Topher and I first found you in Sendecane, we wouldn't be here today," Finnikin said. "I would have left you behind."

"Yes, because you had so much control over the situation, my love." Isaboe laughed.

"Can we get back to why they're here at this time of the morning?" Perri asked politely. "I almost tackled blessed Barakah to the ground."

"Then, let's begin with insanity," the priest-king said. "All great curses do. Because you will always find some sort of genius in it. I found an interesting passage in one of my books from the Osterians. Three thousand years ago, there was a Yut touched by the gods. He was mad — those most touched by the gods are — and his greatest claim was remembering the moment of his birth."

"Mad, indeed," Finnikin said.

The priest-king shook his head. "You didn't see your daughter come into the world, Finnikin. It's our most savage entry into any place on this earth. One that killed your own mother. Imagine the state of one's mind if they were to recall its details. All those months cocooned and then the onslaught of this ugly world. Light and noise and strangeness. It's no wonder we scream with terror at our birth."

"And you found all this in the Osterian chronicle?"

The priest-king shook his head. "Just a mention of the Yut and his theory. So I continued my search. What kingdom has profited most from Yutlind's mess and has become the greatest hoarder and pilferer of its works?"

"Belegonia," Sir Topher said.

"Although it could have been worse," Finnikin said. "The great works of Yutlind could have ended up in the hands of the Sorellians. At least the Belegonians have a love for words."

The priest-king nodded. "Thus Celie's achievement in their spring palace."

"I pride myself on being the greatest spy there is," Celie said. "When I was in the Belegonian capital, I had no such luck finding any foreign chronicles. In the spring castle, however, I found exactly what we were looking for."

"Celie," Isaboe reprimanded. "I told you to find yourself a lover, not hide yourself in a library."

"No, you said we could make these invitations to Belegonia work for us," Celie said.

"Well, I don't know what we would have done without her," the priest-king said.

"Can't you be both?" Isaboe asked. "Someone's lover and our greatest spy?"

"I'll try very hard to please you, my queen," Celie said with a laugh. "But let me start as a spy. I searched the chamber of chronicles in the spring castle every opportunity I could. There's a foreign section. We'll speak later about what they've pilfered from Lumatere. Finally I came across the chronicles of Phaneus of Yutlind. Of course, I couldn't understand a word of it. So I returned home with the chronicles. It had been a strange time in the spring palace, and I told the king that I was sick at heart and needed to be with my family. And here I am."

"And you were able to translate it, blessed Barakah?"

Finnikin asked, and Isaboe heard envy in his voice.

"I promise it wasn't easy," the priest-king said. "Phaneus of Yutlind's writing rants and states that we all speak one tongue before we're born."

"I don't understand," Isaboe said.

"There's no Lumateran, Charyn, Yut, Sorellian, Sendecanese, Osterian, Belegonian, Sarnak," Celie said, excitement in her voice. "He called it the tongue of the innocents."

The priest-king glanced down to where Isaboe held a hand on her belly.

"I listen to you speak to the babe, Your Majesty. But according to Phaneus of Yutlind, that babe does not understand a word of Lumateran. All it understands is the universal language of the innocents. Untainted by life."

"Why can't we remember it, then, according to this Phaneus?" Finnikin asked.

"Oh, Phaneus doesn't have the answer to that. He was barely lucid at times. Dearest Celie had to witness some unmentionable sketches before we reached the pages of the unborns."

"Unmentionable," Celie said, her cheeks pink at the memory.

"How unmentionable?" Isaboe asked, intrigued.

"I'll tell you later," Celie said. "Among other things."

"Celie, you have taken a lover," Finnikin said. "Why is it that Isaboe gets to hear everything and I get nothing but Phaneus the mad Yut?"

Sir Topher made a sound with his throat that meant he was irritated by the chatting.

"Go on, blessed Barakah," Isaboe said.

"My guess would be that we don't remember the language because we don't remember birth. Perhaps the shock wipes it from our memories. Who knows?"

The priest-king swung the chronicle around and pointed.

"The mad Yut's tongue of the innocents," he said, pointing to the strange but familiar lettering.

Isaboe recognized one or two symbols with stems and curves that she had seen in the letters sent by both Froi and Tesadora.

"I found a strange code that matched every symbol to Yut characters I recognized, and then I tried to translate Yut into Lumateran, but the Yut words on both Froi's and the Charyn girl's bodies didn't seem to exist."

The priest-king retrieved the two parchments with Froi's and Quintana's lettering.

"Until I did this," he said, placing them together. They all moved closer to study the words in Yut. "Half of the message was with Froi. The other half with Quintana of Charyn."

"We are incomplete," Finnikin translated.

Isaboe felt her breath catch.

"Is this saying that they're incomplete without each other? Froi and that savage?" she asked.

The priest-king didn't speak for a moment.

"I think it's something even more powerful than that," he said quietly. "It's the spirits of the unborn babes that spoke."

Perri was on his feet, pacing the room, and Isaboe felt the tension from them all.

The priest-king laid Froi's letter out on the table. "We have to go back to the events of the night of our lad's birth. A strange, horrific night when a mother and her son are wrenched apart, a man loses the love of a brother, another man loses faith in his king and himself, a babe loses her mother and twin sister. All those involved, the oracle among them, were so powerful that their loss and pain and fury and grief became a splinter in the soul of a kingdom. We know it's referred to as the day of weeping, when every Charynite woman who carried a child bled it from their loins."

Isaboe held out a hand to Perri and he sat, his fists clenched.

"Look at what Seranonna did to Lumatere," the priest-king continued. "All that rage and anguish. That wasn't planned. It wasn't conjured up in a spell. It came from in here," the priest-king said, pointing to his heart. He flicked through another of the chronicles. "Two hundred years ago, it also happened in Sende-cane. A young girl's passion destroyed the kingdom, and it is still a wasteland today except for the cloister of Lagrami. Five hundred years ago, it happened to an island north of Sarnak, a place that no longer exists. Never underestimate the power of our raw emotions."

Sir Topher was a man of logic, and even he looked spellbound.

"So the two babes and two brothers, and Lirah of Serker and the oracle cursed the kingdom much the same way as Seranonna did?" Isaboe asked.

The priest-king shook his head.

"No. They didn't curse the kingdom. They cursed a day and created the weeping."

"Destroyed only one day?" Finnikin said.

"Then, who cursed the next eighteen years?" Sir Topher asked.

The priest-king looked at them all, his eyes finally settling on Perri.

"I believe the spirit of those bled babes had nowhere to go. Some were days from birth. They had no name, and no way of being called to rest. So they searched for the source. The vessels."

"Froi?" Perri said.

The priest-king nodded. "And the princess. Two vessels more powerful than we can ever imagine. *Come to me. Come to me*, they would have called out, hearing the cries of their lost brothers and sisters. All they wanted to do was protect them. And the spirits did come to them but were splintered." He looked at Perri. "Part of the spirit of your unborn child went to Froi and the other part went to Quintana of Charyn."

The priest-king paused a moment, looking at them all. "It's what takes place during chaos, whether in this known world or that yet to be born. Look at what happened to us here all those years ago. Lumatere was divided in two. Those who were trapped and those in exile.

"And the spirits of those babes have been full of fury and despair all these years. They've wanted the part of them that was lost returned. And now, finally, each has become one again, united in the babe that Quintana and Froi created. Let's pray that it's born, dear friends. Let's pray that it stays safe in its mother's arms."

"Mercy!" said Finnikin.

Mercy indeed, Isaboe thought, placing a shaking hand on her belly. The kingdom of Charyn had not been cursed by evil. It had been cursed by innocence. By the power of the unborn.

CHaPteR 33

Froi heard the words often that day.

"We're going to battle."

They were said with uncertainty most of the time. Although the lads understood that they were going to war for Quintana of Charyn, there was still no guarantee that she would be found in the valley between Lumatere and Charyn. It was where they were heading. But first they had to get through the three hills and Bestiano's army.

That night, they all gathered in the keep to listen to final commands, shuffling for room wherever they could. Froi was on the ground. He looked up at each archway, all the way to the top, and he felt the flatness of everyone's mood. It wasn't the way he wanted these men fighting for Quintana's place in the palace. From the third-floor balcony, Gargarin spoke to them all. He called the next few days the most important hours in Charyn's history. Said that they would be spoken about in years to come. As impassioned as his words were, the men still seemed lost. Froi remembered what Fekra had said. That the Nebian army

Bestiano commanded didn't know what they were fighting for anymore. Nor did these men.

They were about to leave when Dolyn's voice was heard.

"Priestling, can you sing Charyn's ballad?"

Froi watched Arjuro look up to where Dolyn stood. The leader of Lascow was beside Gargarin and De Lancey.

"I heard you once," Dolyn continued. "It was many, many years ago. Your voice rang clear in the crowd. More powerful than any other priestling."

"No," Arjuro said bluntly.

His voice echoed strangely in the quiet space.

"Arjuro—" De Lancey called out.

"My answer is no! It's a song for a Charyn that no longer exists."

"We go to war tomorrow for a Charyn Tariq believed in, sir," one of the Lasconians shouted out boldly from one of the upper balconies.

Arjuro shook his head, his expression weary. "I miss my sisters and brothers in the godshouse," he called back in response. "I don't care whose voice rang clear in the crowd. I sang Charyn's ballad alongside them . . . and now they're gone. I don't sing . . . except for the dead."

"Then, perhaps we can speak it out loud," a Turlan lad said. "As a blessing before battle."

There was a halfhearted mumble and then words were spoken, disjointed and feeble.

". . . the stone we shaped with hands of hope to build a kingdom of might . . . the roads we paved with the blood of our toil . . ."

Something inside Froi's head jolted. He knew this song. The priest-king had taught him. The old man had taught him everything about Charyn. "It's a song of their hubris . . . a song to show off their talents," the priest-king had murmured, but he made Froi listen to it each time they were together. "Sing with me, Froi," he would say. But Froi had refused. He sang for no man. Not since his days on the streets of the Sarnak capital. But now he understood. Had the priest-king guessed who Froi was all along and taught him this song, not to conquer an enemy, but to find his own people? Clever, wicked man. Froi had never loved the priest-king more.

There's a song in your heart, Froi. You must unleash it or you will spend your days in regret.

"I'll sing it with you, Arjuro," Froi called out, and everyone searched for him in the crowded keep.

"I know it . . . I was taught by the blessed Barakah of Lumatere," he said loudly for everyone to hear. "He believed . . . a well-rounded education was the best," he continued to explain, partly with a lie.

A silence came over the room as they waited for Arjuro's reaction. And somewhere in the crowd, Arjuro and Froi found each other and stood side by side. Men crouched around them. From above, Gargarin's eyes seemed to pierce into Froi's. As long as he lived, Froi would never be able to determine his father's thoughts.

He waited for the cue from Arjuro. It was a song for more than one to sing and Arjuro began alone, his voice robust, his warble perfect, a sound still so youthful despite the years. Froi felt a catch in his throat thinking of the young gods' blessed Arjuro, who would have bewitched the hardest of spirits. He was still bewitching De Lancey of Paladozza now. The love on the *provincaro's* face was potent. Catching. Froi waited, ready to commence with the second stanza. His voice had been deep for some years now. Not as a boy. Back then, it was high and pure and it fetched him a price. Back then, he didn't understand the words he sang. All he understood was an empty stomach that needed to be filled. But now, as he started his song, he knew exactly what he was singing, and his voice reached depths that he hadn't known existed. And when Arjuro's voice joined in, it was a communion, a blood tie, and Froi felt the strength that both their voices gave to those listening. He watched men place clenched hands to their chests; he saw tears spring to surprised eyes. He saw Lirah push her way through the men on the balcony above, transfixed. Froi's voice felt like a caress for his battered soul. Because he sang for Quintana of Charyn. He sang for the misery of her life, the poison in her body, the scars on her skin, and the courage in her character. And he sang for the child he would never call his own. He sang for the Charyn he would leave behind, and he felt his hand clench in a fist at the thought of such a kingdom. It made his voice soar with Arjuro's, to a height that matched its earlier depth. And when it was over and he pushed through the crowd, he felt hands clap his back, ruffle his cap, and shake his hand as he moved among them. He felt their euphoria.

He returned to his post on the wall, looking out into the darkness and wondering what the next day would bring. Death. Of course there'd be death. Would it be him? Grij? Who would live and who would die?

Perabo joined him, with Gargarin.

"Your lad here is lethal," Perabo said. "Let's hope a bit of that blood runs through the little king."

"Say it louder and I'll cut out your tongue," Gargarin snapped.

Perabo gripped Gargarin to him, and Froi stepped between them.

"Your secrets, whatever I may believe they are, die with me," Perabo said through clenched teeth. "Doubt me or threaten me again, and you'll have to find yourself another constable."

Gargarin cupped the man's shoulder, his hand shaking. Froi could see that something wasn't right, but to Perabo, at least, Gargarin seemed contrite.

"You're the only constable I want, Perabo. No more doubts or threats. Make sure the names of the lads going into battle are recorded."

Perabo nodded, glancing at Froi. "This one needs to rest. Ariston is going to want Froi by his side."

"He won't be going with Ariston and his men," Gargarin said.

Froi stared at him, stunned.

"What are you saying?" he shouted. "You know I'm as good as a Turlan. You're only doing this because—"

"Because what?" Gargarin hissed. "Because you're my son? You're mistaking me for someone with choices, Froi. I don't have choices."

Froi waited, looking to Perabo for answers.

"I can't have you riding into battle," Gargarin said. "We need you for something else."

Gargarin's stare was deadly.

"You're going to steal into that camp and put him down, Froi."

Froi heard Perabo's hiss of satisfaction.

"We want Bestiano dead."

When the sun rose and every soldier in the fortress was in place, Froi found Grijio in the bailey. The last born was with the Turlans, sitting on his horse, waiting for word.

"Are you frightened?" Froi asked.

"Of course I'm frightened," Grij said, looking over Froi's

shoulder to where De Lancey was watching them from the entrance of the keep.

"Gargarin won't let my father come along," he said. "Dolyn and Ariston agree."

"Well, he's injured."

"It's not that. They can't afford to lose a *provincaro* who will favor the palace in the future. Father ordered that I stay, too, but I told him I couldn't. I made these plans with Tariq and Satch . . . and even Olivier. That we'd save her. I can't do that hiding behind my father's title. And I may not be good with a sword, but I'm fast with a horse."

Froi noticed Mort close by on his mount. Grijio was to travel with the Turlans, who would tear through Bestiano's defenses and get to the Lumateran valley in the hope of finding Quintana there. The Lasconians would stay behind and fight, and if all was true, the Desantos army would decimate the Nebians from the north. Regardless of everything, it meant more dead Charynite lads who didn't know what they were fighting for, judging from Fekra's hopelessness. But Froi couldn't afford to care. He was one step closer to Quintana.

"You take care of him, Mort," Froi said, holding a hand up to Grijio, who shook it firmly.

"*Provincaro* says I not to let Grij out of sight," Mort said.

"Keep safe, Froi," Grijio said.

Froi patted Grijio's mount and then walked back to De Lancey and Arjuro.

"I'm going to see them off from the wall," De Lancey said in a low voice.

Arjuro and Froi watched him walk away.

"Are you ready?" Arjuro asked.

"I've been ready since I left Lumatere," Froi said. He caught the expression on Arjuro's face. "Why look so sad, Arjuro, when I promise I'll return to you with some part of my body to sew up?"

Arjuro didn't have a sense of humor that morning, and Froi walked away because saying good-bye to Arjuro was always hard.

Lirah waited for him by the well, and they sat awhile in silence, watching Perabo organize the Lasconians. Unlike the time at the gate, Florik was ready. He held up a hand of acknowledgment to Froi, and Froi returned the gesture.

He tried hard not to think of what would take place beyond any sort of rescue. All he could think of was seeing Quintana and not letting her go. But what would Froi's place in the new Charyn be? Would he be a foot soldier in the army or one of Perabo's palace soldiers? Would he live in the godshouse with Arjuro and Lirah? And who would he be? Froi of the Lumateran Exiles or Dafar of Abroi? Would he watch his son grow, thinking of him merely as an acquaintance? And what of Lumatere? If he left, did he ever have a chance of returning there again?

"I was born from the union between my father . . . and his oldest daughter," Lirah said.

Froi flinched.

"So my mother was in fact my sister, and oh, how she despised me. Who would blame her? The moment our father died, she sold me to feed her younger children. I was twelve. If I was less beautiful, she would have sold me to a Serker pig farmer who needed the labor, but this face bought me a place in the palace."

"Labor on a pig farm isn't so bad," he said, thinking of what she endured in the palace.

"Yes, I agree, but if she had sold me to the farmer, I'd have been slaughtered with the rest of Serker not even seven years later. So let's just say that this face bought me my life . . . ours."

Ours. Froi belonged to Lirah. *Ours.* He would like that word from here on. It would mean something different, something more.

"There was a woman in the pen with me. It's what they called the cart we traveled in from Serker to the Citavita. The pen, because we were treated like animals. And through all the misery, she said that some of us in this lifetime experience a moment of beauty beyond reckoning. I asked her what that was, and she said, 'If you're one of the lucky ones, you'll know it when you see it. You'll understand why the gods have made you suffer. Because that moment's reward will make your knees weak and everything you've suffered in life will pale in comparison.'"

Lirah stared at him. "Some women claim that moment happens at the sight of their child for the first time." She shook her head. "But I caught a glimpse of you when you were born and then you were gone. I felt nothing except more yearning and despair and misery.

"And then . . . tonight you sang Charyn's ballad with Arjuro and I thought, *Ah, there it is.* That's why I've suffered all my life. For this moment of beauty and perfection." Her eyes pooled with tears. "It didn't come from looking at you or even hearing your voice. It came from seeing the expression on Gargarin's face. He was looking at the wonder of what we made together. Our son, Dafar of Abroi. I'd suffer it all again just to know that moment was there in my life."

She gripped his hand.

"You said to me once that you weren't what I dreamed of. You were right. You surpass everything I dreamed of. Even the rot in you that's caused you to do shameful things. Some men let the rot and guilt fester into something ugly beyond words. Few men can turn it into worth and substance. If you're gods' blessed for no other reason, it's for that."

And then she was gone, disappearing through the entrance

that would take her to the room she shared with Gargarin. But not for long. A new Charyn meant that a *gravina* would lie between Lirah and Gargarin.

They heard a shout from one of the guards on the wall. Fekra had given his signal, which meant that the sentinel he replaced was well out of sight. Ariston and his men rode out first, followed by Perabo, who led the Lasconians. Froi rode last, and his eyes met Gargarin's, who stood at the gate.

"Don't take chances," Gargarin begged. "Do what you need to do, and don't take chances."

Froi stopped, waiting until the others were out of hearing distance.

"Will you promise me something?" he asked.

Gargarin nodded, and Froi could see he was shaking.

"Allow me the honor to name my son," Froi said, his voice husky with emotion. "He'll be called Tariq. Tariq of the Citavita."

CHAPTER 34

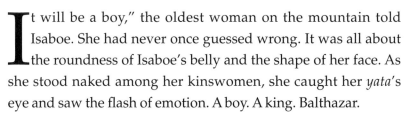

It will be a boy," the oldest woman on the mountain told
Isaboe. She had never once guessed wrong. It was all about
the roundness of Isaboe's belly and the shape of her face. As
she stood naked among her kinswomen, she caught her *yata*'s
eye and saw the flash of emotion. A boy. A king. Balthazar.

The women on the mountain had gathered in Yata's home to
watch the blessing of the unborn. It was a tradition among the
Monts.

"He'll come into this world with secrets," the oldest woman
on the mountain said. "But only few remember what they are by
the time they are old enough to speak. Perhaps yours will be the
one, my queen. Perhaps your son's secrets will cure that which
ails this land."

Isaboe's young cousin Agata held a small bowl of oil from a
Mont olive tree, with a sprinkle of sage in it, and Isaboe shivered
when she felt the old woman's cold fingers on her skin. "Your
milk is strong. It will feed a king."

There was a murmuring of appreciation from the others.
"He's ready," the old woman said. "Wherever he is now, he'll
follow your voice home. Talk to him, my queen."

Isaboe thought for a moment. She remembered her words to Jasmina before her daughter had entered this world. The oldest woman on the mountain had guessed right that time. "You will have a daughter and she longs to hear your voice." Later, after the birth, Isaboe had spoken to Finnikin about it. "I told Jasmina that she belonged to Lumatere's rebirth and that she would be loved for the hope she brought to this kingdom."

But what would she say to this babe, now that she could not get the priest-king's words out of her head? That spirits have their own world and language long before they enter ours? Each night since Celie and the blessed Barakah had come to visit, Isaboe had studied the mad Yut's chronicle and learned to say the words in her heart so that her child could hear and understand.

Be my guide, beloved son. Rid me of my malice and my fury. Don't let it be suckled from my breast.

"I've smelled you all," Quintana said bluntly to Phaedra and the women late that afternoon in the cave. "This whole week. You've smothered me."

"Because our days of bleeding all came at the same time," Cora said. "It's a sign. We need to bathe now that it's over. Together."

"To cleanse ourselves?" Florenza asked.

"There's nothing dirty about us," her mother said. "It's a blessing. We've been given a gift of unity. It's our gift to Quintana of Charyn and her child. The coming of the blood is renewal. So we celebrate it together."

"Bathe?" The princess stared at Cora, all savage teeth. "If you place my head under water, I'll—"

"Yes, yes. You'll slice us from ear to ear," Cora said, dismissively. "We've heard it before. Up you get."

Despite the warmer spring days, the evening air was cool. They undressed by the rocks on the stream, hanging their clothing on the branches nearby.

"I don't like to put my head in the water," Quintana said for the umpteenth time.

"A bit of water over your head never hurts, and if—" Cora stopped, a sort of horror and wonder in her eyes. The others followed her gaze, and in the half light of the moon, they stared in fascination at Quintana's bare, scarred body.

"It's the strangest thing I've ever seen," Ginny said, referring to the belly. Phaedra had to agree. Sometimes when she was walking behind Quintana, it was difficult to believe she was carrying anything. But it was Quintana's scars that made Phaedra want to weep, a cruel reminder of what the princess had endured at the hands of Charyn.

Phaedra suddenly felt conscious of her own bareness. They all did, except for Ginny, who was pleased with her form, as one would expect her to be. Charynite women were not like their Lumateran sisters. It was the way they were raised. Phaedra wondered if the curse had made them all more inhibited or whether it had been like that since the beginning of time.

Florenza was the first to wade into the stream, squealing from the cold. Phaedra thought that she was being precious, and then she stepped in and squealed herself, until they all were there, shushing each other but laughing all the same.

No matter how hard she scrubbed, Phaedra couldn't remove the layers of dirt and grime, but after a while she didn't care anymore. They all seemed bewitched by the moon's glow on the water and they waded toward a place in the center of the stream where its shimmering surface beckoned them. They held on to each other, arms around shoulders, in a circle of something so strange that it made Phaedra feel a lightness of being.

"Did you like Florenza when you first saw her, Jorja?"

Quintana asked, teeth chattering as she gripped Phaedra and Cora around the neck.

"We won't let your head go under, so you mustn't hold so tight," Cora said. At first, Quintana refused to listen, but then Phaedra felt her hold loosen.

"What a thing to ask," Florenza said with a laugh. "Of course Mother liked me."

"What I fear most is that I won't like him," Quintana continued. "I don't know what I'll say to the little king when I first see him."

"You'll know what to feel and say the moment you first see him and not a moment before," Jorja promptly said.

"But what if Florenza was the ugliest babe in the world and you couldn't bear to touch her?" Quintana demanded to know.

"Well, she was quite ugly, come to think of it," Jorja said, and Florenza laughed even more. "All babies are quite ugly."

Jorja pressed a kiss to Florenza's cheek. Despite Florenza's broken nose and bruised face, Jorja still looked at her daughter as if she were the most beautiful creature the gods had ever made. Phaedra remembered her mother looking at her in such a way, those days before the plague took her. If Phaedra had been certain of anything, it had been of her mother's love.

"How did it feel, Jorja?" Phaedra asked. Never had she dared imagine Lucian's child in her arms. It was too cruel a dream. "To hold your babe for the first time, I mean?"

Jorja thought a moment. "I cried for my mother. I was a very spoiled young girl, and my mother and the servants had done everything for me."

They heard a snap of a twig, and Ginny cried out softly.

"We'll be safe. Don't you worry," she blurted out, staring into the semi-darkness.

Despite everything, Ginny seemed more affected than anyone

else by the incident of Galvin the hangman. She appointed herself guard of their cave, disappearing at times to ensure that they were safe from intruders.

"There's nothing strange out there," Cora reassured. "It's the night world scurrying around, going about their chores."

"Go on," Quintana said to Jorja.

"Well, crying for my mother caused much friction between Harker and me," Jorja continued.

"Father's very practical and doesn't like fuss," Florenza told the others knowingly.

"Yes, well, your father grew up with fuss and resented it," her mother said. "He was furious to find himself betrothed to me and threatened to send me back to my mother over and over again."

Phaedra was surprised by the words. "But you love each other," she said. "I saw you together."

"Well, I always loved him, and he grew to love me," Jorja said haughtily. "It's the power I have over him now."

"When did he fall in love with you, then?" Quintana demanded to know.

Jorja thought for a moment. "It was during the drought, when Florenza was five. He said I was resourceful and managed to keep the village fed."

"It's very decent," Phaedra said. "Not many noblemen care whether their villagers are fed."

"Well, that was Harker for you," Jorja said. "Whatever food we had on our table, our neighbors would have on theirs. To be honest, I did it more for him than for the villagers. If it pleased him, it pleased me."

"My father's an idealist," Florenza said proudly. "And my mother is a secret one," she added, feigning a loud whisper. "It's very unfashionable where we come from."

"Never marry an idealistic man," Jorja advised them,

"because one day you'll find yourself dragging your daughter through the sewers of your province or living in a filthy cave with nothing but the putrid clothes on your back." Jorja looked at her daughter. "We imagined a better life for you, Florenza."

"It's good enough for now, Mother. You all did enough, those of your age. Those born in your time and before suffered most because you knew Charyn before the curse and after. Cora would agree."

"No," Cora said, her voice flat. "Not enough." She turned to look at Quintana. "Look at what wasn't done for this one. All of us. Turned our backs on Charyn's last child. We knew what was happening in that palace, and we did nothing. We should have been beating down the palace walls and protecting you. But we turned our backs in bitterness and did nothing!"

"Isn't it the place of men to protect?" Florenza asked.

"Men," Cora said with disdain. "What good are they?"

"That's because you've never had a man," Ginny said.

"Oh, I've had a man," Cora said. "And a more useless species the gods have never created, apart from Kasabian and that young Mont."

"*Luc-ien?*" Phaedra said, surprised to hear such praise from Cora.

Cora snorted rudely. "That idiot? Don't be ridiculous. I mean the Jory lad."

"What happened to your man, Cora?" Quintana asked. "Did he break your heart?"

Cora made a rude sound again. "The only reason I put up with the panting and the grunting was because I was expected to produce a child, and I failed time and time again. Do you want to know when I stopped feeling like a useless woman? When every woman in Charyn was considered useless. Charyn's curse set me free. I left that lump I was wed to, and all I took was four klin tree seeds. Have you seen a klin tree? They hail from Osteria, and their seeds are hard to come by. Osterians say the klin tree flowers hope. So I took hope in my pocket that day I left and joined my brother, Kasabian, on his farm outside Jidia. That year, we felled the trees surrounding his cottage and we grew a garden of wonder. My brother says I have a gift with the land. That I can speak to it."

"Then, why didn't you stay there?" Jorja asked.

"Drought. Plague. The earth stopped listening, and we had nothing to feed us. The klin tree still grew, but I never saw it flower hope and was forced to leave it behind. We were convinced to travel north, where we'd find a new life in Alonso. But Alonso did not want us. It was as though the gods were saying, 'You don't belong to this land.'"

Phaedra looked away, shamed. Alonso was crowded, and her father had refused to allow the travelers in. She remembered those days when people arrived in droves. Alonso land was fertile, and it seemed to promise everything after the curse on the Lumateran border was broken. But her father's people threatened to turn on him if he allowed another traveler in.

"But there's still some land left to share," she'd hear him cry to his lords.

"And there are other men we can find to lead this province," they threatened. And that was how Phaedra's family, whose ancestors had ruled Alonso for centuries, could have lost the province. Not from war or the enemy or even the palace. But because her father dared to allow the landless into the walls of Alonso.

"It may count for nothing," Phaedra said to the women. "And I make no excuses for my father's behavior, turning his back on anyone who begged at Alonso's wall, but there were some nights I'd hear him weep as he prayed to the gods and to my dead mother. I never imagined that a man so proud could weep."

Ginny was already bored with their talk and decided it was time to return to the cave. She waded away with Florenza, and the others began to follow.

"I saw my father weep before me," Quintana said to the others. "When he was dying." She was pensive. "Do you want to know something about tyrants? When faced with death, they weep and they beg just like the rest of us."

Phaedra's eyes met Cora's and then Jorja's, who warned her with a quick shake of her head.

At the rocks, they collected their clothes and wrapped themselves in blankets, hurrying back to the cave to dry. Jorja gripped Phaedra and Cora as they were about to follow the others.

"If you value your lives . . . and hers, never repeat what you heard her say here today," Jorja said.

"She couldn't possibly have—" Cora said.

"Couldn't she? We would always hear of her madness. And these weeks, I've understood it is anything but that. It's survival. She has a madness to survive now. What more could we want from a little king's mother?"

Up ahead, Phaedra saw Quintana shiver despite the blanket covering her body. Phaedra dressed quickly, her body still damp, and hurried toward Quintana. She wrapped her own blanket around the princess, fussing over her. She felt Quintana's gaze, and their eyes met.

"You were his thirtieth, Phaedra."

"Thirtieth?" Phaedra asked absently, leading Quintana along the uneven ground before them. "I don't understand. Whose?"

"Froi's, of course. He said, 'Phaedra of Alonso is kind.' So he chose you to be on his list of those he trusted. It's why I came to you."

Phaedra stopped them both, her hand still gripping Quintana's arm. "You came here for me? Here, in the valley?"

"Well, it's not as if I could have gone to any of the other

twenty-nine on his list," Quintana said bluntly.

"Me?"

"Have I not already said that?"

Phaedra was speechless.

"He was half right, of course," Quintana said.

Phaedra wanted to weep. She would have done a better job if she'd known. She would never have left Quintana alone or snapped at her or rolled her eyes to the heavens. She would have been a better protector.

"There's much more to you than kindness," Quintana continued. "That day after I arrived in the valley and you visited, the other women were all flustered when they saw my baby belly. Until you walked into the cave and you thought fast. And then that time with the queen of Lumatere . . . well, make no mistake of this. She would have used that sword. I've killed a man, Phaedra. I imagine the look in my eye was just like hers. A bit of justice. Self-loathing. Hatred. Pity. We're not so different, me and the queen of Lumatere."

Quintana pulled free of Phaedra's grip and moved ahead to Jorja and Florenza. Both mother and daughter had taken to fussing over her, and Quintana was a cat who went to anyone who showed her affection. Phaedra stood, shivering in her wet shift. And she did weep.

"Phaedra! Don't stray," Jorja called out.

Phaedra hurried to catch up and gripped Quintana's hand tightly.

"You'll have to take your blanket back, Phaedra," Quintana said, stopping to wrap it around her, imitating Phaedra's earlier fussing. "You'll catch your death, and it'll cause hysteria."

Their eyes met for a moment, and Phaedra nodded with a smile.

"Yes, my queen. I think you're right."

CHAPTER 35

Froi watched as Ariston and his men thundered through the Nebian camp, taking the soldiers by surprise. The army had been in the middle of their morning drills and duties, and the Turlans' speed on their horses meant that they were halfway to the second hill before Bestiano's men had even mounted theirs. Froi's orders were clear: to wait until the battle was dragged well away from the camp to enable him a clear path to Bestiano. By then, Ariston and his men would be heading toward the Lumateran valley while Perabo and the Lasconians would join the battle against the Nebians.

From where he knelt, concealed by the old well on the first hill overlooking the camp, Froi could see at least four men guarding Bestiano's tent. Beside him, Fekra was nervous, and Froi had come to learn that a nervous man either had something to hide or made mistakes.

"Who's protecting Bestiano inside?" Froi asked.

"His guard. One of the rogue brigands Bestiano managed to acquire somewhere outside the Citavita. He speaks the language of gold and more gold."

"So, he's not part of the army?"

"No. The army is under the orders of Scarpo, captain of the Nebian Guard."

"Easily controlled?"

"Scarpo is a soldier, so he follows orders," Fekra said. Froi could tell that Fekra liked a man who followed orders. It was why Fekra didn't particularly like Froi.

"But he takes care of his men," Fekra continued. "According to Dorcas, Scarpo did question Bestiano's decision regarding the execution of the riders. And when Bestiano ordered one hundred men to fight the Turlans in the little woods, Scarpo questioned why so many. The lads are merely numbers for Bestiano. For Scarpo, they are more than that."

"It's a pity I'm going to have to kill this Scarpo."

"You may not have to," Fekra said as they watched the Turlan horses trample the clearing just as Perabo and his men entered the fray. "Scarpo may be long dead at the hands of your friends. If Desantos arrives from the north, Scarpo's army will be destroyed."

Froi heard the regret in Fekra's voice.

"Is Scarpo for Nebia or is he for Charyn?" Froi asked.

"Nebia is Charyn," Fekra argued. "Don't judge them harshly. Including the *provincaro*. He's sitting in a province with no protection because his entire army is here. What would the *provincari* of Paladozza or Sebastabol or any other have done if they were kin to the king's First Adviser and he came to them asking for an army after the king was murdered?"

"You're obviously a Nebian, Fekra. So let me rephrase the question. Is Scarpo a madman?"

"He's not one much for talking. But his men will die for him, and he makes sure, in turn, that his men don't die from bad decisions made by others."

Men were dying around them now. Both Ariston and Perabo had succeeded in dragging the battle from the Nebian camp into the valley beyond, where Froi could hear the sickening tune of cries and shouts and the clang of steel against steel. All that was left here were the dead or dying.

"Froi!" Fekra said, pointing down to Bestiano's tent.

A man stepped outside, exchanging a word with those who guarded the tent. He was armed with at least two swords and a dagger at his ankle. He mounted his horse and headed toward the second hill.

"Bestiano's guard," Fekra whispered.

Which meant Bestiano could be alone. But for how long?

"Let's go," Froi said. He slithered down the hill, his eyes fixed on those protecting the former king's adviser. He remembered what Trevanion and Perri would say each time he hesitated. "Dead men don't come back to kill you, Froi. They don't shout out warnings. Make sure you do it right the first time." And that was how simple it was. The type of simplicity that turned his stomach. At the perfect vantage point, he dropped on one knee. One longbow. Four arrows. Four dead men. He heard Fekra's ragged breath beside him.

"You knew them?" Froi asked.

"Does it matter?" Fekra asked. "If I didn't, someone else did." He shook his head with regret. "How do you get used to it? All the killing?"

"Who says you do?" Froi asked, and bolted for the tent.

He reached the entrance.

No mistakes, Froi. No mistakes.

He stepped inside. Bestiano looked up, startled, his hand instantly reaching for his sword, but Froi was faster, leaping on the table and flying across the space to knock him down. *Make it fast. Don't waste time. Don't take chances. Every second counts.* Yet

the sight of Bestiano, with his mottled skin and weak mouth and ever-present smirk, changed everything. Froi wanted every second to last. He wanted to inflict pain. No mercy. And by not using his sword, Froi knew he was making the first mistake of many. But he didn't care. His fist connected with Bestiano's cheek and the man's head flew back, causing him to fall to the ground. Froi leaped, straddled him, and pounded into his nose, mouth, cheek. There was no counting. All rage. Blood, flesh, and might, and cries of pain and grunts of fury. He snapped both the man's wrists, the howl ringing through his ears. And on and on he pounded, landing his blows with precision. Froi wanted Bestiano to feel his rage.

For that morning he witnessed Bestiano in Quintana's chamber.

For not allowing her to make shapes on her wall.

For trying to capture her spirit.

For trying to break it.

For all the times Froi didn't see.

And then Froi's head burst with his own memories of Sarnak. A strike for every man who had held him down under the force of their own weight. A strike for the hatred he would always feel for himself when he remembered Isaboe's face that night in the barn in Sorel. This is what Froi would do to that boy he once was. Blow after blow. He wanted him dead.

A clean kill, Froi. Always a clean kill.

He felt his knuckles crack from the force, but this would not be a clean kill. And when Bestiano had almost passed out from the pain of it all, Froi pulled him forward to speak in his ear.

"You were never able to break her. She is the stone of this kingdom."

Suddenly, there was a sound behind him, and Froi let go of Bestiano and leaped onto the table. Too slow. The blade of a sword tore into the skin at his thigh, and Froi crumpled in pain, kicking the intruder with his other leg. But past wounds betrayed him, and his legs gave way. It was all the time Bestiano's guard needed. Froi felt the tip of a sword pierce the wound already in his thigh, and he cried out, mustering up the strength he had left to kick the man between the legs. And although Bestiano's guard faltered a moment, the sound of another entering changed everything.

"Kill him!"

Dorcas.

What had Gargarin said all that time ago? That he didn't want to die at the hands of someone like Dorcas, who only knew how to follow orders.

Above him, Froi could see Bestiano's man step back to strike.

"Wait," Froi croaked. He closed his eyes a moment, felt the dirt and grime in his tears.

"Dorcas, tell him to wait."

He could hear the heavy breathing of those who stood in the room, but he was too weary to open his eyes. Too heartsick at the thought of never seeing her again. But he needed to find a way to speak a bond to his son and this weak, pathetic rider was Froi's only messenger.

"Listen to me, Dorcas . . . listen well. . . . If all you can do in this life is follow orders, then these are the orders of a man who's to die. Take care of the little king . . . tell him he was made from love and hope. . . . That is your bond to him, Dorcas. If you're good for nothing else, follow a bond that makes him a good king."

Froi raised himself, opening his eyes. He turned to look at Dorcas, who was kneeling beside Bestiano. The palace rider's hand reached out to Bestiano's injured face.

"I said, kill him," Dorcas ordered, looking toward where the

guard stood over Froi. Froi heard the surprised gasp, the gurgle of blood and then felt the weight of the man fall across him as Fekra revealed himself with a dagger in his shaking hand. And then Dorcas pressed a hand over Bestiano's mouth and pushed down hard. Bestiano's body jerked against it with force, but Dorcas held it there for a very long time, until finally he looked over to Froi.

"Tell the little king yourself, Lumateran."

CHAPTER 36

Ginny entered the cave long after she had left to find some kindling.

"Where have you been?" Phaedra asked.

"I thought I heard something and went to look," Ginny said. "We can't be too careful."

"Only squirrels," Cora said. "Our fear will turn us into madwomen."

"And we're not already?" Phaedra watched Ginny fussing with the entrance of the cave, concealing it with some of the shrubs and branches she'd dragged back.

"Come closer and eat before our piglet gobbles everything up," Cora said gruffly.

The piglet didn't defend herself; instead, she tugged at the meat on the bone. Since finding it more difficult to move around outside the cave because of her belly, Quintana had taken to setting traps for the hares that boldly came to their entrance, and there was a glee to her when she held up their lifeless forms.

"There's nothing more harmless than food you catch yourself," Quintana said. "Free of hemlock and whatnot. I've never enjoyed eating so much as I have these past months."

"Wipe your hands and come and sit against me," Jorja said to her. "I'll rub your back. It's a heavy load you carry there."

Phaedra tried to wipe the filth from Quintana's hands and face. The soak in the stream had done little to remove their grime, and it shamed Phaedra to think that Charyn's first child would be born in a cave.

"Harker would rub my back when I was carrying Florenza, and it always was such a relief," Jorja said when Quintana was sitting comfortably between her knees.

Perhaps this was better than the luxury of another place, Phaedra thought, watching them all. Florenza caught her eye and smiled.

And that's how Phaedra would remember the moment before it all changed. In her province, the tailor's wife would speak about before and after the curse. One moment, she was carrying a baby in her belly, and the next, there was a puddle of blood on the ground between her legs and screams sounding across the city. The tailor's wife knew that nothing would ever be the same again. Phaedra understood the truth of those words when she heard the voices outside the cave. She saw the horror of understanding in Florenza's eyes and then chanced a look at the others. They all knew. Because they smelled the violence of the intruders. The malevolence. And when Donashe and his men stormed in with their swords and ugliness, there was no screaming or crying this time. Phaedra and the women clambered around Quintana. Wordlessly, they clasped their hands together as a shield. As if that would be enough, foolish women that they were. They thought that would be enough.

One of the men beat at Jorja's hand with the edge of his dagger until it was a bloody pulp. But still Jorja didn't let go. And worst of all, Phaedra saw Ginny, who was holding no one's hand, but staring at her man Gies with horror, and then

Quintana's eyes met Phaedra's. What had she once whispered in her ear? *"I do believe we're going to have to kill that piece-of-nothing girl, Ginny."* And as long as Phaedra would live, she'd never forgive herself for not cutting the girl from ear to ear.

And then Donashe and his men dragged them out of the cave and forced them to their knees except for Quintana and Ginny, who was weeping her pitiful, treacherous tears. Phaedra felt Jorja's bloody hand take hers and Florenza's because this was how they'd die, with shaking hands, in putrid clothes. But Cora stood. She said there was no way she was going to die on her knees at the feet of a man. Donashe's men trained their weapons on Cora, because it was as she had always said: men would destroy first what they could not control. And Phaedra was begging them, begging, *please, please.* She'd stay on her knees with hands clenched together and beg until her last breath and she could hear Florenza's sobbing and Jorja's voice. *Hush now. Hush now, my beautiful girls.* That would be Jorja's gift to them when facing death. Calmness.

But then they heard a sound so primitive in its savagery that it chilled the soul and stopped the man's blade from slashing Cora's throat. A guttural fury that rivaled the cry of every creature within miles. Through eyes drenched with filthy sweat, Phaedra could see Quintana, could see her madness as the air was pierced with her never-ending roar. Donashe pressed an elbow against her throat and the cry was gagged, but Quintana bit his arm hard, blood on her lips that she spat to the ground.

"I'll will this babe to die!"

Phaedra heard both the gods and the demons in Quintana's voice and the sound frightened her more than the death she was facing.

"I'll bleed it from the inside. Just you watch me. Watch me!"

Donashe stared down at the blood on his arm where her

teeth had cut into his flesh, and he raised a hand to her.

"*Do it!*" Quintana taunted. "Do it and watch what I can do in return."

"Kill them," Donashe ordered the man holding Cora. And Quintana's shrill scream sounded again and Ginny was crying, clasping hands to her ears.

"I've seen what she can be," Ginny sobbed. "She's gods' blessed and cursed, and there'll be no reward for any of you if they die."

Donashe's men dared to look at the filthy princess whose eyes spelled death. Charyn's abomination. Its savage. Its curse maker. And the frightened men shook their heads and stepped away.

"You kill them, Donashe. I'm not doing it."

"She's a mad bitch and she'll burn us all, Donashe."

"They've promised us gold for a living babe. Not for a puddle of blood."

Donashe gripped Quintana's arm and dragged her along.

"You're weak. All of you," he shouted over his shoulder, and the men grabbed Phaedra and the women and followed Donashe to camp.

In the valley, Phaedra saw Tesadora first and then she saw Japhra and the Mont girls and then she saw the valley dwellers. The way they stared in horror and awe at Quintana. The tears on Japhra's face and the rage in Tesadora's eyes as she approached Donashe. Tesadora looked so small, and Phaedra feared for the Lumateran woman's life. Feared for them all.

"You are holding the wife of a Mont leader," Tesadora warned. "If Phaedra of Alonso is not released, the wrath of the Monts will be felt across Charyn. Explain that to whomever you answer to."

Donashe pushed Phaedra and the women toward the stone

steps that led to the highest cave, a place Phaedra knew they would never escape from.

"Did you hear me, Charynite?" Tesadora shouted, following. "These are my demands. Return Phaedra of Alonso to the mountain. Release Quintana of Charyn to my care. Let my girls see to Rafuel's wounds."

Phaedra gasped and swung around, searching for him. Rafuel? How could she have forgotten him?

"Oh, Rafuel. Rafuel," Quintana cried.

And Phaedra truly began to understand the horror of the day as they climbed the steep ascent to the top. In front of the caves below, at the start of the road to Alonso, they saw him. Rafuel was tied to a horse, his face beaten to a pulp, his legs barely able to hold him upright. One of Donashe's men mounted the horse, and it was only then that Phaedra began to weep. Because she knew there was no hope for him . . . the boy with a basket of cats, this man who had never forsaken their kingdom when others had.

"Everything for Charyn," Rafuel cried, and they dragged him away.

Lucian dined late that night with Yata and Isaboe in Yata's private chamber.

"You do us an honor each time you birth your children here, cousin," Lucian said.

Isaboe reached over to take Yata's hand. "I sometimes feel my mother's presence here more than in the palace."

She was teary. Finnikin was settling Jasmina with his aunt Celestina in the rock village, and Lucian knew she missed them both already. She had never spent a night away from her daughter.

"Finn will be here soon," he said quietly.

They heard voices outside the hall, and Isaboe stumbled to her feet. "That's him," she said.

But it was their cousin Constance who entered, the girl's eyes wild and swollen with tears. She had been in the valley, and her distress could only mean that something had happened to Tesadora and the girls. Or Phaedra.

"Constance?" Lucian said, hurrying across the room to meet her just as her legs buckled. They all cried with alarm, and Lucian caught her in his arms.

"Speak, Constance," Isaboe ordered gently.

Yata held out a small bowl of water to Constance, who took it, weeping.

"They've arrested Phaedra."

"Who?" Lucian demanded. *"Who?"*

"Donashe and his men," Constance said. "They knew where to find the cave, and there was a terrible scene as they dragged the women back upstream. Tesadora fears for all their lives. And Rafuel . . . They know he's been hiding the women and they suspect he had a hand in the death of the hangman and they beat him black and blue before our very eyes."

Sweet goddess.

"We can bring them all up the mountain," Constance said, "and protect—"

"No!"

This came from Yata.

"We don't bring war onto this mountain again," Yata said firmly. "If we give refuge to their queen, Charyn will attack. You know that, Isaboe."

Isaboe nodded. "There will be no talk of Quintana of Charyn finding refuge in Lumatere," she said wearily. "I've spent almost four years avoiding war. I won't have it declared over the life of my enemy's spawn."

She stood unsteadily on her feet.

"Where's my king?" she asked, and Lucian heard the desperation in her voice. He didn't want to leave her, but he needed to see Phaedra and he was desperate to go.

"Finnikin will be here soon," Yata said gently. "It's a full day's ride from the Rock, but he'll be here soon."

Isaboe turned to Lucian. "Go," she said firmly. "Take Jory with you. Make Lumatere's presence known."

It was deep into a starless night by the time Lucian and Jory reached the foot of the mountain. A sick moon did little to guide their path to the stream, and once there, they saw the flicker of lights from the caves where the Charynite valley dwellers huddled together in fear. Or perhaps in hope. They may have witnessed horror in the valley, but for many, the sight of Quintana of Charyn had given them hope and there would be little sleep among them this night.

"Lucian!" he heard Harker's voice in the dark once they crossed the stream. "Is that you?"

"Yes, with Jory," Lucian responded. He heard the crunch of footsteps on dry earth, then light from a lantern appeared, and soon Harker and Kasabian were before them.

"Have you spoken to the women?" Lucian asked.

"Briefly," Kasabian said, "but with Donashe and his men at our shoulders, there was no time for anything but a few words."

"What they did to my girls, Lucian—" Harker said, and Lucian heard the break in the man's voice. "My Florenza's face bruised and swollen, and Jorja's hand crushed."

Harker led them to the path that would take them to the highest cave.

"Stay with Kasabian," Lucian said to Jory. "You know what to do if I don't return."

With only Harker's lantern to light the path, they began the climb. Each cave they passed brought with it the sound of whispering. Higher up, they could hear sobbing and cursing.

"Ginny, the traitor," Harker said. "She's hysterical and under guard."

"And Rafuel?" Lucian asked quietly. "Were you able to find out anything?"

"He's a dead man walking, Lucian. A dead man walking."

It was a strange sort of grief Lucian felt for Rafuel. He wondered when these people had begun to feel like kin. When their fate had become his responsibility.

They continued climbing, using their hands to steady themselves, reaching a rock ledge where Lucian made out the shadow of one man, then two. But he knew that they had a way to go if Phaedra and the women were placed in the highest cave. Worse still, he was certain there was little chance of getting past the camp leaders without incident on so narrow and dark a path. But Lucian felt desperate to see Phaedra, and he kept on walking.

"Don't come any farther, Mont," he heard Donashe say. "This is Charynite business, not yours."

"You have my wife," Lucian said as Donashe stepped out onto the ledge, an oil lamp in his hand. "That's my business, not Charyn's."

"Your wife is under arrest for hiding a king killer."

"Why so concerned about a king killer, Donashe?" Lucian said. "The way I hear it, you managed to finish off the rest of the king's family in the Citavita. So what does that make you?"

Lucian saw the fervor in the man's eyes, but also the desperation. With Quintana in his camp, the Charynite was never so close to the prize. But from what Lucian knew, Donashe had been betrayed by his men before and he would be desperate not to take chances.

"I'm going to give you a warning, Mont," Donashe said. "In days to come, Bestiano of Nebia and the entire Nebian army will be arriving in this valley. Don't let me have to tell them that the Lumaterans were hiding the king killer for all these months, because, unlike me, they'll cross that stream and they won't stop at your mountain. They'll follow the path to your palace."

"I want to see my wife," Lucian said, keeping his voice even. "And if I don't see my wife tonight, I'm going to give you a warning. In the hours to come, I can have the whole Mont army in this valley. Don't let me have to tell them that you just made a threat to their cousin the queen, her consort, and their child, because, unlike me, they'll tear you to pieces."

Donashe allowed the threat to register.

"The white witch and her girl is with them. Haven't I allowed enough, friend?" he asked.

"I'm not leaving until I see my wife," Lucian said.

Donashe turned to his companion. Lucian heard the whispering and watched the man leave with Donashe's oil lamp, the light bobbing all the way to the top. It was nothing less than a prison, and there would be no easy way of getting the women off this rock. No hope for their escape.

"*Luc-ien!*"

"Phaedra?" He leaped up the steps, but Donashe was there to stop him.

"You speak to her from here."

"I can't see her!" Lucian said, through gritted teeth.

"Lucian," he heard Tesadora call out. "Don't bring danger to the mountain. For now, do as they say."

"Are you free to come and go, Tesadora?"

"Yes, but Phaedra and the women aren't."

"Phaedra," he called out again, cursing the stars and the moon for being on a tyrant's side tonight. He just wanted to see her face.

"Yes, *Luc-ien*."

"Are you hurt?"

"No, just frightened. I'm very frightened. We all are."

There was a tremble in Phaedra's voice, and it shattered something inside of Lucian to hear it.

"I'll come again tomorrow," he said. "I promise."

Donashe gripped his arm.

"Don't make promises you can't keep, Mont."

Lucian pulled free.

"I never make promises I can't keep, Donashe. And I promise you this: if you so much as lay another hand on these women, I will kill you. It will happen when you least expect it. It will be an arrow to your heart, and its precision will remind you that if my father hadn't been killed at the hands of a Charynite, I would not be leading his people. I would be an assassin in the Queen's Guard because I don't miss a mark."

And with those words, he began his descent down the rock with Harker, taking each step slowly for fear of tumbling into the darkness.

"I hate to be grateful for other people's misfortune, Lucian," Harker said quietly, "but our greatest consolation may have been the death of your father. I can't imagine what would have happened to my people if you weren't leading the Monts."

Lucian stared down the steep stone steps, all the way to the bottom, and his throat tightened with emotion. The valley dwellers stood on each side of the path, holding either a lantern or candle, lighting Harker and Lucian's way.

"My father would never have forsaken a neighbor," Lucian said. "Never."

"Then he taught his son well, lad. He taught his son well."

CHapteR 37

"Nebia! Surrender!"

Froi couldn't hear.

At first he thought the rage of battle was eating the voices, but then he knew it was inside of him. A chilling silence. It made the horror surrounding him all the worse.

He had ridden with Dorcas and Fekra, desperate to reach the battle between the two hills. To put a stop to Charynites killing Charynites. It was under a waning light that the three entered the field of carnage. Once the sun set, it would be next to impossible to put an end to it all, and they were fighting for time. It was his voice that had done it. *"Nebia! Surrender!"* hollered with a might that splintered something inside his ear.

And then all he could see was Fekra's mouth moving, but nothing coming out. He watched Dorcas and Fekra pull off their cloak and tunics, and it was how the two rode into that valley: with white undershirts on their swords.

White flags of surrender.

But it didn't stop arrows from hitting their marks and men falling to their knees, and it didn't stop axes from wedging themselves into the sinews of men's throats, or swords slicing an arm clear off a body. Froi dismounted to stand amid battle rage that had men in a frenzy, their senses attuned to nothing but killing and surviving. Not surrendering. In battle rage, no one was searching for a way to end fighting. It was pure instinct, and the instinct here was to kill. And leading Dorcas and Fekra, Froi knew he had to find a way, and perhaps he spoke the question out loud, because he saw Fekra's mouth holler and he read the instruction on his lips. *Find Scarpo.*

So Froi made his way through the mute scene, not knowing whom he was looking for. And he saw familiar faces sprawled across this blood-drenched piece of land. He was a farmer, and he could tell it was fertile land. It was a place for growing, not dying. And he found Joyner, whose gods' blessed hands had toiled at the etchings on Froi's body, and beside Joyner lay the Turlan lad who had won the tournament against the Lasconians. And on and on Froi stumbled. He knelt by the corpse of Florik's cousin and most loyal friend. Faces that had stared at him as he sang alongside Arjuro.

Don't let me find Grij, he prayed. *Please don't let me find Grij. Don't let me have to tell De Lancey that his beloved son is dead.*

And it was from where he knelt that he saw a mighty soldier to be reckoned with. A mountain of a man, stumbling away from one kill and searching for the next. It was Trevanion, but it wasn't. It was a man born for battle. Captains mostly were. And Froi stood and turned back to Dorcas and pointed ahead, and Dorcas nodded. Froi stepped over the dead, limping his way toward the man, and he thought of the story Gargarin and Finnikin had told them about the Haladyans. His father and his king. A surrender for a surrender, they had said. And Dorcas later said that the gods must have protected Froi, because he walked through the battle like a man in a daze, his weapon in its scabbard, his arms above his head. What was Froi's instinct amid the battle rage? It was what his instinct always would be. From the moment he was born. Find a way to live. And as he limped toward the Nebian captain, he asked himself over and over again, what would Trevanion do? If he saw a lad walking toward him in a futile battle where Lumaterans were slaughtering Lumaterans? Would a captain's pride have him fight on till the end, knowing his men would follow him to the grave rather than give in? Froi knew the moment the captain of the Nebian Guard saw him, because the big man dragged the Lasconian soldier along to where Froi stood with his arms still raised in surrender. He thought he heard Dorcas by his side, but the world seemed a haze.

"Bestiano is dead," Froi said. "Gargarin of Abroi is our only hope."

And the captain of the Nebian army lowered Froi's hands and took the white flag from Dorcas and hollered, and when Froi's hearing returned, his head felt as if it had burst into fragments and he fell to the ground, writhing in pain. But with that pain came the words he was waiting for, from a captain perhaps no different from his own.

"*Nebia surrenders!*"

Later, he watched Dorcas check the corpse of every man they passed, manically searching for life.

"Is he going to be all right?" Froi asked Fekra quietly as they stood under a cruel sun that shone its brilliance, illuminating every fatal wound and blank stare of death.

Fekra shook his head. "We're the last. Of the palace, I mean. Dorcas. Me. Remember all those people when you arrived that day in the Citavita? The king's men and family and palace soldiers? The riders? Everyone's dead, except for Dorcas and me."

"And Quintana," Froi reminded him.

They reached a section of the valley where Perabo and a group of the Lasconian lads were guarding the surrendered army. Gargarin arrived with Arjuro and De Lancey on horseback, and Froi could see De Lancey staring around at the carnage in desperation. With Fekra's arm around him for support, Froi hobbled to them.

"He's not here, De Lancey. You have nothing to fear, for now."

Arjuro stared down at Froi's leg and bent to inspect it. "It's nothing," Froi said. "Just get me onto my horse."

"You're not going anywhere until I see to this leg," Arjuro said.

"There are men dying, Arjuro. See to them."

Gargarin was gravely studying the surrendered Nebian army before him.

"How many dead?" he asked one of the Lasconian lads who was guarding.

"Ours or theirs, sir?"

Gargarin sent the lad a scathing look.

"They're all ours, you fool! They're all Charynites! *How many dead?*"

Froi shivered at a memory of what had happened in Lumatere on the day they entered the kingdom. Trevanion had counted the dead. Young men and not so young. The captain had visited every family who lost a loved one in the battle to reclaim Lumatere. Froi recognized the same pain in Gargarin's face now. He had given the order for this.

Before them, the Nebian army was kneeling in rows, placed in some sort of order that made no sense to Froi. Those who were wounded lay down.

It was here that Froi got a better look at Scarpo of Nebia. He was a thickset man with solemn eyes that made little contact with the world, slightly younger than Trevanion.

"Can you get to your feet?" Gargarin asked.

The captain of the Nebian army rose.

"You surrendered easily," Gargarin said.

There was no response.

"Some will see you as a coward," Gargarin said.

Froi looked at Scarpo's men. Their eyes blazed to hear the words.

"Then, let that title be mine and not my men's, sir," Scarpo said. "They followed orders. They are assembled in the order of rank. All I ask is that you follow the conventions of surrender and that no harm comes to my men, sir. At no time have they behaved disorderly or without honor. If you choose to take their land from them, sir, I ask that you take into consideration those who are sole providers of elderly kinsfolk. If I would also ask that those closest to where we stand are attended to with alacrity, sir. Their wounds are dire and if we are to agree on anything today, it's that Charyn can ill afford to lose another man."

"You have much to say. . . . What's your name?"

"Scarpo of Nebia, sir. Captain of the Nebian Guard."

"Former captain of the Nebian Guard, Scarpo."

"As you please, sir."

"The queen needs a captain," Gargarin said flatly. "And I don't have many candidates, so you're it."

Froi saw the startled surprise in the expression of a man who thought he was to die this day.

"Agreed?"

"Your order, sir."

"Join Ariston of Turla and his men, and bring us back the queen and her child."

Surprise again, and then a grimace.

"The queen, you say?"

"He said the queen," Froi shouted. "Are you hard of hearing?"

The man grimaced again. Froi studied him and walked toward where he was. "What is it you're not telling us, Nebian?"

The captain shook his head with regret. "Bestiano issued an order to every spy, every street lord, and every barbarian outside the province. . . ." Scarpo swallowed hard. "She's not to live."

Froi stared at him, his gut twisting.

"If she's given birth to the child, then grieve Quintana of Charyn," Scarpo said. "Because it means her throat's already been cut."

CHAPTER 38

Almost two days after Donashe's men stormed their hiding place, Phaedra sat in their prison cave with an arm around Quintana and a tremble in her body that refused to stop. Despite Donashe's men standing guard outside their cave, she knew that they were prisoners of a man more powerful than the street lord. Harker had been given permission to see them for a short time that day. He had warned them that a messenger had been dispatched to advise Bestiano that the princess was in the valley.

"Will they take us to the Citavita?" Jorja asked her husband.

He shook his head. "They reveal little."

He glanced at Phaedra. "I've sent word to your father. Perhaps an army from Alonso will secure your release."

"There is no army in Alonso," she said quietly. "And why would my father believe I lived after being told I was dead all this time?"

Harker ushered his wife and Phaedra to the outer cave under the suspicious stare of Quintana. She had been frighteningly quiet since Rafuel had been dragged away.

"One of the men has also been sent to the Sarnak border," Harker whispered. "To find a woman with a babe."

"Why?" Phaedra asked. "Do they think none of us, including Tesadora and Japhra, can take care of a newborn?"

Harker looked away, pained.

"Harker," Jorja asked. "What does this mean?"

They heard a sound behind them and turned to find Quintana leaning against Cora, her hand clutching her belly.

"She'll be here to feed my son," Quintana said. "Won't she?"

Harker didn't respond.

"It's what they do when a mother dies and leaves a babe behind. They find a woman with breasts full of milk."

Quintana's eyes filled with tears.

"I've become greedy. I've always thought it was enough to birth him. But I want to see his face. Promise me I'll see his face."

Later, Ginny entered their cave, fear and pity etched on her face. Was it fear of them or of Donashe and his men who guarded the cave outside? She held a large bowl of a thick substance that she placed in front of Quintana.

"You need to eat, Your Highness."

"Majesty," Cora hissed. "You refer to her as Your Majesty. She's your queen."

Ginny pushed the bowl toward Phaedra.

"They say she must eat. They don't want the little king dead before his birth."

Phaedra heard a pitiful sound come from deep within Quintana, and then a mutter of heart-wrenching desperation spoken so fast that all Phaedra understood was the plea in her voice and the name *Froi* spoken over and over again.

"I meant no harm," Ginny said quietly. "Gies came searching for his friend when the hangman failed to return to camp. It was chance. It was chance," she sobbed. "And I was so happy to see him. I told him to keep our secret as Harker and Kasabian and the Mont were allowed to keep yours." Ginny's hands wrung. "I would never bring harm to you. To any of you. I'm sorry," she wept. "I'm sorry."

Florenza stood and approached Ginny and slapped her hard across the face. Ginny cried out and stumbled, stepping onto the bowl and snapping it in half. Phaedra watched the warm liquid spread against the stone.

One of Donashe's men entered the cave.

"What's taking you so long?" he shouted at Ginny. "Clean up this mess."

Ginny fell to her knees, gathering the pieces in her hands, hurrying to collect the rest. She watched the man leave and looked up quickly.

"They say the Lasconians and the Turlans are camped across the hill from Bestiano's army, two days' ride from here," she whispered before getting to her feet. "And that the Lumateran is traveling with them."

When Ginny left the cave, Cora placed a bony arm around Quintana's shoulders, soothing her.

"See? He's two days' ride from here. He's coming for you, and from the way I see it, watch anyone who gets in the way of the Lumateran and his precious girl."

But Quintana was shaking her head with despair beyond reckoning.

"How long does it take to birth a child, Jorja?" she asked, her voice small and broken.

"Sometimes hours, sometimes almost a day, brave girl."

"I'm not very brave, Jorja," Quintana whispered. "Not at all. When they put the noose around my neck, I was the least brave girl in Charyn."

Florenza crouched before Quintana and took her hands in hers.

"I will cut out the tongue of anyone who says that Quintana of Charyn is not the bravest girl in the kingdom! I will carve it on every piece of stone in Charyn, so everywhere the little king looks he will see the words *Quintana the Brave*."

"What if I don't hold him in my arms?" Quintana lamented. "What if I never get to see his face?"

"You must stop thinking that," Phaedra soothed. "Froi and his army will be here in two days, and when you give birth, you'll have all the time in the world with the little king."

Quintana squeezed her legs tight, and Phaedra saw the water puddle around her. She heard Quintana's whimper.

"Don't fret, my queen. There's no shame in soiling yourself," Phaedra fussed.

But Jorja stared in horror.

"She hasn't soiled herself," Jorja said. "Her water has broken. The babe is coming."

CHAPTER 39

It was a boy, as they had always suspected. They said he looked as if he was sleeping, and it was the only thing that brought any reprieve to them. It was the cord, they said, that had wrapped around his little neck.

He didn't remember much about that day except those who engulfed him in an embrace to comfort him, but then they'd weep themselves. And that the women wouldn't allow him to see his wife until they cleaned the blood from her body and the walls. And then later, people began to arrive on the mountain from Balconio and beyond; August and Abian and Celie arrived from the Flatlands, and then Beatriss and Vestie and the priest-king. His father was coming from the palace, so Finnikin knew it would be some time more before he saw him.

Each time a visitor arrived, the women disappeared inside Yata's home, and the men stayed outside. Some of the younger Mont lads wept; others paced with fury at an unseen enemy. Lucian stayed by Finnikin's side. It's what Finnikin remembered most in days to come. And that the wound at his thigh, created as a pledge among Lucian, Balthazar, and him to protect Lumatere all those years ago, began to seep.

And then Yata was there before them.

"Finnikin," she said, "you can see them now." He felt the tremble in the old woman's hands as she took his. How many children and grandchildren and great-grandchildren had she outlived?

Inside the large chamber, the Mont cousins and aunts stood weeping around a basin, bathing the little, still body in the water they had gathered from the river mixed with the sap of a forest tree and the sage grown on a Flatland farm. It was to prepare the babe for his place in the arms of the goddess who had once come from the ground. Finnikin had told the children of the Rock that story months before. Or was it years? It felt a lifetime ago. One of Isaboe's aunts placed the babe in Finnikin's arms, and he pressed a kiss to its brow, a blessing between a father and a son. And then he returned the babe to the priest-king and followed Yata to where Isaboe lay behind the curtain. Her eyes were closed, not in sleep, but weariness. Apart from everything else, she was exhausted. The birthing had lasted most of the day and night.

"Did you see him?" she asked quietly when she opened her eyes.

He nodded.

"I told Beatriss that I want him buried alongside your sister, baby Evanjalin. It will be good for their spirits to be together."

He nodded again.

"Where's Jasmina?"

"With Aunt Celestina."

"Good. She'll be kept happy. You know what your aunt is like. She'll not let anyone upset her."

Isaboe looked so small and pale, he reached out to touch her cheek. But still he couldn't speak. Everyone had told him to be strong for her, but Finnikin didn't know how to be strong for himself.

He felt one of the women at his shoulder, and Finnikin wanted to shout at them to leave. He wanted to be with his wife. Hold her in his arms.

"And your father? Have you seen him?" she asked.

Finnikin shook his head.

"Make sure you speak to him. You know what he's like. And Sir Topher, too. They're not men for talking, and they'll lock it up inside themselves until it burns a hole in their hearts."

He nodded again.

"And Tesadora?" she asked, her voice wavering. "Has she come?"

He couldn't bear to hear her sound so broken.

"They've gone down to the valley to search for her," he said. "Because I can't imagine anything keeping her away from you."

Isaboe took his hand and placed it on her belly.

"Look. It's still so round," she said. "I'm frightened that I'll wake in the morning and think he's still there."

One of the aunts came to the curtain.

"Finnikin," she said gently. "Come along, now—let her sleep."

"Just a moment more," he said, because he was sick of being strong and talking about the death of their child as if they were discussing the Osterians, and he just wanted to hold Isaboe. He wanted their sorrow to be only theirs, not to share it with the entire kingdom.

"Come, now, Finnikin," another spoke. "You have people to see outside. They've come up to the mountain to express their sorrow."

And so he left and spoke in polite sentences all the night long, and listened to words that brought him no comfort. That his son was in a better place. A better place than Isaboe's arms? That Lumatere had another spirit to take care of them. Didn't they have enough? They had Isaboe's entire family. His mother. His baby sister. The entire village of Tressor. Lord Selric and his family. Every Lumateran found in a mass grave.

Is that not enough? he wanted to shout.

On the floor of Lucian's cottage, he closed his eyes and slept briefly. And when he woke, having dreamed the strangest of dreams, he returned to Yata's home to be with Isaboe, to hold her hands so she wouldn't wake to place them on her belly.

"Finnikin," she said softly when she opened her eyes. "I'm going to have to go down to the valley."

His stomach lurched to hear her say the words.

When the others heard their talk, the women were there hovering around her.

"I'm going down to the valley," Isaboe said to her aunts and cousins, who gasped and cried out in horror.

"What are you saying, my queen?" Cousin Alda said.

"Rest, beloved," Yata said.

Isaboe shook her head and sat up slowly.

"I have to go down to the valley," she repeated, pushing the hands aside and finding Finnikin's to grip. "It's what our son told me to do."

There was wailing and protest, and one of the cousins ran from the room, and soon enough, Trevanion and Perri and Lucian were there.

"Isaboe, you don't know what you're saying," Trevanion said as Isaboe placed her feet on the ground. "Finnikin, help her back onto the bed."

Isaboe held up a hand to stop everyone. "My son begged me to go down to the valley," she said firmly, tears blazing in her eyes. "Are you going to have me defy him?"

They turned their pleas to Finnikin, but he couldn't take his eyes from her.

"Find your queen her clothes, Constance," he ordered quietly. He heard more gasps and cries.

"Finnikin!"

"They've lost their wits. Both of them."

Trevanion took Finnikin by the arm gently and led him away from the fussing, crying women.

"She is distraught," Trevanion said. "You both are. Tell her to rest, Finnikin. She needs to rest or else she will drive herself to madness."

"We're going to the valley," Finnikin said calmly.

"Because you dreamed of your son telling you to do so?" his father demanded, anguished.

"No," Finnikin said. "I didn't dream of our son. Isaboe did. I dreamed of Bartolina. My mother came to me, Trevanion. She's come to you and Aunt Celestina, and I think she's even come to Jasmina, and although I've sensed her in my dreams these past years, she's never spoken to me. Except for this night. And Bartolina of the Rock said, 'Finnikin, you must go down to the valley.'"

Lucian led his cousins to the stream. They were flanked by Trevanion, Perri, Aldron, Jory, and at least six other Monts. There was no room for anger, only confusion and sorrow. Lucian had seen the sorrow when Trevanion arrived on the mountain and Lady Beatriss had been there to meet him by the entrance of Yata's home. She had taken the captain's hand and led him away to a private place. In Lucian's cottage, Aldron and Perri had sat with their heads in their hands.

"I feel useless!" Aldron had shouted, kicking a chair across the room.

As confusing as this journey to the valley was for them all, Lucian was grateful for something to do.

"Don't speak the truth to the Charynites," Isaboe said quietly. "They'll see us at our weakest."

The truth was that the babe had been taken from them. Not in an act of war, or violence, or because of a mistake, or due to an illness. Lady Abian said it had happened to many women before the queen and it would happen again. The gods were cruel, but just. Death chose the powerful and the weak. It chose the seamstress, and it chose the queen. All the wealth in the world made no difference.

"It will make her stronger," one of the cousins said.

"She was strong enough!" Yata snapped.

Regardless of how strong she was, Perri bent and scooped the queen up in his arms and carried her across the water.

The valley dwellers were frightened to see them all. Lucian imagined it had been a terrifying time since the arrest of the women, and despite their hope in Quintana of Charyn's child, they had seen too much death here.

Donashe and his men sat on the landing that led to the high caves. And Lucian wanted to kill him. He wanted to kill someone, and the person he hated most in the world was Donashe. He was an idle man unless he was threatening or murdering someone. Lucian's father had warned him to fear idle men. Without the pride gained from a good day's work, they were left to their vices and the doubts that crowded their head. Their hatred. Their envy. Lucian saw it each time he came face-to-face with the camp leaders.

Lucian led the queen and their party up the steps toward Donashe's men. He didn't want to. He wanted his cousin safe from the malice of idle men, but he had no choice. Donashe and the camp leaders were on their feet in an instant, swords in their hands and suspicion on their faces as they watched Lucian and his people approaching. One of the men whispered in Donashe's ear, and the suspicion turned to surprise as Donashe's eyes fastened on the queen.

"An honor for Little Charyn, Your Majesty," he said to Isaboe when she reached the landing. Finnikin's arm was around her, and Lucian could see that his friend's fists were clenched.

"And so close to the birth of your child."

"The last I heard, this valley is still part of Lumatere," Isaboe said coldly. "Not Little anything." She stared up at the highest cave. "I've come to see Quintana of Charyn. As a sign of peace between two queens."

Donashe laughed.

"A queen? You're mistaken. The girl's no queen. Just a princess."

"I'm not sure what you mean by that," Isaboe said. "My daughter's a princess. Are you saying my daughter is unimportant, Charynite? Are you saying she means little to my kingdom? That she holds no power? That she is worthless?"

Lucian could see the unease in Donashe's expression, the realization that Isaboe could not be charmed into submission. Donashe's eyes met Lucian's.

"Then can I stress to you, Your Majesty, as I did when you sent your Mont to discuss the imprisonment of his wife," Donashe said with a politeness that hid a threat, "that *our* princess is a political prisoner of the acting house of Charyn, and under no circumstances will she be removed from these caves. Quintana of Charyn is under arrest for the murder of her father, the king."

"Be careful, Charynite," Isaboe said. "With news such as that, you're going to make me like your princess, and I'm here for a peaceful gesture, not friendship."

Isaboe went to step past him, but he blocked her path. The sound of every Lumateran sword being removed from its scabbard was sweet to Lucian's ears.

"Regardless of what you choose to do," Donashe said, failing to hide the twitch of nervousness in his cheek as the swords pointed at his face, "there's an army of four hundred men belonging to the acting house of Charyn coming this way. They can be here in days to await the birth of the heir and return him to the palace. And if they arrive to find her gone, I can't promise to keep them off your mountain."

Perri's hand was quick, and he gripped Donashe by the throat. It was only Isaboe's hand on her guard's arm that made him let go.

"I'm here to wish your princess well and to see my cousin Phaedra of Alonso," Isaboe said. "So let me pass. I may not go to war with you over the daughter of my enemy, but I will over a Mont leader's wife."

Donashe hesitated, but then stepped aside as Finnikin took Isaboe's hand and Lucian went to follow.

"Only one of you will accompany your queen," Donashe said, stepping before them. "Who's to know what your real plan is? Perhaps it's to murder Quintana of Charyn before she births the child. We don't take that chance."

Finnikin shoved Donashe out of the way, but Isaboe held him back.

"Let's not make this worse than it could be, my love. Lucian will take me. He needs to see his wife."

Finnikin's rage was potent. He had expressed no grief or emotion at the death of his son, but Lucian saw it all there in his friend's eyes.

"I'll take care of her with my life, Finn," Lucian said.

Finnikin pointed to Donashe and his men. "They stay. If my queen enters that cave unprotected, then no armed man enters with her."

It was a standoff, but finally Donashe agreed.

Lucian gave his weapon to Finnikin and was forced to hold up his arms for a search. When the camp leaders stepped toward Isaboe, the tip of Trevanion's sword pressed into Donashe's arm as a warning.

Donashe and his men stepped back and Lucian took Isaboe's hand and led her up the sheer path to the women's cave. Her tread was slow, achingly slow. He knew it was because she was in pain and weary.

"You go ahead," he said, wanting to be there to break her fall if she was to slip.

He had no idea what Isaboe's purpose was in the caves, but he had faith in his queen and beloved cousin. She was the sister of his heart, and it was only on this climb, with his face turned away from them all, that Lucian cried silent tears for the two people he loved.

On the precipice, he heard the murmuring and furious whispers and he led Isaboe through an archway and then into a second cavern.

The moment they stepped into the dark, dank space, Cora and Harker's women were before him, hostility in their stance. When they saw it was Lucian, they sighed with relief. He couldn't see Phaedra or Quintana of Charyn, but he saw Tesadora step out of the protective circle of these women, her eyes wide with shock to see Isaboe.

"What are you doing here, Isaboe?" Tesadora asked, horrified. "So close to your time. Take her away from here, Lucian. *Now.*"

"What is happening here, Tesadora?" Isaboe asked quietly.

It was Harker's daughter who appeared from behind her mother and Cora to take Isaboe's hand. "I prayed to the god of mercy for a sign and here you are, Isaboe of Lumatere."

Jorja and Cora moved aside, and Lucian saw the princess of Charyn lying on the hard ground with Phaedra kneeling beside her. There was a piece of thick wood clenched between the girl's teeth to stop her from screaming. Her brow was soaked with sweat, her face contorted with pain.

"She's birthing," Isaboe said.

Harker's wife placed a finger to her lips and pointed outside.

"They're not to know. They'll kill her if they know. The order is that the babe lives, but not her. They have a woman from Sarnak who's to arrive soon with breasts filled with milk to feed it. There's talk that your lad Froi and an army is two days' ride from here, but it will be too late to save her."

"The way your camp leaders hear it, there is an army, but not the one you want anywhere near your princess," Isaboe said.

"Take her," Harker's daughter begged. "Give her sanctuary."

"I can't," Isaboe said.

"You mean you won't!" Cora hissed.

"Cora," Tesadora said. "Enough. If Lumatere takes the babe, it will bring Nebia's army onto that mountain. I'll not allow it. We find another way."

Phaedra's eyes met Lucian's. "Arm us, *Luc-ien*," she pleaded. "I'll slit the throat of anyone who comes close to taking her."

"It's what my father says," Florenza said. "It's the only way."

Lucian felt awash with defeat. "There's too many of them, and we'll never get a weapon into this cave," he said. "They searched us, Phaedra. They'll search us again."

Isaboe moved closer to where Quintana of Charyn lay on the ground, the girl's pain muffled, her body convulsing. Lucian watched as Isaboe crouched, and the princess reached out to grip her hand, nails biting into skin.

"You'll never hide her cries or that of her babe from Donashe and his men. If you fear for your queen's life once she gives birth, then give the babe to the army that approaches, whoever that may be." Isaboe hesitated a moment. "Once it's born, I'll give Quintana of Charyn refuge. Perhaps as long as she's out of sight, they may not care whether she lives. They won't storm my mountain for her. She's worth nothing. It's the babe they want. Your camp leader's sentiment, not mine."

Quintana spat out the wedge and Lucian heard a sound so savage and pathetic and heartbreaking.

Phaedra covered the girl's mouth gently.

"Don't let them know, Quintana," Phaedra begged. "If they hear you, they'll know the truth."

"If she wants to live, she has no choice," Isaboe said. "Take my offer and be done with it."

"She won't let them take the babe," Tesadora said.

"And what good is she to him dead?" Isaboe cried. "She can find a way to get him back. If he's alive, she can find a way. All he has to do is live!"

Harker's wife shook her head. "She'll not do it willingly, Your Majesty. You don't understand what Bestiano did to her. She won't give her child to him and walk away to take refuge."

"She must."

Phaedra's eyes blazed up at Isaboe.

"Would you? Give up the child you carry? Do you think a Charynite is made different? That we would love our children less?"

"Phaedra!" Lucian said.

"No, I want to hear what she has to say," Phaedra cried. "You think you're better than us. You think your capacity to love is stronger, but we bleed the same way, Your Majesty. Our queen gives up her son to no man."

Tesadora took Isaboe's hands in hers. "Go," she pleaded. "You shouldn't be here, and the gods help Finnikin and those idiot guards who let you come down that mountain. If they've put you in harm's way, I'll kill them all!"

Lucian placed a hand on his cousin's shoulder. "Come," he said.

Isaboe stepped toward Tesadora and embraced her. Lucian heard Isaboe's murmur, and then Tesadora began to weep, and Lucian had never heard a sound so raw. The two stayed clasped for a long time, and the Charyn women watched them silently. Tesadora's tears frightened them, as they frightened Lucian, beyond words.

Isaboe then stepped away and turned to Lucian.

"I need you to give my king a message."

Finnikin watched Lucian return without Isaboe. He pushed past the camp leaders, desperate for answers.

"My lord," Lucian said to him formally. "You're needed in the cave."

"You all stay here," Donashe said, "and the Mont returns to tell your queen that it's time for her to leave."

"My lord," Lucian said, ignoring Donashe and staring at Finnikin with a strange expression in his eye. "Your child is coming, and your queen needs you by her side."

Finnikin was speechless. He heard the intake of breath from his father and Perri and every other Lumateran around him. Was this a cruel jest?

"Stay," Finnikin ordered the others. He turned to Donashe. "And if you come anywhere near the cave where my wife is giving birth, my guards will kill you, regardless of how powerful the army is that is coming this way."

Finnikin followed Lucian up to the cave, taking the steps two at a time. He caught the warning look in his cousin's eye as he went to speak.

"Not a word," Lucian said quietly.

They entered, and Finnikin heard the muffled cry from

the base of the cave. Stooping, he followed Lucian through a small entrance and saw Isaboe beside a girl who could only be Quintana of Charyn.

"Isaboe—"

"They won't dare enter if they think it's me birthing the child," she said. "We claim it's mine and we take it across the stream. They'll believe the princess is still to give birth, which may keep her alive long enough for her army to arrive, if one exists."

Finnikin couldn't believe what he was hearing. "This isn't right for you!' he said.

But she stepped forward and placed a finger to his lips, and there it was before him. The greatest prayer to the gods he could muster with a heart so broken. *Don't let me outlive this woman. Don't let me exist one moment without her.*

"Is it right for anyone?" she asked, her voice so sad that he had to pray for the strength not to weep before her.

Here was Evanjalin. The girl he fell in love with, who could block out the pain with a bloody-mindedness that shamed those around her. But he remembered the time on the hill in Osteria when she first saw her *yata*. She had held her sorrow for all those years, and then it erupted with a devastation beyond comprehension of anyone present that day. He knew her. He knew her ability to contain everything, but he also knew the girl who still wept in his arms when she spoke of her sisters and Balthazar.

Finnikin turned to Tesadora as Isaboe stepped away. "How could you allow this? It will tear her heart in pieces."

But Isaboe reached out and removed the wood between Quintana's teeth and the girl's cry of pain etched its place into the walls of the cave and drowned out any further talk.

Finnikin was there the whole day long as this strange creature writhed and buckled and spat curses at the gods, and he thought of what his mother had endured to give him life. Bartolina of the Rock, who never lived to see her son. Worse still, he thought of what Isaboe had gone through, and he grieved for his son who would never know a mother. He watched how the Charyn princess gripped Isaboe, their hands clenched, and he knew he'd never loved his wife as much as he did at that moment.

"I can see its head," Phaedra said over Tesadora's shoulder. "I can see its head, Your Majesty!"

And Finnikin saw the women surround Tesadora to look in wonder. Even Lucian.

"I shouldn't be looking, but I can't keep my eyes away," Lucian blurted out, his eyes wide.

"Once more," Tesadora ordered as the girl tried to raise herself again. Finnikin watched as Quintana mouthed a word with a weariness that was heartbreaking.

"*Froi.*"

So Finnikin gently pushed past Isaboe and the women and stepped behind Froi's girl. Pressing himself against the cave wall, he propped her up against him.

"Lean on me. I won't let you fall back," he promised.

And although it gave the princess strength, the pain was too much and her head lolled back against his shoulder.

"Why not just . . . pull it out like we do a calf?" Lucian suggested to Tesadora, who sent him a withering look.

"Once more," Isaboe ordered. "It has so much to tell you, Quintana, and no matter how long you live this life, it will never be enough time spent with your child. So don't you waste a moment."

Quintana hesitated, raised herself again, and in a final burst of strength, she pushed and the babe slipped out into Tesadora's hands. The Charynite women cried with the fright of seeing such a strange creature.

"What is it? What is it?" Harker's daughter asked.

They held their breath.

"It's a king," Harker's wife said. "You were right all along, Quintana. It's a little king."

And they placed the little king of Charyn in his mother's arms, and Finnikin watched Froi's strange girl look at her babe with surprise, almost indignation.

"I know you," she said to her son. "Do you know me?"

And later, when the babe had his fill of his mother's milk for the second time, Finnikin sat in the corner of the cave with Isaboe in his arms.

"Perhaps in a better world, Your Majesty, our little king and the babe you birth will meet as friends and not enemies," Harker's wife said.

Isaboe was silent. It pained Finnikin to breathe.

Finnikin stood and held out a hand to his wife. "We can't stay here. We need to get back to our people, and if there's an army coming, I don't want my queen . . . or your little king in danger."

Finnikin could see that the princess was not going to let go of her son.

"Quintana, if you want to live, you must give him to the queen," Tesadora said firmly. "He knows your love. He'll not forget it."

"But what if he goes hungry?" the princess begged to know.

"He won't," Isaboe said quietly. "My milk will feed a king."

The women stared, confused, and then Phaedra of Alonso covered her face and wept, for she understood the truth of Isaboe's words.

They stepped outside the cave with Tesadora and the babe in the crook of Isaboe's arms. Finnikin held a tentative hand to Isaboe's shoulder as they climbed down the steep descent. He could see Trevanion at the halfway ledge, a place where the earth seemed more stable underfoot. But Isaboe's step was slow and sure. Once or twice she glanced down at the sleeping babe, murmuring a word or two to him, at first in Lumateran, but then she stopped herself and spoke Charyn.

They reached the landing and the men stepped aside, both Lumateran and Charynite. Trevanion's eyes met Finnikin's, but his father and their men dared not give away their confusion at these strange events.

"Let's hope you taught our useless princess a thing or two in that cave, Your Majesty," Donashe said.

Isaboe pressed the babe to her and placed a hand to his ear to stop it from hearing Donashe's voice. And she followed Aldron and Jory down the steps, flanked by Finnikin and Trevanion and the rest of the Guard until they reached the lower caves, where the valley dwellers stood staring up with yearning. Finnikin bit his tongue to stop from telling them the truth.

At the stream, Isaboe stopped to place the Charynite king in Finnikin's arms, and he hesitated a moment. He didn't want to hold another's child. He wanted to hold his own. But he took the boy all the same and watched as Isaboe held a hand out to Harker of Nebia, who was standing close by.

"Your assistance, if you please," she said coolly, as if taking advantage of the closest man standing without a weapon in his hand. Harker looked surprised and took her hand and escorted her across the stream.

"What is it you want from us?" she asked quietly. "You've been boring a hole into my head the moment we arrived."

"Arm us," he pleaded.

"And what if you use those weapons to storm my mountain

and wipe out my people?" she asked. "It is a habit you Charynites have. What then, sir? I've met your pretty daughter, Harker of Nebia. Do I take her and cut out her heart as punishment?"

He flinched, a flash of anger crossing his expression.

"My fight is not with Lumatere, Your Majesty. It is with whoever brings harm to this valley. I know it's your valley, but these are our people and I need to keep them safe."

Finnikin, Isaboe, and Lucian spent the night in a cottage halfway up the mountain. Tesadora woke them once . . . twice to feed the babe, and later, Finnikin held Isaboe in his arms as she wept, sobs that ripped at the core of him. Then they were awoken a third time.

"An army is entering the valley," Trevanion said. "More powerful than we could ever imagine. Take her back to the palace, Finn. Don't even stop on the mountain. I don't want you or Isaboe close if they cross the stream."

"She hasn't lost her hearing," Isaboe murmured, getting to her feet. Trevanion embraced them both.

"Find a way to arm Harker's people," she ordered. "And I want Quintana of Charyn on our side of the stream. She needs to be with her son."

And Finnikin watched as Isaboe took the Charynite king in her arms one last time and pressed her lips to his cheek and whispered something in his ear. She returned him to Tesadora and then took Finnikin's hand and walked outside to where Perri had prepared her horse.

"What say you, Perri?" Isaboe said wearily. "Is it time to go home?"

Perri lifted her onto the horse. "I say what I said in that Charyn woodlands four years past, my queen," he said, his voice husky. "You humble me. You humble us all."

CHAPTER 40

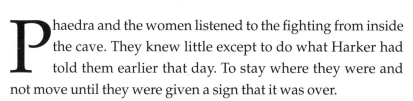

Phaedra and the women listened to the fighting from inside the cave. They knew little except to do what Harker had told them earlier that day. To stay where they were and not move until they were given a sign that it was over.

"It could happen that while we fight Donashe, an army will enter the valley and we won't know who is friend or foe," he whispered when he was granted a visit, accompanied by Donashe, whom Cora kept busy with one of her outbursts. Harker smuggled a dagger into his wife's hand, and she quickly placed it up her sleeve. The Lumaterans had left weapons for Harker's men concealed on their side of the stream, and Phaedra prayed that no one on the Charyn side would be foolish enough to cross beyond the bank. More than anything, Donashe and his men could not suspect that the little king of Charyn was hidden there.

They stayed huddled together all the day long, frightened by the cries coming from outside and below. Sometimes they heard the clambering of footsteps outside the entrance and they'd press themselves into the darkest crevice of the cave, but most times it was a valley dweller finding safer refuge on higher ground.

"It's cat and mouse down there," an old man whispered. "And Donashe's men are not just fighting Harker and the lads; they're fighting each other. There are already corpses floating downstream."

"Father's going to get himself killed," Florenza said, weeping.

They heard wails and shouts, and Phaedra prayed with desperation that Donashe and his men would not take refuge up so high. If they decided to sweep through the caves with their weapons, a single dagger was not going to save Phaedra and the women. Fear was vicious and whispered cruel thoughts into their hearts.

"At times such as this, I'm grateful for the curse," Cora said. "How could we ever have protected children from this?"

Phaedra felt Quintana take her hand, and she gathered her in an embrace.

"If there is one thing I would bet my life on, it's that the little king is safe," Phaedra whispered.

Night brought with it new sounds. A scurry of a rat, or a branch knocking against stone in a grim beat. Sometimes a quick cry would reach them from the world below. And nothing else would follow.

"A dead man," Cora would say. They had learned to tell the difference between the sound of a man with a deadly wound and one that caused pain to linger and sing a maudlin tune. And then they heard footsteps come from the outer cave. No one so much as muttered a word. They heard flint against stone, and a flicker of light appeared. Phaedra could see now that sometime during the night the cave had filled with valley dwellers, their eyes wide with terror.

"The Mont!" someone said and suddenly Lucian was pushing

between those standing before him. Phaedra sobbed with relief as he gathered her to him.

"You've got to trust me," he told the women, whose instinct was to huddle around Quintana. "There's so much confusion, and more than one army is about to enter. I'll find a way to take Quintana to the little king and keep her safe on my side of the stream. I have to do it now, or it will be too late."

"Whose army?" Cora asked.

Lucian shook his head. "Harker sent out a scout, but there's little to see in this darkness. He says it looks like Nebia. So I need to be gone. If they know a Lumateran is on this side of the stream, it could trigger a crossing. Donashe and his men are turning on each other—some surrendering to Harker, others attacking anything that moves and never mind those caught in their way. Trevanion's orders are that the moment I take the princess to safety, the Monts are to return up the mountain. Tesadora will stay with Quintana and the boy."

Lucian pressed a kiss to Phaedra's lips.

"If I get a chance—"

"Don't!" she said. "Just keep her alive."

Lucian picked Quintana up in his arms and the women wrapped her in blankets and cloaks, and then the two were gone.

"If he gets her safe across the stream, I'll never call him an idiot again," Cora said, and Phaedra could hear she was crying.

It was in the early hours of the morning that an army entered the camp. Phaedra heard the shouting, demanding surrender in the name of a united Charyn. Jorja said there was no such thing. Phaedra and Florenza crept to the outer cave and stole a look at the path behind them. A never-ending stream of horses and riders poured from the Alonso road. Phaedra took Florenza's hand and they crawled on their bellies to the tip of the rock that overlooked the stream before them. And they wished they hadn't.

Men lay dead, sprawled over lower cave ledges. The valley dwellers from below began to emerge, searching for their husbands, their sons, wailing at what was to be found. Florenza began to weep, but Phaedra's throat was dry and it felt as though fear had torn and scratched away at its core. Had Quintana and Lucian made it across the stream?

Phaedra and the women made their way down with caution. There were soldiers rounding up Donashe's men and questioning anyone else. The women heard whispers that an army from plague-ridden Desantos had arrived, and those from Turla and Avanosh as well, not to mention those from Nebia. Jorja recognized the uniform.

"Trust no one," Cora said, grabbing a bloody sword discarded across their path. "Plague-touched or enemy."

It was only Jorja's cry of joy when she saw Harker speaking to one of the Nebian soldiers that brought the first hope and certainty of the day. Nebia was not the enemy. They watched as two of the camp leaders were being dragged in chains beyond the caves. One of them had taken part in the murder of the seven scholars. A soldier—Phaedra didn't know if he was Turlan or Lasconian—said Donashe and his men would be handed over to the priests of Sebastabol for execution. The priests would want the seven lads avenged, and they would want to know the whereabouts of Rafuel. She saw Ginny in chains alongside Gies, and Phaedra walked away from Cora and the women and followed the soldiers between the caves to the Alonso road, where Donashe's men and Ginny were being placed in a wagon. Ginny's eyes widened the moment she saw her.

"Phaedra!" she screamed. "Save me, Phaedra, please. Please!"

But Phaedra could only think of being on her knees beside

Florenza and Jorja as Donashe's men held his sword to Cora on the day Ginny betrayed them. Once, her compassion had had no boundaries. The months since Donashe and his men entered the valley had changed that. So Phaedra turned away and walked back toward the caves. But suddenly she was dragged into a crevice and she found herself face-to-face with Donashe. There was a crazed look of fear in his eyes, and he held a filthy, bloody hand to her mouth.

"You tell them that I kept her safe in the end," he said. "You tell them."

He dragged Phaedra back toward the Alonso road, where more soldiers were arriving from the south.

"You tell them or I'll make you pay," Donashe threatened, his mouth close to her ear.

But when the new arrivals stopped to tether their horses, Phaedra broke free with a cry and it was then that she saw a figure limp toward them, an ax in hand. And his eyes met Phaedra's, and she saw the vengeance that they promised, and knew exactly who he was. He was not a boy anymore, this lad who had placed her on his list of those he could trust.

"Keep running and don't turn back, Phaedra," Froi of Lumatere ordered, and she did as he asked, but stumbled, falling forward into the dirt.

"Did I not tell you I never forget a face, Donashe?" she heard Froi say and then there was a cry and the sick thud of ax hitting bone. And Phaedra lay there on the ground, weeping, until she felt a hand on her shoulder. She stared up to see another lad caked with mud before her. She took his hand, and he helped her to her feet.

"Don't look down, miss," he said, as he led her back to the camp. "It's not a pretty sight."

And then a sound rang out across the valley that unfroze

hearts made of Charyn stone. A babe's cry. And the newly arrived soldiers hurried to the sound and it led them to the stream. Phaedra followed. The cry rang out again, and the valley was still and those from the caves appeared, their eyes searching.

But the cry was drowned out by a roar of Quintana's name that ripped through the camp, a cry so hoarse that Phaedra could have sworn the ground rumbled beneath her. She saw Froi of Lumatere drop to his knees. The wildest men she had ever seen circled him in sorrow and still the babe's cry echoed across the valley, mingled with Froi's pain.

"She dead?" one of the wild Turlan lads asked Phaedra. "If there's king born, Scarpo say our Quintana dead, for sure."

Before Phaedra could answer they heard a voice.

"Froi?"

Phaedra watched Froi freeze at the sound of his name. He stumbled to his feet, searching to see where it came from.

"Froi?"

It was Quintana's voice from across the stream, and Froi of Lumatere walked toward it, his hands to his head, almost dazed in wonder. And Phaedra and the wild Turlan lads followed, and she heard the breath catch in their throats when they saw Quintana of Charyn across the stream, holding the little king. As Froi dragged himself across the water, Phaedra marveled at the look on the face of her queen.

"Do you think you love him?" Phaedra had once asked.

"I don't know really what that is," Quintana had responded in her cold, practical way.

Yes, you do, my queen, Phaedra wanted to say now. Quintana's love was unabashed. Wondrous. The type of love that lit a strange, strange face and turned it into a beacon. Every man and woman in the valley saw the joy on the face of their king's mother that day. He was born in love, this king of theirs. Phaedra watched as Froi reached Quintana and then he fell to his knees before her, weeping, his arms circling her waist as she held him to her with one hand, the screaming, squirming babe with the other. And there were sighs all around her, and she smiled to hear them come from such savage lads.

But everything changed so suddenly as the captain they called Scarpo of Nebia and his soldiers came riding across the stream in frenzy.

"We need to get you to the palace, Your Majesty," he said, bellowing orders to the soldiers surrounding him. And they pushed Froi aside and wrested Quintana and the little king from out of his arms, and the savage lads beside Phaedra flew across the stream, shouting and cursing.

"Let him hold them! Let him!" one shouted.

"Froi!" Quintana cried.

One of the Nebian riders picked Quintana up in his arms; another tried to pull the babe from her grip.

"Froi!"

"You're hurting her!" Froi shouted, trying to get to her. "She's scared!"

Scarpo of Nebia leaped from his mount and stood before Froi. "They are my orders," Phaedra heard him say. "We need to get them both to the Citavita and secure their place there. You stay here, Lumateran. Gargarin's orders are that you stay in Lumatere and wait. In weeks to come, do not make contact with the Charyn palace. You wait. 'Trust me,' he said. These were Gargarin's words."

But Froi fought like a madman, and the Turlan lads tried to protect him, tried to hold him down.

"Don't hurt him. Please," Quintana begged as she pulled free of the soldier's arms and cowered on the ground, covering her babe's head with her arms.

And then things got worse and Phaedra watched as Lucian and Jory and the Mont lads came charging out from between the copse of trees, swords in hand, ready to cut down any man who was a threat to Froi, and when the Turlans saw the Monts, they cocked their bows and raised their swords and Phaedra cried in fear of the blood that would be shed in this stream.

"Stop!" Froi shouted, stumbling between the Monts and the Turlans, arms outstretched. "Stop!"

And then there was silence. The Turlans stepped back across to the Charyn side of the stream, and Lucian and his Monts stood beside Froi.

Phaedra pushed through the Nebian soldiers and reached Quintana, who rocked in the mud with the screeching little king in her arms.

"Shh," Phaedra said calmly, looking up at the captain of the Nebian army and his men. "You're going to hurt her and the babe if you don't restrain yourselves."

Scarpo of Nebia hesitated and then nodded.

Phaedra looked across the water, and her eyes met Lucian's. Their needs came second. It came from the privilege of being trusted.

But that doesn't mean I love you less.

And she held a hand down to Quintana, who took it and stood, and they followed Scarpo of Nebia to the waiting cart that would take them back to the Citavita.

part three

Tariq of the Citavita

CHAPTER 41

Froi began each day counting the moments that made his life breathable. The feel of soil in his hands. The colors of autumn in Lumatere. The murmuring between Lord August and Lady Abian on the porch each night. The sight of their eldest son, Talon, relieving one of the village women of the hay bale she carried. The priest-king's belly laugh. The sound of Vestie's voice when she asked about Kintana of Charyn. And then the next count would begin. Of everything that made his life unbreathable. And each time, it outnumbered the first.

It had been four months since he had arrived back in Lumatere, and most days he was able to put aside the ache and complete his work on Lord August's farm. But today was different. It was the curse day. Their birthday. Charyn's day of weeping. *Let her be happy.* Perhaps this would be the first of the birthdays she'd enjoy, for she had his son in her arms. The image of the two was etched in Froi's memory, and although they had only those few moments together in the valley that day, he missed Quintana more than ever. And try as he might, Froi couldn't get the scent of the boy off his hands. He began to understand Lirah and

Gargarin, and the way they had coated their hearts with ice so they wouldn't feel.

As if Finnikin had sensed his pain that morning, he came riding by with Jasmina.

"I'm going to teach her to swim," Finn said. "Come with us. I'll enjoy the company." By the look on Jasmina's face, the invitation was not extended to Froi, but he agreed all the same.

Trevanion joined them later. He kept a river cottage in Tressor, which was beginning to look like a village now, after all these years of grieving the Tressorians who were slaughtered in Sarnak. Froi watched the three from the riverbank and even found himself chuckling once or twice to see the authority the princess had over her father and Trevanion. Later, when the captain left, Froi and Finnikin lay on the grass under the last moments of the afternoon sun, Jasmina asleep in Finnikin's arms.

"How is she?" Froi asked, and they both knew he was speaking of Isaboe.

"Bad days. Good days. Bad days."

Finnikin looked at his daughter, pressing a kiss to her cheek.

"She doesn't want Jasmina to see the bad days."

Froi saw the dark circles of weariness under Finnikin's eyes.

"You're not trying to do it all on your own, are you, Finn?" he asked. "You should ask the women for help. Lady Beatriss would understand, and Lady Abian."

"Oh, I'm not against begging," Finnikin said. "I went to see Tesadora, you know. Me?" He laughed. "We've rarely exchanged a civil word. But I asked her if she would come to the palace and stay awhile." Finnikin shrugged and smiled. "And she said yes. And then Celie returned, as you'd know. For this week anyway . . . especially for the feast tonight. And I asked her to stay, too, and she said yes."

Tonight would be Isaboe's first public outing since the death of the child, and Lady Abian had been preparing for weeks, demanding that those most loved by the queen attend. The whole week's talk in the village had been about the feast and Celie's return.

"Lord August thinks that Celie is spying for you in Belegonia," Froi said quietly.

Finnikin glanced at him. "Celie *is* spying for us in Belegonia."

"Don't tell Lord August," Froi said with a sigh. "Thinking is one thing. Knowing for sure is another. And then there's the matter of the castle castellan searching Celie's room when he suspected that she'd stolen a chronicle from the library and Lord August remembering the castellan of the Belegonian spring castle as a portly older man with a lot of facial lumps, and of course when he visited Belegonia three weeks past, he met the new castellan."

"No facial lumps?" Finnikin asked.

"None at all. Nor was he old. Nor was he portly, and now Lord August is questioning how he would dare be in Celie's room."

"Ah," Finnikin said, nodding. "No wonder Isaboe and Celie were locked up in our chamber all the day long when she arrived. They weren't talking about Belegonian fleece. They were talking about the castellan."

"According to Lady Celie, no," Froi said. "She wants to outsmart him, not bed him."

"And you?" Finnikin asked softly.

"No, Finn, I don't want to bed the castellan of the Belegonian spring castle."

Finnikin laughed, but soon his expression was serious.

"We don't speak of it," he said, "but I can't imagine it being easy for you, Froi."

Froi shrugged. He had received a letter from Lirah. It came via the valley one day, out of what seemed nowhere. Froi had opened it with shaking hands. Lirah had sketched him an image of Quintana and his son. And one of Gargarin. He knew it was his father and not Arjuro. Not because of his solemnity, but because of the look in his eyes. Froi would always recognize the desire in Gargarin's eyes when he was looking at Lirah.

"It's hard to explain . . . what they mean to me," Froi said.

Finnikin's smile was faint. "I can imagine."

"Can you?"

"Froi, you have my wife's name etched on your arm, and the only thing that stops me from skinning you are the other two names."

Froi laughed and shook his head ruefully.

"Not many men can read the words of the ancients, my lord. I'll have to remember that next time."

They rode together until they reached the village of Sayles. The beauty of his home village always forced Froi to think of Gargarin. What would Gargarin think of the Flatlands? Would he be impressed by the water pipe that ran from the river into the fields? Would he ever share his plans for a waterwheel with Lord August? How would the two men get on? But with all those questions came bitterness. Not once had Gargarin attempted correspondence. And Froi couldn't understand why. When Scarpo of Nebia had passed on Gargarin's orders for Froi to stay behind that day at the stream, Froi hadn't questioned it. Because Gargarin had once begged Froi to trust him and Froi had. But these days he felt like a beggar each time he visited the palace, asking if anything had arrived for him.

"Don't forget the priest-king tonight," Finnikin reminded.

"Why does everyone presume I'm going to forget the

priest-king?" Froi said, irritated. He'd been feeling like the village idiot lately. His only chore for the night was to collect the priest-king, and if it wasn't Lady Abian or Lord August or Trevanion reminding him, it was Finn.

"I'm just saying," Finnikin said.

In the royal residence, Isaboe watched Tesadora pour more water into the tub.

"What say we wash that hair, beloved?" Tesadora said, her voice gentle but firm as she began to lather it. Tonight was special, Isaboe reminded herself. She would make the effort.

"Finnikin says he hasn't seen it out for months," Tesadora said practically, "and hair such as this should never be hidden."

Isaboe tried not to think of her hair, because then she'd have to remember the red-gold strands of her son's.

"I miss the color of mine," Tesadora admitted. "Sagrami punished me for being so vain. It was brown and gold. Do you remember that, or were you too much of a child?"

"I don't remember you," Isaboe said. "I wish I did, but I know you're somewhere there in my memories. I remember your mother, of course, but you were Seranonna's mysterious half-wild daughter living alone in the forest of Lumatere."

"Put your head back," Tesadora said, and Isaboe felt the warm water blanket her head. She closed her eyes a moment.

"My brother, Balthazar, said he saw you once," Isaboe said. "When he tried to describe you to my mother, he wept and she asked him why. He said it made him ache inside, and my sisters teased him for days. He would have been a romantic, my brother. Unlike Finnikin and Lucian. He would have worn his heart on his sleeve, and we would have found him sitting with the women and listening to their woes."

"Yes, he would have been a romantic and a kind, kind man," Tesadora said. "But this kingdom needs a great leader, and you, beloved, are a great leader."

Isaboe swallowed hard. "My people are in despair," she said, trying to conceal the break in her voice. "I sense it in their sleep."

Tesadora brushed a strand of hair out of Isaboe's eyes. "Your people can be selfish, indulgent grumblers at times, Isaboe. And you may feel the hardship of their sleep, but you are the reason they sleep at night. Because they know that their queen will never forsake them. And they grieve that little babe for more reasons than losing a future king. Your people are sad, beloved, because they know your sorrow and they feel helpless. 'How can we help?' I hear them ask throughout the kingdom."

Isaboe looked away, to the corner of the residence where the crib would have stood.

"Sometimes I think I can bear it," she said, "and then Jasmina will look at me with so much confusion and she'll touch my belly and ask me where it's gone. 'Where's baby?' she cries. She looks for it everywhere we go." Isaboe felt the tears bite her eyes. "On the mountain just the other day, we went to visit Yata and one of the girls had just birthed and Jasmina threw the mightiest of tantrums and insisted we take the babe home, because she believed it to be ours. In her sweet mind, I went to the mountain to have a baby and I came home with none. So she believes we left it behind."

She looked up at Tesadora in anguish. "And later that night, I heard him weeping. My king is not one for tears. I only saw him cry once, when we came across the fever camp in Speranza. But that night on the mountain, he wept and it broke me to hear it."

Isaboe stepped out of the tub, and Tesadora helped her dress, securing the ties of her gown at her wrist.

"You are strong and young, and you will find a way out of this darkness. But that path will belong to you. No one else."

They heard a sound at the door, and Isaboe quickly wiped her tears and turned to the entrance, where Finnikin stood watching her with Jasmina drowsy in his arms.

"And don't let me ever have to admit this out loud," Tesadora said in an exaggerated whisper, walking toward the door, "but you lead this kingdom with a good man by your side . . . as stubborn and annoying as he is. A man who has proven himself to have courage and compassion. The Charynite valley dwellers believe that if they could find a man as good as yours to marry Quintana of Charyn, their kingdom would stand a chance."

Isaboe watched Finnikin grip Tesadora's hand as she passed him, pressing a kiss against it.

Jasmina woke up, sleepy and shy, and looked up from her father's shoulder.

"Tell Mama what you did today," he said, approaching Isaboe. Jasmina hid her face in his neck, and he chuckled and whispered in her ear until she looked up again.

"Tell Isaboe," he urged. "Go on."

Isaboe leaned closer to hear Jasmina whisper, "I put my head in the wiver."

Isaboe gasped with delight. "Do I not have the bravest girl in the kingdom? Did Fa tell you that I didn't put my head in the river until I was a grown girl in Yutlind Sud?"

Jasmina was pleased by the attention and held her arms out to Isaboe, and then Rhiannon was at the door.

"She put her head in the river," Isaboe told her.

Rhiannon gasped on cue and held out a hand to Jasmina.

"Then I think Miss picks out her own dress for tonight."

Isaboe watched them leave and felt Finnikin's eyes on

her. Sometimes she felt as shy as Jasmina with this man. Grief stripped her of a veneer. Sometimes she wanted it back.

"You're beautiful," he said, and it surprised her to hear those words. She always felt his love when he was present, but Finnikin wasn't one for words of endearment. It was because he came from the Rock. People there were practical and very contained.

They heard Jasmina's laughter from down the hall, and she caught Finnikin's smile at the sound of it. Isaboe pressed fingers to his lips. He didn't smile enough, and the sight of it always caught her breath.

"What if she's all I give you in this life of ours, my love?" she asked quietly.

"Then I'll shout at the goddess in fury," he said fiercely. "I'll beg to know why I've been given so much when other men have so little."

"We're going to be late," Froi told the priest-king, trying to shuffle him quickly out the door of what was now the shrine house of Sennington.

But the priest-king was fumbling with the key.

"Let me do that," Froi said. "You know Lady Abian hates people being late."

"You want me to hurry, do you?" the priest-king asked. "An old man like me?"

Froi placed the oil lamp in the priest-king's hand and hastened them toward the horse and cart he had prepared. Although the priest-king's house was in use all the day long, most of Sennington village was still empty, and once the sun set, there was nothing but the moon to light their road to the village of Sayles.

"Froi, slow down," the priest-king said.

"Half the mountain's come down, blessed Barakah, and you

know the Monts. They'll eat all the food before we get there, and Lady Abian's made those rolls of pork and cheese."

"Wonderful. I'm going to be forced into my deathbed because of pork-and-cheese rolls," the priest-king said, stopping a moment to wheeze. Froi flinched to hear the sound of it. Much had changed since he left, but he had only realized now just how frail the priest-king was.

When they reached the feast, most of the guests were already inside, except for some of the Guard, who merely raised a hand in acknowledgment. Things had changed among them, Froi thought. In the past, there would have been mockery or jest, but it was as if they could barely look him in the eye. Did they see him as a Charynite now? Would he be a stranger in every land? Not a Sarnak or a Charynite or a Lumateran?

"You're gritting your teeth," the priest-king said as they made their way to the entrance.

"I liked it better when they used to call me a filthy little feef," Froi said bitterly.

"And they probably liked it better when you had little control," the priest-king said. "You've become a surprisingly formidable young man, Froi. Nothing's more frightening to others."

On the porch, Perri was organizing another shift of the Guard. Froi could understand the caution. Lord and Lady Abian's home had little protection for such a royal guest list, and Trevanion's men had to ensure that every entrance and corner of the village was secure. Upon seeing Froi and the priest-king, Perri pointed to the hall, which was rarely used except for large gatherings. One of the guards pushed past them and hurried along without so much as a grunt of apology. Froi bit his tongue and held out a hand to the priest-king, who moved slowly. It made Froi wince.

"I want you to see Tesadora now that she's spending a little time in the palace," Froi said to him. "She may be able to give you something."

"For being old? There's a cure, is there?"

"And don't stand around too long," Froi ordered. "Everyone's going to want to talk to you, and next minute you'll be tottering."

"I've never tottered a day in my life. You're annoying me, Froi."

"Yes, well, I'm annoying everyone these days."

They reached the hall and stepped inside. They all were suddenly standing in silence. Staring at him. It was awkward, and it made him feel uncomfortable and a stranger. Angry tears burned at the back of his eyes.

He saw the queen first. Froi had seen little of her since arriving home, and knew it would take her some time to heal. But tonight there seemed more of a bloom in her cheek. She bent to whisper something in Vestie's ear. Vestie took Jasmina's hand, and they ran to Froi, beckoning him to bend to their level. Bemused, Froi crouched beside them.

"Happy birthday, Froi," Vestie said proudly.

And then everyone was shouting it, and the priest-king was pushing him forward, not weak at all, and Froi was engulfed in embraces and kisses, with friends pressing gifts in his hand.

Jasmina clutched his arm all night, abandoning her reserve from earlier in the day.

"It's all about your gifts," Finn said. "She thinks they're hers. She's stealing everything. Even letters addressed to us. She loves the pretty seals."

Froi laughed, caught Lord August's eye, and shook his head.

"You, sir, are deceitful."

Lord August embraced him, and then Celie was there with Talon and his brothers.

"Mother's been planning it for weeks," Talon said, laughing.

"And if anyone dared to say a word, I think she would have had the boys strung up," Celie said.

Froi was jostled from one person to another until he found himself with Lucian, quietly watching the revelry. Finnikin had expressed a suspicion to Froi that Lucian was in love with Phaedra of Alonso and missed her deeply. From what he had heard these past months, Froi knew that Phaedra had been everything he imagined her to be. Kind. Loyal. And currently, Quintana's only companion. Froi itched to ask.

"No," Lucian said, reading his mind. "Only letters from the priests of Sebastabol. They want to know how the seven scholars died. Every detail. Why would you want every detail of the way seven men died?" he added, irritation in his voice.

"They're the priests of Trist," Froi corrected. "And if one of the Monts died in Charyn, wouldn't you want to know every detail? It's the same for them. One of the lads, Rothen, was the grandson of the head priest."

"Rothen. I remember him," Lucian said quietly.

"Then, tell them everything you know. It's not a trap, Lucian. It's just people wanting to know how their loved ones died."

"You know them?" Lucian asked. "The priests?"

Froi nodded. Lucian looked at him shrewdly. "You seem to have had a very busy year, Froi."

"Almost as busy as yours, Lucian."

Lucian was steered away by one of the Flatland lords, and Froi caught Isaboe's eye as she excused herself from speaking to Beatriss. He fought hard to stop the wave of emotion that always came over him in the queen's presence.

"Will your husband come charging across the room if I do this?" he said, catching her in an embrace. He felt her fists clenched with emotion against his back, and the shudder in her breath. They hadn't spoken about the death of her son and her part in the birth of his. There were no words, just the certainty that he would love Isaboe of Lumatere for the remainder of his life.

"So you heard about his outburst in our residence?" she asked huskily, stepping away after a while and eyeing Finnikin across the room.

"Yes, well, he did beat me black and blue on the Osteria-Charyn border."

"Strange that he left that part out," she said dryly.

They were awkwardly silent for a moment or two.

"Thank you for all of this," he said, looking around the room, knowing she was involved as much as Lady Abian. Then his eyes met hers. "Thank you . . . for everything you did . . . for her."

Isaboe's stare was fierce. "I did it for you. I don't do Charynites favors."

"I'm a Charynite," he reminded her softly.

She shook her head emphatically. "I don't care what your blood sings, Froi. You belong to us. You're a Lumateran."

And he was. How could he feel both so strongly?

She took his hand, and they walked to where Jasmina was playing under the long table with the village children. The little girl was giddy with the sort of hysteria he noticed in those her age.

"All the laughing will end in tears," Isaboe said, sitting down while the children crawled between her feet. Froi sat down beside her.

"Did blessed Barakah tell you about the spirits and the Yut madman's theory?" she asked quietly.

"Oh, yes," Froi said, his tone dry. "He decided to tell me in front of Perri, who didn't cope at all."

They both laughed at the thought, but then she was serious again.

"Is it true that you can sing spirits home, Froi?" she asked.

He didn't know how to answer that.

"I don't know what's true," he said, awkward at hearing the words. "I know my . . . uncle . . . Arjuro can."

"Can you tell . . . if a spirit is lost?" Isaboe asked.

Froi saw the sadness in her eyes.

"Is that what you think?" he asked. "That your boy's spirit is lost?"

She winced, but he could also see her confusion. "When I was carrying him in my belly . . . I'd sense her . . . Quintana . . . but not like when I walked the sleep with Vestie and Tesadora. This was different. More distant in a way, and I think it's because . . ."

She couldn't finish. She looked away, pained, and Froi tried to search the room for Finnikin because he knew his friend understood Isaboe's despair better than anyone. But Finn wasn't there, and Froi could see that Isaboe wanted to speak.

"Do you still walk her sleep?" he asked softly.

She shook her head. "Quintana and I do not have a connection, Froi. But I think our sons walked each other's sleep . . . and I don't know whether I was desperate for a sign or whether all this talk of spirits has played with my mind, but I sensed him. . . . I sensed my boy in your boy's eyes. Isn't that what you wrote in the letter about the husband and wife you shared a barn with? She said the half-dead spirit of her child lived in you."

He nodded. Tesadora told him how Quintana had spoken the same words to her. Froi's mind had been filled with sorrow for the families of the lost Charynite babes. He wondered if they still would sense those spirits within him or Quintana now, or had they been passed to Tariq?

"I think you're wrong about Quintana and you," he said to Isaboe. "Because I first heard a voice four years past in Sarnak. It was on the bleakest day of my existence, at a time that I almost gave up. Almost. Until I heard her song. I didn't know what it was at the time. But it told me to go to Sprie. *Sprie?* You saw it. Why such a nowhere place in Sarnak? I could have chosen any place in the land, but not Sprie. And it's taken me all these years to realize that she was singing me to you. And Finn. And Sir Topher." He looked around the room. "And this, Isaboe. And all this, led me to Charyn. Blessed Barakah says our paths aren't straight, and they make little sense. But Quintana heard my pain, and she led me to you. Which means that your connection with her existed long before the sons you both carried."

"You don't know that, Froi," Isaboe said, her voice cool.

"No, I don't. But your plan for revenge on Charyn led me straight into Gargarin of Abroi's path. And I crossed a *gravina* to be with Arjuro of Abroi, and I climbed a tower to be with Lirah of Serker. Call it coincidence, but I've spent a year questioning what I know and what I sense, and sometimes what I sense over-powers everything."

Isaboe sighed. Jasmina's head popped up between her feet again, and they both laughed.

"Well, let's hope they're making a fuss over your Quintana today," Isaboe said, gathering her daughter to her.

Froi grimaced. "She's not very good with . . . fuss," he said.

"Every princess is good with a little fuss," she said, kissing Jasmina. "Aren't you, my love?"

Froi sighed. Yes, but Quintana wasn't exactly the most normal of princesses.

"Perhaps they've thrown her a party."

Sagra! He couldn't think of anything more frightening for her. Or for those who tried.

CHAPTER 42

Y ou're not thinking of throwing me one of those odious surprise parties, are you?" Quintana asked coldly, clutching the little king. "If you do, I'll lock myself and Tariq in our room and never come out."

Phaedra looked from Quintana to Gargarin of Abroi. "Well, it's not as if you don't already do that, Your Majesty," Gargarin said. His eyes met Phaedra's. They had managed to coax Quintana out of her self-imposed prison and into the courtyard to greet those who now lived in the palace. Phaedra and Gargarin hoped they could lead her farther, to the portcullis and perhaps down the drawbridge and into the Citavita.

"Could I suggest that we visit the town square and greet those who have traveled here for your birthday?" Phaedra said.

"The town square?" Quintana asked. Phaedra watched Gargarin wince, as if he knew the following words would not be pleasing to the ear.

"The town square where they once set up the gallows and jeered when the street lords placed a noose around my neck? Brayed for my blood?"

And this was how they had begun each day since they had arrived all those months ago.

"It's about time and compromise," Gargarin of Abroi had said to Phaedra outside Quintana's chamber one morning. He had said those words after yet another failed attempt to have her join them outside the palace. "Let's give her the time she needs."

Time, Phaedra noted, was spent in Quintana's cold, sparse chamber. Its only appeal was a balconette that looked over the *gravina*. Phaedra was fascinated with the way the godshouse opposite tilted toward them, not to mention the hollering that took place between Quintana, Gargarin, the priestling Arjuro, and Lirah of Serker. The *provincari*'s people who had settled in the palace tower on both sides of theirs complained the whole day long about the early-morning and late-night shouting. Phaedra would have died of boredom without it. As she would have without the nocturnal visits from the godshouse residents.

On the second night in the palace, she was introduced to two priests, both in robes and cowls. She was soon to discover that one was Arjuro and the other Lirah of Serker. Perabo, the keeper of the keys of the palace, had smuggled Lirah in with Arjuro, far from the prying eyes of those they called the *provincari*'s parrots.

Lirah of Serker was the most beautiful woman Phaedra had ever seen apart from Tesadora. They reminded her of each other. Especially in their disdain for the world, until they were in the presence of someone they loved.

As long as she lived, Phaedra would never forget the first moment Lirah of Serker held the little king in her arms.

The queen allowed only Phaedra, Lirah, and Arjuro to hold the child. And Gargarin, but he refused each time, preferring to admire the little king over the shoulders of others.

"Is he not the most perfect thing you've seen, Lirah?" Quintana asked. "Is he not just like Lirah, Gargarin?"

"Thank the gods for that," the little king's regent murmured. Phaedra knew that Gargarin and Lirah were lovers. It was whispered in the hallways of the palace by the guards. But Phaedra hadn't realized the two loved each other until Gargarin watched Lirah of Serker with the sleeping boy.

"You can stay the night with Phaedra and me, Lirah," Quintana said. "We can watch Tariq sleep."

Lirah and Gargarin exchanged a look, and Arjuro snorted a laugh.

"Yes, I'll sit with Gargarin and speak of waterwheels and privies."

Today, having lost the battle of Quintana leaving the palace, Phaedra watched as Gargarin decided to bring up the issue of chambers when they returned to her room.

"There's been enough time to settle in," Gargarin said. "You can't stay in here, Your Majesty. It's not big enough for you all."

"But I can," Quintana said dismissively. "This has always been my chamber."

Gargarin grimaced. "It holds bad memories for you, Your Majesty," he said. "Awful."

Quintana picked up Tariq from his basket and clutched him to her. She did it often. Up and down he went. From her arms to the basket and then back into her arms. Sometimes Phaedra would see Quintana place an ear to Tariq's lips to check for breathing.

"This chamber holds the best of memories, too," Quintana said quietly. "You forget that."

Gargarin sighed. "It's best you take the solar. It's large and well lit and the most comfortable place in the palace."

Quintana wanted to hear none of it. Instead, she held out Tariq to Gargarin. "It's about time," she said. She tried at least once a day to have the little king's regent hold him, but always failed.

"You move to the solar," he said firmly instead.

Phaedra believed that Quintana had all but lost this fight.

"My idea is better," Quintana said. "You take the solar, Gargarin. There's the secret passage through the cellar that leads to it, and on the nights Perabo is on watch at the gatehouse, Lirah can visit you more easily there than meeting you here. She certainly won't be seen by the parrots of the provinces. When he's old enough, we can place Tariq in the chamber next door to here. We can hack an entrance just there," she said, pointing to the wall. "We can place a desk near the window, just for you. The little king will have to get used to you, so it's best you use his chamber as a study during the day. It means you'll still be able to use it when the sun comes up to greet Arjuro and Lirah."

"Your Majesty—"

She shook her head and placed her hands over the little king's ears. "I slit my father's throat in the solar, Gargarin. Not exactly the room I want my son sleeping in. And anyway, think of your satisfaction. You get the dead king's sanctuary. You get what Bestiano wanted for himself. Lie back and relish it."

Gargarin was silent. Most of the time, Phaedra was frightened by him. Not that he had ever shown a violent trait and not because of words he had spoken, but because of the silence. He had a wounded spirit, and the only time she saw him happy was when he was in the company of Lirah and his brother and Tariq, despite not wanting to hold him. But then again, everyone was happy in the little king's presence. Phaedra couldn't bear to start her day without having him in her arms. He soothed her aching heart.

"And I've made a decision about my title of *Queen*," Quintana continued. "I've decided to relinquish it. In years to come, when

Tariq marries, it will belong to his betrothed, and I'll despise her enough for taking my son from me. It could get quite ugly if I get used to the title, and I may hate her twice over. I might want to kill her, and we do want to avoid future bloodshed in the palace."

There was a strange, twisted smile on Gargarin's face. Phaedra didn't understand their humor. It bordered on wicked when Arjuro joined them.

"Then, Princess—"

Quintana shook her head. "I can't say I enjoyed being princess of this kingdom, either. It's best that the people of Charyn forget that title until I have a daughter. She can be the spirited princess. The gentle princess. The sweetest princess in the land. The bravest. The feistiest. But when the people of the Citavita think of me as princess, they'll remember the cursed princess. The Princess Abomination."

They waited.

"I'll be referred to as Quintana of Charyn, mother of the king. And Lirah of Serker will be referred to as *shalamar* of the king."

Gargarin sighed and then nodded, and then gave a twisted, shy smile again. It made him quite striking. "When did you work all this out?" he chided gently.

Quintana looked down at Tariq. "Quite some time ago. Tariq loved the idea. We just thought we'd wait until you were ready, Gargarin. It's about time and compromise."

Gargarin looked around the room, already imagining how the residence would be if they made an entrance between the two rooms. He walked to the wall and knocked hard.

"In the fortress beyond the little woods where we hid with the Lasconians and Turlans, they had fireplaces on every floor without so much as a chimney," Gargarin said. "They used vents in the wall. We'll put fireplaces in both these chambers." He liked the idea. "And I daresay I think we can make another entrance into the room adjoining the next. All three could make a strange private residence."

Quintana seemed pleased. She held Tariq out to Gargarin.

"My arm—" he said.

"You won't drop him, Gargarin. Froi would want you to hold him."

Phaedra wondered what had taken place when Quintana escaped with Froi, Gargarin, and Lirah all that time ago. They shared a bond, a secret. She knew that Froi was the father of the child. Very few did, except for Lirah, Gargarin, Arjuro, Perabo, and the *provincaro* of Paladozza. But there was more, and she knew the answer lay with Froi of Lumatere.

She tried asking once.

"Better that we don't tell, Phaedra," Quintana said.

"We'd have to kill you," Arjuro added, "and we don't really want to do that."

But regardless, Phaedra knew she was trusted by them all. She liked the priestling best. Arjuro was besotted by the little king and visited as often as possible.

"Did you see that?" he asked Gargarin one time. "He stared straight at me with understanding when I explained the symptoms of gout. Pure genius."

But despite some of the compromises, Phaedra could see that Gargarin and Lirah and Arjuro feared for Quintana. The way she had imprisoned herself in the castle with Tariq, and her belief that an enemy had been sent to kill him. It meant that if Phaedra wanted to walk the streets of the capital, she did so with a guard, and not Quintana. At first she had been frightened that the stone walls would come tumbling down on her. As time passed, she was accompanied by Lirah, and she warmed to the people and wished Quintana could hear the yearning in their voices when they asked Phaedra and Lirah about the little king. But no one could convince Quintana. Not even Lirah, whose only means of seeing Tariq was through her nightly visits.

"I'd love to see him during the light of the day, Quintana," Lirah said one night.

"But you see him from across the *gravina*, Lirah," Quintana said coolly. "I hold him up every morning."

"You know that's not enough," Lirah said. "And you know that Dorcas and Fekra and Scarpo and Perabo and his men would never ever let anything happen to Tariq. Even I trust them. How many people have I trusted in my life?"

Gargarin blamed it on the little sleep Quintana had. Arjuro and Lirah said they'd seen her this way before and were lovingly patient, despite not seeming to be lovingly patient people.

"If I don't guard Tariq, Lirah, they'll kill him," Quintana explained. "They'll kill my guards to get to him."

"The only person I know who'll get through those guards is Froi," Lirah said. "Do you want him to return to this? To a frightened Quintana and an unwashed babe?"

The washing of the babe had become an even bigger issue.

"It's been months, Quintana," Phaedra pleaded. "It's not enough to clean him with a cloth. You need to bathe him."

"I don't want his head to go under the water," Quintana whispered. "You see awful things down there. Those from the lake of the half dead are desperate for him."

Gargarin later explained to Phaedra about the soothsayer. The ritual that had happened each year before the day of weeping. And it shamed Phaedra even more to have known so little of Quintana's suffering in the Citavita for all those years. It made her want to take back every moment of their time hiding in the valley when Phaedra and the women had dismissed her as nothing but a delusional, half-crazed girl.

But memories of the valley were dangerous for Phaedra. It was deep in the night when she allowed herself to think of Lucian. Was he thinking of her? Had he moved on with his life? And she thought of the valley and realized that it was more of a home to her than Alonso was and that she missed its people in a way that she hadn't missed those of her province. When she was young, she had been kept protected from the world outside her father's compound. In the valley and mountain she had truly begun to live.

And on one such night, Quintana lay beside her, tense with fear of what the unseen enemy would do to her little king. Sometimes when the breeze spoke from outside the balconette and the shadows played with their eyes, Phaedra would hear the hope in Quintana's voice.

"Froi! Is that you?"

And then the disappointment. Phaedra would take her hand. "You need to sleep, dear friend."

"And dream of what, Phaedra?" Quintana asked, getting out of bed. "The *provincari* are beginning to make suggestions for a consort. Should I dream of choosing the one that turns my stomach least?"

After Quintana had checked Tariq's breathing for the umpteenth time, she crawled back into bed, exhausted.

"I'll never leave you," Phaedra said, tucking the blanket around the princess. "The consort can find himself another chamber."

"I know you'll never leave me," Quintana said. "But when it comes to you, Phaedra, I'm afraid of worse."

CHAPTER 43

Froi was led through the gilded doors and into the palace throne room. He had never been in here before and marveled at the rich tapestries of fierce men battling impressive boars with bare hands. On the ceiling was a fresco of women, stupendous in their girth and beauty, with serpents they had conquered beneath their feet. Froi understood with great clarity why he wasn't meeting Finnikin and Isaboe in their private residence. But he had been waiting for this day. Regardless of his time spent with Finnikin, riding around the kingdom; and with Trevanion, fishing in the river; and with Perri and Tesadora down in the valley, laughing with the camp dwellers; and blessed Barakah, translating a journal in the shrine house; and with Isaboe, suggesting changes to her garden; and with Sir Topher, beating him in a game of kings—today they weren't those people to him. They were the queen, her king, the captain of the Lumateran Guard and his second-in-charge, the queen's First Man, and the priest-king.

And he wasn't Froi. He was their assassin who had spent nine months in an enemy kingdom. He had a head full of information they wanted, and this was the time to give it.

"Was the palace exactly as Rafuel of Sebastabol sketched?" Finnikin asked when they were finally seated.

Froi didn't answer. He didn't expect them to begin with that question. He had thought they'd skirt around things before they asked him that.

"Froi?" Sir Topher prodded.

"Do you not trust us with that information?" his queen asked.

"I trust you with my life," Froi said. "But if I answered your question, then the people I love in Charyn would never trust me again." His eyes met hers and then Finnikin's. "And in my whole time there, I never once betrayed Lumatere. So if there's no reason for you needing to know how to enter my son's home, I'd prefer not to speak of the Charynite palace."

There was silence. Perri was already on his feet, pacing the room.

"Then, what shall we speak about?" Finnikin asked.

"The weather is always a safe topic," Froi said pleasantly. "It could lead to some vital information about the storage of rainwater and growing produce. We have different terrain from Charyn's, and what we grow, they want, and what they grow, we may want."

"Anything else, Froi?" Finnikin asked dryly. "Any other suggestions?"

"Well, you have invited me here for a reason," he said with a shrug, "and I have become used to people asking my opinion, so it's a bit difficult to hold my tongue."

Sir Topher sat forward in his seat. "And you gave your opinion readily?" he asked. "With them?"

"Most times. I did lose my confidence once . . . after I was injured," he said, remembering Gargarin discussing Froi's self-doubt with Lirah that time in Sebastabol.

"After you were betrayed by a Charynite . . . friend?" Isaboe asked.

"Yes."

"An opportunist? This traitor friend?" Finnikin asked. "Did he do it for money? Lucian mentioned what greedy, ignorant Charynites they were, those who placed themselves in charge of the camp dwellers. Do most Charynites betray for money?"

Froi felt himself bristling. "Well, first, I tend to refer to him just as a traitor these days," he said. "Not a friend. And . . . no. Most Charynites don't betray for money. Most Charynites want to stay alive and hold their children in their arms."

He regretted the words the moment he spoke them. Caught the pain in Isaboe's eyes. But there was understanding there as well.

"He—the traitor—didn't do it for money," Froi said quietly.

"And you know this for certain?" Sir Topher asked. "Someone just wakes up one morning, Froi? And decides to betray those who trust him? But not for money? And you believe that?"

Froi sighed. "No, sir. I'll explain to you how betrayal happens. A bunch of lads come up with a plan. Quite noble, if naive," he said, thinking of Grijio and Satch and Olivier. "And then what happens is that one of the lads gets kidnapped as part of a plan hatched between a neighboring enemy kingdom and a very secretive organization. . . ."

Finnikin sighed. "If it's Lumatere and Rafuel's people you're referring to, then let's get rid of the cryptic references. I get so confused when I haven't slept."

"Yes, let's use names," Isaboe said.

Froi nodded. "I took Olivier's place at your instruction, and meanwhile, he was held captive underground, guarded by a man, Zabat, who convinced him that he could make a difference.

Except Zabat had switched sides and believed Bestiano of Nebia was the best chance for Charyn. And when Olivier of Sebastabol was released, he became what Zabat, not his original captors, wanted him to be. Which led to betrayal."

"In what way?" Sir Topher asked.

"Olivier withheld the truth," Froi said.

Isaboe made a sound of annoyance.

"He doesn't seem so naive after all," she said. "If you're ever writing to the Charynites, Froi, tell them not to execute the smart ones. They do come in handy."

He looked up at her again. Would Froi's rotten corpse be lying somewhere in a ditch in Sorel if Froi were less smart?

Yes, of course it would be, her eyes told him.

Froi smiled, half bitterly, half in amusement that he would think she had lost any of her fight or backbone. That he would think that Lumatere's charming, loving queen and her king were any less than they presented. But they didn't lie about who they were. They just omitted details.

Finnikin retrieved a letter and passed it to Froi. Froi's heart hammered at the thought of Gargarin finally writing.

"This came to us yesterday, addressed to you."

Froi opened it, recognizing the writing from a letter Simeon had sent to Lucian.

"The priests of Trist," Froi said, reading quickly, his heart heavy by the end.

"Rafuel?" Finnikin asked.

Froi nodded. "They obtained information from one of Donashe's camp leaders and found Rafuel outside Jidia in a mine shaft with no food and only a little water trickling from a stone—skin and bones. They don't expect him to live. They want me to pass on the news to the women of the valley as well as Japhra and Tesadora. The priests of Trist found mad ramblings on the walls imprisoning Rafuel, and the names of the women of the valley were among them."

Froi heard Perri's sound of regret.

"Tell us about your correspondence with these priests," Finnikin said.

"The priests of Trist wrote to Lucian first, and I replied on Lucian's behalf. They wanted to know how the scholars died."

"Why didn't that order come from the Charyn palace?" Finnikin asked.

"Because the palace is taking care of political traitors, not personal vengeance, and what happened with the scholars . . . and Rafuel is about personal vengeance. The priests had five camp leaders in their prison. They wanted to make sure those who murdered the lads were tried and executed, and they didn't want to get it wrong, especially if there was a chance that Rafuel lived."

"Is Rafuel of Sebastabol's being alive your business?" Trevanion asked, looking at Froi. "You hardly knew him except for the week he taught you about Charynite customs. You smashed his nose, last I remember."

Froi felt the regret he always did when he thought of Rafuel these days.

"Let's just say that Rafuel and I go back . . . nineteen years. If you remember anything about the events I spoke about in the letter I gave to Finn—Your Highness, it was that I was smuggled out of the palace as a babe."

"By a boy."

Froi shrugged. "Rafuel was that boy. So yes, his being alive is my business. And for all of your information, it won't do us any harm finding allies in the priests."

Isaboe stood and walked to Froi, then sat facing him.

"And that is why we need you, Froi. Talk us through it. What if we want to take a step toward peace? Who has the most power? Gargarin of Abroi? The *provincari*? The godshouse?"

"The *provincari* united have the power," Froi said. "My advice is that you go to Gargarin but that you also establish a relationship with the individual *provincari*. Deep down, they're slightly impressed with Lumateran nobility. Take advantage of that. And then remember that the godshouse is important to the people and if you're going to impress Charyn, you're going to want to impress the godshouse." He looked at the priest-king. "They want nothing more than absolution from the blessed Barakah. They understand the pain that took place here at the hands of Charyn's army and they know they can't change the past, but they want to acknowledge it."

"How strong is their army now, Froi?" Trevanion asked.

Froi was dreading that question. His eyes met Trevanion's.

"Very strong. United, it's even stronger."

"If they were ever to attack . . . ?" Isaboe asked.

"We wouldn't stand a chance."

He heard the sharp intake of breath around the room.

"So the way I see it, we try very, very hard not to be attacked by them," Sir Topher said.

"Well, we could see the situation from the side of wonder," Froi said.

"Oh, there's a side of wonder in all of this?" Finnikin asked, sarcasm lacing his words. "Charyn has a new army large enough to decimate us, and he tells us we're going to look on the brighter side."

They all stared at Froi as if he were some foolish child.

"If we make friends with them, we'll have a powerful ally in Charyn," he said.

"Very simplistic," Isaboe said.

Froi shook his head with frustration. "It's the way I see things now," he said. "The simpler it is to keep peace, the better our lives are. You don't want Lumaterans to die, my queen. They don't want Charynites to die. Trust me on that. A powerful Nebian captain surrendered and was on his knees because he didn't want one more Charynite to die. He knew the man he surrendered to was a good man who did not want one more Charynite to die. So when good leaders don't want their people to die, they spend quite some time trying to work out how to achieve things without going to war. It's that simple!"

He needed to walk. He needed to count, because his blood was jumping. But most of all he needed to show them that he had control over himself. *No counting. You can do this without the counting.*

"At the moment, Charyn has a stable alliance among the *provincari,* and the way I see it, they want peace," he continued. "They need it. They may have the power to decimate a neighboring kingdom, but they need that power to mend their own decimated people."

Isaboe took his hand. "You'd be our perfect envoy to them, Froi, and regardless of whom . . . she is married to, you would still have an opportunity to . . . see her. Each time you visit."

"An arrangement that would work for us all," Finnikin said with a shrug. Froi shook his head, wondering if his king would ever understand.

"That's very easy for you to say, my lord," he said in an even tone. "You're married to the woman you love, and your daughter sleeps between you."

"Well, if you'd really like to know, she's getting used to her own bed now, and I wish everyone would stop going on about it," Isaboe said.

"Froi—" Finnikin said.

But Froi stood. He needed air.

"Sit," Finnikin ordered. Gently.

Froi sat.

"So you get half the dream, Froi," Finnikin said. "You can't have the whole thing because they won't let you. Not us. So why the anger toward Lumatere?"

"I'm not angry at you, Finn," Froi said, frustrated. "But you can't go around expecting me to spy and be happy with halves and whatnots while you get the whole dream."

"I don't get the whole dream," Finnikin said. "My whole dream is that my wife wakes in the morning and doesn't have to worry about an entire kingdom. That all she has to worry about is—I don't know—looking after her husband and child."

Isaboe choked out a laugh.

"Or her husband looking after her, then," Finnikin said.

"Wonderful. I get reduced to either a slave or a helpless idiot," she said with a smile toward Finnikin. But then she was all seriousness. "In the games of queens and kings," she said to Froi, "we leave our dreams at the door and we make do with what we have. Sometimes if we're fortunate, we still manage to have a good life."

She thought about her own words for a moment and smiled.

"We don't want you in the Charyn palace to spy, Froi," she said. "Regardless of what you think of the situation with Celie, she is in Belegonia to provide us with an opportunity to talk. Without talk between past adversaries, we don't stand a chance."

"If you want peace, you begin with the valley, then," Froi argued back. "You begin at the foot of your mountain, Isaboe!"

"But there's more to all of this than the valley, Froi," Isaboe argued. "If Gargarin of Abroi is as smart and noble as I'm sick of hearing he is, why has the man not written to us? To you?"

Why indeed? Froi wondered angrily.

"When the time comes, will you travel to Charyn and begin talks between the kingdoms?" she said.

"When?" Froi asked.

"Not now. Let's take the time to get the treaty right. As you said, perhaps we speak his language first. Water and land and how we can learn from each other. In the meantime, you can write Gargarin of Abroi a letter—"

"No," Froi said.

They all stared at him. Regardless of Froi's fury and betrayal, it had been Gargarin's order not to make contact with any of them, and Froi's pride demanded he honor that.

"I'll write the letter," Finnikin said. "Let it be seen that Lumatere was the first to make contact."

In the weeks that followed, Froi found himself traveling to almost all corners of the kingdom. In the forest of Lumatere, he attended a remembrance ceremony with Tesadora and the novices of both Lagrami and Sagrami. During his first year in Lumatere, Froi had spent much of his time with Perri guarding Tesadora, the priestess, and the girls. He had accompanied them when they moved their cloister back to the forest of Lumatere after ten years near the Sendecane border. Froi knew back then that he had earned trust from these women at a time when he was desperate for it, and each year when they had the remembrance ceremony, they invited Froi along.

The tree of remembrance had been planted in honor of the Charynite who had smuggled the Lagrami novices out of the palace village. It meant more to Froi now, knowing that Arjuro had been part of the escape. That morning, he stood with the priestess watching Perri carry earth to the separate plots surrounding the cloister. The novices had grown a spectacular garden of healing, and Froi knew that Lumaterans from across the kingdom came to these women to cure their ailments.

"Tesadora says you're acquainted with the Charynite

holy man who took us to her," the priestess said.

Froi nodded. "His name's Arjuro," he said. "He never spoke of his time in Lumatere."

"Yes, well, who can blame him?"

"What happened?" Froi asked.

The priestess held out her hand and he took it, escorting her for a walk around the gardens.

"We met him through John, the Charynite soldier who smuggled us out of the village," she said. "The lad was working as a scout for the impostor king and heard of the heinous plans in the barracks. They wanted women in the palace as their . . . playthings, and what better girls to have than those of the Lagrami cloister, who were close by in the palace village and not protected by fathers and brothers?"

"How did this . . . John make Arjuro's acquaintance?" Froi asked.

"Earlier that month, John had been sent on a scouting mission by the impostor king's captain to check the rest of the kingdom. The Charynites were hoping that the Sendecane and Sarnak borders were free of the curse. Your friend the holy man was camping close to the Sarnak border when John came across him. Despite the distance to the cloisters on the Sendecane border, Arjuro took John to meet Tesadora, for no other reason than that the holy man had read an instruction in his dreams to lead the boy to the novices. It would be a most symbolic meeting between them all because weeks later John of Charyn made a decision that would cost him his life. He smuggled us out of the village, for he had found the perfect place to hide us. He took us to your friend the holy man first, but the palace riders had followed and we had little time for further acquaintance. The man we now know as Arjuro of Abroi drew us a map to where Tesadora was hiding the Sagrami novices, and then he and John became the decoys.

We never saw them again. John of Charyn was seventeen years old when he died. Strange to think he'd be a man of more than thirty today."

Froi looked out at the garden so similar to Arjuro's on the roof of the godshouse.

"Well, Arjuro survived. He's a brilliant physician," Froi said, "and if there's ever peace between Charyn and Lumatere, he'd welcome some of your girls as his students of healing. Your novices are smarter than the *collegiati* I came across in Charyn."

Tesadora and Japhra joined them soon after, and the priestess took Tesadora's hand. Two very different women stood before Froi, but the respect between them was fierce.

"Are you ever going to allow him a bonding ceremony?" the priestess asked shrewdly.

"Who? Froi?" Tesadora asked, and Froi laughed.

"You know who she's talking about," he said, looking over to where Perri was working.

"She asks you every year," Japhra said, her voice soft.

"I don't need a ceremony," Tesadora said.

"And what if a child comes to your union?" the priestess asked.

Tesadora sent her an annoyed look, but the priestess persisted.

"The end of the curse for Charyn means the end of the curse for you, Tesadora," she said.

"I'm past the age," Tesadora said. Japhra made a sound of disbelief.

"My mother birthed me at the same age as you," the priestess said. "And the queen's beloved mother gave birth to her fourth and fifth children well past your age. He's very virile, Tesadora."

As if Perri suspected he was being spoken about, he looked across at them from where he was digging.

"If you allow that man into your bed, be prepared to hold a child at your breast one day."

"Remember what John of Charyn said, Tesadora," one of the novices joined in. "That his mother was a midwife and women came to her at all ages."

"Yes, and his father was a man of horses, and old mares dropped dead when they were carrying," Tesadora said, her tone tart. "Enough. All of you."

Froi accompanied Tesadora and Japhra and two of their girls back up to the mountain that afternoon, his mind going over the talk of the day. There were names and facts he couldn't get out of his head for some reason.

Japhra was quiet, and when they were well ahead of the others, he asked her about Rafuel.

He had spoken to Japhra about Rafuel, the last time he was in the valley and she had introduced him to Quintana's women of the cave.

"Do you love him?" he had asked. "Rafuel?"

"Does it matter?" Japhra said. "My heart belongs here with Tesadora and my work, and his heart belonged in Charyn with the priests and their work." She smiled. "But he helped me heal, and one day I want to do something to repay him."

Down in the valley, he was taken again to the women who once shared Quintana's cave. Froi always found it hard to believe Quintana had bonded with these three: two who grumbled and argued, one who giggled and preened. But Cora, Jorja, and Florenza loved his girl, and they had taken care of her. If there was any reason to spend time with them, it was that. More than anything, he loved the valley. Because the valley was Lumatere and Charyn. Forest and rock and mountain.

"If I write a letter to the palace," he said quietly to Cora, "will you sign your name to it?"

"Why can't you sign your own name to it?" she demanded, making a rude sound any time he attempted to take a blade to one of the weeds in her vegetable garden that now lined the path along the stream.

"Because I promised I wouldn't," Froi said.

Florenza of Nebia nudged Cora.

"Of course, you'll do it, Cora. Or I will. I want to write to Phaedra, anyway."

Cora grumbled.

"Don't you go upsetting our little savage," Cora warned. "That's all you men are good for. Upsetting women."

"What's the letter about?" Jorja asked.

"It's just a story I heard that may interest them," Froi said. "About a young man named John. John of Charyn."

CHApteR 44

I start my day counting. And it slows down the rage. And only then, when the rage is a melody, do I go see the little king, so he'll hear a hum of joy the moment I speak. He knows me, this strange little creature. And it feels good to be known this well. It makes me less lonely. Because I think I've lost my song to Froi. It was taken when the spirits of the unborn babes went away. I miss them. I miss blaming them for the rage and my cold, cold heart. In the end, the sum of my vices is all me. I was sired by a tyrant and a gods' blessed. Sometimes, I've no idea which part of me is more frightening.

And most days we're fine, the little king and me. Phaedra is by our side. "Because I'll never leave you," she says, and she fusses and loves, but I hear her sadness deep in the night. There's sadness all around. During the days, I watch Gargarin write and talk and fight and limp from one tower to the other. Those *provincari* parrots are the bane of our lives. He goes to appease, to convince, to plan, to build, to try the guilty and release the innocent. Because the trials have begun and there's death in the air. The *provincari* have sent a judge from every province to assist

Gargarin in sentencing the Charynites who acted dishonorably, or worse. They want to try to execute them on palace grounds, but I don't want their cries heard by my little king, because the cries of the wretched always find a way to wedge themselves deep in the marrow of one's spirit. I don't want that for my boy. And Gargarin wins this first battle and we adopt the Lumateran ways. Our traitors are executed out of plain sight of those from the Citavita.

Olivier of Sebastabol does not become one of those condemned to die. Much to my despair. The *provincari* pardon him. *Brave, brave Olivier*, they say. But I remember the eight arrows that pinned Froi down to that rock outside Paladozza. And when he's a free man, Olivier kneels at my feet and tells me he'll spend the rest of his life in my service, even as a lowly soldier. Last borns don't play soldier, I say. They play nobleman. They play merchant. They play landowner. But Olivier will do anything to prove his worth, he tells me.

"Where do you want him?" Perabo asks.

"In the dungeons," I say. "Because everyone knows the dungeon master is as much a prisoner as those he guards."

And weeks pass and a letter arrives from Cora. It's traveled from the valley to Alonso and to Jidia and then it reaches us. The scribe reads it aloud in the great hall because there are to be no secrets from the *provincari* in Charyn. It's the story of a lad named John of Charyn, hanged as a traitor fourteen years past. Hanged by his own men for saving the lives of twenty-three Lumateran novices. It's a letter requesting that the mother and father of such a lad be told of their boy's courage. But I see the letter, written in penmanship so alike to Gargarin's that I know it's Froi's, and later I show it to the little king so he'll know his father's hand. And I see the names of John of Charyn's kin and I shudder at the power of the gods who steer our paths.

"Do you believe in fate?" I ask Arjuro when he comes to visit and reads the letter with watery eyes. He laughs, shaking his head.

"You ask that of me?"

And more weeks pass and nothing changes, except Phaedra's cries in the night are more muffled, hidden by her love for Tariq and myself.

"Are you happy here, Phaedra?" I ask one day.

And she looks up from loving Tariq's perfect face, and I see the fierceness in her eyes.

"I will never leave you," she says.

"It's not what I asked."

And most nights there's no sleep to be had. There are too many things keeping me awake. Tariq's cries. The shadow on my balconette that makes my heart leap with one name on my lips. And the cells where the traitors are imprisoned. I wish I could keep away, but I can't.

Olivier of Sebastabol tells me he knows why I'm there, hovering in the bowels of the palace. He sits at a bench with no more than a flicker of candlelight, recording his facts, his once-handsome face pale and thin.

"Don't read my mind, traitor."

"You're here about the girl, Ginny," he sighs, looking up. "She cries for you often."

"Ah, you know her well," I mock. "She's knelt at your feet, has she?"

"She's condemned to hang a week from now," he says. "That's all there is to know."

But they gnaw at my sleep, these two, and I travel there each day before dawn, hovering at the entrance, praying to the gods that Ginny will batter her head against the stone so her death will be at her own hand and not mine.

"This is no place for you," Olivier of Sebastabol says.

"Do you think your concern for me is going to change my mind about you?" I demand to know.

"No, but I'll still express it," he says. "Whatever has happened, my actions will always be determined by my need to keep you safe, my queen."

"I'm not a queen."

"You were Tariq's bride," he says. "Tariq was a king. You are his queen in my eyes."

Olivier stands and lights a lantern. "Come," he says quietly. "You need to say your piece before her death, or it will haunt you for the rest of your life." And I let him guide me through the damp darkness. It's a place to get lost, this labyrinth of misery. But I know the way because I've been here before. Waiting for a noose. I know the terror that taunts, and the piss that stains your legs from fear. I know the stench wedged deep in the stone. I know the sounds of the rats scurrying, the touch of their whiskers on your skin.

And when I hold up the light and see her huddled in the corner of her filthy chamber, my hatred for her is even stronger.

"I despise you," I say. "I always did. I despised your lamenting. I despised your need to blame everyone for lost dreams. Poor, poor pathetic Ginny. What a life she could have had if not for the last borns," I mock. "I despise your weakness. Your desire to satisfy the needs of men, but not your own. I despise that I can't remove from my memory the image of Phaedra and Cora and Florenza and Jorja on their knees waiting for death."

And I'm weeping because I'm weak in that way. It's another unwelcome gift the unborn savage spirits left me with: the need to cry for everything and everyone.

Ginny crawls to the iron bars to speak.

"Not a word," I say. "I never want to hear your voice again, you wretch. I never want to see your face again."

And the day is announced by the cock that crows and she's on her knees begging, sobbing, and I remember the time with the street lords when they took this palace and wiped out my bloodline. I remember the begging. Aunt Mawfa. The cousins. The stewards. The uncles. All begging for life and Gargarin in the cell beside me saying, "Close your ears, *reginita*. There's nothing you can do to save them. We're powerless."

But I'll never be powerless again.

"There's a tailor passing through from Nebia," I tell her, because today is not a day for dying. My son spoke that to me with his smile. "The tailor needs an apprentice, and you're going to join him. And you're going to learn everything you believe was taken away from you by the last borns. So when you fail again, you will have no excuse but your pathetic self."

And I reach a hand inside the bars and grip at the filth of her hair till it binds to my hand. "Don't dare show your face in this Citavita or in Phaedra's valley as long as I breathe, or I will have you cut in pieces and fed to the hounds."

"Phaedra's valley."

I wake with those words on my lips on the day Grijio of Paladozza arrives and I know it's a sign. I count so I can find a way to breathe, watching Phaedra of Alonso hold Tariq in her arms, and I know I have to do what is right, so I speak the words. And she weeps and she weeps and begs me, but I numb my heart to her cries.

"Go back to where you came from, Phaedra," I say. "You're not needed anymore."

◆ ◆ ◆

And for days after, I walk through that strange sleep with Tariq in my arms and he takes me places I don't want to go. Searching for her. Isaboe of Lumatere. She with the stealth and she with the strength. And my son promises me that if we find her, I'll sing my song again. He knows, because there's a spirit inside him seeking her. But in Tariq's waking hours, he wails, and it curdles my blood because I know what is true. They've poisoned my son. So we stay in my chamber, Tariq and I, day in and day out, a dagger in my hand as he wails with all his might. Until Gargarin comes and sits by my side and I see the sadness in his eyes and for the first time I've known him, Gargarin of Abroi weeps.

"You're letting the demons win, Quintana," he says. "He won't want this for you. Froi won't want this for you."

And he holds out a hand and takes me down the tower steps to the courtyard, where travelers have arrived. A man and a woman, their faces gaunt and pale.

"You sent for them," Gargarin said. "Be gentle, they're frightened."

And clutching Tariq to me, I walk to them, because I know who they are.

"Your son was a traitor who was executed," I tell them, and I hear Gargarin's intake of breath beside me. I see the woman's legs crumple beneath her as the man holds her upright.

Tesadora says to coat my words. So I try again. I try a gentle voice. I use the voice that belonged to the *reginita*.

I tell them about their son who was taken to Lumatere fourteen years past. I tell them that he and Arjuro hid the young novices of Lagrami, who went on to save the lives of many. I tell them their son was arrested and sentenced to hang while Arjuro was imprisoned for ten long years. And I tell them that I want to understand. I beg them to share it with me.

"How do you raise a boy of substance?" I ask her. "Will you

stay and teach me?" I look at them both. "Soon we'll have a stable of the best horses in the kingdom, Hamlyn of Charyn. Is that not what you were known for? The best horse trainer outside Jidia? Will you and Arna stay and teach me how to raise a good man?"

My son wails in my arms. The little king wants to know, too. He wants to be that son.

And Arna holds out her hands to take Tariq in hers, her fingers going to his mouth, holding up his perfect lips, and I see the rawness of his gums.

"Your boy's teeth are bringing him pain," she says quietly. "It's why he cries. And he needs to be bathed."

And so we bathe him, surrounded by his guards, just in case his little head slips. Tariq gurgles with laughter, his arms and legs flailing like the strange sea urchins I've seen in the books of the ancients. And Arna of Charyn places the cloth in my hand. "They love water," she says gently. "You try."

We take Tariq from the tub, and Dorcas holds up the blanket to wrap him, all the guards fussing. Arna shows me how to wipe him dry, and I let Dorcas hold him. Because Dorcas is my favorite. He choked the life out of Bestiano of Nebia.

"Can I hold him?" Fekra asks.

"Can I?"

"Can I?"

But then I place Tariq in the crook of his *shalamon*'s arms, and Gargarin's mouth twists into its bittersweet beauty.

"When a king hides behind the walls of a castle, his people are frightened," he says quietly.

So with Lirah and Arna by my side, surrounded by the riders, I travel through the Citavita and we jostle through the people, more people than I've ever seen except for the day of the hanging.

I hear the weeping and the joy, and I dare not look for the noose because Gargarin says it is not there to be found. But when a woman grips my arm, I jump from fear.

"I've not bled for months, Your Highness," she sobs. "I'm weary all the time, and I don't know what to do. I'm frightened to squat over the privy in case a babe slips out."

Dorcas gently guides me along, but I pull free.

"Are you a fool?" I demand to know of her. "It won't be slipping out for months!"

So I order the girl up to the godshouse, where Arjuro will soften her fears, but the next day in our chamber, I hear a bellow from across the *gravina*.

"Quintana!"

And I step outside to the balconette and see a furious Arjuro standing on the other side of the *gravina*.

"Here. In the godshouse. Now!"

When we reach the path up to the godshouse with our guards, Gargarin and Arna and I stop in shock.

"He'll kill you," Gargarin mutters, and I see the road is lined with women, weeping. Desperate. Every woman carrying a child in her belly, from the Citavita and beyond, is waiting to see Arjuro. And inside, we push through the long line of people and suddenly Lirah is there, taking Tariq in her arms.

"Arjuro is furious," she said. "And to make matters worse, the *collegiati* arrived today, and they may be good at reading books about women carrying babies but they have no idea how to speak to women carrying babies."

Day after day, we spend our mornings at the godshouse. There's too much confusion and shouting and crying, most of it coming from the *collegiati*. And then a week later, while Arna shows the women how to hold Tariq so one day they'll know how to hold their own, we hear a voice outside from the godshouse entrance.

"I'm here, my loves. No need for despair," Tippideaux of Paladozza says, and by that afternoon, she's created rosters and assigned chambers and shouted orders and terrorized the *collegiati* into submission. She tells us all, because she does enjoy an audience — that since the betrayal of Olivier of Sebastabol, she has no trust in men except for her father and brother.

"I swear I'll die a barren woman and give my life to those whose wombs bear fruit."

I see Arjuro and Lirah exchange a look.

"Make peace with Olivier the traitor," Arjuro mutters. "Or I'll kill you all."

Later, Arjuro walks us down to the Citavita, and I let him hold Tariq because it brings them both pleasure. We pass more women with swollen bellies hurrying toward the godshouse, and Arjuro presses a kiss to Tariq's outstretched fingers.

"She's mocking me, runt of our litter," Arjuro tells him. "The oracle is mocking me for choosing a man to share my bed. And her punishment is that I spend the rest of eternity staring between the legs of women."

And for the first time since I can remember, I laugh, and I watch my little king leap in his uncle's arms at the sound of it.

CHAPTER 45

When Perri arrived at Lord August's farm one morning while they were fixing the fence, Froi knew it was time.

"Can we borrow him, Augie?" Perri asked.

"For how long?" Lord August said, not looking up from his task.

Perri didn't respond.

"Last time you rode by to 'borrow' him, we didn't see him for nine months and he returned with a body full of scars and an awful Charynite accent," Lord August complained, glancing at Froi. "When do you get to be ours for always?" he asked, his voice low.

"Do I have to be here to belong to you?" Froi asked. "Can't I belong to you wherever I am?"

In the kitchen making honey brew with the village women, Lady Abian had the good sense not to ask too many questions.

"Is August blustering out there?" she asked quietly.

"A bit," Froi murmured. "A gentle early-winter bluster, I'd call it."

She pressed a kiss to his cheek and he went to speak, but she held up a hand.

"Don't make promises you can't keep."

❖ ❖ ❖

At the palace stable, Perri insisted on Froi taking Beast as Trevanion fitted him with his weapons.

"Your—Gargarin never wrote back," Finnikin said, standing
beside Isaboe and Sir Topher.

"After the letter Finnikin wrote promising to share ideas with
Charyn about reservoirs and waterwheels and anything else
we've been able to translate from the chronicles Celie stole—
I mean, borrowed from Belegonia," Isaboe said.

Froi was confused. "Gargarin loves talk of reservoirs and
waterwheels."

Sir Topher handed him a satchel of documents. "Tell him we
don't beg, and if he chooses not to respond to our attempts of
peace, we won't offer again."

Finnikin nodded. "First time. Last time."

Froi placed the satchel in the saddlebag.

"You travel through the Osterian border. It's quicker from here
than if you travel from the mountain through the valley," Perri said.

Too many abrupt instructions.

"You tell them that under no circumstances will the queen travel
to Charyn, so not to make that part of their terms," Finnikin said.

"Anything else?" Froi asked, mounting Beast.

"Yes, you can at least look upset about leaving," Isaboe said.

Froi rolled his eyes.

"Did he just roll his eyes at me?" she asked the others.

"I'll be back in two weeks!" Froi said.

"Yes, I think you said that last time we sent you off to meet
with Gargarin of Abroi and he cast a spell on you," she said.

Froi held out a hand to her, and she looked away.

"I don't shake hands. I'm not a Charynite."

He sighed and dismounted, embracing her.

"Trust me when I say that Gargarin of Abroi's spell has well
and truly worn off."

CHAPTER 46

Phaedra and Grijio reached the rocky outcrop that marked the beginning of the road from Alonso to the Lumateran valley. They had left the Citavita days ago, and Phaedra's heart had hardened the farther they traveled away from the palace. She didn't know what faced her in the valley. It had been more than six months since she'd left, and she was frightened that everything had changed. But how could it have stayed the same, when she herself had changed? Who was Phaedra of Alonso after all this time? She had lived her entire existence as a last born, controlled by Quintana of Charyn's curse.

"Are you sure you don't want to visit your father?" Grijio asked as they glimpsed the walls of Alonso in the distance.

Phaedra nodded. "I need to write to him first. There is much distance between us, and it won't be solved with a visit."

They continued riding toward the valley, and she felt the anger build up inside her.

"I hate her," she suddenly announced.

Grijio stared at her, taken aback by the outburst.

"You don't mean that," he said patiently.

"Oh, I do," Phaedra said. "She's cruel and she's cold and she doesn't understand love. Look at the way she treated you, Grijio. You come for a visit and she sends you away instantly."

Grijio shrugged. "I can see her anytime. Gargarin's offered me a place in the palace as an envoy. And anyway, I jumped at the chance to see Froi."

Grijio dismounted his horse and shuffled through his pack. When he found what he was looking for, he held out a letter to her.

Phaedra recognized the writing and refused to take it. She refused to be controlled by another's cruel plan or by a pledge made before she was born. But Grijio continued to hold out his hand.

"Quintana gave me four absolute instructions," he said firmly. "And I'm not to return until my work is done."

Phaedra walked away and sat on the rock face that gave her a view of the caves. On a clear day, she'd be able to see Alonso to the west, and she wondered if she would be better off there. Grijio came to sit beside her. He took her hand and placed the letter there.

"She's playing with you, Grijio," Phaedra warned. "It's what she'll do now with the little power she has."

"If you say another word, Phaedra, I think you'll have much regret," he said sadly.

Phaedra refused to open the letter. In the distance, she could see Lucian's mountain, and she kept her gaze fixed ahead. The sun was setting early and her body was beginning to feel the cold, and all she could think of was Lucian's fleece that made him resemble a bear.

"Did I tell you that once I sat out on a rooftop in early winter and got a chill and almost died?" Grijio said with an exaggerated sniff. "We're very fragile, us last borns."

She glanced at him and could see that, despite the soft, fair curls and gentle face, this lad was steadfast in his decisions, and she knew he would not move until she read the letter. So she opened it.

Dearest Phaedra,

I asked Grij not to give this to you until you reached the ridge before the valley, so you wouldn't turn back. Because I know you well, and I couldn't bear your not taking the journey back to the valley where I know you belong.

I remember on the day I was separated from Froi outside Paladozza, I learned that I could be loved. That was his greatest gift to me. From you, I learned that I could love my people. Don't ever underestimate the power of that. I needed to learn. How can I guide the little king without that lesson?

We speak the words gods' *blessed again and again in this kingdom. I'm not sure what they mean. But know this. That what you have in spirit is a gift indeed, Phaedra of Alonso. It's a true blessing from the gods. It's one I will be grateful for each day of my life. My king will be raised with the privilege of his mother having known you.*

When I saw the list of consorts, I knew I would never have true happiness in my spousal bed. But you love your Mont, Phaedra. So it's only fair that one of us finds deep happiness. You said repeatedly that you'd never leave me, and I knew you'd keep that pledge. But what I feared most is that you'd come to hate me for trapping you in the Citavita.

As I write this, I feel as if I'm broken in all these pieces that only you and Froi and little Tariq can put together. I will miss your presence every day of my life.

Quintana of Charyn

Phaedra stared at the words. Read them again and again. She scrambled to her feet, hurried to her horse, and mounted it.

"Take me back, Grijio. I'm begging you."

Grijio shook his head and got to his feet.

"She said that if I returned you to her, she'd never speak to me again."

"Take me back," she cried. "*Please*. You don't know her, Grij. You don't know how lonely she can get."

"I've lost too many friends, Phaedra," he said. "Through betrayal or distance or circumstance. I couldn't bear to lose her."

Grijio was resolute as he mounted his horse. "My pledge to Quintana was that I'd get you to your valley."

They arrived later that afternoon, and her heart leaped to see the busyness of the camp dwellers' day from where they were standing on the path behind the caves. Their lives seemed full of talk. It's what she had noticed these past months. That Charynites had found their voices. But she wondered how long the valley dwellers would stay here. Perhaps a new Charyn meant there was a place for them across the kingdom. Gargarin's focus was to bring the dry lands back to life for farming. It would take the pressure off the overcrowded provinces. In the months to come, when children were born to this valley, the people would have to leave and find a home, not a temporary camp. Phaedra wondered what would become of them all.

She led Grijio between the caves and saw Cora and Jorja in a vegetable patch crowded with produce and color. Close by, a few of the men were roasting a boar on a spit, and women were scrubbing clothes by the stream. Phaedra's heart leaped to see one or two of the camp dwellers with swollen bellies. She gave a sob of laughter, and then someone pointed up to where she sat astride the horse, and as Phaedra dismounted, the valley dwellers rushed to greet her from caves above and below. Cora and Jorja heard the commotion and turned, and suddenly she was running toward them and she was clasped in their arms, weeping.

"Look at you," Jorja said.

"You've a bit more weight," Cora joined in.

"Well, there's a bit more food to be had in the palace." Phaedra laughed, looking back to search for Grijio.

"How is she?" Jorja asked. "How are they both? Is he as beautiful as they say?"

Phaedra held a hand to her chest. More tears because there would never be words to describe the little king.

"Enough of the crying," Cora snapped, but she hugged Phaedra all the same.

Grijio reached them as Harker and Kasabian approached and Phaedra completed the introductions.

"We've met, sir," Grijio said to Harker, shaking his hand. "On the day you took this valley."

"How are things in the Citavita?" Harker asked.

"Hopeful, sir."

Grijio searched through his pack and handed Harker the mail. "These are for the Lumaterans. Is there a chance they can reach the palace soon? Gargarin of Abroi was very insistent."

Harker shook his head. "When it comes to messages and mail, we have to wait for the Monts to visit, and then it's up to chance when they next visit their palace. Sometimes a week passes. But we'll do our best."

"I'm presuming that I'd be expecting too much if Froi of Lumatere was here in the valley?" Grij said.

Harker shook his head again with a grimace. "He's on his way to Charyn, the way we've heard it."

Phaedra turned to Grijio, understanding his disappointment.

"Rest first and then go," she urged, knowing he'd want to see his friend. "You may catch him in the Citavita if you're lucky."

"And which of you is Cora?" Grijio asked.

"Me," Cora snapped. "Why?"

He retrieved a tiny purse from his pocket and held it out to her. Everyone crowded around Cora, curious to see what it was.

"She's rewarded you with gold," someone murmured.

"Perhaps a trinket."

They waited as Cora emptied the contents into the palm of her hand, and soon there were sighs of disappointment. But Cora looked up and caught her brother's eye, and Phaedra saw a smile on both their faces as they studied the seeds.

"Where would she have found herself a pair of klin tree seeds?" Kasabian asked as Cora placed them in his hand. He clenched a fist and pressed a kiss to it. "These seeds grow hope," he said.

"I have one more letter," Grijio said. "Quintana said I had to deliver it by hand. To Florenza of Nebia."

"My daughter?" Harker asked, perplexed.

"By hand, you say. Why?" Jorja asked.

Grijio shrugged. "Quintana said I could not leave until the letter was read out loud, and then I had to wait for Florenza of Nebia's response. So then Her Highness would be sure it was delivered."

"I'll go find her," Harker said

More of the valley dwellers came to greet Phaedra, and she introduced them to Grijio, who seemed fascinated by the way they lived.

"For now, every family is assigned to their own cave, with ample privacy," Jorja said. "It was difficult for us during the time of Donashe and his friends. Families were separated."

"But still a blessing that our Quintana found herself in a cave with you women," Grijio said.

"Phaedra!" they heard Florenza cry, and, the next moment, they were in each other's arms, laughing and crying.

"I was with the Mont girls when we heard the news," Florenza said. "Are you back for good?"

"I am indeed."

"And how is she?" Florenza asked solemnly. "I dream of them both. All the time, I do. Is she happy?"

Phaedra didn't know how to answer that truthfully.

"The little king is the most beautiful creature I've ever seen in my life," she said. "Is that not true, Grij?"

Grij was staring at Florenza, who was now staring at Grij with a hand held to her face to hide her nose, which had survived its ordeal in the caves with quite a large bump.

"Yes . . . yes, of course," he said, flustered, clearing his throat.

"Father said you have something," Florenza said, and Phaedra watched as Jorja's hand brushed a leaf from Florenza's hair surreptitiously. Cora exchanged a look with Phaedra.

Grijio removed a letter from his pack and handed it to Florenza.

"She requested that you read it aloud before me," he said. "So then she'd be sure that it was read."

"Why?" Cora asked bluntly.

"Hurry up and read it, Florenza," Jorja said.

Florenza broke the seal of the letter.

"Dear Florenza,

"I hope all is fine with you. Phaedra will tell you more about life here. The weather is quite unspectacular and so are most of those who live in the palace—"

"They are," Phaedra agreed.

"Of course, I'm yet to meet a girl such as you, Florenza, who crawled through the sewers of Nebia to save the life of those Serkers and whose nose was broken as she fearlessly fought a man who was a threat to myself and the future king of Charyn. . . ."

Florenza touched her nose again self-consciously.

"You crawled through the sewers?" Grij asked in awe. "To save the Serkers?"

"And broke her nose as she fearlessly fought a man who was a threat to Quintana and the future king of Charyn," Jorja reminded him.

Florenza removed her hand from her nose and continued reading.

"Anyway, enough of all that. I was wondering if you'd like to come and visit sometime. You can give your response to Grijio, the brilliant scholarly son of the provincaro *of Paladozza and one of the heroic masterminds of my rescue in the Citavita."*

Phaedra burst out a laugh and stared at Cora. This time it was Florenza who looked up in awe.

"You were the mastermind?" Florenza asked Grijio.

He waved a hand in embarrassment. "One of them, anyway," he murmured.

"Our little savage has turned matchmaker," Cora muttered. "What have they done to her?"

Lucian finished helping Orly with the fence post, and they both stood back to assess the work. Lotte joined them soon after and handed Lucian a hot brew. There wasn't much talk among them, although he could sense that Lotte was dying to say something and Lucian knew exactly what that was.

"Lady Zarah," Lotte said politely. "She seems a fine girl."

"Yes, indeed," Lucian said curtly. He was sick and tired of being asked at every turn if it was true that he was betrothed. *No,* he wanted to shout. *Fabrications from an overzealous lord who wants a cut in our fleece market!*

But he held his tongue.

"Some are saying she'll be your new wife, Lucian."

Orly muttered something rude, and Lucian had to agree.

Lotte peered beyond him toward the path that ran through the mountain.

"Is that one of your aunts?" she asked, somewhat alarmed. "Is she running? Sweet goddess, Lucian. Something's happened."

Lucian leaped over Orly's post to reach his aunt.

"Lucian, Lucian," she called out, her face lit with excitement. "Phaedra's returned to the valley!"

His mouth was suddenly dry. His heart was pounding too fast, his face felt aflame. Lotte and Orly caught up with them, Lotte trilling with excitement. He had to get away from them all to think clearly. He had to work out what to do and how not to ruin things. But he couldn't do it here, and it was clear to Lucian that there'd be no more work done with Lotte and Orly, so he gently steered his aunt back home.

"Too much work to be done around here to be wasting time," he said to her calmly. They passed Jory and the lads, who were rounding up the sheep on Yael's spread.

"See?" he said, pointing. "The lads have got the right idea. Work and no talk."

"Lucian," Jory hollered, jumping from his mount and running toward them. "Phaedra's back."

"Be quick! You'll lose her again!" another cousin shouted.

In the Mont market square, Lucian was surrounded instantly. By everyone. He hadn't seen such a gathering since Isaboe had returned for the first time since the death of her child. The mountain had celebrated that day. Finnikin had begged Lucian, "Tell them that their sorrow will break her. She's come for their joy." And the Monts had tried.

Today, he saw a truer version of that joy.

"I'm going down to Lumatere," he muttered, and there was a collective sigh of annoyance.

"Lucian, don't be ridiculous," his cousin Alda snapped. "If you're going to betroth yourself to that useless Tascan's daughter, you'll be insulting the women of this mountain and the memory of your poor mother."

"Don't know what was wrong with the first wife," Pitts the cobbler said.

"Yes, yes," most agreed.

"I always said that if Phaedra of Alonso's people weren't cursed, those hips of hers were made for childbearing," Ettore the blacksmith piped up.

Lucian caught his *yata*'s eye, and he could see she was seething about something. She turned to them all, fire blazing in her eyes.

"When Lady Zarah visited last, the little miss turned up her nose at the food on our table! I jest you not!" she said.

There were gasps of outrage all around.

"A good riddance to her now that Phaedra's back!"

There was a cheer at Yata's words.

Goddess forbid, Lucian had to get off this mountain.

CHAPTER 47

Most things had changed.

At the bridge leading to the Citavita was a guard station. No one was permitted to cross without dismounting. A garrison was camped on a piece of land by the road, swarming with soldiers asking questions and allowing entry onto the bridge, one person at a time.

"What's your business?" Froi was asked. He recognized no one among the guards.

"I'm from Lumatere," he replied. Lies only created problems. Even so, the man looked at him suspiciously. He indicated that Froi was to raise his arms.

"Shoulder, ankle, and here," Froi said, patting the sword in its scabbard at his side. "All weapons revealed. Is there a rule about being armed?"

"No, but there's a rule about having a smart mouth."

And some things stayed the same.

Unlike every other person before and after him, Froi found himself escorted across the bridge. Beast was just as disgusted. Halfway across, Froi stopped, daring to look down the *gravina* and then ahead through the mist at the splendor of the Citavita's stone piled high.

How could he have imagined that Gargarin's sigh that first time they arrived here was of anything but pleasure?

He continued walking, his heart thumping with anticipation. *Home,* it sang. You're home. But he argued back with that part of his heart that couldn't let go of the Flatlands. Until he stepped onto the Citavita. *Home,* his heart sang.

He steered Beast off the bridge and looked around. There were no street lords demanding a coin for use of the bridge. There was no wretched line of Citavitans desperate to leave the carnage behind. Instead, a marketplace was set up at the base of the rock and there was haggling and shouting. And laughter. Froi had never heard laughter in the Citavita.

He saw the sentinels instantly, guarding the roof of the Crow's Inn. He imagined Scarpo's men would be swarming the capital now that most of its people were returning to their homes. As he was led toward the walls of the city, a dozen or so soldiers came striding toward him.

"Now, that doesn't surprise me," the guard escorting him said. "A welcoming party."

"My favorite type of party in the world," Froi muttered.

Could he expect less, leading a Serker horse?

"I'm actually on my way to the godshouse to see the priestling Arjuro," Froi explained. He wasn't much in the mood for being interrogated by a group of soldiers who didn't know him and wouldn't believe a word he said.

"The priestling's a busy man."

Before they could exchange another word, one of the approaching soldiers broke free and lifted Froi off the ground in an embrace.

Mort.

"Where you been, Froi?"

Mort was shoved out of the way, and Florik was there.

"We've been taking odds to see whether you'd return," the Lasconian said.

Froi looked from one to the other, laughing. "You're both on the same duty?"

Mort and Florik placed arms around each other's shoulders. They looked strange in uniform, but it suited them.

"I'm teaching him a thing or two," Mort said. "Lasconian lads know nothing."

"Except how to speak better than Turlan lads," Florik said. "So I'm teaching him a thing or two."

Within moments, more of the fortress lads were surrounding him, and Froi embraced and shook hands with as many as he recognized.

"We take things from here," Mort told Froi's guard. Mort moved in closer. "I got rank," he whispered. "Turlans outrank everyone on this rock."

"Who says?" Froi asked.

"She say. She don't get much power, but she picks whoever protects Citavita, and our Quintana pick the Turlans."

Smart girl. No one would protect Quintana and Tariq better than her kin.

"How are things here?" Froi asked.

How are Quintana and Gargarin and Lirah and Arjuro and my son? he meant.

"Gettin' there slow-wise," Mort said. "But gettin' there all the same."

"What you doin' here, Froi?" another Turlan asked. "You here for the—"

The lad was nudged into silence. Froi saw their unease, so he held up his pack. "Palace business from Lumatere," he said.

Mort shoved Froi playfully. "Told you lads this one no soldier boy. He's a palace big man."

Froi laughed at the description.

"We'd take you up there, but Scarpo would skin us if we left our post," Florik said.

Mort pointed up to the roof of the Crow's Inn. "That's where I aim from, and if there a problem, fastest lad in Charyn here races to the castle and let 'em know," he said, shoving at Florik's head.

Florik looked slightly sheepish. "Second fastest."

"Did you see Grij on your travels?" one of the lads from Lascow asked. "He was on his way to Lumatere to deliver Phaedra of Alonso back to the valley."

Froi shook his head, annoyed to think he missed seeing Grij in Lumatere of all places.

"He would have traveled another path," he said. "I came through Osteria."

"He'll be back soon," Florik said. "So you wait for him, Froi. He'll not like missing you twice."

"And come see us at our post."

Froi promised to return to the inn and made his way up the city wall to the road that led to the godshouse. He couldn't avoid seeing the castle battlements, but he forced himself to look away.

On the path above the caves, toward the godshouse, he was bewildered to see a cluster of women coming and going.

The priestling's a busy man, the soldier had said. Busy doing what?

Inside the godshouse, it was stranger still. More women, as well as the *collegiati* Froi recognized from his days in the caves under Sebastabol. The entire lower level of the godshouse was bustling with activity. Questions were being asked; orders were being given. And then Froi noticed the swollen bellies and understood why.

He gently pushed past the women, up the steps, and at each floor, Froi glimpsed well-lit rooms and once-empty cells now decorated with a sense of home. He thought of these steps. Where he had first discovered that Gargarin was his father. The cells where he had found out for certain that Lirah was his mother. Each flight he climbed was a memory, and the closer he got to the top, the more hurried his steps became. Because he had missed them all with an ache that had never gone away, and he was desperate to see them. That was it, he convinced himself. Just one glance at them all. The higher he climbed, the less noise he heard, and by the time he reached the Hall of Illumination, the godshouse had returned to its quiet self.

Inside the room, he could see through the windows out onto the Citavita, and from the balconette out onto the palace.

Arjuro sat at a long bench, head bent over his books; plants and stems spread across the space before him. Froi caught his breath.

"If you're here about the Jidian invitation, tell them I'd rather swive a goat," Arjuro murmured, not looking up.

Froi stepped closer.

"Must I, blessed Arjuro?"

Arjuro looked up in shock.

Froi grinned. "For those of us at the godshouse are well known for swiving goats, and I'd prefer not to give them weapons of ridicule."

Arjuro stood and grabbed Froi into an embrace, his arms trembling. Froi pushed him away, unable to get rid of the grin on his face.

"Sentimental, Arjuro? You of all people."

Arjuro studied his face. "Me of all people can be as sentimental as he pleases."

And then he was taking Froi's hand, leading him to the steps of the roof garden.

"Lirah," Arjuro called out. "Come down and greet our guest."

Froi caught his breath again.

"If it's about the Jidian invitation, I said no," she shouted back.

"The Jidian *provincara*'s in town, I'm supposing," Froi said quietly.

"They're all coming to town," Arjuro said with a grimace. "And everyone wants to visit the godshouse."

Froi nodded, and suddenly he understood. It's what Mort and Florik stopped the lad from saying outside the inn.

"They're here for her betrothment?" Froi asked.

Arjuro nodded. "Five days from now, they decide who he is."

"Lirah!" Arjuro bellowed again. He pointed up, rolling his eyes. "They say the ambassador of Nebia's wife has taken over Lirah's roof garden in the palace."

"Lirah's prison garden, you mean," Froi said.

"Lirah says it's her garden. She's livid. So she's determined to make our garden better."

Our? Froi shook his head with disbelief. The idea of Arjuro and Lirah having something together was too strange.

"Are you not going to come down for me, Lirah?" Froi called out softly. "I've come a long way, and I'd hate to return to the Lumaterans and tell them how inhospitable you are here in Charyn."

There was no response, but suddenly Lirah peered down the steps, the sun behind her illuminating her face. She had kept her hair short, and without the grime of travel and with her sea-blue dress, she looked regal.

She descended the steps and Froi helped her down the last few, and then she was there before him.

"What's this?" she asked gruffly, touching the fluff of hair on his chin.

"A pathetic attempt at a beard," he said. "It's not working, is it? Which is so unfair when you think of the face of hair Arjuro had when I first met him."

She smiled. "Regardless of their might as warriors, the Serkan lads could never grow one."

Lirah reached out and touched Froi's face as if she couldn't believe he was standing before her.

"Wait until you see him," she said, and there were tears in her eyes. "Wait until you see the wonder that's our boy. Sometimes when they smuggle me into the palace, we lie there, Gargarin and I, with this little bundle between us and we count all his fingers and toes. And in all the joy, it's only a reminder of how much we lost and there are some days that I don't think he can bear the memory."

Froi took her hand and pressed a kiss to it.

"Gargarin thought he found a way," she said. "But now he believes it's lost and he's bitter, Froi. Why were your Lumaterans so cruel? If they loved you, they would not have been so cruel."

"Cruel?" he asked. "Lirah, Gargarin left me behind without a thought. That's cruel. The Lumaterans have proved themselves to me over and over again. What has he done?"

Arjuro joined them with a jug of brew and a bowl of broth.

"Have you seen our guest?" Lirah asked quietly, and Froi shook his head and followed her into a chamber. Its walls were adorned with rugs on one side, books stacked high on the other. A cot and fireplace occupied one corner. At first Froi thought there was a child lying on the bed, but then he realized the truth.

"You can speak to him. He can hear you."

Froi took a step closer, wincing at the skeletal figure that lay before him.

"Hello, Rafuel. Do you remember me?" Froi asked, his voice catching to see the man in such a state.

Lirah took Rafuel's hand. "He's to save his breath and get himself well," she said. "If anyone can get you back on your feet, it's Arjuro, isn't that so, Rafuel?"

There was no response. Just the stare. Rafuel was all eyes in a shrunken body. His left eye was half-closed, and there was a scar across his lip.

"Let's get you seated upright," Arjuro said to Rafuel. Froi helped, suddenly overcome by emotion. He couldn't recognize Rafuel as the same animated man who had shown him the way a Charynite danced, even though he had been in chains. Froi sat down beside Rafuel on the bed.

"This one loves nothing better than when the little king visits," Arjuro said, placing a spoon to Rafuel's mouth. "His eyes light up like a beacon."

Froi looked away, unable to watch. He had never seen a man look so much like death. It almost seemed too cruel to keep him alive.

"How did you come to be here, Rafuel?" Froi asked, knowing that it would be one of the others who would answer. But he didn't want to insult the man into believing he didn't exist.

"Gargarin demanded it the moment we found out he lived," Lirah said. "Rafuel belongs here with us. It all began with him, didn't it, dear friend, with those silly cats? Where would we all be without Rafuel?"

"I can take over here," Froi said, holding his hand out for the bowl. "I've got much to tell you, Rafuel. About the valley and the women who beg for news of you."

He returned to where Lirah and Arjuro sat in the hall, his emotions ragged.

"Will he get better?"

Arjuro shrugged. "We don't know what's broken inside of him up here," he said, pointing to his head. "We don't know how much of it came from the beating he received upon his arrest or from being left for dead in that mine shaft."

"But when he arrived, he could barely open his eyes," Lirah said. "Quintana visits with Tariq every day, and it's been a revelation to see how much he's changed in the presence of the boy."

Froi was suddenly envious of them all. Even Rafuel with his decrepit body. They had each other, despite the fact that they lived in separate places. Quintana and Tariq and Lirah and Arjuro and Gargarin and even Rafuel hadn't needed Froi. They had begun to thrive without him.

"Will she want to see me?" he asked quietly.

Lirah didn't respond.

"Would that stop you?" she asked.

"That means she doesn't want to."

"I didn't say that at all." Lirah sighed. "I think . . . I think Quintana believes you've forsaken her."

"Me?" he asked. "I've been waiting for Gargarin to do something. He promised to do something! I've been waiting."

"Gargarin said he wrote," Lirah said.

"Well, he didn't. He lied."

"No," Lirah said firmly, "he doesn't lie to me."

Froi made a sound of disbelief.

"Especially about our son!"

Froi was on his feet pacing.

"Do you think you can get me into the palace without the *provincari*'s people knowing?" he asked

Arjuro chuckled. "It's our favorite sport," he said, winking at Lirah. "And you've picked an easy night."

❖ ❖ ❖

An easy night, Froi learned, was when Perabo was on watch. The keeper of the keys studied him intently at the gatehouse, a lantern in his hand held up to Froi's face.

"You took your time," Perabo muttered as he escorted him to the second tower. "Head down. Let them think you're Arjuro."

It was Fekra who guarded the second level of the second tower. His eyes flashed with surprise to see Froi.

"We have to be careful of the *provincari*'s people," Fekra told him. "They don't have a life of their own, so they're fascinated with everyone else's."

Once they reached her chamber, Fekra poked his shoulder with a finger.

"Don't wake the boy. It took Dorcas all night to get him to sleep."

Froi tiptoed into her room. At first he wondered why Gargarin would have kept her in this chamber and not a larger residence. Until he saw the fireplace and then the archway between Quintana's chamber and the room Froi once shared with Gargarin. He crept to its entrance. He knew what was in there . . . who was in there. He could hear the steady breathing of the boy, the strange little sounds of sleepy satisfaction.

An arm was instantly around his neck. A dagger to his throat. A savage noise in his ear. *Sagra.* How he missed her.

"You'll only make a small hole there," he whispered. "Not fatal. Inconvenient, really."

He leaned his head back onto her shoulder, exposing his throat to her blade. He felt her arm linger, her cold cheek against his. They stayed there for a time with trembling bodies.

And then he turned to face her. How could he ever have thought this face plain? How could he ever have imagined that the savagery would leave her, just because she birthed a child?

"You're a stranger," she said coldly, but her body spoke of warmth, pressed so close that the thin fabric of her shift seemed not to exist.

He saw tears in her eyes, anger. Sadness. He searched her face in the light from the godshouse across the *gravina*, his fingers on her cheeks, mouth.

"Who do you see?" she demanded. "Am I a stranger in return?"

He took her hand and linked his fingers with hers.

"Why say that?" he asked.

"Because I calculated," she said coolly. "I've become good with your counting. You and I have known each other for fewer days than we haven't."

"Does that matter to you?" he asked as she clenched their hands together. He sensed his arousal, knew she felt it strongly pressed against her.

"I can live without you," she said. "I can live without a man I've only known for one hundred and eighty days."

"And how have those calculations helped?" he demanded to know.

She didn't respond except for a look down her nose at him and a curl of her lip. So much for the angry half spirits being responsible for the savages within them both. This was pure Quintana.

"Then step away," he taunted. "If you can live without me, step away."

He felt her warm breath on his throat.

"Because you can't," he said. "You think you can, but we're bound, and not just by the gods or by a curse or even by our son. We are bound by our free will. And you can't step away, because you are not willing."

He bent, his mouth close to hers.

"Step away," he whispered. "If you step away I'll learn from you. I'll find the desire in me to live without you. Much the same as you want to live without me."

"I didn't say I wanted to live without you," she said, angry tears springing in her eyes. "Only that I can. I've practiced. I've been very good in that way."

She stepped away, but not too far, and his eyes traveled down her nightdress, transparent in the moonlight. He could see the fullness of her beneath it all. He reached out a tentative hand to her breast, but she flinched and this time he stepped away.

"It's full of milk, fool," she said. "It's tender. You'll have to find another place to put your hand."

"You tell me where?" he said, his voice soft. "Because it's not in me to be gentle."

"Then you'll just have to learn, won't you?"

She swayed toward him, playing with him. Had she turned temptress, this cat of his? And then their mouths were fused, the cloth of her nightdress bunched in his hands, his arm a band around her body, lifting her to him as one tongue danced around the other, until her legs straddled his hips and he dragged the shift over her head, desperate to remove anything that lay between them, his mouth not wanting to leave hers as he fumbled with the drawstring of his trousers. Soon they were skin against skin and he tried to be gentle, chanting it inside his head while saying her name, and they rocked into each other with a rhythm played out by the gods who had guided their wretched way. *Where have you been? Where have you been? I've lost our song,* he thought he heard her cry inside his heart, until finally Froi felt her shudder, her fingers gripping the place her name was etched across his shoulders.

"Our bodies aren't strangers," he said, his voice ragged. "Our spirits aren't strangers." He held her face in his hands. "Tell me what part of me is stranger to you, and I'll destroy that part of me."

And she wept to hear his words.

Later, as they lay in silence, Quintana kissed each one of his scars from the eight arrows.

"Do you want to see him?"

He nodded like a hungry man, and they shivered naked in the cool night air as she led him into the other room.

"We're not to wake him," she said firmly. "I'm very strict about rules, you know."

She lit a candle, and Froi stared into the crib and saw the most amazing creature he had ever seen, the babe facing them, his arms outstretched.

"What kind of rules?" he whispered.

"Well, I don't wake him just because I want to hold him. I wait until he wakes on his own. And I only give him four or five cuddles a day. Sometimes a few more if he's fretful. We don't want to spoil him."

He smiled.

"And look," she said. She pointed above the little king's crib where a cutout piece of parchment hung from the ceiling. Froi's eyes followed her finger across the ceiling to the wall, where the light from the moon made a shape of a rabbit.

And because Froi was overwhelmed with emotion, he buried his head into her shoulder.

"Are you crying?" she asked.

He didn't respond, but his tears were wet against her and he felt her pat his back. "He likes me to do this," she said, her voice practical. "It calms him down if he wakes up with the night terrors."

They watched Tariq for a long time until he woke and

Quintana reached out to pick him up, and Froi's son suckled as she fed him on her bed.

"Does it hurt?" he asked, fascinated.

"It did to begin with."

When she was finished and Tariq burped in a way that would have made Arjuro proud, she held him out to Froi. He took his son gently, and Quintana placed his hand securely against Tariq's head.

"It used to roll all over the place if I didn't put my hand there. Sometimes I fear it still will," she said, and he stared in amazement as Tariq stared back at him.

"Sagra," he muttered. "You've gone and stolen Lirah's face, you thief."

The three fell asleep in one another's arms, and when the sun began to rise, Froi woke and kissed Quintana and Tariq, then dressed quickly. He stepped out into the hallway and found himself face-to-face with Gargarin.

"So it is true," Gargarin said, furious. "I thought the guards were making up stories."

Froi shoved past him. Six months without a word and that's all Gargarin could say to him.

Gargarin dragged him back. "Where are the Lumaterans?"

"In Lumatere! Where else?" Froi said, pulling free and walking away.

"So they had to have you all to themselves?" Gargarin demanded. Froi stopped and turned back to face his father. There was no amount of counting that could control him.

"They have me all to themselves because my real father doesn't want me! He never did. He regrets not tossing me out—"

"Don't!" Gargarin shook his head with disbelief. "Don't say those words to me."

"If you weren't a cripple, I'd beat you senseless," Froi said.

"What would it have taken for you to acknowledge me? That's what I wanted. To hear those words from you. And all you could say to me through Scarpo was that in weeks to come, not to make contact with the Charyn palace. 'You wait,' Scarpo said. 'Trust me. These are his words.' I know them by heart, Gargarin. And I waited and waited."

Gargarin gripped Froi's cloak, pulling him closer, tears of anger in his eyes.

"I begged them for you because I thought I found a way," Gargarin whispered. "That despite never being able to claim you as mine or Lirah's, I found a way for my son to get everything he wanted. Here. In this palace."

"You're lying."

Gargarin shoved him away.

"Go back to your greedy dishonorable people who'll do anything to keep you away from those who love you. And you tell them that Lumatere has made an enemy of me, and they'll regret that for the rest of their lives."

CHAPTER 48

Phaedra spent the next few days in the valley being visited by the Monts. Many of them. All expressing disappointment in Lucian.

"He's an idiot," Constance said to Phaedra. "I've said it once and I'll say it again," she continued, taking one of the honey cakes Florenza had made. They were sitting inside Jorja and Harker's cave with Tesadora and anyone who came to put their thoughts into the matter.

"What's she saying?" Cora demanded.

"Lucian's an idiot," Tesadora translated with alacrity.

Cora sighed. "I'm biting my tongue because of a vow I made when he carried our little savage to safety," she said.

Phaedra had refused to condemn Lucian's absence. She had made the choice to follow Quintana to the Citavita. It was Lucian who had been left behind. He owed her nothing.

"I understood his pride," she told anyone who asked. "And I've changed. I'm a different Phaedra," she said with determination. "No more weeping. No more begging the gods for what I want and can't have. We learn to live with our disappointments. It's one thing I've learned from our brave Quintana."

The others, Charynites and Lumaterans alike, stared at her disbelievingly.

Goddess. Gods. Anyone listening, she cried all the night long. *Let him come down the mountain tomorrow.*

Tomorrow came and there were more Mont visitors. Jorja borrowed rations from the other valley dwellers because it was rude to have visitors, especially foreigners, and not feed them. They were all forced to move outside the cave, where there was more room. Harker built a fire, and everyone seemed happy enough discussing Lucian out in the open.

"Is that Orly and Lotte?" Sandrine exclaimed as they watched the Mont couple cross the stream, leading a cow.

"Orly doesn't come down the mountain," Constance said.

But today Orly and Lotte had decided to pay their respects.

"A gift," Orly said to Phaedra. "She belongs to Gert and Bert."

Phaedra embraced them both. She understood the significance and worth of this cow.

"The milk will come in handy once you all start breeding like normal people," Orly said, pulling away from Phaedra, not liking the fuss. "I'll be off now."

"Orly! Stay awhile," Constance argued, rolling her eyes at the awkward ways of her kin.

"We're to go now," Lotte said woefully. "He's feeling this very strongly, Phaedra. He thought the moment you returned, Lucian would take you back up to the mountain, but the lad's gone to the palace village and we are fearing the worst, we are. The worst," Lotte cried.

"What is she saying?" Cora asked. "This one talks too much."

"That Lucian is still an idiot," Tesadora said.

◆ ◆ ◆

Another day passed. Another set of visits from the Monts. The Charynite valley dwellers also joined the discussion. The men lay bets.

"Five days," one said.

"Ten," another argued. "She was the one who left him this time."

"But he sent her back the first time, so he'll feel contrite for that. Seven."

It was neither five nor ten nor seven days. Kasabian guessed it right.

"When the lad sorts out what he needs to sort out, he'll come for you, Phaedra."

Everyone was on their feet in shock and surprise when Lucian appeared on the third day. Phaedra watched him cross the stream, his eyes taking in the large party staring his way with curiosity. She could see by the set of his shoulders that he was dreading whatever he was about to face.

He greeted them all politely with a nod of his head.

"I want to speak to Phaedra," he said, his eyes firmly on hers. She could read nothing in them. No, there it was. Panic.

"Alone," he said, holding out a hand to her.

No one moved.

"Don't be ridiculous," Cora said, pulling Phaedra away. "Kasabian's her chaperone in the place of her father."

Florenza snorted out a laugh. "That is so not true—"

But Jorja hushed her daughter.

"What you have to say to Phaedra you can say in front of everyone, cousin," Constance said. She received instant approval from the camp dwellers, who understood exactly what she was saying.

"I agree," Pitts the cobbler said. He came down most days to enjoy Jorja's hospitality.

Phaedra took pity on Lucian and held out her hand. He looked too nervous for any of this to turn out right, and she had an awful feeling that she was going to cry in front of everyone.

"This is a matter of privacy between two people," she said firmly.

There was a chorus of disapproval at the suggestion, but she could feel the tears burning her eyes and she wanted to leave. Lucian was staring down at her, horrified.

"Enough!" he shouted at the crowd. "You've all made her cry."

"I'm not crying," she cried.

"You're the one who made her cry, running off to the palace the moment she arrived," Constance said.

Lucian was shaking his head with exasperation.

"I thought it best that we make our marriage official," he blurted out. "The first time it was in Alonso and . . . quite a miserable affair. My cousin insists we make it less miserable, and I couldn't agree more."

"Your cousin Jory?" Phaedra asked, her heart hammering to hear the words.

"No," he said with a sigh and Phaedra could see how uncomfortable he was under everyone's scrutiny.

"What cousin?" Cora asked.

Lucian pointed across the stream. Isaboe of Lumatere stood on the other side of the stream with her child on her hip and her consort by her side, surrounded by the Lumateran Guard.

"That one."

The queen looked annoyed. "*Lucian!*" she called out. "What's happening over there?"

Lucian turned back to Phaedra and the others. "The priest-king is coming, too. To conduct the ceremony," he said.

Lucian waved the royal party over, and suddenly Jorja was

taking deep breaths from the shock of seeing the queen of Lumatere walking toward her cave.

"I don't want any fanfare," Lucian said gruffly when his cousin reached them. "Nor does Phaedra. Is that clear, everyone?"

"You can't speak for her," Constance said.

"I don't want any fanfare," Phaedra said, and she caught Lucian's grateful smile.

"No, none at all," the queen of Lumatere joined in, accepting Jorja's invitation to sit down. "Although we'll have to wait for everyone on the mountain to come down. Balconio, too. They've all promised to travel up . . . and down for the wedding. As has August and Abian and their lot and Trevanion and the rest of the Guard. Very small. Compared to ours."

The queen turned to her consort.

"I think the whole kingdom came to that one, didn't they, my love?"

"No, some of the Flatland lords boycotted it because they thought you were marrying beneath you," Finnikin of Lumatere advised her.

Jorja was looking flustered, and Phaedra knew she had little to serve as refreshments.

"The groom's family is responsible for the feast," Isaboe of Lumatere said, "and they'll be arriving with the food soon."

Phaedra knew the tradition was the exact opposite in Lumatere, but she didn't dare challenge the queen.

"While we wait for the arrivals, we thought we could take time to speak of matters," Finnikin said to Harker, and Phaedra watched everyone's stillness as the valley dwellers gathered close.

"To be honest, it'll be a long time indeed before Charynites live in Lumatere. The wounds cut very deep. But we—" Finnikin looked at the Queen. "My queen and I thought we'd speak to you about ideas for this valley. Perhaps it's time to build and make plans . . . for permanency."

There was silence from the valley dwellers.

"It needs a leader, Harker," Isaboe said. "And you seem to be that man."

Perhaps it wasn't exactly what Harker and Jorja and the rest of the valley dwellers had journeyed here for, all that time ago, but they were interested in what the queen and her consort had to say.

"The way we see it, this valley will have the best that Lumatere and Charyn have to offer," the queen said. "It could become a thriving place of progress. A place where both kingdoms meet."

Jorja suddenly gasped and jumped to her feet. "How could we have forgotten? It's a good thing you've visited, Your Majesty," she said. "The Charyn palace has sent a letter. Go get it, Florenza. And then we'll find you a pretty dress, Phaedra, for the ceremony."

"Well, if I may," the queen of Lumatere said, "I brought a dress that belonged to my sister, Evestalina. Lucian was her favorite, do you remember that, cousin? She'd let you get away with anything. Even more than our brother, Balthazar."

Phaedra saw the emotion on Lucian's face. The queen rarely spoke of the past, and everyone present knew the importance of her speaking her family's names on the Charynite side of the stream.

"Well, she would have wanted your wife to have it." The queen looked at Phaedra. "It shames me that it has taken me so long to acknowledge you, Phaedra of Alonso."

Phaedra shook her head. "It shames me to have spoken to you the way I did in the caves after you put your life at risk for Quintana of Charyn."

"Enough said." The queen's voice was brisk but filled with emotion.

Florenza returned with the letter and handed it to the queen. The princess Jasmina cried to have it.

"Jasmina likes the pretty seals on the letters," the queen explained, "especially those that are red." There was much oohing and aahing from the valley dwellers, who were besotted by the little princess.

The princess Jasmina took a liking to Florenza, gripping her hand tightly, trying to drag her away.

"Be careful," the queen said firmly. "She'll try to control you."

"Has she a gift?" Florenza asked.

"Yes," the queen said, her tone dry. "The gift for . . ."

"Stubbornness," Finnikin said.

More people arrived from over the mountain, and on a cold night under a full moon, Phaedra found herself wed to Lucian for the second time. He wore a royal-blue doublet and his trousers tucked into his buskins, and Phaedra's dress was fitted to the waist, in soft pink. She wore flowers from Yata's garden in her hair. He was very solemn; she wasn't. Phaedra couldn't stop smiling.

While the celebrations continued well into the night, they sat by the stream alone.

"I think this party will last for days," he said. "And we'll never be alone together."

"Soon enough," she said. "I don't think tonight is just about us."

He pressed a kiss to her lips.

"We'll have to visit my father, Lucian. There's too much anger between us all, and I can't begin my life with you this way."

He nodded. "Then we'll visit your father soon," he promised.

Suddenly Finnikin was at Lucian's shoulder.

"Lucian, we have a problem," the queen's consort said, holding the letter from the Charynite palace in his hand. "A big one."

"Can it not wait until the morning?" Lucian asked.

"Apparently some of our mail has gone astray."

Lucian laughed, his eyes never leaving Phaedra's.

"Finnikin, unless it affects the future of this kingdom, I'm going to have to say no to whatever you're about to ask me to do," her husband said firmly.

Finnikin placed an arm around them both.

"Cousins, I'm afraid it affects the future of both our kingdoms."

CHAPTER 49

On the day the *provincari* of Charyn were to choose Quintana's consort, Froi sat on the roof of the Crow's Inn with Mort and Florik, the lads staring down at every potential suitor who arrived in the Citavita. Each candidate brought with them a large enough entourage to impress, and Froi's heart sank with every step they took closer to Quintana and his son.

"The Osterians," Florik said somberly, indicating the procession crossing the bridge with great ceremony. Froi had come to realize that the more banners a kingdom had, the more useless they were.

"They say he could be the one," Froi said. "The Osterian."

"Why?" Mort asked.

"Apparently no mad blood or inbreeding for the past hundred years." Froi watched the Osterian prince as he stepped onto the rock of the Citavita.

Mort stood and walked to the edge of the roof. "Easy if a bolt flew out of my longbow, right between Osterian's legs. Accidents happen, lads."

"You'd start a war with the only kingdom who hasn't gone to war for its whole existence," Florik said. "Not your best idea, Mort."

Mort looked back at Froi and managed a grin. "Gods are smiling, Froi. Think I see our Grij."

It was both Grij and Satch who arrived, and Froi had never been so happy for their company.

"Why did you stay, Froi?" Grij begged to know as they made their way up to the castle, arms around each other's shoulders.

"She w-w-won't want you th-th-there," Satch said. "T-too painful."

"Then what are you both doing here?" he asked.

Satch shrugged.

"C-couldn't bear for her to b-be alone this day."

When they reached the drawbridge, they lined up behind a crowd of foreigners waiting to enter. They had left their weapons with Mort and the lads, knowing that only the little king's palace guards would be allowed into the palace armed. Everyone who traveled through the gates, whether prince or servant, was checked for weapons. Today, every soldier in the palace was on guard and tension was high among Scarpo and his men. Froi finally reached the portcullis, but Olivier appeared before him. He had seen glimpses of the last born since his arrival five days ago, but it was the first time they had come face-to-face.

"Let me pass," Froi said, his tone cold.

Olivier looked beyond Froi to where Satch and Grijio stood.

"You call yourself his friends and you bring him here?" Olivier demanded.

"You try stopping him," Grij said.

"It's not right!" Olivier said.

"Let me pass," Froi said again, but he couldn't find the anger anymore. He just felt the tears biting at his eyes.

Inside the great hall, there was barely room to move. Froi and the lads found themselves close to the back, fighting for space among horses and hounds. Some of the suitors had animals with them, until Perabo ordered anything on four legs to be taken to the stables or their two-legged owners would be removed themselves. The fool Feliciano of Avanosh joined them soon after, and Grijio, always diplomatic, allowed him to stay.

When Quintana entered the great hall holding the little king, a hush came over the room. Some had never seen Tariq before. As the only babe in Charyn, people were in awe of him wherever he went. The *provincari* followed, and each acknowledged Quintana and the boy with a bow before being seated on a raised platform. Froi was pleased to see Ariston and Dolyn there to represent the rights of Turla and Lascow. He watched Tariq squirm in Quintana's arms, and she placed him on the ground and Dorcas and Fekra had a hard time trying to keep up with him as he crawled among the *provincari's* feet.

"They're saying the prince from Osteria will win the day," Feliciano said.

"We've heard," Froi muttered.

"He's brainless, according to my father," Grij explained.

"Exactly what the *p-provincaro* wants," Satch said. "Someone they can all control."

"And why aren't you in contention?" Froi asked Feliciano coldly.

"My uncle owes money," Feliciano admitted. "A lot of it. He believes we have a better chance of paying his debts if I marry the daughter of the Osterian archduke. We're in with a very strong chance. They're taking marriage requests for her in three days' time."

"Then why are you here?" Froi asked.

"Avanosh has been accepted as a province. My uncle will have a vote in the decision."

Another candidate and his entourage entered through the great doors behind Froi and his friends. They were from Sarnak. Froi would know a Sarnak in his sleep. They had ruddy cheeks and high foreheads. And they married young.

"I don't have much experience determining the age of people younger than us," Grij said, catching a glimpse of the new arrivals, "but is he—"

"Twelve. Possibly thirteen," Froi said.

"F-F-Froi," Satch said quietly. "L-let's go. This will only end in heart-b-break."

Froi dismissed the suggestions. Whether he stayed or went, the heartbreak would be the same.

They saw Olivier again, pushing through to oversee the ever-growing crowd by the doors.

"Olivier!" Grij called out. "Olivier. What are they saying? We can't hear a thing."

Olivier reached them, trying to catch his breath after being squeezed between two large Sorellians.

"The Yuts of the Nord walked out," Olivier said. "Your father, Grij, asked them what they had done with the heir of Yutlind Sud. They didn't like the question."

The crowd surged forward. There seemed to be a commotion at the entrance. Olivier was gone within moments.

Froi's eyes followed him.

"What's happened to his family? The *provincaro* of Sebastabol claimed to have expelled them from the province."

Satch and Grij exchanged a look.

493

"Desantos has t-taken them in," Satch said. "I will always underst-st-stand your anger, Froi, but in t-trying to make amends, he risked his life again and again."

"He'll never be the same lad," Grijio said. "He refuses to befriend any of the Guard and keeps to himself. He's a stranger, this Olivier. I don't think he'll ever forgive himself for what he did."

There was a surge forward again and shouts of exasperation. At the front of the hall, people were oblivious to the disturbance at the back.

"Probably another mountain goat from Osteria and his herd," Grijio muttered.

The noise at the entrance became louder.

"Something's happening back there," Grijio said. "Hitch me up so I can see."

Froi and Satch hitched Grijio up onto their shoulders, and he peered over their heads toward the grand entrance. Grij's peering turned into shock as he looked back down to Froi.

"What is it?" Feliciano asked.

"Froi," Grijio said calmly. "I think I recognize your queen's cousin from my time in the valley after the battle. He's just shoved his way into the hall."

"*What?*"

Grij climbed down, and they lifted Froi up onto their shoulders. He looked toward the crowded entrance. He could see nothing but an irate crowd being pushed forward. Olivier and one of the guards were attempting to shove their way through the crowd to see what was taking place.

And then Froi saw Lucian.

And Finn.

And Perri. The three of them were searching above the heads of those around them.

494

Sagra!

"Here!" Froi shouted, holding up a hand. *"Lucian!"*

The Lumaterans had managed to cause a small riot near the entrance, and there was too much noise to be heard. Meanwhile, the onlookers standing around Froi yanked him down.

"We can't hear a thing, you fool," one snapped.

Froi climbed back up again, slapping away at the hands that were pulling at him.

"What can you see?" Grij shouted.

Froi could still see Olivier shoving his way toward the entrance to investigate the small brawl that seemed to have taken place.

"Olivier!" he shouted. The last born must have heard, because he turned, and Froi pointed toward the entrance and then to himself.

"Lumaterans! They're with—"

He was yanked off Grijio's and Feliciano's shoulders before he could speak another word. So he pushed headfirst into the crowd, telling himself he could have imagined one, but not all three. Close to the entrance, he hit a wall of a man. One who was determined Froi would not pass him by. Until a hand covered the face of the man and shoved him out of the way.

"Lucian? What are you doing here?" Froi asked.

Grij, Satch, and Feliciano had followed, staring at the Lumaterans just as incredulously. Lucian waved away the question with irritation.

"You," Lucian said, pointing to Feliciano. "Get your jacket off," he ordered the Avanosh heir. Feliciano pointed to himself, stunned. Lucian stared down at Feliciano's tights. "Just the jacket."

When Feliciano was too slow, Finnikin was there, yanking Feliciano's arms out of the sleeves.

"Follow everything we say, Froi," his king said. "Put this on. Ask no questions."

And then Lord August stumbled through the crowded entrance, followed by Lady Abian and Talon and the younger boys, their faces soaked with perspiration. And just when Froi thought nothing could shock him more, he saw the priest-king.

The Lumaterans looked disheveled. Froi was so confused, his arm half stuck in a jacket that was far too small.

"You," Lucian said, pointing to Olivier. "Get us to the front."

"Just agree with everything," Finnikin said. "Let me do the talking. There's no time for an explanation. Do you trust us, Froi?"

"With my life," he said.

The path to the front seemed never-ending.

"Excuse me."

"Excuse me."

"Out of the way."

There was shoving and cursing, and Froi's heart was pounding. Lady Abian was adjusting her dress and hair and swiping at the dirt on Lord August's face.

"Blessed Barakah is going to faint," Froi said, trying to hold on to the old man's arm.

"They dragged me off the carriage as if I were a sack of potatoes," the priest-king complained as they stumbled to a standstill at the front, facing a shocked *provincari*.

There was furious whispering all around him. Froi heard someone gasp.

"It's the queen of Lumatere's consort."

"No!" another replied.

"Yes. Look at the hair."

Froi glanced at Finnikin, and already his friend's face was a mask of arrogance. Finn said it worked well in negotiations.

Isaboe said she hardly recognized him when she first saw it appear with the Belegonians.

Before them the *provincari* and the other leaders were staring their way. Quintana stood to the side. Tariq was on the ground, tugging at Gargarin's leg. Gargarin's stare was fierce. Angry. Hopeful?

"Introduce me," Finnikin ordered Froi in Charyn.

Froi cleared his throat.

"My lord Finnikin, consort of Her Majesty Queen Isaboe of Lumatere, may I present to you the *provincari* of Charyn."

Froi held out a hand to indicate the Lumaterans.

"Lord August of the Flatlands. Lady Abian of the Flatlands; the lords Talon, Duret, and Ren of the Flatlands. Lucian, leader of the Monts. And the blessed Barakah of Lumatere."

There was a stunned hush as the *provincari* leaped out of their seats to offer the priest-king one of theirs. But despite his limp, Gargarin beat them to it.

"You're late," he hissed, glaring at Finnikin.

"We had a slight problem . . . locating the letters you sent," Finnikin whispered back. "Explanation later," he added. "Go. Away."

The *provincari* were staring at the visitors, intrigued.

"I'd prefer to speak Charyn so there'll be no misunderstanding of our intention," Finnikin said to the *provincari*. "I will be translating for Lord August and Lady Abian of the Lumateran Flatlands."

Lord August stepped forward while Lady Abian was still swiping at his face with her kerchief. Finnikin gave the nod for Lord August to speak.

"As stated, my name is Lord August of the Flatlands. Today, my wife and my family present to you our eldest boy as a prospective consort to Quintana of Charyn."

Froi was speechless. He thought he would be sick on the spot. He could hate anyone, but not Talon, who was a brother to him. Finnikin translated and glanced at Froi, who hadn't taken a breath. Froi felt a pinch on his arm.

"Don't you dare faint," Finnikin whispered.

Lord August continued.

"My eldest boy may not share my blood, but he is part of our life and has been since the rebirth of our kingdom. When we chose four years past to give him our name, we never imagined that we would be presenting him to a foreign court."

August caught Froi's eye. Him? They were talking about him. Not Talon. But Froi had never been given Lord August's family title. Who had hatched up this lie?

Before them, the *provincari* were bewildered by the turn of events. Gargarin wasn't.

"That doesn't count," Vinzenzo of Avanosh said.

"How does that not count?" Lucian asked politely.

Finnikin nudged Froi. "Which one's Paladozza?" he whispered.

"Fourth from right."

Finnikin stepped forward.

"My father is the captain of the Lumateran Guard," Finnikin said coldly. "Don't let me have to go home and tell him that the child he calls his own is not a daughter to him just because she doesn't share his blood." He looked at De Lancey. "Provincaro De Lancey," he continued. "I've been told your children are not of your blood. Do they not count?"

De Lancey was livid. "They're my children," he said through clenched teeth. "Regardless of blood ties, they have my name. They have my land. They have my title." De Lancey stared across at Avanosh. "Are you questioning the rights of my children?"

"No one is questioning the rights of your children, De Lancey," the *provincara* of Jidia said, trying to placate him.

"It's not enough," Vinzenzo of Avanosh shouted.

"He's the son of a Lumateran Flatland lord," the *provincaro* of Sebastabol said. "How much more do we want? The Belegonians turned down our invitation to be here today. It will turn them green with envy to have our Quintana wed to the son of a Lumateran Flatland lord."

"Don't trust a Lumateran," the *provincaro* of Alonso said, eyeing Lucian. "They lie."

This time Lucian stepped forward.

"For the sake of my beloved wife, I will forgive my father-in-law's words," Lucian said. "And offer a hand of friendship to my neighbors in Alonso."

"Your wife?" Alonso shouted. "The one you sent back and then claimed was dead? And then let go to the palace? And where is she now? Is my daughter a toy to be passed around?"

"Your daughter is a woman who makes her own choices, sir," Lucian said. "And it was her choice to sacrifice her safety for Quintana of Charyn in the valley, and it was her choice to rightfully travel here and settle the first mother and child of Charyn into their home. I would never ask my wife to choose me over her king."

Lucian stepped forward and bowed to Quintana. "And I will always be indebted to Quintana of Charyn for allowing Phaedra to return."

Froi was most impressed with Lucian.

"So you married her again?" Quintana demanded to know.

"Yes, I did."

"Good," she said, looking away.

"We don't trust this lad," Vinzenzo of Avanosh said, pointing to Froi. "He's lied and he stole the princess from under us in Paladozza. I was there."

There was more hushed talk.

"Louder!' someone from the back called out. "We can't hear."

Froi felt as if he were part of a pantomime, placed in front of a crowd hungry for entertainment.

"I was there, too," De Lancey said. "And I don't recall her being stolen." He looked across at Quintana. "Stolen, Your Highness?"

The Nebian *provincaro* spoke up. "If I may be so bold as to say that our Quintana may not be the best person to ask whether she was stolen or not?"

Finnikin made a rude sound of disbelief.

"Can I be even bolder and ask why she can't be asked?" he shouted, for those at the back. "All we hear about is Quintana the brave, Quintana the mighty who broke the curse. It turns my queen's stomach to hear all the praise. Yet here, a *provincaro* calls her a dimwit who can't answer a question about whether she believes she was stolen or not!"

Finnikin received a round of applause. The crowd liked the ginger king.

"A dimwit?" De Lancey asked the Nebian *provincaro*.

"I didn't call her one at all," the man protested.

"What of a dowry?" the *provincara* of Jidia demanded to know. "What has your son got to offer Charyn, Lord August?"

Finnikin translated, but first answered himself.

"The benevolence of Lumatere," he said. "Is that not enough?"

"And an invitation to your little king's regent into the Belegonian court," Lord August said. "If I understand rightly, the Belegonians refused your offer to be part of today's proceedings."

Finnikin translated. The *provincari* exchanged looks with one another.

"Nothing more than what the Osterians are offering," the Nebian *provincaro* said. "Haven't they promised to assist making peace with the Belegonians?"

Froi couldn't imagine what else Finnikin had to offer.

"The valley," Lucian said, exchanging a look with Finnikin.

Froi shook his head with disbelief. "One moment!" he shouted, ushering the Lumaterans aside. There was a sound of irritation from some of the *provincari* and furious talking from the crowd. They wanted to hear every word.

"Land?" Froi whispered. "You're giving them land? I'm not worth the valley."

"You're worth a kingdom," Finnikin said, turning back to the crowd. He had a better chance of impressing them.

"We offer the valley between Lumatere and Charyn," Finnikin shouted to the crowd.

There was a hushed silence. Even the *provincaro* of Alonso was speechless.

"With a stipulation," Finnikin said.

"Charynite people, governed by Lumaterans?" Vinzenzo of Avanosh scoffed.

"Charynite people governed by their own *provincaro*," Lucian said.

"And the stipulation?" Gargarin asked Finnikin.

"That under no circumstance will the valley ever accommodate an army. Yours or ours."

"And what will you name the valley? Little Lumatere?" Sol of Alonso scoffed.

Froi noticed Arjuro push through to the front of the crowd. He wondered if one of the lads had gone to find him. Arjuro had professed that he'd have nothing to do with this day, but here he was.

"They will name it the Valley of Phaedra," Quintana said, her eyes meeting Lucian's. Froi could see that Lucian was moved by her words.

"I think my queen will approve," Lucian said quietly.

Vinzenzo of Avanosh was whispering to Sol of Alonso. Froi knew that Avanosh could poison any bitter man's heart, regardless of what was being promised.

Froi sighed loudly. "We need to hasten these proceedings, Father," he said to Lord August. "And my king," he added to Finnikin, who looked at him curiously.

Play along with me, Finn.

"Remember? The Osterian archduke's daughter is receiving suitors in three days' time, and we may have a better chance with her. You did spend many years in exile among the Osterians with Sir Topher of the Flatlands. And they do love you so."

"True, true," Finnikin said.

"No!" someone in the audience shouted.

Froi chanced a look at Quintana and saw a show of vicious little teeth.

"Let us go, Lumaterans," Finnikin said, enjoying himself.

"No!" someone else in the crowd shouted out.

But it was Vinzenzo of Avanosh who was on his feet in an instant.

"No need for that. No need at all," Avanosh said, adopting a good-natured tone. "Only testing your worth. I say we talk about this. Have we seen all the candidates?"

"One more question," Orlanda of Jidia demanded. "What was the son of a Flatland lord doing in Charyn?"

Everyone stared at Finnikin and Froi, waiting. Finnikin stepped up to the platform and managed to address both the crowd and *provincari*.

"Why question what Froi of Lumatere was doing here?" he asked. "When you should be questioning what would have happened to Charyn if he hadn't been here. Who else would have saved Gargarin of Abroi from the street lords? He's now the little king's regent," he said, pointing to Gargarin. "Who would have saved Quintana of Charyn from hanging? Who would have rescued her from Tariq of Lascow's compound? Who would have sent her to a safe place to birth the curse breaker? Blah, blah, blah. I'm bored now," Finnikin said, looking around. "Are we here for a wedding, or are we off to Osteria for the archduke's niece?"

"Daughter," Froi corrected.

Finnikin stepped toward the *provincari,* and Froi could sense his friend's anger.

"My queen offers you peace. Your dead king ordered the slaughter of her family, and his army tortured her people. *This* is our peace offering," Finnikin said, pointing to Froi. "Take it or leave it. We're busy people."

He turned his back on the *provincari* and joined the Lumaterans.

The *provincari* and the other leaders rose and walked to a corner. Froi watched them argue vehemently. Suddenly Arjuro was there beside Froi and the Lumateran lot.

"This is all too much for me. My heart is hammering."

The priest-king stood and the two men embraced and then Gargarin was there. He bowed to Lady Abian and turned to Lord August. Both men acknowledged each other with a wary nod.

Finnikin held out a hand. "How could you take such a risk?" Gargarin whispered angrily, shaking it hard. "I wrote to you months ago and you sent him here on an errand about water fountains."

"He said you loved water fountains," Finnikin argued, but when he saw the fury on Gargarin's face, he sighed.

"We had an issue," Finnikin said.

"What type of an issue?" Gargarin hissed.

"A very substantial one," Finnikin said. Froi and Gargarin waited.

"If you must know . . . your letters went astray."

"The Belegonians?" Gargarin asked.

Finnikin shook his head ruefully. "My daughter likes . . . red seals. She chews at them. She must have come across your correspondence in our residence."

Sagra.

"Jasmina stole the letters he sent?" Froi asked.

"Ridiculous," Gargarin whispered.

"Yes," Finnikin said, leaning closer, "And your grandson is chewing the *provincara* of Jidia's pearl shoes. Equally ridiculous. Try controlling him."

Finnikin stepped away. "Now if you don't mind, I'd like to speak to the king's mother. Can you reintroduce us, Froi?"

Froi did just that, and Finnikin bowed to Quintana.

"A trinket from my wife to your son," he said, holding out a little purse.

Quintana stared at it.

"A trinket?" she said. Froi could see she was hurt. She wanted more from Isaboe. "I would have preferred a letter addressed directly to me. If the queen of Lumatere wants a friendship between us, then she must learn to communicate, not send trinkets."

"Hmm, yes, I'll pass that on," Finnikin said. "She's always so appreciative of being told what to do."

The *provincari* returned, and when they were all seated, Orlanda of Jidia stayed standing. Not a good sign, Froi thought. If it was good news, De Lancey would have been chosen. Not Orlanda. Froi's stay in Jidia was disastrous. Lirah had attacked Orlanda; Orlanda had insulted Quintana and Lirah. Gargarin had rejected Orlanda. It couldn't get much worse.

"We have many strong young men presented here today," Orlanda said over the noise of the room. "All with so much to offer us, in what we call . . . our infancy. For we are infants in many ways, and we must choose well."

She looked back at Quintana.

"If there is one thing I am certain of—we are all certain of, based on the events of this kingdom during the months before the little king's birth—it's that we need to ensure Charyn's safety. There's no better way of doing that than to keep the king well taken care of under the guidance of his mother's consort . . ."

Her eyes met Froi's.

"The Lumateran has already played a great role in Charyn's peace and will play a greater role in our future."

There was silence. Froi's eyes met Quintana's and then Gargarin's. He blinked. Once. Twice. And there it was. The moment Lirah had spoken of that day in the fortress beyond the little woods. Froi shook his head with wonder. But then he saw Quintana's face. She was confused. Disbelieving.

"One moment," he called out.

There was an uproar.

"What? What's he doing?" the Nebian *provincaro* asked.

"I would just like to speak to Quintana of Charyn. Can we have a moment or two? Talk among yourselves," Froi suggested.

He leaped onto the platform and took her hand.

"What is it?" she whispered.

"Do you want this?"

"What a thing to ask, you fool!"

"I just want you to feel normal for a moment."

She shook her head, confused. "Normal? Why are you using that word? To taunt me?"

He laughed. Only Quintana would consider being called normal a taunt.

"Will you be my wife?"

She looked taken aback.

"You're asking me?"

"Well, no one else is."

They turned back to see the entire room watching them.

"What are you doing over there?" the *provincara* of Jidia demanded to know. Froi shrugged.

"I just wanted to ask her to be my wife."

"And what say you, Quintana?" the *provincara* of Jidia asked.

"Well, if the truth be known, I'd very much like him to be my husband," Quintana said coolly.

And then everyone was shouting and jostling to surround them and Froi was separated from Quintana, and he found himself embraced by Lord August and Lady Abian and the boys, stunned by how quickly the events had unfolded.

"We lose you, Froi," Talon said. "How can we celebrate when we lose you?"

"You will never, ever lose me," he said.

Lord August took him by his shoulders.

"I'm angry at myself, Froi, because it wasn't my idea," he whispered. "It should have been. I should have done this years ago, but I didn't. It was his. Gargarin of Abroi. In his letter, he wrote that I owed him because of the water system introduced by the Charynites that saved our first crop. He wrote, *Give my son a name that will buy him happiness.* Have I done that for you, Froi? Is this what you want?"

"It's everything I want."

And then the Charynite last borns were lifting Quintana on their shoulders and the Lumaterans had Froi on theirs, and she was laughing and he thought he'd never seen her look so beautiful. And over everyone's head, Froi could see Gargarin and Arjuro staring up at her with their bittersweet smiles, and Froi imagined two boys with the same face all those years ago in a filthy cave beneath the swamps of Abroi, praying for a better life.

Later in the night, Finnikin was there, gripping his arm.

"We'll be leaving tonight, Lucian and I, and Perri. We've invited the *provincaro* of Alonso to travel home with us, and Lucian wants to see Rafuel before he leaves. The others will stay."

Froi nodded, his throat constricting. He wasn't ready for this so soon. He hadn't even had a chance to speak to Perri.

"Come," Finnikin said, leading him outside of the great doors. Finnikin retrieved his dagger, and a moment later they were surrounded by Scarpo's men, who were surrounded by Finnikin's guards, all ready to attack.

"Sagra!"

"Mercy!"

"Go. Away," Lucian shooed the guards back.

The three stood alone in the alcove. Finnikin cut into both Froi's hands and then into one of Lucian's and finally his own. Froi clasped both their hands.

"A pledge, with your blood mixed with ours," Finnikin said.

Froi nodded, unable to speak.

"Brothers always. Balthazar is with us, too. We make this work," Finnikin said fiercely. "We bring peace to these kingdoms. We deserve it. Our women do. All of us have lost too much, Froi. We've lost the joy of being children. Let's not take that from Jasmina and Tariq and those who come after them."

The three embraced and Froi felt the tremble in their arms and then he followed them to the stables, where Perri was waiting for them with their mounts. And it was only then, when Perri gripped a hand to Froi's shoulder and pressed a kiss to his brow, that Froi wept.

❖ ❖ ❖

He stayed there awhile at the portcullis until he could see nothing more of his friends in the darkness. Behind him, he heard voices, and Gargarin, Arjuro, and De Lancey approached with Tariq in Arjuro's arms.

"You may need to go inside," Arjuro said. "She's surrounded by the *provincari* parrots and she has that caged-animal look that's beginning to frighten everyone."

Arjuro placed Tariq in Froi's arms.

"Tell Lirah we'll visit with the Lumateran Flatlanders tomorrow," Gargarin said quietly. "We'll celebrate among ourselves then."

They watched Arjuro and De Lancey leave, and Froi felt awkward alone with Gargarin. He didn't know what to say. Not after the last furious words he had exchanged with his father. But it was Tariq's strange little chatter with himself that made them both smile.

"At least I get to be with Quintana and Tariq," Froi said quietly as they returned to the great hall. "What will you possibly get out of all of this, Gargarin? You don't have Lirah. You hold such little power, and you're as much a prisoner here as you were nineteen years ago. It's like the dead king won."

Tariq had recognized his name and chortled. It brought a soft smile to Gargarin's mouth.

"I get to raise a king, Froi. We all do. We'll make a good king. And when he comes of age, his *shalamar* will live with us in the palace because I can't imagine Tariq wanting it any other way."

Gargarin reached out a hand and touched Tariq's face. "Your priest-king told me just now that he once dreamed that you would hold the future of Lumatere in your hands. Perhaps Tariq is Lumatere's future. As a powerful neighbor, he will ensure that Lumatere will always be protected. Because regardless of everything, yours is still a small kingdom and any one of us larger kingdoms can crush Lumatere at a moment's notice."

Gargarin's eyes met Froi's. "They know that. It's why their queen gave you to us. Because she and her consort trust that you can raise a good and powerful leader. That's how I'll win against the dead king, Froi. We share a grandson, and I'll live to see him become a great leader."

Froi remembered what Lirah once told him. *Don't ever underestimate him. He's the most powerful man you'll ever know.*

Gargarin turned toward the revelry. "It's best that we get back to your Lumateran family."

"They're good people," Froi said.

"Very demonstrative," Gargarin said. "All that embracing Lord August does with you. Are all Lumaterans like that with their sons?"

Froi shrugged. "That's just Lord Augie. He's like that with everyone. He says he wasn't embraced enough as a child and he's making up for it now."

Froi stepped forward. He pressed a kiss against Gargarin's brow much the same as Perri had kissed his. Then he pressed one against Tariq's.

"That's how Lumaterans give thanks between fathers and sons."

Gargarin looked away, overwhelmed.

"You make sure our boy learns the Lumateran ways, then," he said.

epiLogue

There's a song that I hear at the back of my heart that I feared for so long, when I sensed you were there. And I think of those times when you crept into my dreams and I thought you a threat to curse my sweet king. But it was the boy in your belly that whispered to mine, and even before that, you lived in my spirit.

Because I think of those times when I was a child. I prayed to the gods and I begged for a sign. I know that they sent you, despite the blood of all those you loved shed at the hands of my kin. For you were the one who found him in exile and though it took time, you led Froi to his home.

And you've sent me this trinket that hardened my heart, because I wanted your words and a sign of true peace. But I've opened it now after all these long weeks, and Froi stares at it, speechless, when I hold out my hand. And we see it before us, our spirits shaking. The brilliance of color: the same ruby ring.

Oh, you've outdone me twice now, you queen of forgiveness. The ring's a promise of peace, and I'm greedy with hope. It's a song that we sing in a tongue that we share. And though you say it's a gift from a king to a king, I say it's a sign from a queen to a queen.

❖ ❖ ❖

In the palace of Lumatere, Finnikin woke to the sound of Jasmina crying.

"I'll pay you all the gold in the land if you get out of this bed and see to her," Isaboe said sleepily.

"I don't want all the gold in the land," he said, placing his pillow over his head. "It's your turn, anyway."

He felt her lift the pillow to place lips close to his ear.

"I will do anything you want."

In her little bed, Jasmina stared up at Finnikin from under the blankets, refusing to surrender their warmth until she was certain to get what she wanted in return.

"Isaboe," she whimpered.

If there was one thing Finnikin understood, it was the yearning in his daughter's voice when she spoke her mother's name. He held out his arms to her, saw the smile of satisfaction on her beloved face. He chuckled at her brazenness.

"You'll make a brilliant queen one day, my love," he whispered.

"Finnikin!" Isaboe reprimanded from across the residence. "Remember our rules."

Finnikin kissed his daughter's cheek. "But for now, there's room for only one queen in this kingdom."

He waited until she slept and then returned to their bed.

"So you'll do anything I want?" he asked, trapping Isaboe, a knee placed each side of her body. "Can we play any game?"

"Which game were you thinking of?" she said with a laugh.

He pretended to think deeply. "The one where you are a novice named Evanjalin."

In the dark, he kissed the smile from her lips.

"And you're a farm boy named Finnikin?" she asked.

"No," he scoffed with arrogance. "I'm the king."

"Ah," she said. "That game."

◆ ◆ ◆

On Lucian's mountain, someone hammered on the cottage shutters.

"It will be for you," he said drowsily.

"No, it will be for you," Phaedra said, wrapping the blankets around her.

"It's your turn," he insisted.

Phaedra pulled the blankets from the bed, leaving him cold and exposed as she wrapped them around herself. She was back soon enough.

"Sheep. Looting. Cousins."

Lucian cursed and got out of bed.

It was too cold a morning to be settling disputes between two neighbors over marked sheep, but he knew he would have to see to it. The mountain was still dark, but down in the valley he could see the twinkle of lantern light as they woke to milk the cows.

Back inside their cottage, the fire was lit and Phaedra was dressed. As always, she left for the valley before first light.

"Can they not go one day without you?" he asked gruffly.

"Can yours not go one day without you?" she asked.

She took his hands and wrapped them in a cloth warmed by the fire. "They're ice," she murmured.

"You're going to have to learn to ride a horse on your own, Phaedra," he said. "It will make the journey faster."

"The mule and I have an agreement."

"The mule and you have similar traits," he said.

He helped her with the fleece Yata had made for her, and then he warmed her face with his hands. "If I don't get called to the palace and if Raskin's sheep don't take all day to birth and if the Mont cousins don't create a drama, I'll come down the valley to collect you. The days are getting shorter, and I don't want you to travel in the dark."

She pressed a kiss to his mouth, and then she was gone. Sometimes when he watched her ride away on these cold mornings, he'd want a better life for her, but then she'd return at night and they'd dine with

Yata or visit the cousins or feast with friends and Lucian would hear her laughter, and he imagined that this was the better life.

In the Citavita, Froi lay beside Quintana, both knowing that any moment now a cry would be heard from the other room and one of them would need to leave the warmth of their bed.

"What's creasing your forehead this morning?" he asked.

She turned on her side to face him. "I was thinking of all the babes to be born today in this kingdom and what if you and I were to have another and it was a girl with Solange of Turla's eyes or a boy with Arjuro and Gargarin's face?"

"I can see your concern," he said, nodding. "An awful thought. The idea of a babe born with Arjuro's beard."

She laughed. "Fool."

He kissed her dimpled chin. "Let's not worry about having to explain the past. If the palace does the right thing by the people, they won't care who our children resemble."

"It's still a worry, isn't it? All this talk about balance of power and neutral consorts and neutral regents and there's nothing neutral about this household at all."

"Everything's a worry if you let it be, Quintana."

"But what will you do today when the Nebian ambassador's wife asks you if her garden is better than Lirah's? Will you choose hers over your mother's?"

He was trying not to think of that.

"How did I get to be the judge?" he asked, suddenly worried.

"Your Lord August was speaking to the Nebian ambassador's wife about your skills in the garden when he was here, and one thing led to the other."

The cry sounded from Tariq's chamber.

"I'll go," Froi said. "He may shine light on the matter."

"He'd choose Lirah."

❖ ❖ ❖

Froi stepped out into the cold morning air with Tariq in his arms. Gargarin was already on the balconette beside theirs and the palace was beginning to stir.

"My lord," Froi heard Dorcas call out from the battlement above.

"Yes, Dorcas."

"You're going to have to cover his head. He'll catch a chill. Fekra made him a cap."

"Thank you, Dorcas."

Gargarin laughed softly.

Quintana joined Froi soon after, placing a thick woolen cap on Tariq's head, and then she took him and wrapped him in a blanket against her, murmuring to their son. Sometimes when she spoke to Tariq, she sounded like the reginita.

"Good morning, Gargarin," she said.

"Good morning, Quintana."

She looked above to the battlements. "Good morning, Dorcas," she called out.

"Good morning, Your Highness."

"Good morning, Fekra. The little king loves his cap."

"Good to hear, Your Highness."

Froi wrapped all three of them in his fleece, and they watched Lirah and Arjuro step onto the balconette across the gravina. *Today Rafuel was there, leaning on them both. But he was standing, and that was enough for now.*

Little steps led to big achievements, the priest-king would always say, and sometimes Froi had to remind himself of that. The days here were long and full of work to be done and worries to be had. Today no less than any other. There were talks with Osterians about a cotton crop, and arranging with Perabo and Hamlyn about the arrival of Serker horses from Lumatere, and the first planting of maize across the bridge, and helping Scarpo train the riders, and scribing for Gargarin's well project, and provincari *demands, and merchants to be placated. And, of course, the impending births. They frightened and thrilled people at the same time. And then soon they would take Tariq into Charyn's provinces. Quintana wanted to meet the men and women who had lost their babes on the day of weeping. She wanted to introduce Tariq to them because she believed he would bring the living some sort of peace. They would also visit Serker. After months and months, Lirah had recorded as many of the names found in the journals Perabo gave her that night in her province as she could. Arjuro had promised to sing those names home.*

"Why are you smiling?" Gargarin asked Froi from across the balconette. "When you're going to have to learn a lesson in diplomacy today and choose between the gardens of two women?"

Froi laughed, his chin resting on Quintana's head, his eyes taking in the joy of their son, despite the ridiculous cap that covered the babe's eyes. He looked across at Lirah and Arjuro and Rafuel, and then back to Gargarin, who was smiling himself, because he knew the answer to his own question.

"Because today, I think I'm leaning on the side of wonder."

ackNOWLeDGmeNts

First, a big thank-you to my readership for the passion you've shown for this trilogy. I may not respond to all the letters, but I read every one of them and your words become part of the space I work in.

Thank you to my editor Amy Thomas and my publisher Laura Harris and designer Marina Messiha, and my U.S. editor, Deb Noyes Wayshak at Candlewick. Also to my agents, Sophie Hamley, Jill Grinberg, Cheryl Pientka, and Jennifer Naughton.

For everyone who has been in my creative world in some shape or form during the past year or so, especially Cathy Randall, Joanna Werner, Samantha Strauss, and Sue Taylor.

For Kristin Cashore, who is as enthused about catacombs and underground cities and medieval ruins in Italy as I am. Thank you to Olivia Stewart for your warm hospitality in the Roman hills

Thanks Kirsty Eagar for the late-night telephone angst. Much appreciation to Anthony Catanzariti and Barbara Barclay for feedback on the manuscript. And thanks to Anna, Barbara, Brenda, Janet, Liz, Maria, Pelissa, and Philippa, whom I'd take into the cave with me.